Like False Money

Like False Money

Penny Grubb

ROBERT HALE · LONDON

© Penny Grubb 2010
First published in Great Britain 2010

ISBN 978-0-7090-8980-3

Robert Hale Limited
Clerkenwell House
Clerkenwell Green
London EC1R 0HT

www.halebooks.com

2 4 6 8 10 9 7 5 3 1

Typeset in 10/12pt Sabon
Printed in Great Britain by the MPG Books Group,
Bodmin and King's Lynn

PROLOGUE

THE FILM HE shot the day before yesterday plays through Terry's head. A dull, malodorous corridor thick with stale dust. A locked door. That awful close-up. Bile rushes the back of his throat. In the dark and the panic, he must have caught the zoom control. His clenched fists drive fingernails into palms. When he gets back he'll edit that bit out.

Forget what it shows. Remember only that it's worth big bucks. Terry peers through the windows of the killer's house, but it still lies empty. He isn't in control, can't threaten someone he can't find.

'Where the fuck are you, Balham?' He kicks out at the wall in frustration before he turns back to the road and makes his way down the hill.

A door slams. Terry glances across. Sees the woman on the doorstep. The adulteress.

'Beckes split over brook,' he murmurs. Catchy title. He thought at one time he might see his name in big print over that. Stares lock for a microsecond. Lying bitch.

He cuts through to the alleyway. Incredible what that creaky old git, Balham, has been up to, but the evidence is plain on the film.

A small figure meanders ahead of him. He watches for a moment, lengthens his stride and catches up.

'Hi,' he says. 'I just went to call on Mr Balham. Do you know where he'll be?'

'Out in the fields.'

'No, I've tried all over. He's not been at home the last couple of days.'

'Gone walkabout then. He does that. He goes off.'

'Where does he go? How long for?' *Long enough to kill.*

'Dunno.'

'So who'll know? Who should I ask?'

Terry leaves the small figure behind and heads for a new target. He feels good now. Back in control.

There's a ritual to go through. 'Good turnout for the show at the weekend.... They were lucky with the weather.... Nice day....'

Once that's over he goes right to the heart of it. 'I went to call on Mr Balham but he wasn't in.'

'Anything I can help with?'

Terry laughs inside himself. *No, there's no one can help Balham out of this one.* He pauses a moment, wondering what line to take. He has an old damp squib of a story he tried to follow at one stage. It'll do for bait.

'It was about his church work.'

Church is a good topic to stoke discussion in Milesthorpe. Everything in Milesthorpe leads to the church like every road once led to Rome.

Terry bats the conversational ball back and forth as the image of a killer plays in his mind. He's known all his life that knowledge is power. Now he feels it as a reality in his gut. Balham's going to pay, just as soon as he can find him.

In the glow of anticipation he loses the thread of the dreary chat. 'Sorry, what did you say? You've … oh yes, I see. Just a sec, I'll get it.'

As he bends forward, the hint of a latent instinct nudges him to turn his head a fraction. Not enough. And not quickly enough.

In the third of a second that's left of awareness, Terry sees the sturdy wooden bar close in. His thoughts zip ahead, dart back, unravel the whole of the story he's wrestled with these last few weeks. Yes, of course … so simple.… A burst of fear almost dulls its edge on something close to pride. He's found the killer.

There's time to feel wonder at the clarity of his thoughts, at the razor sharp precision with which they home in on the facts.

What there isn't time for is to sidestep death.

CHAPTER 1

THE JOURNEY FROM King's Cross to Hull's Paragon Station allowed Annie a couple of hours with only strangers and her own thoughts for company.

A flutter of unease, the same that had plagued her all week, unsettled her again. It was Vince Sleeman, the man who'd interviewed her. Each time she thought of him she experienced a gut-crunching what-if over her recklessness when he'd stepped out of the room. What if he'd caught her? The coldness of his pale-blue eyes made clear he wasn't a man to mess with, even without the rugged features and misshapen nose, or the sheer solid bulk of him. He had disappeared from the room and she'd clicked open his briefcase and taken a peek inside.

The recollection generated a shiver, but she'd got away with it. The memory shouldn't spook her. Vince Sleeman would play a six-week bit part in her life, then be gone forever. She knew from the laziness of his questions at the interview that she would be no more than a filing clerk but it didn't matter. On paper, she was to cover the sick-leave of one of the firm's directors. And boy, would this six-week placement boost her CV.

Sleeman had barely glanced at the certificates she'd thrust under his nose, which came as a relief because she was fed up with trying to justify the thinness of her qualifications.

Then he'd really floored her. 'So you've wanted to be a private investigator all your life, have you, since your father hired one to catch a burglar?'

He didn't have the facts straight, but he'd touched on a closely guarded secret. Anger had blazed inside her; not at Sleeman but at her flatmate, Kara, and her loose tongue. Kara had taken the call when Sleeman rang to set up the interview.

Sleeman followed his crack about her father with a series of questions about a temporary job she'd had in a nursing home. Irrelevant and easier to answer, but not great in terms of impressing him.

As the train rattled through a landscape beginning to lose clarity with the fading light, Annie thought ahead to the end of this six-week stint. She'd made it up with Kara but refused to promise she'd be back. Where she'd go was a bridge to consider later. It wasn't easy finding decent accommodation with her credit rating.

Determination to make an impression on Sleeman had been at the root of her impulsive raid on his briefcase, but it had told her nothing. All she'd seen was a thin newspaper, the *East Yorkshire* something-or-other, the title semi-obscured by a fold in the page, showing a posed group-photograph flanking the text, 'Glorious weather for Milesthorpe's tenth annual show last Sunday.' She'd snapped the case shut and leapt back to her chair as she heard him return.

He needled her a bit about not having the Security Industry Authority licence.

'I'll get it as soon as I have a proper footing in the business. I'm only twenty-two.'

'I can't contract you out though, can I?'

She acknowledged the point with a tip of her head. Her unlicensed status had been plain on her application.

It hadn't looked good, but then out of nowhere he'd ended the interview with the incredible words, 'Six weeks cover for Pat Thompson. You'll do whatever she needs you to: filing, making coffee, whatever. She's laid up with a broken leg, but you can stay with her so no bother about accommodation. You can drive, can't you?'

The real status of the job and that it was hers hit simultaneously. Pat Thompson was one of the firm's directors. She fought for nonchalance as she answered Sleeman's question. 'Uh ... yes. Five years. Clean licence.'

And that was it. A contract had been thrust into her hand and she'd signed it.

No need to worry over Sleeman, and any residual guilt about walking out on Kara at such short notice would soon dissolve. She shut them both out of her mind as the scenery changed from the warehouses and railway sheds of Doncaster to fields, then waterfront and finally back to cityscape as a booming announcement told her, *We are now arriving in Hull. This train terminates here. Thank you for travelling on Hull Trains….*

Annie lugged her cases on to the platform and struggled to get her ruck-sack on her back. Hull's station turned out to be a buffered terminus, no through track, just like London except that where King's Cross led out into the noise and bustle of vibrant city life, this was strangely lifeless. Banks of shop windows reflected the streetlights and duplicated the stillness. More a dead-end than a gateway to somewhere new.

Despite her tiredness, she felt the thrill of adventure as a cab sped her through the empty streets. The city had the newness of unfamiliarity and a nautical air. Boats with high masts wobbled just by the road and the fading horizon seemed to show a giant liner tipping up as though about to slide beneath the waves, but there was no air of panic about it so it must be some-thing else. Then they were swallowed up into a smart housing estate and Annie fixed her stare on the meter willing it not to move.

Outside a waterfront apartment block, Annie parted with a handful of her dwindling funds, and watched the taxi execute a swift three-point turn to head back towards the main road. After Vince Sleeman's factoring in board and lodging this was the worst-paid job she'd ever had bar none.

Pat Thompson's apartment was on the first floor. There was no lift. The weight of the cases fought with her all the way up the stairs. She knocked briskly on the wood-panelled door and waited.

After a minute she knocked again, and immediately heard locks clicking open and a voice snap out, 'Bloody hell, give me a chance.'

The door opened on a mountain of a woman balancing on a crutch and with an enormous plaster cast from toes to thigh on her left leg.

'Pat Thompson?' asked Annie.

The woman nodded.

Annie held out her hand. 'I'm Annie Raymond.'

The woman looked blankly, first at Annie then at her two enormous cases. 'Not interested, whatever you're selling,' she said, and shut the door in Annie's face.

'No … No, wait!' Annie leapt forward, but her bulky luggage prevented her getting a foot in the door.

As she banged her hands on the wooden panel, she remembered the cold blue of Sleeman's eyes and the mental alarm bells they'd set ringing. But why? Annie was a stranger to him. Why would he lure her to this godfor-saken place just to strand her here?

Annie banged on the wooden panel again, this time using her fist. 'I've come to work for you,' she shouted. 'Vince Sleeman sent me.'

After a pause, a muffled voice answered, 'Who did you say?'

As the door reopened, Annie scrabbled through her bag for the paper-work.

'Vince sent you?' Pat Thompson held the door only half open. 'At this hour on a Sunday? To do what?'

'He told me to arrive this evening. He's hired me to cover while you're … uh … off sick. He said I'd be able to live here.'

Annie pushed the contract at Pat Thompson who took it with a terse, 'He did, did he? Wait here.'

The door shut in her face again. Annie waited longer than was comfortable, but eventually Pat Thompson reappeared with a phone in her hand which she stared at with exasperated disbelief, before looking Annie up and down. 'Bloody hell. Well, I suppose you'd better come in.'

Feeling a surge of relief, Annie lifted her cases once more. In the wake of her lumbering new boss, it was a slow journey across the apartment's small inner lobby and into the living area where a huge LCD screen played speckled fog into the room. A picture window framed a ribbon of lights in the far distance beyond a dark stretch of water, the scene disjointed by the multiple reflections of moonlight on the river and that the view was from a lighted room out into darkness.

Once she'd slumped herself into the settee, Pat Thompson looked up at Annie with a shake of her head. 'I suppose it might make some kind of sense,' she said. 'Spare bedroom's that way. You'll find bedding in the cupboard. Dump your stuff, then we'll talk.'

Annie shoved her cases into the tiny bedroom, threw some bedding at the bed and returned to the living room where she sat in an armchair. She'd counted on some conventional hospitality; an offer of something to eat or drink, but then she'd counted on Pat Thompson expecting her.

Pat clicked the TV remote and the screen blanked. She shifted her bulk on the sagging cushions of the settee, sat upright and turned to face her new employee.

'Let's be clear on one thing,' Pat opened. 'If you're here to work, you're here to work for me. Not Vince Sleeman. You report to me. How well do you know him?'

'Not at all. I met him when he interviewed me, that's all. Why hadn't he told you I was coming?'

'Hadn't got round to it … he said.' There was a pause Annie couldn't bridge, and then Pat looked her in the eye and began to rattle out all the questions she'd expected a week ago. Gathering up her wits, Annie batted back the answers as efficiently as she could, fighting not to let her inner squirming reach the surface as her lack of experience was laid bare.

'I've done self-defence and I did the conflict management course in Birmingham.' She passed across her meagre stack of certificates and watched Pat Thompson's left eyebrow rise higher as she scrutinized them. 'So what will I be doing exactly?'

'Not sure what I can give you to match this lot.' Pat gave the paperwork a hard stare. 'Where did you say Vince picked you up?'

Annie drew herself tall in her chair. 'Through a recruitment agency,' she snapped, pulling out the crumpled advert.

Pat blew out her cheeks and shrugged. 'Why London, for pity's sake? Oh well, nothing ventured … It'll be on his head. There's only the one case I was working on when this happened.' She gave a nod towards the giant cast. 'Some bother on an estate in the city. I can give you the gen tomorrow. Have a look through the notes if you want.'

Annie reached for the folder as a rush of anticipation grabbed her. Despite her flaky CV, Pat was going to let her have a go at the real job. Her tiredness vanished as excitement mingled with anxiety. She swallowed to moisten her suddenly dry throat and ducked her head over the papers as she pulled them out and scanned them.

'Just the one case?' She asked the question at random. It wasn't what she wanted to know. What she wanted to know was who would be out there with her? Who would show her what to do?

'Uh … yeah. That's right.'

Annie looked up at the hesitation in Pat's reply. Pat met her eye impassively. Annie turned back to the papers in her hand. There was precious little to read, a few scrawled notes, a name and address and an unsigned contract. As Pat yawned and began to gather together a mass of scattered tissues that she shoved in her bag, Annie couldn't stop questions tumbling out. What was it about? Who was Mrs Earle? Why was the contract unsigned?

'She lives in a tower block and some kids have taken over her landing. Dealing drugs by the sound of it. She wants them cleared out.'

'Why doesn't she go to the police?'

'Small-time drugs dealing is way down the list. You're used to London ways, I suppose. Humberside Police don't have London resources. So unless we hit a drugs crackdown initiative, Mrs E isn't going to get more than a crime number from her local nick and that only if she gets her door kicked in.'

'So what are we supposed to do?'

Pat shrugged. 'I hadn't got that far.' She indicated her leg with a glance. 'Find out who they are, then get a handle to move them on.'

Annie's tongue hovered over a question about the giant plaster cast, but she decided it would be unprofessional during a discussion of the case.

'People learn to live with it,' Pat added. 'If you want a drug deal round there, just throw a brick. This Earle woman's got some particular reason for calling us in, but I hadn't got round to finding out what it was. Anyway, we'll talk in the morning.'

With that, Pat heaved herself to her feet, grasped her stout metal crutch and hobbled out of the room.

*

The next morning, Annie surfaced from sleep and felt the strangeness of new surroundings. Silence hung all around, no engines revving, no hum of traffic, no bustling city waking up with her, and no friend in easy reach. She tasted adventure, but also insecurity; climbing without a rope. The face of the bedside clock emerged from a haze to a neat set of figures, and she pulled herself up to sit on the edge of the bed.

The early morning light danced on the walls. The bedroom window was small, giving the room a cell-like feel. From this first-floor apartment there was a good view of the water and mud flats. This was one aspect of the area she hadn't needed to research. One of her teachers, an avid naturalist, passionate about the ecology of the north-east coast, infected them all with his enthusiasm. Thanks to him, she could tell a coot from a moorhen, but couldn't imagine a use for such a skill in Pat Thompson's world. She stood up, stretched and peered out across the Humber. A small boat forged its way up the estuary. The water ripped apart and mended as the craft sliced through. The sun's heat warmed her face. A scorcher of a day in the making.

Neat, but practical, she thought, rummaging through the clothes in her case for jeans and T-shirt. Once dressed, she went through to the living room where the settee, Pat's territory, still bore the indentation of her new boss's form from the night before. She listened to the background rasp of snores from the master bedroom and wondered if she was expected to get things moving on her own initiative. If so, she had no idea where to start, hadn't even a street map of Hull.

Facing her, the big window gave a broad canvas on to the estuary and far bank. The small craft she'd seen from the bedroom had vanished upriver. The treachery of the Humber showed itself only in the snaking patterns on the water's surface.

Despairing of the snores ever stopping, Annie went to explore the kitchen. The worktops gleamed up at her, the neat layout posed like a show-room. She opened cupboards and found them packed. One held nothing but tins of Campbell's soups; another contained a stack of cellophane-wrapped French bread. She broke off a large chunk and chewed it hungrily. A shower of crumbs speckled the floor round her feet. Her search eventually turned up a kettle and cups but no coffee, only a packet of Yorkshire Tea. She settled for a drink of water.

Wandering back to the living room, her gaze lighted on a wooden side-board, one of its two drawers not quite shut on its bulging contents. The stuff trying to escape looked like official paperwork.

She'd got away with snooping in Sleeman's briefcase. Here was easier prey and her chance to find out about this odd outfit she'd come to work for.

Alert for any break in the rhythmic snores from Pat's bedroom, she ran her tongue over her lips, eased the whole drawer silently out of its housing and set it on the floor. Keeping her mind focused, she went through it sheet by sheet running a mental commentary.

Sleeman asking for something to be signed ... what? Doesn't say. Pat must have signed it and sent it back to him. Account with a taxi firm. KC ... Kingston Communications, bill for broadband services. Bills, bills, bills ... Here's a flyer for the firm ... Jed's Private Investigations ... who's Jed? Remember to ask Pat. Hospital appointment card ... must ask about her leg, too. I wonder if it was anything to do with the case....

As she worked her way down the heap, the story became more structured. Jed turned out to be Jed Thompson, who she tentatively categorized as Pat's father before finding confirmation in a letter to him from Pat that started 'Dear Dad'.

There were no case notes. No sign of activity on Pat's part other than as a payer of bills. This random set of papers didn't fit the mental model Annie had built of Pat as a dynamic operator.

At the bottom of the drawer were copies of legal documents. Certificate of Incorporation of the company, its original Memorandum and Articles. She ran her eye down the list of shareholders: George – presumably Jed – Thompson, Vincent Sleeman, Patricia Thompson and Barbara Caldwell. And tucked at the very bottom, a death certificate for George Thompson dated just over a year previously, cause of death myocardial infarction. He'd been 62. If he were the size of his daughter, premature death from heart disease wasn't so surprising.

The Mem and Arts listed George Thompson as managing director and Barbara Caldwell as company secretary. According to the Companies House information she'd looked up before her interview, Vince Sleeman held both these positions now.

And what did any of this say about her own role? Last night, she'd felt the excitement of stepping into a real job no matter how lowly the pay or odd the circumstances, but the morning light brought a disturbing clarity with it. A single case? Did those few notes she'd read really constitute six weeks' full-time work? Sleeman had had a contract drawn up that assumed whoever signed it would live in, but she'd seen no sign of six weeks' worth of work to be covered.

Had Sleeman brought her here to look after Pat? He'd asked as much about her ability to care for others as about her thin CV. But if he'd wanted a carer, he would simply have brought one in from a local agency.

What other role could possibly fit the facts? Part of the puzzle was that Pat herself didn't seem to know.

A bodyguard to keep Pat from further harm? If so, she was an unlikely choice.

A prison warder to make sure Pat stayed put? Hardly.

To be here as an independent witness? But witness to what?

None of it fitted. As she tried to find a credible answer, she dealt herself a mental slap. Bodyguard? Prison warder? What a drama queen!

She replaced the papers, carefully recreating the chaotic jumble at the top of the heap, and slid the drawer back into place.

What she'd seen was a random snapshot. It wasn't official paperwork in any bookkeeping sense. It was clear from what she'd read that Pat's father had founded the firm. Was that why Pat was a director, why she was still a part of it? The real work of the agency went on in the office in town, at the address on the letterheads, wherever that was. Somewhere else to look up as soon as she got her hands on a map. Maybe Pat was just dead weight. Weight being the operative word. Vince Sleeman was clearly in charge. Pat wasn't the experienced PI of Annie's imagination. She was just a hanger-on in her late father's firm.

It was close to midday before Pat emerged hobbling on her crutch and with a huge bag over her shoulder. She heaved her bulk to the settee and slumped into the cushions. Pat in the flesh, stripped of her glamour as an experienced PI, was simply gross. Annie felt a stab of revulsion as she said, 'Nice morning,' and nodded towards the big window.

Pat grunted an indeterminate reply, then said, 'Get me a coffee and something to eat, will you? You may as well earn your crust while you're here.'

Annie tensed, annoyed at Pat's tone, but it was too early to burn bridges, and Pat's order held the promise of coffee in a secret stash, so she held back a sharp retort. 'There isn't any coffee. I looked.'

'Freezer, top shelf. And put some soup on. Cupboard over the sink.' As she spoke, Pat fished a remote control from under the cushions and the television blared into life.

Annie threw Pat an exasperated look. Whoever heard of keeping coffee in the freezer? The blare of the television turned the flat from sterile and empty to overcrowded and busy. Annie stomped through to the kitchen, made coffee for them both and heated a tin of asparagus soup which she carried through on a tray with one of the French sticks and a giant carton of Anchor Spreadable.

Pat shot her a narrow-eyed glance. 'Thanks.' She spoke tersely, but seemed to make an effort to take the rough edge out of her tone. 'Look, I don't do mornings, OK?'

As Pat broke the bread and lavished it with butter, Annie savoured the taste of real coffee and tried to ignore the lip-smacking and crunching from the settee. A crackle of paper made her look across. Pat had taken a packet of chocolate digestives from her bag. Annie's gaze was riveted as Pat dunked the biscuit in her soup and stuffed it in her mouth. The thought of living in close proximity to this hulk of a woman was impossible.

Annie's thoughts were interrupted by the click of locks from the lobby, followed by the slam of the door and locks sliding home again. She twisted round. Whoever had come in had relocked the outer door. Was that to keep intruders out, or someone already here from leaving? As the living-room door opened, she found herself staring at the rugged misshapen face she'd last seen in a London office.

'Ms Raymond,' Vince Sleeman greeted her. 'Annie, isn't it? Settling in?'

'Mr Sleeman.' She acknowledged his query, taking in the coldness of his eyes, the unnatural flatness of his tone.

'Vince, please. I hope you two have got to know each other, sorted things out. You'll work here with Pat, Annie. I'm sure she's made that quite clear. There's no cover needed elsewhere.'

'You can give me those keys back now,' Pat mumbled, through a mouthful of bread.

Sleeman said nothing as he slipped the keys into his pocket. Annie intercepted a shaft of venom in the glance Pat shot at him. She looked into his cold blue eyes to the backdrop of Pat gulping soup and crunching bread and biscuits. She'd walked into the clutches of two strangers without a clue about either of them, blinded by the chance to get something solid on her CV. And now she sat locked in an upstairs apartment with them.

Vince's head turned to Pat but his stare stayed on Annie right to the point when he started on a new speech that didn't include her. It felt like an order to leave the room and had her on her feet before she could think.

'Excuse me,' she muttered, and slipped through to the inadequate refuge of the tiny bedroom.

Deep breath. Think this through. She was sure Vince Sleeman had brought her here for some purpose of his own. The memory stood before her of the phone call she'd walked in on back at the flat in London. Kara's gossipy chat with Sleeman. How much had Kara told him about Annie's family circumstances? A father she hadn't met in years, an aunt now in sheltered accommodation. Had Sleeman read it as no one to notice if she disappeared? It was time to bail out. She took out her phone. She would let Kara know she was on her way back. It gave her a fallback, someone who knew, in case her imaginings had substance.

The voice that answered was unfamiliar.

'Could I speak to Kara?'

'Sorry, she's out. Can I take a message? I'm her new lodger.'

Annie knew she shouldn't be surprised. She'd made no secret about the prestigious new job and maybe she'd exaggerated the wonderful things it would lead to. There'd have been a queue for her old room.

'It's OK. It wasn't important.'

As she ended the call, Annie realized that she'd known all along she was never going back. The bridges behind her were well and truly ablaze. The duo the other side of the closed bedroom door lost their sinister gloss. They became an obese thirty-something woman and an ill-tempered hulk of a man whose agenda Annie neither knew nor cared about. They didn't give a damn if she stayed, or where she laid her head tonight. It was time to grow up, cut the drama and make something special out of this scrap of a job.

She faced herself in the mirror and flicked her fingers through her hair making it bounce back into shape, then she pulled in a breath, straightened her shoulders and marched back through.

Pat lay back into the cushions, the picture window framing the curve of the river behind her. 'Oh, there you are. I wondered where you'd got to.'

Annie shot a glance around the room. Sleeman had gone. 'Should I go down to the office? I know what Mr Slee— uh … Vince said about working from here, but I'll need paperwork. You'll have your own templates, affidavits and so on.'

'Vince won't want you down at the office.'

'OK, no problem. As long as you have everything we need, I'll work from here.' Annie knew her smile was too bright, her manner too chirpy, but she couldn't tone it down.

'You think you're going to stay, do you?' Pat's voice mocked her.

'Yes, of course.' Annie looked at Pat in alarm. 'Why on earth wouldn't I? What's Mr Sleeman said?'

'Don't you know? I assumed you'd been listening at the door.'

'No, of course I wasn't. What do you take me for?'

'I thought you wanted to be taken for an investigator. In your place, I'd have listened at the door.'

Annie dropped her gaze, annoyed with herself. 'Look,' she said. 'I know Vince Sleeman thinks I'm an airhead. I may not have all the bits of paper, but I can do a good job. This drug dealing …' – she pointed to the folder – 'you give me the equipment, camera and so on, and I'll soon get to the bottom of it.'

Pat laughed. 'So you came here to do a real job? Well, I think I'd have let you run with the Orchard Park case, but that's one of the things Vince came to say. He's called the job off. So, though he seemed to think I should keep you on anyway, there's nothing for you to do any more. You may as well pack up and go.'

'But he can't do that.' Annie felt indignation rise. This was her case, not Sleeman's. 'Why?'

'I can't say he came out with a very convincing reason,' Pat conceded. 'I think someone called in a favour, and Dad's cronies have their own ways of doing things.'

Dad's cronies? Was the ghost of Pat's father still a key figure round here? 'That doesn't mean they're right,' Annie muttered, half under her breath.

'You really want this job, do you?' Pat turned away, almost seemed to ask the question to herself. 'But there's no need for anyone now. The agency can handle all the work that comes in. It was only because this one came directly to me that we needed anyone.'

Annie's fingertips drummed on the arm of the chair. Questions rushed her. Why would a case come directly to Pat? What was the dynamic between Pat and Sleeman? What did she need to say in order to keep this berth for long enough to sort herself out?

'Why does he want you to keep me on if there's no work?'

'He seems to think I need someone here to look after me.'

'I'm no good at that sort of thing.' The words were out before Annie weighed her immediate need for accommodation, but it didn't matter. She couldn't play carer to this woman for any price. 'Isn't it worth waiting to see if something else comes in? Just a day or two?' A day or two was enough time for her to re-find her feet. 'I could go shopping and that sort of thing.'

Shopping. She could do shopping, but none of the personal stuff, helping her move about, touching her, all that. Just one more night. If she could wangle just one more night, then she'd have all of tomorrow to get her head together.

For the first time, Pat's face relaxed into a real smile, and then she grimaced as she shifted position yet again. Annie held her breath and looked out across the river until the rustle of paper brought her gaze back. Pat had pulled another folder from her voluminous bag. 'As it turns out there is another case. I hadn't got round to telling Vince about it. Came in yesterday just before you arrived. An odd one. Nothing to it really, but I could let you run with it for a day or two. Maybe.'

Annie kept her tone even. 'I'll make a good job of it.'

'You don't know what it is yet.'

'Even so …' Annie subsided, but under the surface she bubbled with anticipation, a mix of anxiety and excitement. There was no going back. It was time to let go of the sides. Of course she could do it. What did lack of experience matter? It was time to test the confidence she'd always claimed to have in herself. She waited as Pat slid a sheet of paper from the file.

'It's a Mr and Mrs Martin,' said Pat, reading from the page in front of her. 'Their son died in an accident on a building site. They want to know how it happened.'

'Here in Hull?'

'No, in Milesthorpe, one of the outlying villages. You can go out and see them this afternoon.' Pat looked again at the paper. 'Terry Martin. The son was called Terry Martin.'

CHAPTER 2

'MILESTHORPE?' ANNIE CLOSED her eyes to grab the memory. A headline … upside down text. The half-glimpsed newspaper in Vince Sleeman's case.

The Martins' file comprised a single sheet of paper; handwritten notes Pat had made when she took the call. Annie read it through. Terry Martin had been found dead in Milesthorpe the previous Tuesday evening and had last been seen at his parents' home in Withernsea last Sunday.

'Last seen by whom?' she asked.

'His mother, Martha Martin. He left after Sunday lunch. Didn't come back. They didn't hear a thing until they had a visit from the police Tuesday night.'

'Was it a regular thing, Sunday lunch? Would they have expected to hear from him during the week?'

'Oh yes; he lived there. As far as I could gather he'd never left home, not properly.'

'So did they report him missing or anything?'

'No, they didn't. And that's something to look at. I assume it wasn't unusual for him to stay out – hell, he was thirty-seven years old – but she was a bit hazy about it when I asked.'

Annie scanned across the scribbled words. Scaffolding collapse … trespassing?

'What sort of site is it? What are they building?'

'She didn't know. Or rather couldn't remember. She wasn't focusing on anything really except a sort of desperation not to face the fact he was dead. It won't take much digging to find out.'

'And was he trespassing?'

'I assume so. She said he wouldn't have gone there without good reason. She said it before I'd had a chance to ask, and I don't think she just meant Milesthorpe in general. It wasn't a long call, she cut it short. Sad really. They've no other children. She wasn't going to break down for me to hear, but she was right at the edge.'

Annie looked again at the notes.

Police … Health & Safety … work suspended … Surely everything that could be done was already in hand.

'What exactly is it she wants from us?'

'Like I said, it's an odd one. Probably nothing to it. She's lost her son and she's grabbing at straws; kept telling me, everyone says it was an accident.'

'And she thinks it wasn't?' Annie felt a frisson of something close to excitement run through her, but Pat's next words damped it down.

'Yes, she accepts it was an accident, but what was he doing there, that's what she wants to know.'

'Won't the police investigation find that out?'

Pat threw her a raised-eyebrows glance. 'What investigation would that be? If it was clearly an accident they'll leave it to Health and Safety who'll be all over the site. If they find anything that warrants criminal charges, it might go further. They might investigate the builder, but no one's going to put resources into finding out what Terry Martin was doing there. No one except his parents, that is, and they've come to us.'

Annie's mind raced through the angles looking for ways in. 'Can we get at any of the official reports? Witness statements, that sort of thing.'

Pat nodded. 'I'll get hold of the post-mortem report. You'd be better talking to whoever found the body than reading their statement. And the

Martins'll know who that is. They know far more than I got out of the mother. Like I say, she was on the edge, cut things very short. They're your starting point. Get the name of the coppers who dealt with them as well. It might be useful to talk to whoever went out to Milesthorpe that night. They could well have picked up gossip about what Terry Martin was up to.'

'Wouldn't they have put it in their statements?'

'You are wet behind the ears, aren't you? Look, if they got a whiff anything was dodgy about the death, I'm sure they'd have reported it. Well, most of them would. But they're not going to go digging for complications. When a body's found on your watch, you want it to be a clear-cut accidental death. Suspicious deaths are a nightmare all round.'

'So how many police officers would have been involved?'

'Mrs Martin said "they" came to tell them on Tuesday night, so I assume two. They likely dredged up a second officer from somewhere to go and break the news. It'd be unusual for more than one to have gone out to Milesthorpe initially.'

'Even for a body being found?'

'You need to grasp the scale of things round here, Annie. We're not even talking Hull resources. Milesthorpe's East Riding. Factor in people off sick, people called to cover elsewhere and you're lucky to have two coppers on duty at night in that area. Might only have been one. That's something like a thirty-mile stretch of coast. It's a big area.'

Annie felt the weight of her bottom jaw. One police officer covering a thirty-mile stretch? It felt more as though she'd crossed continents than come a mere 200 miles north.

'What did Terry Martin do? For a living, I mean.'

'His mother said he worked as a journalist, but I don't think he did. Not as a regular job anyway. I think he just bummed off his parents really.'

'OK, I'll see what I can get out of them face to face. Shall I ring and see if I can go now?'

Pat pushed her hands down into the cushions of the settee, shifting position in what seemed more of a habit than a real need to move. 'I wouldn't mind having a go at her myself, but it's a bother getting anywhere with this blasted thing.'

Annie followed Pat's gaze to the giant plaster cast and opened her mouth on the question she'd been at the brink of asking since she arrived. But before she could speak, Pat went on, 'I suppose I could get you to drive me, but I'm not sure it's worth the bother.'

Drive? Annie's mouth shut as she lost the thread for a moment. She'd told Vince she had a clean licence. He hadn't dug deeper and she hadn't explained. In the five years since she'd passed her test in the driving school Corsa, she'd driven maybe half-a-dozen times. But – she straightened her shoulders and sat up – all cars were more or less the same and the roads were quiet round here. Not like London.

It struck her then what Pat had said ... unless Mrs Martin had changed her mind. One wrong word ... she's on the edge ... clutching at straws. If Mrs Martin backed out, there was no job for Annie.

When a man's voice answered the phone Annie knew she'd been handed an advantage and mustn't let it slip. His tone was weary but in control. She must deal with him and not let his wife into the conversation. 'Mr Martin? My name's Annie Raymond. I'm calling from Jed's Private Investigators. You contacted us yesterday.'

There was a pause. 'Oh yes. That was the wife. I'll get her—'

'No, no. That's OK. I'm just ringing to say I'm on my way out to see you.'

'Martha,' she heard him call. 'It's that investigation firm. About that disk. What shall I...?'

Annie strained to listen but his voice tailed away and the response was muffled. Then he was back in her ear. 'Just wait a sec, love. The wife's on her way.'

'No, that's OK, don't disturb her. I'll be with you in ... in twenty minutes. Bye.' Annie raced the words out and put the phone down. If she could just get them face to face she'd convince them they needed her. *About that disk* ... So there was more to this case than just a nebulous need to know what had happened that night in Milesthorpe.

She told Pat about the disk, but Pat just said, 'Twenty minutes? You'd better bloody not be there in twenty minutes. If you're clocked speeding, you're paying the fine.'

Annie left the flat in a more buoyant mood than she'd have thought possible just an hour ago and clicked the key fob in her hand. It was no Corsa-clone that winked its lights back in reply: it was a sleek, silver monster that unlocked its doors and ran its BMW logo across her consciousness. She felt her shoulders tighten but took in a deep breath.

Pulling away from the kerb was a jerky affair with frantic wheel turning to avoid the car parked in front, and her halt at the end of the street was rather too abrupt, but, despite her clumsy-handedness it was a smooth ride and the biggest, glossiest car she'd ever been in. The afternoon sun bathed her in a warm glow. She imagined every passer-by followed her progress with envy. Soon, she was out on the main road heading for the coast.

'Head east and follow your nose,' had been the main thrust of Pat's directions. She'd pooh-poohed Annie's assumption that she could just key the address into the SatNav.

'SatNav's OK in town. It would have got you to Mrs Earle's, but don't try it in East Yorkshire, you'll end up in a ditch.'

The bulk of the Salt End chemical works, a 'can't miss it' landmark appeared through a tangle of concrete legs that hoisted a road over a large roundabout. The bright lights on the cooling towers and skeletal metal infrastructure lit the near-horizon like a vast pleasure beach. It lacked only the screams of revellers and booming beat of loud music from extravagant rides. If she tried to turn in here, Pat told her, she'd find the road blocked by gates and uniformed guards. She glanced across as she approached the island: an innocuous exit from a roundabout that sparked a feel of something hidden below the surface.

The road east out of Hull went on for longer than seemed possible, bypassing the town of Hedon, snaking through unlikely sounding villages, past interminable speed camera warnings and even through a pseudo-town large enough for complex junctions and civic flowers. How was it possible to travel so far east and not fall into the sea? If the signs hadn't continued to say Withernsea she'd have been convinced she'd taken a wrong turn.

Forty-five minutes after her call, she found herself on a doorstep that led directly from the street and up against a hatchet-faced woman who made no move to invite her in. 'Twenty minutes you told my husband,' the woman said. 'And anyway, I rang back and told the other woman—'

From the corner of her eye Annie saw a curtain twitch next door. 'How do you do,' she interrupted in strident tones. 'I'm Annie Raymond from—'

'Come inside.' Mrs Martin grabbed her arm and with a murderous glare dragged her into a gloomy hallway where a man with lined features drooped in the background. A dark-wood hallstand crowded the space, but played no functional role except to hold a small white card the print of which Annie couldn't read without staring, but first she must consolidate her position. Clearly Mrs Martin had contacted Pat and Pat had decided to give Annie free rein to try and retrieve the job.

'Miss Thompson must have just missed me. But I'm here now. Let's at least talk it through. Don't you want to know … uh … what really happened?'

Mrs Martin pursed her lips. It was her husband who responded, his tone gentle, resigned. 'We know what happened, love.'

Annie knew she'd lost them. Martha Martin had changed her mind just like Pat predicted. Mr Martin, she judged, hadn't wanted them in the first place. If I can just get them face to face, she'd said to herself. Now she was here and had nothing to hold them.

Nothing. She glanced round the hallway. Wood panelling gleamed at her. The white card still shimmered just out of range. Dust particles danced in a shaft of sunlight. Nothing except Mr Martin's words. A long shot that might alienate them more, but it was all she had.

'I could just take a look at the disk while I'm here.'

Martha Martin spun round to give her husband an outraged glare. He turned helpless eyes upon Annie. 'But how did you know about it?'

For a second, Annie thought he begged her not to let on that he was the culprit, the one who'd spilt the beans. But then she saw he was sincere. He'd never noticed his slip over the phone. She turned to Mrs Martin. 'Didn't you mention it when you spoke to Pat Thompson yesterday?'

'No. I never said anything about … about any disk. We hadn't made up our minds.' Behind the words, Annie heard uncertainty. Martha Martin hadn't been sure what she'd done or said since she'd heard the news about Terry.

'It might help.' Annie tried to speak gently. 'A trouble shared and all that.'

'The lass has a point, Martha.'

Martha Martin fixed her steady gaze on Annie for a moment, then seemed to come to a decision. 'Come through here.'

The musty aroma of age and sweet smell of polish wrapped itself round her as she followed Martha across the hallway and through to a small sitting room. A tall-backed two-seater settee and matching pair of armchairs clustered round an elaborate fireplace that housed a small electric fire.

'Sit down,' Martha ordered, 'but we've not made our minds up.'

Annie hesitated. The end of the settee nearest the fire was undoubtedly Martha's; her territory marked out with a non-matching cushion placed to support her back, reading glasses balanced on the settee's arm, a worn footstool. The armchair at the other side of the fire was marked equally clearly as Bill's.

The other chair must have been Terry's. Annie hesitated before sitting in it, but the only alternative was the other end of the small settee that would put her in awkward proximity to Martha.

Despite the weather, the room felt chilly, but Annie would lay money the fire wasn't switched on from April to October. Unless, she thought suddenly, Terry had demanded heat. They'd have switched it on for him and never mind the cost. The room was too small for the three of them to remain standing, but their old-fashioned courtesy demanded they wait for her to sit. She took in a breath and sat in Terry's armchair, seeing Martha stiffen as she did so.

Martha sat down with a small gesture to Bill. 'Tell her about his disks.'

'Our Terry did them for the newspapers, love,' Bill told her.

'Did what exactly?'

'He took photos and wrote articles. Quite the roving reporter was our Terry. He did all the village shows.'

'And it was always his stuff they printed, you know,' Martha added with a spark of pride. She gestured towards a tiny television tucked almost out of sight by the side of the settee. 'It was because of his films. He took moving pictures and then made photographs out of the good bits. He said it was the only way to get good shots of the livestock.'

Annie looked at the television. Both Martha and Bill would have to twist awkwardly in their chairs to be able to see the screen. Only Annie, in Terry's chair, had an unimpeded view.

'And this disk?' she prompted.

'It was by his camera. We didn't find it right off, so we didn't tell the police when they came.'

'And they wouldn't have been interested,' Martha muttered.

'Did he have the camera with him when…?' Annie let the question fade.

'No, love. He just had his notebook. The camera was in his room.'

'What's on the disk?'

'We don't know. Our Terry had a special machine to play his disks.'

'Any idea what he might have been filming?'

'He was set to do a story about Spurn, so it might be that. We're not sure. It says "Spurn" in his book, the one he had with him.'

'Spurn Point?' Annie smiled as school memories surfaced. 'A cyclic coastal landform,' she recited.

Both Bill and Martha stared. It was Martha who spoke. 'Do you know Spurn? I thought from your voice you weren't from round here.'

'Oh yes, we learnt all about it at school. One of our teachers took us on a trip there. He was a keen naturalist. We loved it; great stretches of beach and sand dunes.'

'Terry loved Spurn,' Bill said to Annie. 'We used to take him there when he was a lad.'

'It's a wonderful place. It'll be a real shame if they let the sea take it.' For the first time Martha's expression was friendly. By chance, Annie had said the right thing.

This was the time to slip in questions about who had found the body, what were the names of the police officers who'd broken the news, where exactly had it happened? They were too conventional a couple not to give her information now they'd invited her in. On the flip side was the resentment she'd build if she antagonized them. They hadn't signed up to the job yet. She decided to keep quiet.

'You'd better come and see.' Bill got to his feet. 'I'll take her,' he said to Martha. 'You stay here.'

'There's the notebook too,' Martha said. 'She can look at it but don't let her take it away.'

'The notebook?' Annie queried, as she followed Bill out of the room.

'He must have had it in his pocket. They brought us back his things after … afterwards. There was mud on it and that.'

He stopped abruptly in the tiny hallway and Annie prayed he wouldn't break down. She wouldn't know what to do; how to console him. Impulsively, she reached out and put her hand on his arm. He gave her a smile; his eyes shone brightly through tears that didn't quite fall as he said, 'They all say it'll be better when the funeral's out of the way.'

Annie felt shock prickle her skin. 'You haven't had the funeral yet?'

Her eye was drawn to the wooden hallstand and the card that had been in her peripheral vision when she arrived. It was an order of service for the following day.

'Funeral's tomorrow. Things was delayed. They had to do a post-mortem with it being an accident on that site.'

She worked it out. Seven days from death to burial was too short a delay for there to be any doubts that the death was anything other than an accident.

He took her up the narrow staircase and led her into a large front bedroom. 'This is our Terry's room.'

She paused for a mental inventory of the dimensions of the house. This was the main bedroom. Martha and Bill must be squashed into a box room at the back. They'd never change things now though. This would remain a shrine to Terry for as long as they were here to look after it.

Bill opened a cupboard that was stacked with DVDs. 'These are his disks, love. And this is his last one. It wasn't in the cabinet with the rest.'

She took the shiny circle from him. 'You say you haven't watched it?'

'Oh no, we wouldn't know how. They're special disks that our Terry got for his camera. He had a machine for getting photos out of them. We'd have loved to see them, but he couldn't play them for us.'

Annie knelt down by the cupboard and looked closely. They were standard DVDs. And in the corner of the room sat a PC with a larger screen than the television downstairs. She could have this disk in the slot and playing for Bill Martin within a minute, but he'd already lost his purpose in life. She had no reason to destroy him completely by exposing his dead son as a liar. Still, it could be useful to know what Terry had kept on his PC.

'May I look at his computer?' she asked.

Bill hesitated. 'He didn't like folks meddling with his stuff, but you can have a look if you're careful.'

Annie smiled her thanks, walked across and clicked the machine on. It hummed to life and invited her to enter a password. Damn. She tried all the combinations she could think of in case he'd picked something obvious, but without success, and reflected not for the first time that none of the IT courses she'd done had ever been of practical use. She shut the computer down.

'Have you got what you need?'

She gave Bill Martin a smile and a nod and looked round the room. Terry's presence hung over the house. Best seat downstairs, best bedroom. She did a swift calculation. Terry had been born in the late 1960s. His parents looked as though they'd been married forever and must be well into their 70s, touching 80 probably. She imagined Terry as an unexpected late baby, over-indulged all his life. Their illusions about their son were like some precious, bone-china tea-service, irreplaceable and fragile. Annie must be sure that nothing shattered whilst in her care.

'You said there was a notebook?'

Bill Martin pointed to a bookcase where A5 notebooks were neatly stacked. 'He made them to go with the disks.'

As she knelt down to look, she asked, 'Why exactly did you contact a private investigator, Mr Martin?'

'To tell the truth, love, I don't know that Martha knew what she wanted when she rang.'

'And now? Do you want me to look into where he was and what he was doing?'

'I don't know. That'll be up to Martha. The police weren't interested in his notebook, so they won't want his disk. But you can check it out if you like and let us know what he was working on. That'll be a comfort to us.'

It wasn't much comfort to her, but Annie gave him a sympathetic smile. Watching a single DVD wasn't going to provide her with six weeks' gainful employment.

'What made you call Pat Thompson?' she asked. 'Call her direct, I mean, rather than call the agency.'

'We don't know anything about an agency. We got the number off one of our Terry's friends. He called round after … after it happened. He hadn't heard. Martha asked him if he knew anyone. It were just a whim really.'

'Who was he, this friend?'

'I've no idea, love. Our Terry mixed with some dodgy types. He had to, you know, with the line of work he was in for the newspapers. This one were only a young lad. From Hull by the accent. Said our Terry owed him money. Of course, we weren't standing for that. Martha asked him straight out did he know a good private detective. You could see he was the type to mix in that sort of world and he give us that number for Pat Thompson. I think Martha slipped him something for that. He's not been back. We didn't encourage our Terry to bring riff-raff like that home with him.'

'And you've no idea who he is or how to contact him?'

'No, and we wouldn't want to.'

Annie picked a notebook off the shelf at random and pulled it out. She had to grab at it to avoid it coming to pieces in her hand. The sheets were all loose.

'Sorry, love, I should have warned you. Our Terry tore the pages loose when he'd done with them.'

Annie picked out a couple more and carefully flicked through them. From the varying thicknesses she surmised that a lot of pages had been thrown away. The final book was easy to identify. Its cover was twisted and torn, its page edges ragged and smeared with mud. It, like the others, comprised headings and a few scribbled notes. Spurn was there along with a list of village shows, the last being Milesthorpe Show just over a fortnight ago. She wondered if Terry Martin had written the report she'd glimpsed in Vince Sleeman's paper.

'It must have come out of his pocket when he fell,' Bill Martin said.

The final page was torn, a few random markings around the tear suggesting its missing half had been written on. Annie looked a query at Bill.

'We told the policeman about that,' he said. 'We thought it might have been destroyed on purpose with it being the only one missing, but he didn't think there was anything in it.'

Annie looked at the book again and gave Bill a neutral smile. It had survived a fall that had killed its owner, so there wasn't anything remarkable in its being torn. She flicked through it once more, concentrating on where the pages fitted into the spine and felt a glimmer of surprise. Bill Martin was right. That last half page was the only piece completely missing.

CHAPTER 3

ANNIE DIDN'T HURRY back to Hull. The roadside signs with their nationally recognizable camera icons were a useful excuse to keep her speed down. She wanted the time to think. How should she report to Pat? The Martins had cancelled the job, but Pat, who could easily have called Annie up and told her to turn back, must have decided to let her have a go at keeping them on board. And how far had she succeeded in that? Only insofar as they'd given her the DVD to watch.

It wasn't just her own need to carve out a useful role that drove her, but also the need she'd identified within the Martins. As things stood, they would never move on, not a millimetre from the huge frayed end that was their son's death. His funeral wouldn't bring closure. Maybe nothing would, but the only chance they had was to find out why Terry had gone where he'd gone the night he died and just what had happened there.

Annie felt a flicker of pride. Her instinct had led her away from the direct questioning she'd gone out there for and, as a result, she'd made a real connection with the Martins. Martha with her granite features, her hard outer shell that repelled all offers of sympathy and help, had to a tiny extent allowed Annie in. Her spontaneous comment about Spurn Point had been the trigger.

Could she explain any of this to Pat? And would the Martins give the go-ahead for a full investigation into the circumstances of Terry's death? If they did, would she find anything beyond the official version? Had his fall ripped half a page from his notebook? But she knew nothing of the physical circumstances of his accident, had no parameters on which to pin a theory about how a notebook might tear.

She'd packed a lot of baggage into agreeing to watch this DVD and report back on it. Would Pat say she'd overstepped her delegated authority? Idle imaginings over the years had danced around what her first autonomous decision as a PI might be, but her wildest guesses had never come close to this.

As she drew up outside the flat, her mind rested briefly on Bill's words about the 'young lad' who'd given Martha Pat's number. Who was he? Why Pat's number and not the agency's?

Pat, from her accustomed position slumped in the cushions of the big settee, pulled herself upright and greeted Annie with a hard stare, her tone sharp. 'Why did you turn your phone off? I expect to be able to contact you any time when you're working for me. If you need your phone off, you tell me so I know. If you're out in the field and I can't contact you, it might be a sign you're in trouble. I could have had the troops out looking for you.'

'But I didn't. I ...' Annie scrabbled through her pockets for her phone and pulled it out. A blank screen looked up at her. 'Oh hell, I'm sorry, I don't know how that happened. I must have caught it by mistake.'

She sent up a silent prayer and held her breath as she pushed the on-switch. The phone flickered to life with a tinny jingle. Her phone had been on the blink for weeks, but just trust it to let her down now.

'The Martin woman rang the moment you were out of the door,' Pat said. 'Could have saved a journey if you'd had the blasted thing on.'

Annie realized the phone hadn't let her down at all. She rubbed its casing like a good luck charm as she put it back in her pocket.

Pat sighed and shifted position. 'OK then, how did you get on? Did you manage to talk them into giving you the job?'

'Well, sort of.'

'Go on.'

Annie outlined the events of the visit as accurately as she could, trying to give Pat a feel for the ambiance, the sense that the Martins really did need this job to be done. She looked out over the river as she spoke. The water spread out calm and smooth, just the twists and turns of the sunlight dancing on the surface giving a hint of the turbulent currents beneath. She felt as though she'd seen those shafts of sunlight dancing on the grave Terry Martin wouldn't inhabit until tomorrow, but of course tiny snags disturbed the surface of the calmest settings at times. It didn't necessarily mean anything.

Pat let her finish her account before she held her hand out for the DVD. When Annie passed it to her, she held it up to the light and twisted it from side to side. 'It's been well-handled,' was her verdict.

Annie imagined Bill and Martha clutching it as though it were some precious silver coin whose currency they didn't understand, studying it from every angle, wondering what to do with it. The last link to their son's life and one more segment still hidden from them.

'And you think you can get a job out of them on the back of this?'

'Yes, I've a good chance. I made a connection with them. I don't think they've got anyone else.'

'I'll make a copy of it when I go through.' Pat nodded her head towards her bedroom. 'Keep the original as untouched as possible when you work with anything like this. You realize what you've done, don't you? If you're to have a chance of talking them round, it'll have to be face to face. You've committed us to another round trip to Withernsea. Vince and his cheap labour. Huh!'

Annie noted Pat's comments with interest. Equipment that would copy a DVD must mean a PC and access to e-mail and internet when she needed them.

'Right then, the funeral,' Pat went on. 'What time is it? Where?'

Annie closed her eyes to recall the Martins' hallway so she could retrieve the details she'd read on the tiny card and recite them to Pat.

'Nine o'clock in the morning? You'd better leave by eight. The traffic'll be bad.'

'You want me to go?'

'Oh yeah. You show your face at the funeral. Make sure you look sad, caring, all that kind of stuff. Check who turns up. With luck there won't be many there so you'll stand out for making the effort. Don't make a nuisance of yourself, but talk to whoever's there, see what you can find out. Then, when you contact the Martins, you'll be in a stronger position to ease them into agreeing to the job. We'll give them a day or two. I hope you've something suitable to wear.'

'Uh … yes. Yes, I have.' She'd brought every stitch she owned. 'By the way, I asked Bill Martin how come he'd chosen to contact you.' Annie told Pat about the young lad whose name Bill didn't know, who had passed on Pat's number.

Pat looked blank. 'No idea. I suppose he must have seen the advert.'

The advert? Any adverts would surely have the agency number not Pat's. Annie looked the question at Pat who shrugged.

'I shoved an advert in one of the local rags a couple of weeks ago. Mrs Earle was the only answer I got, until yesterday that is when Martha Martin rang. I only needed the one. I wasn't expecting anything after the first couple of days. Those things have a short shelf-life and it was only a one-off. Maybe this kid, whoever he was, had the page wrapped round some chips or something.'

'But why did you put the advert in? Surely the agency advertises.'

'I was having a go at Vince, if you must know, giving him a nudge.'

'About what?'

'About the work he was passing on to me. Nothing you need worry about.'

'Did it work?'

'Well, who knows? I went and picked this thing up.' Pat gave a nod towards her leg. 'We'll see when I'm up and about. And don't get the wrong idea: Vince is OK, just needs a nudge now and then. We're OK, me and Vince.'

Annie knew she'd get no more by direct questioning. She changed tack and asked, 'How did it happen? Your leg, I mean.'

'I fell down some stairs. Going too fast, not taking care. I probably slipped.'

'Probably?'

'I slipped, OK?'

'The stairs here?'

'No.'

'It looks to be a nasty break.'

'It is, but I can manage.'

'That's what Vince brought me here for, isn't it? It wasn't to cover for your cases; it was to look after you.'

Pat gave a mirthless laugh. 'It took me about two seconds to suss him. And I'll tell you this, if I'd seen so much as a hint in you of this caring bollocks I'd have had you down those stairs so fast you'd have broken both bloody legs!'

'But you could have got someone in from round here if you'd needed anyone.'

'Which is just the point I can't get across. I don't need anyone. I can look after myself. I can't abide people fussing about. It's not only Vince behind this; it'll be Babs, too, though she denies it. Someone to cover the work was a different matter. I agreed to that. Just didn't expect him to land me with a houseguest.'

Babs? Annie remembered the name she'd seen on the company papers. Babs must be Barbara Caldwell. She wouldn't query the name immediately in case a flicker of guilt at her snooping showed through. 'Is that why he picked me, because I'd have to live in? I mean I could have found some-where to rent for the six weeks.'

'Could you? On what Vince is paying you? Or are you rich enough not to have to worry?'

It was too good an opportunity to miss. Annie confessed her parlous financial circumstances. 'It's the car that worries me,' she ended. 'When it needs petrol I'm not sure I've enough cash to fill a tank that size. I don't want to risk my card. It's right at its limit.'

Pat's laugh this time was genuine. 'Broke enough to have to live in, desperate to get PI experience and, on Vince's scale, an airhead. Do you think he knew all that before he saw you?'

She felt herself colour up, remembering the chatty conversation she'd walked in on as Kara passed on her life story to a stranger who'd rung to arrange an interview. 'Yes, I'm sure he did.'

'Then I imagine he just stumbled upon you and snapped you up. They knew I wouldn't have anyone in to look after me, but I wasn't going to object to someone in to cover the work. Anyway you're here, Vince is paying, and there are a couple of cases for you to get your teeth into. If you try any of the caring malarkey, mind, you'll be out quicker than you came.'

'A couple of cases?'

'Yes, I had a call from Mrs Earle on Orchard Park. She wants to know why the hell no one's been back to see her.'

'But Vince said—'

'I know, but he can't have cancelled the job, so maybe he's changed his mind. Oh, and that doesn't mean we need to go blabbing to him about it.'

Annie digested this. A nub of excitement grew inside her. From nebulous bits of jobs that might evaporate and leave her in limbo, things were beginning to look up. And what was this thing between Pat and Vince? Pat might say the two of them were OK, but her words were a clear warning to Annie that they would do this behind Vince's back. 'Vince expected you to cancel the Orchard Park job, didn't he?'

Pat tossed her a sideways glance. 'He told me it was cancelled. Not my fault if no one told the client. I've said you'll go round tomorrow. Give her a ring on your way back from Terry Martin's funeral to make sure she's there. She's horribly unreliable.'

The funeral the next morning was a quiet affair. Annie arrived ahead of the coffin to see only a thin sprinkling of others in the church. Three young girls sat near the back where they whispered and stifled occasional giggles. An elderly couple sat midway down; the man pulled continually at his shirt collar and cast worried glances at the woman beside him.

Just settling into a pew at the back was a tall woman about Annie's age, her small features framed by mid-length dark hair. There was something graceful about the way she moved as she tried to create more legroom, yet she looked ungainly too. Annie identified the awkwardness as her clothes. She wore a tweedy suit more suited to someone Martha Martin's age and far too fussy a style for her majestic form.

She was an obvious initial target. Annie slid into the seat next to her, gave her a nod of acknowledgement and whispered, 'Are you here for Terry Martin's funeral?'

'Yes, I am. You too?'

'Yes.' Annie held out her hand. 'I'm Annie Raymond. How d'you do?'

The woman looked surprised but returned Annie's handshake. 'Jennifer Flanagan.'

'Were you a friend of Terry's?'

'Oh no, I never met him … um … saw him until he was … well, you know … dead. I was involved the night he died. I'm a police officer. Did you know him well?'

Bang on target, thought Annie, as she replied, 'I didn't know him at all. I'm a private investigator working for his parents.' It felt good to label herself.

'Working for the Martins?' Jennifer said, an edge of suspicion shading her tone. 'Is it about what happened?'

'Well, no, not really.' Annie back-pedalled, realizing that good though it had felt to boast about her profession, it hadn't been a smart first move. You'll meet suspicion, she'd been told often enough, if you dip your toes into police territory or anywhere that might muddy their waters. 'Mr and

Mrs Martin have just employed our agency to look at some of Terry's things. Were you in charge of the investigation into his death?'

Jennifer gave a soft laugh. 'Oh no. I'm only a probationer. PC Greaves – he's my tutor – says it's good public relations to show your face at this sort of thing. I went with him to answer the emergency call.'

So there had been two of them, despite Pat's assessment. 'Not the sort of call you want, is it? A body on your watch. Did you know it was an accident when you went out there?'

'Frankly, we didn't know what we were going to. The old man who found him was in a terrible state. From the message we didn't know if he'd found a dead cat or unearthed a massacre.'

Jennifer would assume the Martins had provided the facts about the night Terry died, so wouldn't mind speaking about things she thought Annie already knew. Aiming a bow at a venture, she nodded to the pews opposite. 'What's-his-name over there, you mean?'

Jennifer followed the line of Annie's gaze and looked at the nervy man the other side of the church who bent over on the wooden seat, a few silver strands of hair stretched across his otherwise smooth scalp. 'Charles Tremlow. Yes, that's right.'

While they watched, the man pulled again at his collar and gave a hunted look at the woman next to him. Annie made a lightning character assessment and chanced a further comment. 'I'm surprised he made the call. He looks the sort who'd just panic.'

'Oh, you're right. He didn't call us straight away. He called a friend.'

A friend? 'Oh? I thought *she* was there,' Annie murmured, looking at the woman beside Tremlow.

'Yes, she was. She went round for some reason of her own, but he'd already called Ludgrove. And, of course, by the time we got there, we had three of them to deal with and all with a different story.'

Annie mentally filed this and risked a question that displayed her ignorance. 'Isn't she his wife?'

'Oh no. He isn't married. I think he's divorced. She's just … well, to be honest I think she's just the village busybody.'

Annie itched to ask for the woman's name and address. Milesthorpe's resident busybody who'd been on the spot the night Terry died was just the sort of contact she needed, but the question would signal a fishing trip too clearly, and she reminded herself that she didn't yet have the job of looking into Terry's death. Instead, she asked Jennifer, 'Were you one of the ones who went to see the Martins that night?'

Jennifer nodded. 'It was awful. It's the first time I've done anything like that. You learn how to break bad news and what you should do, but the reality was nothing like it. I wasn't the one doing the talking, but I thought I'd be able to give some support.'

'Were you with PC Greaves, the one you mentioned before?'

'No, another colleague went with me to the Martins. PC Kerridge. I was glad about that. PC Greaves isn't ... well, he's not the most sympathetic man I've met.'

Three of them involved on the night, Annie noted. Positively over-staffed from what Pat had told her. 'It's terrible the way it's hit them, isn't it?'

'Oh yes, and they don't seem to have anyone. They wouldn't let us call anyone. He was just stunned. It was as though we'd hit him so hard we'd barely left him conscious. I felt I could have reached him somehow, said something, but he didn't seem to be with us at all. And she brought down the shutters like nothing I've ever seen. She made me feel we were prying, like some sort of ghoulish voyeurs.'

Annie could see from Jennifer's expression that her encounter with the Martins still preyed on her. 'I can imagine it,' she said. 'It took some hard work for me to make a dent and I had the advantage that they'd invited me in.' Hard work? No, just a lucky break. And maybe this was another one. Pat had asked Martha a few questions over the phone and had no useful replies. Pat assumed Martha knew the detail of what had happened but had been too upset to talk about it. Maybe she didn't. Maybe it wasn't just that she couldn't bear to talk, she hadn't been able to ask either. 'They didn't ask you anything, did they?'

'No. They answered our questions. She did, anyway, but she wouldn't let us tell her anything. It was as though she couldn't bear us to know things about him that she didn't. Wouldn't you think "How?" would be the first question you'd ask? You could see her close her mouth on it, then she just held us off, kind of gritted her teeth until she could get us out of the house. We told her to get in touch if she wanted to, but she hasn't.'

Annie saw her chance. 'I don't think she's kept your contact details. Could I take a card? I might get the chance to pass it on and I'm sure she will want to talk to you. She needs to know what happened that night.'

Annie hoped this might prompt Jennifer to say something about the events in Milesthorpe, but she nodded without speaking and reached into her bag. As she passed Annie a business card, she said, 'Can I take one of yours?'

'Uh ... yes, of course. Only I'm afraid it's my boss's. I'm new in the job, haven't had any cards made up yet. My number's on the back.'

Pat would be pleased with progress so far and Annie decided to devote some time later to the map of Milesthorpe and the electoral register. She'd like to build a mental image in her mind. She had two surnames to work with, Tremlow and Ludgrove, and might have more before the day was over.

She looked over at the three girls. The tallest raised her head and raked the church with a lofty glance. Annie wondered if they were relatives and, if so, why they sat in an isolated bunch. 'Not much of a turnout, is it?'

Jennifer shrugged, then shushed Annie with a gesture as canned music started and there was a flurry of movement at the church door. Annie hoped to see a crowded funeral cortège enter, but the half-dozen pallbearers outnumbered the following mourners two to one. Behind Bill and Martha Martin came a woman Annie was certain must be the sister of one of them, but they were all so alike she couldn't have said which.

Bill caught her eye and gave her a nod and half a smile. Martha looked neither left nor right as she followed her son's remains towards the altar.

Just as the coffin settled on its trestle, there was a commotion from across the aisle and Annie saw the smallest of the three girls scramble to her feet and rush out. Neither of her friends made a move to follow, so Annie got up and crept out after her.

The girl, ashen-faced, leant against the wall of the church. Straggly dark hair hung forward partly obscuring her sallow features. Annie looked for any familial resemblance to the Martins but saw none. The girl, eleven or twelve years old, breathed in great gulps. Her cheeks were tear-streaked.

'Hey, hey, relax. Come on, deep breaths. These things are never nice. Did you know him well?' Annie smiled and put a hand on the girl's shoulder.

'I didn't want to come. I hated him. I can't bear to think about it. His head all bashed in. I think I'm going to be sick.'

Annie took a step back. 'Come on now. Breathe deep through your nose. You'll be fine.'

The girl turned big trusting eyes up to her. 'I'm sorry, I didn't think. I shouldn't have said I hated him, not with him being ... you know. My mother says I should think before I say things.'

'That's OK. I don't always think before I get myself tangled up in things. There are worse faults. My name's Annie Raymond.'

The girl took her hand in a limp handshake. 'I'm Laura Tunbridge.'

'How old are you, Laura?'

'I'm twelve. So were you his girlfriend?'

Annie smiled and knew she could harvest the names of everyone in the church, and maybe a few who weren't, from a garrulous child like Laura. She had an easy hook to reel the girl in. 'No, I didn't know him at all. I'm a private detective. I've been hired by his parents.'

A grin lit Laura's tearstained features. 'Oh wow, a private detective. That's so cool. Anyway, I don't think he had a girlfriend.'

No, thought Annie, it doesn't look like it. 'How did you know him, Laura?'

'I didn't know him. Not really. Not like introduced and that. I mean I so didn't want to know him. He just hung about. Mally knew him best.'

'Mally's one of the ones you came here with?'

'Yeah, the other one's Kay. Kay's my best friend. I so wouldn't have come at all if Kay hadn't. Only Mally's grandad said it would be a kindness to Mr Tremlow, to show him some support, so me and Kay got a lift with Mrs Kitson.'

Annie employed no subtlety as she questioned Laura for her friends' surnames – Dearlove and Fletcher – and confirmation that Mrs Kitson was the woman with Tremlow in the church. The colour crept back to the girl's cheeks and her face broke out in a delighted grin.

'But wow! A private detective. That's so cool. Will you wait and tell them? Mally'll so not believe me. She'll say I made you up.'

Annie laughed and pulled one of Pat's cards from her pocket. 'That's the agency I work for.'

'That says Patricia Thompson. You said your name was Annie.'

'Pat's my boss. I borrowed some of her cards. My name and number are written on the other side.'

Laura scrutinized the card front and back, then put it in her pocket with an air of importance. 'I'll let you know if I find out who did it.'

'The police are satisfied it was an accident,' Annie said gently.

'So what do they know?' Laura dismissed the official investigation with a wave of her hand before giving a great gasp and staring up at Annie. 'Oh look, it wasn't us. It so wasn't anything to do with us. Mally didn't mean it.'

'What didn't Mally mean?'

'When she said she'd kill him. She so didn't mean it. Not like really kill him.'

'Why did she say it? What had he done?'

Laura's gaze slid away to one side, her whole body radiating wariness. 'Oh nothing. He was just a creep.'

Annie smiled, amused. Some childish transgression preyed on Laura's mind. Interesting that she knew Terry Martin well enough to dislike him. A thirty-seven year old impinges on the lives of a group of twelve year olds from a village almost ten miles from his home. Her amusement faded. The implications weren't pleasant.

'Come on,' she said. 'Do you feel strong enough to go back in?'

It was late morning when Annie drove across Hull towards Orchard Park.

As Pat instructed, she'd rung Mrs Earle who'd said through an exaggerated yawn, 'Yeah, anytime. I'm not going anywhere today.'

The neat rural scene with twisty roads and huge expanses of crop fields changed first to pockets of buildings crowding the road and then to the industrial landscape that was east Hull. The road surface deteriorated as she neared her destination. The tarmac gave way to concrete slabs that sat uneasily as though disturbed by something beneath. Narrow roads threaded through open spaces surrounding low rectangular terraces and towering blocks up to twenty storeys high. The concrete landscape sucked in the sun's rays and held them tight creating an arid desert. Nothing rural about the grass here. It was short, tamed town grass trodden to dust along well-used paths, and strewn with litter. Two boys ran back and forth around the skeleton of a burnt-out car. A scrappy feel. Just like Terry Martin's send-off. His parents, one elderly relation and remnants of people he'd only half known. The only ones remotely near his own age had been Annie and Jennifer neither of whom had met him.

She bounced Pat's car over speed bumps and wondered how on earth a funeral procession left this area with any dignity. Bill and Martha had at least been spared the ignominy of speed bumps, though their pathetic cortège, a hearse and a black car that swallowed the three of them into its huge interior, had been forced to an abrupt halt as it tried to leave the churchyard for Terry's final journey.

Annie felt anger rise as she remembered the red Fiat that had screeched up packed with adolescent boys, blaring loud music from its open windows and caused the hearse to stop. Their antics were more suited to the battered environment of this edge of Orchard Park, but it had been Terry's funeral they'd disrupted briefly while the few mourners stood awkwardly about waiting for the Martins to go so they could slip back to their everyday lives.

The car had been gone in seconds in a squeal of tyres and a hail of shouted comments that were drowned by the booming beat from within. It was over too quickly for anyone to do anything. Annie had seen Laura slap out at one of her companions who'd laughed. 'It so isn't funny!'

Annie had tried to shake off the emptiness she felt, and the guilt that she could walk away while the Martins started a life sentence without their son. Maybe she could unearth the big story that he'd been after. Or more likely make one up. Would posthumous publicity be any consolation? To Martha perhaps. And she couldn't do that unless she could make the leap from watching Terry's last DVD to getting them to agree to an investigation.

Annie pulled up in the shadow of one of the tower blocks. A group of children slouched at the fringes of the car-park. They looked Laura Tunbridge's age but tougher, more worldly-wise. Slowly she turned her head in the direction of their bold stares, but kept her own gaze on the row of houses across the way, until at the last moment when she snapped her eyes to meet theirs – an imitation of the tactic Vince used with her. She felt gratification in seeing their stares drop as she climbed out of the car. Body language was wary now more than defiant. Fine. Let them think her a drug dealer with an army to call on. It might keep Pat's car in one piece while she interviewed Mrs Earle on the sixth floor.

A crowd at the entrance jostled about laughing. Annie slipped inside in their wake, noting a security system that should lock the doors against all comers. Probably it hadn't worked in a long time. A uniformed guard sat behind a glass wall in a security booth. Annie took in the shabbiness of the over-elaborate jacket and complete lack of interest in anything but the newspaper on his lap.

The stench in the lift made her pinch in her nose, but six floors meant twelve flights of stairs. No joke in this heat. It wasn't as complex an estate as some she'd seen. She'd rented a room in a block in East London which had been a nightmare of complicated walkways, twisting streets and alley-ways providing cover and escape routes.

This was on a smaller scale, but clearly had its hotspots. The question was what could she do about it? She and Pat didn't have the muscle behind them to go after any perpetrators and warn them off. Find out who they are, Pat had said, and get a handle to move them on. Or if she found real wrong-doing, and could produce the evidence to match, it would surely be a police job.

A large man in shirtsleeves and rumpled trousers answered her knock.

'Annie Raymond. I'm here to see Mrs Earle.'

'She ain't here.' The man made no move to elaborate the bald statement or to invite her in.

Annie looked at her watch. 'But I arranged it with her on the phone less than an hour ago. Will she be long? Can I come in and wait?'

'You from that private eye place?' He looked her up and down and grinned. 'I suppose you'll fall lighter than the fat bint. Broke her leg, didn't she?'

Annie stiffened. So this was where it had happened. Involuntarily she glanced back towards the concrete staircase she might have climbed on a cooler day. She didn't like it that this man knew about Pat's accident, much less that something in his tone implied it hadn't been an accident at all.

'So will Mrs Earle be long?' she asked again.

The man shrugged and yawned. 'She went off with her mate. No point waiting. She might stay over. Says she doesn't like it here with all the bother at nights.'

Annie let out a huff of exasperation. 'That's what I'm here for. Where does her friend live? I'll call and see her there.'

Another shrug. 'Somewhere Sutton way.'

'Do you have an address?'

'Nah.'

Annie stared. Was that the best he would offer when she'd gone to all this trouble? 'If you see her, tell her I called. I'll give her a ring later.' She snapped the words out as she turned on her heel and retraced her steps.

With an unexpected gap in her day, she decided to drive into town and find Hull's main library. She could spend an hour with Milesthorpe's electoral register and telephone directory.

When Annie returned to the waterfront apartment an hour and a half later, it was with a dissatisfied feeling of business undone. The funeral had gone to plan as far as talking to people was concerned, but it was all for nothing unless she could find a way to bring the Martins back round to the idea of an investigation. And the Orchard Park job had hit an unexpected dead end. Horribly unreliable, Pat had said of Mrs Earle. The comment was spot on.

'Hi, d'you want coffee?' she called, as she made straight for the kitchen and flicked the kettle on.

No reply.

She set out the cups and went through to the living room. 'That woman on Orchard Park, she …'

An empty room lay before her. 'Pat,' she raised her voice and called through towards the bedroom. Nothing. She was alone in the flat.

Annie made coffee for one. No reason Pat shouldn't go out, of course, and she was under no obligation to tell Annie her movements, but it felt unsettling. It hadn't occurred to her that Pat could get herself down the stairs and where would she go then? Annie had the car and anyway Pat couldn't possibly drive with that thing on her leg.

What should she do now? She decided to raid Pat's store of French bread and make a sandwich, but as she turned towards the kitchen, sunlight speared through the big window and caught a pool of silver on the top of the TV. A disk lay there. The Martins' DVD.

Pat had been going to make a copy. Annie's obvious next task was to do it herself, but the PC was in Pat's bedroom and it would mean breaching the boundaries of Pat's personal space, something for which she should get the OK first. She decided to play the disk anyway.

She slid it into the DVD player and sat back to watch. If Mrs Earle continued to play silly buggers there was little else for her to do.

Crash! A silver-foam-topped rush of waves flooded the screen making Annie sit up in alarm, her hands gripping the chair arms as though the water were a here and now threat. A voice that must be Terry Martin's, a slightly nasal whine, filled the room.

'Spurn Point,' he announced, over jerky shots of the pebbly beach.

The camera drew back at dizzying speed, the water receding, the pebbles rushing away, becoming sand dunes and tough grasses. Annie tried to recognize the scene, but couldn't.

'Ah bollocks!' The profanity broke the mood as did the sudden disorientation of the camera angle, swooping up to face the sky, then taking a dive into an unfocused close-up. Terry Martin had tripped.

After the contrived drama of the opening sequence, the following shots of beach, grassland and marshes lacked continuity. Terry's few remarks sounded lacklustre as though he knew he would bore his audience. He began a couple of commentaries on the breached road; on the isolation of life in the tiny community, but they petered out, incomplete. Annie thought back to the schoolteacher whose enthusiasm might have imbued her with a love of natural history if her heart hadn't been long sold to the world of private investigation. She wasn't sure why Terry Martin bothered. It was a big enough story in its way, the instability of life on this outpost with the North Sea's constant battering that might separate it from the mainland at any moment; the debates over whether the sea would inevitably claim it and what would happen to the shipping lanes in the Humber if Spurn were swallowed by the waves. But it was a story done to death and Terry Martin had no new angle to hook it on.

An abrupt cut took the film from landscape to close up. 'Rumour has it this place sees some interesting night-time activity. Let's see what evidence we can find.' Terry Martin's voice dropped to a whisper with a sly undertone. Annie stared as the camera closed in on a small concrete bunker. A war relic, she thought.

The camera approached the opening and Terry Martin lowered his voice further. His words were carried away on the rush of pebbles under the waves. Annie strained to hear, but couldn't make out more than the occasional phrase. 'What goes on ... dead of night ...' She found herself at the edge of the chair as the camera swung round into the dark interior.

An empty McCoy's crisp packet flapped gently in a corner. 'Naff all,' whined Terry Martin back to normal volume.

The film cut to a different time of day, indoors now, a close-up of a giant onion filling the screen. The following shots swung from smiling faces to prize-winning entries; a proud smile, a marrow, then a pot of jam with a frilly top and rose-patterned label. Over it all Terry Martin intoned a laborious roll call of winners, spelling out some of the names.

After ten minutes of this, Annie's eyelids grew heavy and hunger gnawed at her so she turned up the volume and went through to the kitchen, leaving the door open so Terry Martin's commentary made a backdrop to her breaking bread rolls and slicing cheese. These sorts of shots, she had no doubt, were the basis of the reports that appeared under Terry Martin's byline in the local press. Local show reports had to be accurate. They might record someone's sole claim to fame and mustn't do so with a misspelt name.

As she balanced a pyramid of three sandwiches on a small plate, Annie realized that Terry Martin had gone silent. The thought had barely formed when a woman's voice from the living room screeched, 'Just fuck off!'

She jumped with the shock and had to juggle the sandwiches to keep them on the plate. She raced back through to a momentary view of a face contorted with rage before the scene snapped to a sunlit field crowded with vehicles and ponies weaving their way through brightly dressed people, trestle tables and flapping tapes.

'Milesthorpe Green,' Terry Martin's voice announced, as Annie grabbed the remote and froze him.

Her mind leapt to touch disconnected ideas as she took the film through jerky backward movements to the jam and fruit affair. She let the film play again.

The mundane recital of show winners cut abruptly to an outdoor scene at dusk. The camera faced a house front, the only background noise the soft wheeze of Terry Martin's breathing as he zoomed in on one of the windows.

No sign or sound of life anywhere near him. When he spoke, his voice was back at the surreptitious level he'd used to stalk the disappointing concrete bunker at Spurn. Without the rush of the sea Annie could make out his words.

'Beckes split over brook.' That sly undertone again and a soft laugh.

The picture wobbled. He stopped zooming in on the house from a standstill and approached on foot.

'Mrs Becke's secret affair.' Something about the furtive satisfaction in his tone made Annie's skin crawl. 'Who's the lucky guy? And how much does Mr Becke know, I wonder.'

'Just fuck off!'

Though she'd heard it before, the shriek still made Annie jump. From the gasp and the jolt Annie was sure Terry Martin had thought himself alone. The lens swung at dizzying speed, gave one brief shot of the enraged woman. Late twenties, maybe thirty. A small slim woman. Her face filled the screen for just a second then the film cut from the still of dusk to the crowds and noise of a sunny afternoon on Milesthorpe Green.

Mentally she flagged the episode and noted the surname it had given her. She sat back with her sandwiches and watched the crowds who might be contestants in a garish colours competition. What on earth was she to tell the Martins about this disconnected collection?

She remembered the notebook with its torn page. What she looked at on the screen now was surely Milesthorpe Show. He'd filmed these sequences on the Sunday of the show. And he'd died nine days later, exactly a week ago. As he'd strolled across Milesthorpe Green with his camera Terry Martin had nine days left to live. A cold shiver ran through her.

The scene changed again. Still Milesthorpe Show but this must be a different part of the green. Small children clad in huge hats and padded protective clothing raced through the heat on their ponies like old-fashioned knights in miniature.

The crowds were incidental background now. Terry Martin concentrated on the ponies, mostly at a distance. Occasionally, a horse and rider flew by close at hand and leapt a pole balanced across a line of concrete blocks. He might cull some good action shots from this sequence to accompany his show report. Suddenly, events hit closer to home. Two ponies raced at the obstacle. Terry Martin was unprepared for them to swerve out at the last moment and almost run him down. Annie couldn't help laughing as he backed off hurriedly and went over backwards in a tangle of legs as the ponies flew by. No good stills from the close up of hoofs and flying clods of mud.

Cut again to a familiar sequence. The winners in groups. She smothered a yawn and wondered how long this would last.

The sight of a grinning Laura Tunbridge grabbed her attention for a moment. Laura sat astride a small brown pony and accepted a red rosette and a cup.

Annie waited for Terry Martin to speak and maybe spell out her name, but he remained silent. Of course he already knew her, but he seemed to lose interest. The camera swung away from the winners, raked the crowd, then drew back. She realized he'd filmed this from quite a distance away. The background boom of tannoy announcements was audible but not clear enough to make sense. He'd get no words or pictures in print from this one.

The camera swung in lazy arcs and zoomed only occasionally, once to focus on a group of three girls leaving the field. Two rode ponies, the other a bicycle. Annie recognized Laura Tunbridge again, but couldn't say for certain whether the other two were Kay Dearlove and Mally Fletcher – the best-friend and the one who'd said she'd kill Terry Martin. She felt uneasy that Terry had chosen to pick them out of the crowds.

Another close-up was on a couple talking by the dismantled remains of an awning. The woman was the one who'd told Terry Martin to fuck off, presumably Mrs Becke. Maybe the man was the secret lover.

Annie wondered what had first brought Terry to a village ten miles from his home, and what connection he had with the people there.

It took a moment to realize that one of Terry's random cuts had taken the film away from Milesthorpe Green, away from the sunny outdoors. One moment the screen had shown the tired crowds, the next it was dark and all background noise had gone.

Terry Martin was in a cellar. Annie had to squint at the screen to compensate for the lack of light in the shot. She made out a corridor and ragged lengths of timber hanging from dilapidated walls. The only sounds were Terry Martin's breathing and a steady drip of water.

'Got you now, Mr Balham.'

Annie allowed herself a sigh of exasperation. That was Terry Martin's surreptitious voice again, but constrained as though something restricted his breathing.

There was a flurry as the camera wobbled. Annie had the impression he'd swapped it to his other hand.

A wooden door swam into focus from the shadow. The shot dropped to floor level and steadied at an angle. Terry Martin had put the camera on the ground while he dealt with the door. Annie watched as the Martins' son appeared from behind the camera. She stared closely, curious to know what he looked like, but in the gloom he was little more than a silhouette, a small man bent over in the darkness, his back to the lens. Sound as much as movement told her he wrestled with a key in the lock. Then the camera was hoisted to shoulder level and the door pushed open. The murkiness lifted a little as though the light were better beyond the door.

Annie took in the briefest impression of a largish room as ramshackle as the corridor before the picture dropped.

'Oh my God!' Terry Martin's cry choked itself in a gasp.

A flurry of movement. The camera slewed through bizarre angles. Terry Martin retched and choked as he fought for breath.

Annie heard his feet slip on the rubble of the floor, saw his backward stumble in the sudden upward swing of the lens. Then it steadied. One clear shot into the room. A second and a half.

'Oh my God!' The words came involuntarily, as Annie clapped her hands to her mouth and echoed Terry Martin.

A large woman, Pat's size at least, slumped backwards. All elements of the scene hit simultaneously. The splayed legs, the skirt ridden high, the hint of lace beneath it. The woman's head lolled at an impossible angle, her eyes stared, her tongue protruded gross and blackened. And at her neck a ligature bit deep.

The camera's incoherence charted Terry Martin's fight to escape; to keep to his feet. His frantic flailing must have caught the camera controls. There was a sudden zoom. A momentary close up of what was left of an eye in a gaping socket. A fat white worm wriggled and took centre stage.

Cut.

CHAPTER 4

ANNIE STOOD IN front of the television, no memory of the move that had taken her from sitting to upright. Barely noticed, her bread and cheese bounced on to the carpet, a plate clattered against the leg of the coffee table. For a few seconds, the screen played a frantic blizzard into the room, then it blanked leaving no trace of the bloated features now etched on Annie's mind.

He'd found his big story. The thought whirled in her brain. Terry Martin of all people had uncovered a murder.

A part of her wanted to pull out the disk and smash it to pieces. The Martins didn't need this. They'd seen Terry's big story in terms of a learned treatise on Spurn Point, him as a David Attenborough figure giving a weighty commentary. Annie thought of Terry stalking a concrete bunker, looking for evidence of sinister night-time activity; creeping up to Mrs Becke's house at dusk with his sly comments about a secret lover. Uncovering a gruesome murder was exactly the sort of thing he'd dreamt of doing. Then she remembered his panic as he'd entered that cellar. Living the dream hadn't been so good.

And how on earth did she tell his parents what he'd found?

At the same time, a small part of her mind stood back and began to analyse. What had he unearthed? Whose remains had he found? Had he filmed the woman alive? If Annie were to rerun the film would she find the victim in an earlier scene grinning from behind a giant onion, or wandering about in the crowds on Milesthorpe Green?

The woman's body had begun to decay, but given the sweltering weather, not that much. Her death wasn't ancient history. Whoever strangled her had done it recently. Terry Martin had filmed Milesthorpe Show on the Sunday and nine days later he'd died. Sometime in that nine days he'd found and filmed the woman in the cellar.

'Oh my God. Pat …'

But Pat wasn't here. Annie was alone. She grabbed at her phone and dialled Pat's mobile only to hear the tone sing out from the empty bedroom.

'Yeah, great,' she shouted out at the chirpy ring-tone. 'So much for keeping your phone on at all times.'

She paused to take a deep breath, rerunning the advice she'd given Laura Tunbridge outside the church. What were her options? Easy answer. There weren't options, plural. She knew exactly what she had to do. This had crossed official boundaries without ambiguity. She had to call the police.

Still she hesitated. It seemed wrong that she, the new employee, the temp who hadn't been employed to get involved, should call the police into the heart of the agency's business. Pat should be here to take the reins, to make the call. What would Vince say when he found out?

The television hummed gently, ready to spring to life and replay the disk at the press of a button. Annie retrieved the remote from the floor so she could turn it off. She watched herself hold it away from her body between thumb and forefinger as though the images had leaked out to infect it.

Get a grip. Do what has to be done. She stood up straight. There could be no question of ersatz drama here. And anyway, she had no need to speak to an anonymous voice in a call centre. She grabbed her coat and scrabbled through the pockets. Where was that card?

Her fingers felt the size of fat sausages and the buttons on the phone shrank to pinheads, but she fumbled through the number and listened to the ring tone. Charles Tremlow, the nervy man at the funeral, hadn't managed to get out a coherent story when he'd phoned in a panic to report finding Terry Martin's body. Jennifer implied they didn't even know how many bodies he'd found. There was something about talking to a stranger … maybe Tremlow had felt it too. Calm. She must be calm.

Answer. Please answer. Don't let it be voicemail.

'Hello? Jennifer Flanagan here.'

'Jennifer, it's Annie Raymond from the PI agency. We met at Terry Martin's funeral. I need your help.'

Annie paced back and forth wearing a track across the longest stretch of carpet the flat had to offer. Jennifer had promised to come out with a colleague as soon as she could. But why weren't they here? She paused to stare out at the estuary where rippling patterns in the water wove around and through each other painting the surface of one of the world's most treacherous shipping lanes. So much hidden beneath the surface. Then she rushed back to the other side of the flat, to the kitchen where the window looked out over the road, where she'd see Jennifer arrive, or Pat.

Annie kicked herself for not sounding more panicked on the phone. She'd gone to the opposite extreme from Tremlow, but now realized she'd been every bit as incoherent downplaying the enormity of what she'd found.

'But how urgent is it? What is it you've found? I don't understand.'

'It's evidence of a crime. A serious crime. One of the cases I'm working on.' The memory of the decomposing body inhibited her. She didn't want to try to describe it, couldn't even bring herself to say Terry Martin's name aloud.

'We have to come into Hull to get a witness statement. We could call in. About half an hour … maybe an hour. But if it's really urgent then you should call direct.'

How urgent was it? Too late for the woman in the cellar. 'That's fine. Half an hour's fine.'

Only it wasn't. *Pace – pace – pace.*

The sound of a car slowing to turn the corner had Annie at full stretch straining to see. Not a police car. She followed the course of the large blue people-carrier as it approached and pulled up across the road.

Pat!

Annie was out of the door and taking the stairs in huge three and four step bounds. Thank God Pat was here first so she could explain what she'd done. 'I didn't know how long you'd be,' she would say. 'I had to call the police.' She arrived on the street to see a large woman heave herself out from behind the wheel and on to the pavement.

Was it Pat? No … yes … no … It looked like Pat but …

No, definitely not Pat, because there was Pat, granite-faced in the passenger seat, pushing off the hands that tried to help her swing the plaster-cast round and on to the tarmac. Sunlight glinted off the roof of the car. Sweat glistened on the faces of the two women as they bickered their way out of the vehicle, wrestling with each other and bundles of bulging Sainsbury's carrier bags. Annie watched a mime show as the stiff breeze from the estuary took their voices out of reach. The other woman had to be Pat's sister, if not her twin, and was so intent on pressing unwanted help on Pat that Annie thought they were sure to fall into a squabbling heap on the roadside long before they reached her.

They came near enough for Pat's words to reach Annie, 'And there's no need to …' just as Pat spotted her and stopped.

'Annie?' Pat frowned puzzled, then took a closer look and hobbled nearer. 'What is it? What's happened?'

Annie had barely started a reply when the sound of another car spun her attention to the far end of the street. A police patrol car turned in and sped towards them.

Both Pat and the Pat-clone at her side stared first at the patrol car then at Annie. 'Are they here to see you?' Pat said, reading the answer in Annie's face.

The other woman pursed her lips. 'I knew it meant trouble. I told Vince we should get you a proper woman in, but—' She stopped abruptly.

Pat turned a triumphant glare on her. 'I knew it! I knew you were in on it.'

'Well, someone's got to look out for you. You can't look after yourself.'

'Says who? Don't answer that. Vince says. Well, when did you start taking notice of him?'

'And that's another thing. I called into the office. He's changed the lock on Dad's safe. I'm not at all happy with—'

'It's nothing to do with you anymore, Babs. And if you're so unhappy with him, why did you gang up against me?'

'He was right about you needing someone in. He should have left it to me. Someone to cover the work, huh!' The woman's gaze raked Annie from head to toe. 'Just look what she's done and she's only been here five minutes.'

The woman looked across to where the police car had parked and now disgorged two uniformed officers, Jennifer and a dark-haired man.

Annie's mind grabbed at the disjointed information and pulled it together. Babs? So this was Barbara Caldwell who'd been a director of the firm and its original company secretary and who was clearly Pat's sister.

Pat turned to Annie. 'Come on, you can play carer for thirty seconds and help me in. Let Babs deal with this lot.'

In the time it took to help Pat inside, Annie gabbled out a swift explanation. It was barely coherent but Pat took it in her stride, only raising her eyebrows a little when Annie touched on the punch line to Terry Martin's film. Behind them, Annie could hear Barbara greeting a clearly puzzled Jennifer and her colleague.

'E Division, are you? I knew Sergeant Ready for years, you know.' Barbara's voice oozed geniality as though she were greeting guests at a formal event.

'Jim Ready retired a while ago,' Jennifer's male colleague replied.

'Oh yes, I know. He and his wife went off to Spain. Lovely little apartment they have there. He was a good sort, didn't you think so?'

'Oh, I never knew him,' said Jennifer.

'Didn't know Sergeant Ready. Good Lord, he's a legend.'

'PC Flanagan only joined the force a few weeks ago,' her colleague pointed out.

Annie had expected a police presence to bring some order to her turbulent thoughts, but their arrival was untidy. Barbara had loaded them with super-market carriers and kept up her social chit-chat as she told them to 'Just put them down there. I'll see to them all now. You go and sit with Patricia and her assistant. I'll make some tea.'

Jennifer, maybe in an attempt to wrest control back from Barbara, leapt in with introductions. The man's face remained serious as he nodded first to Annie, then to Pat. He'd have a nice smile, Annie thought, if he ever lost that grim expression. His name, she learnt, was PC Scott Kerridge.

Pat took charge. 'Sit down. I'll just give you a bit of background before Annie shows you what she found.' She outlined the Martins' case.

'So what is it you've found?' Scott Kerridge said to Annie. 'Evidence of a crime, a serious crime you told my colleague. Did the parents warn you about it?'

'Oh no.' Annie reached for the remote control. 'No, they didn't even know how to play the disk. I hope they never have to see it. It'd destroy them.'

'And what's the crime?'

'I think it's ... well, I'm sure it's murder.'

She was aware that Jennifer's eyes opened wide at her words. Scott Kerridge appeared unmoved and she felt his disbelief. Maybe her announcement lacked drama. Well, too bad. He'd see for himself in a moment.

'Give us a brief summary, Annie,' Pat said. 'We don't need to see it all. They can watch it when they take it away.'

Swallowing a knot of apprehension, Annie clicked the machine in her hand and the waves of Spurn crashed into the room. 'This is just ... well nothing. Spurn Point.' She fast forwarded, saw the concrete bunker flash past. 'He did village shows and things.' Giant onions jumped in and out of shot followed by jerky pictures of prize-winners.

'What was that?' Scott Kerridge had spotted Mrs Becke's angry face as she ambushed Terry Martin.

Annie took the film back to the dusk sequence. 'It's nothing really. Seems he was always on the lookout for some scandal to expose. Must have made himself really unpopular in Milesthorpe.'

'Are you suggesting his death wasn't an accident?'

'Oh no. Nothing like that. I just don't think people liked him much. He pried into things. I haven't met many people who actually knew him.' She remembered Laura Tunbridge outside the church.

Oh look, it wasn't us ... Mally didn't mean it.

She fast-forwarded again until the scene cut to the damp cellar. 'This is the bit.' Her voice wasn't as steady as she wanted it to be.

Annie sensed a moment of extra attention as Terry Martin came out from behind the camera. Then the door opened on the nightmare. She heard an 'Uh!' from Jennifer and saw her wince. She felt her own finger-nails dig into her palms. Only Pat and Scott Kerridge sat impassive to the end though she sensed his flinch at the unexpectedly explicit close-up that ended the scene.

There was a silence as Pat reached across and took the remote control from Annie's hand.

Scott Kerridge spoke first. 'Whew!' He blew out a breath. 'You say the parents haven't seen this?'

'I know they haven't. I … Look, they had the funeral today. They're quite old. They're on their knees with him dying as it is. Will they have to see it? I doubt they knew anything about what he was really like.'

'And you do?'

'Call it instinct, intuition, what you will.' She wouldn't mention the three girls. Let them dig out that connection themselves if they had to. 'I think he was a nasty piece of work, but I also think his parents thought the sun shone out of his backside. I don't think they'd cope with this.'

Scott Kerridge gave an indeterminate gesture that Annie could only hope was a concession to the Martins, then he looked right at her. 'Do you know where he filmed this?'

'No, but he had his own suspect. Someone called Balham. Mr Balham. You heard him when he was in that corridor. I thought he must be in the guy's house. In his cellar.'

'You're not from round here, are you? Holderness, the East Riding, is a big plain of clay. Very few houses have cellars. I doubt there are any in Milesthorpe.'

'Should make it easier to find then.' Jennifer made her first contribution since the film started. Annie looked across and saw Jennifer's gaze still held to the TV just as her own had been.

'Mmm.' Scott Kerridge gave his colleague a glance and turned back to Annie. 'What about when? Have you any idea how old this footage is?'

'Not to the day, but he must have filmed it after Milesthorpe Show and before he died, so sometime between nine and eighteen days ago.'

'And she'd been dead a while when he found her,' Pat said.

'I don't know,' said Scott. 'In the weather we've been having, it wouldn't take long for a body to get to that state.'

In a quiet that followed his remark, Annie became aware of cupboards opening and shutting in the kitchen, water running. She caught a flash of Marigold gloves as Pat's sister zipped across her peripheral vision wielding a cloth. Irrelevantly, she realized why the kitchen worktops gleamed. She'd known it couldn't have been Pat who took such care of them.

Her attention came back from the activity in the kitchen to see Scott Kerridge move across to sit next to Pat and engage her in intense conversation. Annie turned to Jennifer. She felt an odd sort of bond had developed between them strengthened by Jennifer's reaction to Terry Martin's film.

'I hope I haven't caused you a problem with calling you direct,' she murmured.

'No no, that's OK.' Jennifer cast a glance towards Scott and Pat.

'Uh … It's silly I suppose but I needed to speak to someone I knew rather than an anonymous voice in a call centre.'

'Really, it's no problem. I'd have known nothing about it if you'd just rung in direct. This is the biggest thing I've been involved in by the looks of it. Though I suppose it'll all go to CID now. And what about your job with the Martins?'

'I don't know. Nothing like this has ever happened to me before. But I'm glad the Martins didn't get to see the film. It would have been too much after Terry getting killed. How exactly did it happen? No one ever told me.'

'He fell off some scaffolding. It's a private house. The owners are on holiday.'

'They said he didn't have his camera with him.'

Jennifer shook her head. 'No, he didn't have anything apart from the usual stuff in his pockets, wallet, notebook, keys … He knew they were away and Milesthorpe's the sort of place where people don't always lock up.'

'Don't lock up when they go on holiday?'

Jennifer laughed. 'You'd be surprised. I'm sure she did lock up, but the neighbour had a key, her father had a key. There were people popping in and out, looking after plants and such. He'd have had a good chance of finding it open. As it happens, it wasn't. Still, no point speculating now. We'll never know. And whatever he was up to, he paid a heavy price.'

Annie nodded. 'Do you know why he fell?'

'It's possible the scaffolding wasn't as secure as it should have been, but I doubt there'll be a prosecution.'

'I don't think it matters to the Martins how it happened, they just want to know. It wouldn't be any better or any worse if it was foul play or whatever. It can't be reversed.'

'Oh, I'm sure it wasn't foul play.'

'No, I'm sure it wasn't. There's been a post-mortem and everything, hasn't there?'

It wasn't us. It wasn't anything to do with us. Mally didn't mean it.

Pat's voice reached her. Pat was still talking to Scott Kerridge, but Annie felt she'd raised the volume because she wanted to be heard. 'We know the score,' Pat said. 'And you've known the agency for years. Anyway, this one'll stay between me and Annie. There are no records in town.'

Annie understood that they were asked to keep quiet. She wasn't sure if it was about the whole thing, or certain aspects of it. That wasn't a problem. Who would she tell? And anyway, like Pat said, she knew the score.

'Would you mind,' Scott asked apologetically, 'if we saw the final stretch through once again, only I thought …' Whatever he'd planned to say, he changed his mind and stopped.

Annie picked up the remote and set it to track through the disk. 'Which bit do you want?'

'The very end. The close up on the face and neck.'

They all watched as Terry Martin played his final panicked shots. Jennifer's face drained of colour and from the prickle on her own skin Annie thought hers did the same.

Pat sat opposite, face emotionless. Scott beside her watched intently as though he'd seen something the rest of them had missed.

Please God the Martins never had to see this. Then a thought struck her. Maybe they knew where it was. If they were shown edited stills they might identify the cellar. Was there a cellar in that little house in Withernsea? No, it couldn't be there. The smell would have permeated the whole building.

Into the silent aftermath of their watching a fat white maggot wriggle in the decomposing flesh of a murdered woman, Barbara walked in with a laden plate.

'Jam sponge, anyone?' she asked, proffering a cake oozing white and red goo.

CHAPTER 5

BARBARA DIDN'T OUTSTAY the two police officers by more than a few minutes and, after she'd left in a flurry of domestic instructions that seemed aimed as much at Annie as Pat, the two of them sat in silence for a moment. The blank TV screen seemed a huge presence. Pat picked up the remote control, but it was an automatic gesture that died as she looked across at the television.

'Had he filmed her earlier in the footage?' she asked. 'Alive, I mean.'

'I wondered about that. Not that I saw, but I wasn't paying that sort of attention.' Annie remembered the tedious stretch of vegetable show winners, the roll call that had played as background while she delved for food in the kitchen. 'He might have but I didn't play it through again.'

'No, I don't think I would've wanted to straight off. And it's not our problem now. Let the lads in blue deal with it.'

'With her face all distorted like that, it might be impossible to say.'

'It wouldn't be easy,' Pat agreed. 'Hard to say how old she was either. Did you notice her legs? They weren't a young woman's legs. And the clothes, micro skirt and lacy underwear.'

Annie's mind rested again on the memory of the bloated features and she felt just a glimmer of an urge to watch the film again, to analyse what she'd seen. Pat was right. It hadn't been a young woman. Nor had she been slim enough to carry off that outfit. Her size wasn't all post-death bloating. Now she thought beyond the horror of it, she was certain she could find her if she was there in those earlier scenes, or find out a lot about her if she could watch it through again.

'Pat, do you think that guy, PC Kerridge, saw something before he asked to rerun it?'

'Not sure. He certainly thought there was something there to see, and important enough to have us rerun it here rather than wait to get back to the station.'

'What sort of thing would that be?'

'Something he wants to say when he hands it on to CID. Maybe he recognized her from a missing person report. Here's what happened to so-and-so. Or maybe the MO of the killing alerted him to something. It looks like the cellar strangler's struck again … that sort of thing.'

'Cellar strangler!'

Pat laughed. 'I made that up, but for all we know there's a matching killing still live on the books. Anyway, what are you going to tell the Martins?'

'I don't know, but I want to go out and see them. Now, I mean, before the police go back.' She tried to explain thoughts that hadn't properly crystallized in her own mind; why it was so important she get to talk to the Martins face to face before the police got there. 'It's as though I've broken confidence already, but I want them to hear it from me, not the police.'

'It's good to have a real connection with the client, to care about them even, it keeps you sharp, but you'll not stay in business if you don't make it pay at the same time.'

'Are you saying I can't go?'

'Oh yes, you can go. I'm going to bill Vince for this job and he's going to cough up every last cent. He'll learn just how cost-effective cheap labour is and he'll not interfere in my affairs again.'

The fierce red of the setting sun followed Annie as she drove east. Shadows lengthened as fire blazed across her rear-view mirror. A repeat of yesterday's journey but darker. In the nine days between filming Milesthorpe Show and falling to his death, Terry Martin could have travelled the length of the country or crossed continents. But he hadn't. He worked close to home. The rotting body he'd found lay somewhere nearby. She might drive right past the house that concealed it and never know.

She thought of the blackened tongue, the bulging eyes, the beginnings of decay. Her mouth was suddenly dry; her throat constricted making it hard to swallow. Someone had deliberately twisted a cord round that woman's neck as she fought and gasped for air.

Speed camera sign. Concentrate.

The house was in darkness when she arrived, but in answer to her tentative knock a light snapped on and a moment later Martha swung the door open.

'Oh.' Martha seemed taken aback as though half expecting someone else. The awful thought came to Annie that Martha was used to waiting up for Terry. This was the evening of his funeral. Martha wouldn't think of sleeping, going to bed, yet maybe she'd dozed in that small front room as the light faded, and been woken by a knock at the door. Half asleep, half hoping, she'd come to see who was there.

'I'm sorry to call today,' Annie said. 'But there's something I need to tell you. Can I come in?'

Again, she sat uncomfortably in Terry's chair between Martha, now wide awake, and Bill who nodded in acknowledgement of her but whose eyes never focused on her face.

In contrast to her husband, Martha Martin's whole attention directed itself to Annie and homed in on the purpose of Annie's visit before she could speak.

'It's about our Terry's disk, isn't it?'

'Uh … yes. Yes, it is. The thing is I've had to give it to the police.'

'The police? What would they want with it?'

'It seems that Terry was on the trail of something quite big. He's used the disk to record evidence. We had to hand it over.'

Annie expected indignation, even if muted, but the Martins nodded in silent acquiescence. They lived in a world where authority ruled. If Annie said it were a police matter, it wouldn't occur to them to argue. She didn't even have to field questions on what exactly Terry had filmed. They took it for granted they'd be told when the powers-that-be decreed the time to be right.

Before she left, she warned them that the police would visit again.

As she walked to where she'd parked, Annie saw a police patrol car turn in at the far end of the street. Instinctively, she ducked out of sight and watched from the shadows as it drove past. Two men in uniform. One of them was Scott Kerridge. The bastards! They couldn't leave the Martins alone even for today. Thank heavens she'd made the trip out here to warn them. She watched the car pull up; saw the two uniformed men at the door of the Martins which swung open. A short mime show and they disappeared inside, their bulk too large for the tiny house.

Annie carried on to Pat's car where she climbed in and waited.

Scott Kerridge and his colleague stayed inside just over twenty minutes. When they emerged, Scott held an armful of DVDs and his colleague carried Terry's PC.

Annie hesitated. Should she go back and see that the Martins were OK or should she leave them in peace? As she weighed the options, her phone rang.

'Hello, Annie Raymond.'

'You on your way then?'

'Who is this?'

'You left yer number. Said you was working on it now.'

'Oh … yes. Mrs Earle.' Annie heard the slur of one too many drinks in the woman's voice and closed her mouth on a sharp retort. *Am I psychic!* 'I'm on another job at the moment, not sure when I'll be finished.'

'Well, it's Tuesday night, so this is your chance.'

Annie glanced at her watch and did a quick calculation. Back to Pat's for a break then on to what might be a long and uncomfortable night. 'It might be Wednesday morning by the time I get there.'

'Whatever … Nowt'll kick off till two or three o'clock. Plenty of time.'

As she snapped her phone shut, Annie became aware that a background noise had cut off with the call, a busy rumble of voices as though Mrs Earle shared a space with hundreds of people.

CHAPTER 6

A S THE BRIGHT lights of the chemical works at Salt End lit her return to the city, Annie thought of the dank, smelly cavern that was the way in to the tower block. It resonated in her mind with the image of a damp cellar and a rotting corpse. She reflected on the twists and turns of the day – Terry Martin's funeral and the odds and ends of people she'd met.

It wasn't us … Mally didn't mean it …

Jennifer Flanagan, the rookie in whom Annie sensed a core of strength; the later introduction to her more experienced colleague, Scott, the guy whose so far unseen smile was the thing she remembered most about him. And those stupid joy-riders in their ten-to-one stolen car swerving into the way of Terry's cortège. Bill Martin had looked puzzled, struggling to interpret it as normal behaviour, an unconventional tribute to his son.

For all the miscellany that made the day, one woman dominated. Location unknown, identity unknown, time of death unknown, murdered by person or persons unknown. Words came back to Annie. Words she'd heard more than once as she'd struggled for a foothold in her chosen career.

People see us as having the boring leftovers. … Even now we're seen as the slightly shady second-best. … If you want real respect in this profession, cross the pond.

She'd uncovered a murder and handed the evidence on. All that about second-best made sense now in a real-life way that theory could never teach. After all, how had the Martins found her? They'd gone to a shady character who they deemed moved in the sordid underworld that private investigators inhabit. But there were no regrets. She recognized the perceptions she saw in others; felt pride at being the target of them. It meant she was really here, doing the job she'd chased for so long.

The background chatter of the television met her entry into the flat.

Pat raised a lazy hand in greeting. 'Hi,' she mumbled, through a mouthful of something as she brushed crumbs from her ample chest. 'Nice work talking her round. She rang about half an hour ago.'

Annie wondered why she was credited with talking Mrs Earle round. 'Yes, she rang me, too. She wants me to go round tonight. I wanted to talk it through with you before I went.'

'I didn't mean the Earle woman; I meant Martha Martin. She's talked it over with her husband and they want you to find out what their precious son was doing when he got himself killed. She insisted it was you. No one else would do.'

Pat's smile bore no resentment that they'd plumped for the inexperienced operative. Annie didn't know what to say. She felt a sense of achievement, though wasn't sure what she'd done to get this result. She'd let instinct guide her when she was with the Martins. Low key, not pushing for every scrap of information. It seemed she'd played it right.

Pat laughed. 'It'll be ironic if you turn out to be good at the job Vince pretended he hired you for.'

Annie felt herself bristle a little. It wasn't that unlikely. 'I'm a better PI than I am a carer. I could have told him that from the start if he'd been honest with me.'

'I can vouch for that. You're a piss-poor housekeeper. You leave the kitchen like a bomb's hit it. Still I shall laugh like a drain if Vince offers you a job at the end of this. And if he does, you be sure you hold out for a proper basic and good bonuses.'

For a moment, Annie was lost in a world where Vince Sleeman offered her a proper job. Real work, a living wage.

'I wish I'd taken notes when I'd watched Terry Martin's film,' she said. 'I could do with going back over the early bits now.'

'You can. I made a copy.'

'I didn't realize,' Annie said, surprised. 'I didn't think you'd got round to it. Should we have told them?'

'They didn't ask.' Pat shrugged. 'Anyway, leave that for tomorrow. Mrs Earle's the priority right now. Don't ever leave the car there at nights. We've an arrangement with a cab firm. The number's on the side there. Put it in your phone. Use them if you need to do night work where you can't take the car. They know the score. They'll turn out quickly if you need them to, but don't take advantage of that unless you have to. We pay for the privilege.'

Annie got up and found the number. While she put it into her phone, Pat outlined the detail of the case. There was little more to add to what Annie already knew.

'The trouble doesn't kick off till two or three in the morning. That's the early hours of Wednesday and Saturday. According to her those are the only times. It's some kids that set up shop on her landing. It's not a massive operation or anything, but if you've seen the state of a place after a couple of hours of people shooting up, you can see why she wants them cleared.'

'And the police won't do anything even though it's so regular?'

'Not so much won't as can't. There's pockets like this all over the show. Mind you, these kids are so blasé it's not real. They're daft to be so bloody regular you can set a clock by them, but they're obviously sure enough of prior warning of any raids that they're not bothered. I reckon it's just a gang of kids who can get their hands on some gear on a regular basis. They want a bit of extra cash. There's a reason they do those two nights. And I'd take bets they answer to someone who knows nothing about it. It might be as simple a matter as finding out who their parents are.'

'You make it sound like somewhere out of an old movie. Cut out the dealing or we'll tell your dad.' Annie laughed. 'And chances are they haven't got dads around anyway.'

Pat reached for the biscuit packet at her side and pushed two chocolate rounds up to the open end. 'My parents split up when we were at school. It didn't turn us into helpless junkies, and I'll tell you this, I took notice of what my dad said up to the day he died.'

Which wasn't so long ago, thought Annie, as Jed Thompson's death certificate came to her mind. She remembered her own upbringing, her one tangible memory of early childhood, that her father had hired a PI. She felt no regret at the premature loss of her mother; no trauma from her father's palming her off on to her aunt. It was just the way it was. Either you got on with it, or you made your life a real mess by dwelling on how it might have been.

'I suppose all that early stuff shapes you somehow,' she said vaguely. 'But it's a deprived area, isn't it, where Mrs Earle lives? Doesn't that make a difference?'

'It's not black and white. Nothing ever is when you get down to it. Sure there are pockets where I wouldn't leave my car overnight. But if you want to find a community where they still let the little kids out to play on the street because they know the neighbours'll keep an eye out, and where the kids keep out of trouble because they know they'll be reported back to their dads if they don't, then you'll find that on Orchard Park, too. You'll find a sense of community there that you'll not find in a lot of well-to-do areas with all their high fences and big gates. Never judge a book by its cover, Annie. You've been told that often enough, I'm sure. It's doubly important in this business where you've got people out to show you the face they want you to see.'

'How far did you get with this case before you had your accident?'

'I didn't get off first base. I was round there checking the lie of the land when it happened.'

Pat looked relaxed, ready to talk. Annie took a chance. 'It wasn't an accident, was it?'

Pat showed no surprise at the question. 'I don't know. I never found out what I tripped on. The timing was pretty handy for them, couldn't have been better if they'd known just where I'd be.'

'But how would they know?'

'I suppose the Earle woman might have blabbed too loudly. But to know exactly where I intended to wait to try to clock them that first night ... well ... that's a good question.' Pat heaved a sigh as she shifted her weight in the cushions of the settee. 'Someone from the agency would have known.'

'You're kidding me! Why would your own colleagues do that?'

'I went and got that job for myself. I wouldn't let anyone else take it off me.'

Annie recalled Pat's words. She'd advertised privately ... given Vince a nudge ... just a one-off ... 'But, surely your own people wouldn't have put you in that sort of danger? I've seen those stairs. You could have broken your neck.'

Pat shrugged. 'Oh, I don't think they realized what would happen. I think someone called in a favour. This woman's queering our pitch, can you tip us off when and where, that sort of thing. I've told Vince. He plays his cards close, but he doesn't like what happened. He'll sort whoever it was did the dirty. But that's as it may be, let's just keep this quiet and see how we go.'

Annie was struck by a sudden sense that Pat pinned more on her than she realized. Pat wanted revenge for what had happened. If Annie turned into a competent operative, maybe she could deliver it.

'Right then, the practicalities,' Pat said, and outlined the course she wanted Annie to take.

Annie listened attentively, then went at Pat's bidding to collect the camera and lenses from the master bedroom. She sat and checked through the equipment, admiring its quality. Just what the financial damage would be if she wrecked this lot she didn't like to think.

'Get there before anything kicks off,' Pat cautioned. 'And don't go all the way to six in the lift at this time of night or you'll have to walk right across the sixth floor landing. Use the stairs from five and get yourself to the Earle woman's door quickly and quietly. You're safe enough inside the flat, but you can't see much. Just don't take any chances. Stay safe, see what you can see. If you go on to the landing to have a look-see later on, make sure you put the sneck on. Those doors swing closed and lock. Get what you can, then we'll see.'

'How do I get out again?'

'If it kicks off, don't walk out into the middle of it. If you manage to clock the kids before they set up shop on six, then get yourself out; use the stairs. Otherwise, settle yourself for a night with Mrs E.'

Annie stood up and stretched. She ought to feel tired, but the buzz of genuine night obs, not just role play, buoyed her up with both anticipation and apprehension.

Pat nodded towards the folder. 'If you think you can run with it, see if you can get a signature. Let's at least commit her to paying before we go any further.'

A waning moon joined the glow from streetlamps to light the approach to the tower block. Annie climbed out of the taxi and stood in the car-park. She stared hard at and around the entrance as she listened to the vehicle reverse out, leaving her on her own. She started forward. Mrs Earle's home offered only dubious sanctuary but she should make her way there as quickly as she could.

The entrance door jarred her arm as she pushed at it. The security system worked after all. She peered inside and saw only the black sheen of an empty security booth. She clicked the buttons on the intercom and wondered if this would become a repeat of her first visit. Would the moron in the rumpled shirt tell her Mrs Earle had vanished again? Would anyone answer at all?

When the machine crackled into life, it was Mrs Earle who answered and her voice was friendly. 'Hi. Wondered when you'd get here. Come on up.' Again that background roar almost as though Mrs Earle spoke from inside a crowded football stadium.

Annie took the stairs from the ground floor, wanting more of a feel for the place. Lights blazed on the communal landings, except as she approached the sixth floor where an eerie darkness hung in wait above her. As she climbed the final staircase, she saw that most of the bulbs were gone – smashed or disappeared, she couldn't say which – and a familiar sound began to swell. The roar of a crowd, incongruous in the darkness, grew louder with every step. The shadows in the darkest corners were too deep for her gaze to penetrate. A creeping sensation up her spine told her she wasn't alone. She strode the few steps from the staircase to Mrs Earle's door trying to radiate a confidence she didn't feel.

Don't mess with me. I know you're there.

The door swung open and a wall of pounding noise hit Annie in the face. She flinched back from it. Mrs Earle stood there, glass in one hand, cigarette in the other, oblivious to the deafening cacophony and waved her inside. Without warning, the noise subsided and became a single booming voice instead of thousands.

A TV, a football match. Mrs Earle had been watching football or something similar with the sound at murderous levels, but thank heaven it had just finished. Maybe she'd turn it off, or at least down now Annie had arrived.

The woman led Annie down a short corridor past an open door. Annie glanced in to see an enormous television screen. As she carried on to a bedroom, the noise from the other room changed to the bouncy commentary of a quiz show.

The bedroom door muffled the sound and Annie had her first proper look at the woman who thought nothing of arranging a meeting then clearing off. Her age was hard to guess, her skin ravaged and fragile. Brittle, over-bleached hair frizzed around her head in muted shades of orange. If she'd lived a largely quiet and sober life, Annie could have believed her in her sixties. If she'd dedicated her life to alcohol, she might be in her thirties. Mrs Earle yawned extravagantly and slumped down on to an unmade double bed where she half-sat half-lay back into the pillows. The room's only chair stood beneath a towering mound of clothes. There was nowhere for Annie to sit unless she perched on the edge of the bed so she remained on her feet.

'You can see outside when they arrive,' Mrs Earle said with a vague sweep of her hand.

The origins of the woman's mellow mood were clear in the row of wine bottles on the bedside table. If this were the only safe place from which to mount any sort of surveillance, Annie decided she must sort things out so she didn't have to rely on this wreck in human guise. Tucked in her inside pocket was the contract. She'd have a signature before she left, and if she could wangle it she'd have a spare key, too.

Mrs Earle, engrossed in reaching for a bottle to replenish her glass, paid Annie no attention, so Annie moved back to the corridor to glance into the living room. The bulky man of her earlier visit now lounged in the cushions of a large settee with his back to her, the television flashing coloured lights at him from little more than a metre away.

Annie returned to the bedroom. 'Tell me what happens at nights?' she said, as a burst of laughter from the other room drew her glance towards the door.

'He won't bother us.' Mrs Earle gave a contemptuous sniff and gestured with her glass, slopping wine on to the rumpled duvet. 'Shit!' She tried to focus on the wet patch then giggled. 'Yeah, trouble at nights. If I knew what happened, I wouldn't need you here, would I?'

'How many of them? Where do they come from?'

'How would I know? I'm not going out there to count, am I?' She rolled herself sideways across the bed to grab a bottle by the neck and refill her glass. 'It's only one or two on a Tuesday. Friday nights is when they really go to town. It's disgusting come morning. I want things back the way they were. I've a lovely little niece and nephew. I want them to come and stay like they used to. This is a decent area. Decent people. We shouldn't have to put up with it.'

Annie kept her mouth shut about what she thought of the area. 'What does your husband think about it?'

Mrs Earle laughed and wiped her mouth. 'Which one? I've had three.'

Annie tipped her head towards the door through which the intrusive booming of the television still came.

'Him? Give over. That layabout's nothing to do with me. Even I had better taste than that when I wed them. He's my brother.'

Mrs Earle sat up suddenly alert. 'There. Any minute now. Quick or you'll miss 'em.' She signalled Annie to go to the window.

Annie pushed the window open letting in a rush of cool air and sounds of the city at night. Sure enough, a car zigzagged its way down the street far below. She glanced at her watch – 2.30 – and pointed her camera. For a moment she couldn't work out what on earth the car was doing, then she realized it was a fast, well-practised, slalom to avoid the speed bumps as it careered down the narrow street and swung into the car-park. Tyres squealed as the car spun on the concrete at the base of the tower. She stood on tiptoe to look down. The battered yellow and black saloon put on a show with sudden starts and stops, the high screech of dramatic parabolic skids and a bang that sounded terminal as it left the concrete, bounced down a stretch of grass and out of sight. These guys, whoever they were, didn't do discreet. So blasé it's not real, Pat had said. It had been an under-statement.

'Joy riding just a sideline,' she murmured.

'What?' said Mrs Earle from behind her. 'Oh, them little bleeders. Oh, sod them. That's just kids playing about. Isn't there a van, a white van?'

As Annie's gaze searched the area, a small white van came into view. It drove unobtrusively up the road, turned into the car-park and pulled up near the entrance. Either Mrs Earle had superhuman hearing to have detected its approach over the roar of the television and screeching of the joy-riders, or she possessed some sense beyond the norm.

Annie watched through the camera lens. The angle was difficult but she recorded what she could of two men removing something from the vehicle. The distance and the awkward angle made the forms indistinct and remi-niscent of trying to make out the figure of Terry Martin when he came out from behind his camera to wrestle with that door. These two were tall and slim, but beyond that she couldn't have said if they were black or white, old or young, dark or fair.

She strained to see more of the detail of the packages, expecting that the shapes would made sense as the objects came into view. They didn't. Large, well-wrapped, but couldn't even be termed boxes in the conventional sense. Not as heavy as the size implied or the men would struggle more. She watched the way they moved, the mime show of talk between them. Cigarettes balanced on lips showed in spots that glowed a brighter red as they drew on them while they manhandled the packages. There was some-thing amateurish about the scene. Clearly the two men didn't want to advertise the delivery, whatever it was, but this was hardly a great way to keep the movement of goods under wraps. Stolen gear to be stashed in one of the flats perhaps? Not drugs, that was certain. Had it been drugs in those quantities they'd be weightier and worth too many millions to risk in this way.

'Do you know where they're heading?' she asked, as the two figures approached the building and the steepness of the angle hid them from view.

'Yeah. Here. This landing. Why do you think I called you? I wanted someone a bit more on the ball.' The tone was tetchy. The woman seesawed on the alcoholic brink of belligerence. Time for Annie to make her move.

'OK.' She raised a hand without glancing at the bed. 'I'll take a look.'

As she left the room, Annie knew the few pictures she'd taken already could count as having done the job for tonight. Now was the gap into which she should slot her getaway, before the two guys reached floor six. Her few photographs were just enough to allow her to leave, but just enough wasn't good enough. She had no signed contract, no useful new information.

She walked through to the tiny hallway, clicked off the light and eased the outer door open a fraction. Darkness pooled; the background glow of light from the lower landings made no dent. The whine of the lift was audible. If she slipped quietly out on to the communal landing she'd get a better view of whoever was on their way up. Mindful of Pat's words, she felt at the lock on the door and wondered if she could trust Mrs Earle or the scruffy brother not to lock her out, close off her bolthole.

A rush of anticipation heightened her senses as she grasped the door more firmly and began to ease it further open. A grating sound stopped her as a sudden pinprick of light flared in the gloom across the way. Against the flame of the match, Annie caught a glimpse of the screwed-up face of a young woman who drew in on a cigarette, then flicked her gaze towards the lifts. Human wreckage waiting in the shadows.

The whine of the lift continued uninterrupted, clearly going on up beyond Mrs Earle's floor tonight. Annie heard a muttering of curses in the darkness. The woman wasn't alone. That brief glimpse in the glow of the match had shown her the gaunt features of someone who hadn't reached twenty and probably never would. She eased the door shut.

Where had they gone? How long before they arrived on this landing? Realizing her escape route wasn't yet blocked, Annie darted back inside to the bedroom where Mrs Earle slumped on the pillows, eyes closed.

'OK,' Annie rapped out making the woman on the bed start up from a doze. 'I have all I need for now. Do you want this job doing? Do you want them clearing out?' She packed self-assurance into her voice, her aim to get that signature. How to do the job was a bridge to be crossed later.

'Are you saying you can get rid of them? You've seen what they're up to. They're peddling shit out there. On my bloody doorstep.'

Annie nodded. 'I know.' Not that drugs explained the real reason those two men were here. That was somehow tied up in those odd-shaped packs that had gone on up in the lift. But it was the drug-dealing on the ill-lit communal landing that was Mrs Earle's bugbear.

'Yes, I can get rid of them if you want me to.'

'Well, of course I want you to.'

'Fine.' Annie slid the form from the folder. 'Just sign here and here. And I'll need to come back, so unless you're going to be in round the clock or you don't mind it dragging on, you'd better give me a key.'

'It's been going on forever as it is. What's a bit longer?'

Annie shrugged. 'It'll cost more.'

'Oh all right.' Mrs Earle spoke petulantly and snatched at a crowded key ring that jostled for position with the empty bottles. With difficulty she extracted the necessary keys and tossed them across to Annie. Annie swapped them for the all-important contract but wondered how much legal weight a signature carried when the client was this drunk. She'd let Pat worry about that.

Keys and contract safely tucked away, Annie rushed for the door and opened it a crack. She caught the whine of the lift slowing. In seconds the light from the lift would illuminate the landing. It would all kick off. She'd be trapped. As the thoughts formed, she slipped through the door and strode silently to the staircase. Laboured breathing rasped nearby. The image came to her of a hand reaching out from the shadows. Her nerve cracked and she sprinted down two flights of stairs. No one followed. She modified her pace and tried to slow her breathing as she clicked the buttons on her phone to call the taxi.

At ground level, Annie stayed in the darkness at the base of the building. The immediate area was quiet now but not deserted. Indistinct figures slouched in the glow of the streetlights. The early hours of every Wednesday and Saturday? It was a stupid time and place to peddle drugs and surely just an afterthought. She had to look at the full picture, to target their real reason for coming here.

When she saw a taxi in the right livery approach, she stepped out on to the concrete pathway.

A burst of loud music made her leap back. With a squeal of tyres and spray of turf the battered yellow car she'd seen from upstairs and assumed long gone pulled out in front of her. The suddenness of its reappearance stood the hairs on the back of her neck to attention as a leering face loomed from the driver's window.

'Hey, bit late for playing detectives, innit?' A burst of exaggerated laughter and the car took off again swerving round the taxi as it drove in.

What the hell…?

'Bloody kids!' the taxi driver snapped, pulling up beside her. 'You going back to Vikky Dock?'

Vicky who? Annie stopped the question on her lips. It must be the local abbreviation for the riverside where Pat lived. Victoria Dock. She nodded and settled herself in the cab, her gaze never leaving the yellow car which slalomed back up the road then snaked round a corner and out of sight.

The heat of real anger rose in her. Different car, but she knew the driver. That was the grinning face which had yelled obscenities outside Terry Martin's funeral.

And now he was here outside Mrs Earle's. The only common factor she could think of was herself. And the boy had seemed to know her. How? She thought of the upset he'd caused to the Martins, and vowed to nail the little bastard if she did nothing else before she left Hull.

CHAPTER 7

DESPITE NOT GETTING to bed until dawn began to spread the promise of daylight across the sky, Annie was up and wide awake again before nine o'clock. She woke with a feeling of frustration, of business unresolved, and remembered she'd gone to bed angry.

That boy and his mocking laugh. She'd never wanted to slap someone so badly. Her mind played an image of Laura Tunbridge outside the church slapping out at one of her companions who'd laughed at the antics of the boy joy-rider.

Mally didn't mean it … Me and Kay got a lift with Mrs Kitson …

As she splashed water on her face in the small shower room, Annie was aware of someone moving about. Surely Pat wasn't up at this hour.

It wasn't Pat; it was Barbara, who looked up from where she bent over a chair sorting clothes. 'Oh … hello.'

As Annie returned the greeting, she felt a dart of hostility shoot her way. What was that about? It was Barbara, with Vince's connivance, who'd brought her here. OK, so she didn't conform to Barbara's view of a *proper woman* in housekeeping terms, but whose fault was that? They should have been straight with her.

'Would you like coffee?' she offered as an olive branch.

Barbara chipped off a tight-lipped, 'No, thank you,' rebuffing the gesture.

Annie went through to the kitchen, made coffee for herself and leant back against the fridge door as she cradled the cup and sipped the steamy liquid. Her reflection in the mirrored veneer of the cupboard opposite looked at her, its expression pleased, satisfied. No trace left of last night's anger. Here she was, a real life PI with two cases on her books.

Two cases that needed preparatory work before she settled on a next move. A real PI with work to do who would now stride through to the living room, take out her folders and spread the papers across the table as she planned her day. The flat hummed to the roar of a vacuum cleaner. Last night in a semi-deserted car-park in a run-down area of town, she would have grabbed that boy out of his car without a second thought, but she balked at disturbing Barbara's routine.

A boss who slept late every day was disconcerting. It put the onus on her to make the kind of decisions that had always been someone else's. From working at the level of general factotum who couldn't replenish the office coffee jar without a signed chit, she owned a caseload that involved sudden death and late night drugs deals. The feel was of being pushed in at the deep-end having only ever read up on the theory of how to swim. It sent waves through her that were equally anticipation and anxiety. Her reflection grinned back from the mirrored surface. She was way out of her depth and relished every second. By the time Pat was up and about, she would have strategies worked out for both cases.

Orchard Park. Drug dealing on landing six was the symptom she must cure, but what else brought the two men there in their van? What were the peculiar packages? What was and wasn't normal human traffic late at night and what was different about Tuesday and Friday nights? Annie remembered the rush of adrenalin that had flooded her as she'd stepped out into the darkness of the sixth floor lift bay. She wanted more of being right at the edge, of pitting her wits against shadowy wrongdoers in the dark labyrinth of the tall block. The plan she would put forward would be a week-long surveillance. Tonight and every night for a week. To observe, maybe to follow, to suss out just exactly what went on. If Pat recognized the perpetrators from the photographs she'd taken and found an easy route to close the case, it would be a terrible anticlimax.

At any rate, she had a signed contract. That would please Pat.

And while her nights were taken up with Mrs Earle's problems, her days were the Martins. Mrs Kitson, the busybody who was there the night he died, was the obvious lead, but Mrs Becke was her number-one target. It wasn't enough to get the what and when, she needed the why. Why did Terry Martin go to Milesthorpe in the first place?

Beckes split over brook …

Mrs Kitson might be useful for the mundane detail but Mrs Becke was the one mixed up in Terry Martin's real agendas.

The next move on both cases needed the technology in Pat's bedroom, to print out the photographs from last night and to make some more copies of Terry Martin's DVD.

She thought back to her time in Birmingham and the sense of belonging it gave her to be amongst people who took her ambitions seriously. *Never assume you know all the answers*, one of the guys had said to her. He wasn't a course tutor; he'd been in the business for years and come to get himself the bits of paper. *Don't hem yourself in. … Spread your material however wide of the mark it looks.*

She would split the film and create a carefully labelled set of DVDs, so she could show different bits to different people. Spurn Point and those few seconds in a deserted concrete bunker. One of just the fruit and veg show; another of Terry's encounter with Mrs Becke. Then the crowds on Milesthorpe Green. There were no useful shots in the following stretch, mostly filmed at a distance, where one of the few close-ups was of Terry Martin escaping flying hoofs, but she wouldn't exclude it just because it looked wide of the mark. Then the final sequence where he'd filmed some of the prize-winners in amongst random shots of the crowd. Leaving out the useless footage would save time, but who was she to predict what anomalies a Milesthorpe resident might notice? *The guy who filmed this? Oh yes, I remember the guy with the camera ...* A careful operator covered all the angles.

But not a single frame or still of that dark cellar, because there must be no chance of accidentally showing the wrong person the wrong bit of film. There was no ambiguity in this case where the PI/police line lay and she had no intention of going near it.

A mental map of Milesthorpe sat in her head, dotted with the dwellings of the people she'd looked up. She planned to drive around first and get a feel for the place that had drawn Terry Martin to his death. She'd seen her prime target's house already on his film.

And after Mrs Becke came Tremlow, Kitson and Ludgrove, the trio on the spot when Terry's body was found. Any of them might lead to new avenues. Her other names were Laura Tunbridge and her two friends, Kay Dearlove and Mally Fletcher, all of them under sixteen. She crossed them off the list. Her job was to do her best for the Martins not to destroy their son's reputation. The sleeping dog would never wake again, it was best to let it lie.

Mally didn't mean it ...

She would unearth every last twist of his final hours, all fifty plus of them. It would be more than a bare skeleton of a story of where and when. She would smooth away the unknowns and show the Martins the real picture of Terry's last act.

Realizing that the noise of the vacuum cleaner had stopped, Annie broke her self-imposed exile and slipped back through to the living room. She walked in on Barbara bent over the sideboard drawer rummaging through the company paperwork.

Barbara swung round, giving Annie a hard glare as though daring her to make anything of it. Annie pretended an interest in the view across the river as Barbara with difficulty forced the drawer completely shut, locked it and marched through to the kitchen without a word. Sounds emerged of water gushing and cupboard doors banging shut.

Now their locations were reversed, Annie sat down and spread her case notes on the table. There was little she could do with them, but she let them float across her consciousness as she hardened up the plans she would put to Pat.

It was midday before Pat emerged. Annie, who had learnt the morning routine, prepared coffee and soup. Barbara had disappeared but her bag still sat on the worktop so Annie knew she'd only popped out to the bins or to see a neighbour. The surfaces gleamed; everything had been stowed away behind the pristine cupboard doors. Annie tried not to make any mess but the bread was crumbly and spread bits everywhere. Guiltily, she swept them on to the floor where they crunched underfoot.

Annie allowed Pat ten minutes with her breakfast before she began to outline her ideas for the two cases.

Pat met her plans for Orchard Park with a moment's silence then commented, 'Let's see what you got on camera first. You might not need to go back at all. And every night's a bit OTT anyway.'

On Terry Martin, she chewed her way through a substantial chunk of bread as she ruminated on Annie's suggestions. 'Mrs Becke? Yes, I see where you're coming from. She didn't like the little toerag, but you'll need to tread softly. There might be something in the secret lover story that she won't want to shout about.'

'That comment he made, "Beckes split over brook", any idea what he might have meant?'

'Sounds like a headline to me. Fits with his journalistic ambitions. Clever enough if the lover's called Brook.'

'But who's going to care enough to print a story about it?'

'If she's big in village politics, there might be something for the red tops, and I suppose he could have hit the Sundays if one of them was a celebrity.' Pat laughed. 'I can't see it though. Not in Milesthorpe. OK, what else?'

'Can we find out what he had in print over the last few months? I don't see how it might help yet, but ...'

Pat sat up and gave a nod of approval. 'That's a good idea. Yes, I can do that. I know most of the editors locally. I'll chase that up while you're out and about.'

The animation in her boss's tone surprised Annie, giving her an insight into how frustrating it must be for Pat to sit about doing nothing. Surely Vince could have found something for her to do, but then according to Pat he'd starved her of work before this had happened. It was the reason she'd gone out and got the job that led to the broken leg.

'You should be resting, getting that leg better.' Barbara's voice made Annie jump. She looked up at the stern face Barbara turned on her sister and saw something of the struggle Pat had to carve out a role for herself against the combined efforts of Barbara and Vince.

'I can make phone calls. It's only my leg, for God's sake.'

'Even so ...'

Annie saw them square up for a spat, so slid herself off into Pat's bedroom to access the PC to print out the photos she'd taken last night and make edited copies of Terry Martin's DVD.

It was just two o'clock. Annie had been back in the living room ten minutes, sorting last night's photographs and shutting her ears to the high-tension, dual monologues that were Pat and her sister organizing an outing later in the day.

With an inner sigh of relief, she became aware that Barbara had gathered her belongings together ready to leave.

'I'll call for you at five prompt. Make sure you're ready. We want time to eat before the film starts.'

Pat grunted a response as the door buzzer sounded.

'I'll get that on my way out,' said Barbara, 'and if it's Vince—'

'It won't be Vince. He hasn't given me back those keys you let him have.'

'Don't go on at me about that! What was I supposed to do…?'

Annie sank herself lower in the cushions of her chair to shut out the bickering and concentrated on the prints of the scene from Mrs Earle's bedroom window. She was aware of a door opening behind her, of Pat looking up, but the voice in her ear shot her up in surprise.

'Annie, how could you!'

The words blazed with fury and loosed her grip on the prints which floated to the carpet. Her hand automatically reached down to retrieve the fallen pictures as her stare rose to look at Jennifer Flanagan, whose face blotched with anger.

'Jennifer?' She tried to pull her thoughts and her photographs together enough to frame a coherent question.

'How could you? I trusted you.' Jennifer spat the question out again.

Annie wanted to say, I didn't know you did anger. Surprise robbed her of clear thought. Her hand floundered in the weave of the carpet.

'How could she what?' A creak from protesting settee springs turned their attention to Pat, a solid immovable presence, who fixed Jennifer with a stare.

'Everyone knows! You promised to keep it quiet. I've seen the girl. Scott was with me. You're lucky it wasn't Rob Greaves. What were you thinking of!'

Annie exchanged a bewildered glance with Pat who spoke firmly. 'Sit down, Jennifer, and cool down. Let's have it from the top. You can start with the assumption that neither Annie nor I have a clue what you're on about.'

'*You* might not, but Annie does. I've talked to the girl.'

'What girl?' asked Annie.

Pat stopped them both with a raised hand. 'I said sit down, Jennifer. I'm getting a stiff neck looking up at you.'

Jennifer sat.

'Right then. What's happened?'

Jennifer glared at Pat and let out an exasperated sigh. 'It's all over Milesthorpe that we're looking for a body in a cellar. We're swamped with phone calls and stupid theories and everyone's out looking. Someone'll stumble over it and probably the whole of Milesthorpe'll traipse through before the SOCOs get there. And all because—'

Again Pat's raised hand stemmed the flow. 'Exactly what is the rumour? Do people know about the film?'

'No, but you know how these things travel. It's Chinese whispers now. Anyone who hasn't been seen for a couple of days is assumed dead in a cellar. Scott and I got talking to the kids.'

'Kids?'

'It's all very Pony Club out there. The kids' network drives everything. And this one girl—'

'Name?'

'I couldn't possibly give you that information.'

'Laura Tunbridge,' supplied Annie.

Jennifer looked from one to the other of them clearly wondering how she'd slipped from attack to defence so quickly. 'A couple of other kids quoted her as the source of the rumour so we tackled her about it. Not formally, luckily for you. We were just going round the place chatting and trying to find out what the hell was going on. But if we have to interview her properly … well … anyway her version was that Terry Martin killed Edward Balham and put his body in a cellar. We asked where she'd heard it and she said it had come from a private detective who was investigating Terry Martin's death. She showed us your card.'

'But that's ridiculous.' Annie spread her hands wide and tried to voice her bewilderment. 'I only spoke to Laura once. That was at Terry Martin's funeral. That's when I gave her the card. I hadn't seen the film then. Look, whatever she's got hold of, it hasn't come from me. I'd hardly have said it was a guy's body anyway.'

A wariness so fleeting Annie wasn't sure she'd seen it flashed across Jennifer's expression. 'The funeral's the only time you've spoken to her?'

'Yes.'

Jennifer knew she hadn't seen the film at that stage. Annie saw the woman's certainty melt as her anger vanished. 'But she told us … Scott said he thought she was lying … Look, you've got to tell me what you know about this.'

Pat spoke. 'We will. If we know anything, you can have it. Now let's get the facts straight. How have you been conducting this search?'

'Checking cellars. Very discreetly of course. We haven't said anything about what might be there.'

'But it'll be an empty house,' Annie pointed out. 'No one could live with that under them and not know. Look how Terry Martin reacted.'

'And a lot of people'll be on holiday now. How are you checking their houses? How do you know who has cellars anyway?'

'Look, we've thought of all this, you know. We *are* professionals. It isn't easy. We're really low on manpower.'

'But this is a murder enquiry. Surely you've drafted in extra people from other divisions.'

'Not yet.' Again Annie thought she caught a flash of wariness in Jennifer's eyes as she replied to Pat and then went on quickly. 'There aren't many houses with cellars anyway. We've checked it out with the planning department.'

'So it's not Balham's house then?'

Jennifer shook her head. 'We've been through it obviously, but he doesn't have a cellar.'

Pat focused her eyes somewhere distant as though thinking something through. 'I suppose Balham's your prime suspect. He's not turned up, has he?'

'No, but he's done this sort of thing before.'

'What? Murdered women in a cellar?'

'No.' Jennifer's pursed lips admonished Pat for inappropriate levity. 'Disappeared for a few days.'

'It's more than a few days this time. I'd say he knows you're on to him. Did he know Terry Martin?'

'He'd been seen talking to him.'

There was a pause, then Pat heaved herself to a more upright position and fixed Jennifer with a hard stare. 'I suppose you're watching the house in case he comes back?'

'We're doing everything we have to.'

'And you're trying to find out where he goes when he does his disappearing acts?'

'We know how to conduct an enquiry.'

'OK, let's just get this straight. You've watched his house. You've asked around to find out where he is. You've made enquiries about him and Terry Martin. You've searched people's cellars.' She paused to let the point sink in. 'And you're telling us you're surprised the village grapevine cottoned on to a body in a cellar. Of course they think Terry Martin murdered this Balham guy. I think that's just about where I'd get if you gave me that set of clues.'

Jennifer looked uncomfortable. 'But the girl—'

'Just wanted to make herself important probably. My information is from a good source, that sort of thing.'

Jennifer looked across at Annie, caught her eye and looked away. 'Sorry. I shouldn't have jumped to conclusions. Scott did say he thought she was a liar.'

'That's OK.' Annie had no problem with Jennifer feeling in her debt. 'But what about the woman in the cellar? Do you know who she is? I was expecting to hear something on the news today.'

Pat laughed. 'Never heard of the north-south divide, Annie? It takes more than a body to get East Yorkshire in the news.'

'But surely, the local news…?'

'An odd mix of prurience and prudery. On the one hand, she isn't young enough to be a juicy story. On the other, she might be the wife of some local worthy they don't want to get the wrong side of.'

Jennifer shot Pat a disapproving look. 'It's all still under wraps officially. We want to be the ones to find it.'

'But do you know who she is?' Annie asked again.

And again Jennifer's eye slid away from hers. 'Maybe. Nothing's confirmed yet. We can't be sure of anything till we find the body.'

'I wonder if Terry Martin locked the cellar door when he left,' Pat said.

'If he did, we have the key. We found one in his things that we're pretty sure matches the one he used on the film.'

Keys and cellars and bodies are your side of the line, thought Annie, looking across at the woman who was as much a rookie in her profession as Annie in hers. The difference was that Jennifer's status gave her the upper hand when it came to access to the Milesthorpe residents. Jennifer and her colleagues could demand people's co-operation. Annie could only ask. Annoyance welled up against Laura Tunbridge for damaging her credibility, painting her as the sort of person who passed confidential information to children.

After seeing Jennifer out, Annie sat down again opposite Pat and said, 'That's put paid to me going out to Milesthorpe, hasn't it?'

Pat nodded. 'For today, yes. There'll be a police presence out there. Maybe later in the week. With all Milesthorpe on the lookout, they'll get their hands on that body pretty soon if it's anywhere in the area.'

Annie picked up the Orchard Park photographs again. She rifled through them to pull out the ones that showed the two men and their van and held them out to Pat. 'These are the guys peddling shit on Orchard Park last night. Any idea who they are?'

Pat took her time holding the prints up to the light, squinting at them from every angle before she shook her head. 'I can't even say for sure they're the same guys I tried to clock, though I suppose they must be.'

'Does that mean I can keep watch like I wanted to?' Annie tried not to look too pleased.

'Yeah, I suppose.'

Annie pulled all the pictures together and shuffled them as though they were a deck of cards. They showed the van, the men carting their awkward-shaped packages, and that battered yellow car with its insolent payload. She looked at the blurred image, remembered the fracas at Terry's funeral and saw again the image of Laura Tunbridge slapping out at one of the other two. *It so isn't funny ...*

She looked up and blinked her eyes to refocus on the scene outside the window where sunlight played on tiny waves, shading the path of the underlying currents. The river was as busy as she'd ever seen it, one of the vessels making its way upriver the largest she'd seen so far, though even its huge tonnage was dwarfed by the expanse of water.

'Pat, can I run something past you? This joy-rider. Why was he at Terry Martin's funeral?'

'He wasn't, was he? He just turned up outside. Disrupting funerals might be a hobby. What about it?'

'It's the girl, Laura Tunbridge. She hit out at one of the friends she was with. One of them laughed when the joy-riders stopped the hearse. Laura hit out and told her to shut up.'

'Fair enough, but what of it?'

'They were with strangers, well more or less. In a church. At a funeral. What are they, twelve year olds? You don't go laughing at some random kid messing about at a funeral, not if you're twelve years old and off your own territory. It doesn't sit right.'

'You're saying they knew the kid in the car?'

'Yes, I think so, the one who laughed anyway.'

'That's quite a leap, Annie, on a flimsy premise.'

'No, there's more. It's been niggling at the back of my mind all day. Laura Tunbridge told me she and Kay got a lift with Mrs Kitson. I remember her saying it. Me and Kay. Not the third one, not Mally.'

'You're saying the one who didn't get the lift with Mrs Kitson knew the lad in the car and that's how she got there?'

The one who said she'd kill Terry Martin.

'Yes, I think that's what I'm saying. It could explain how he knew who I was. She could have met up with him later and told him. Of course I could be way off. Maybe she's just an obnoxious little cow who got there by bus.'

'Milesthorpe to Withernsea? You must be joking. One bus a week if there's any at all. No, she had a lift all right.'

A minute before five o'clock, Pat hoisted herself out of the settee and hobbled through to her bedroom. As the hour struck, Annie heard the key in the lock and smothered a sigh. Pat would be at least half an hour getting ready.

The chair was comfortable. Annie didn't want to go and sit in the small bedroom or hang about in the kitchen, but there'd be no comfort in listening to bad-tempered mutterings.

As Barbara bustled in and glared at the empty space on the settee that should have been Pat all ready to go, Annie leapt in with the first topic that came to mind. 'Pat tells me you used to be a key figure in the agency,' she lied. 'What made you give it up?'

Barbara swivelled her gaze to Annie. Her expression smoothed from cross towards smug. 'Did she now? Well yes, I was. I used to be the company secretary, you know.'

'Oh, really? That's quite a responsibility. But you decided to give it up?'

'I served my apprenticeship, learnt the business. Decided it wasn't for me, so I went away to university and left Pat to take up the reins. It was more suited to someone of her temperament.'

'What did you do at university?' Annie asked, determined to keep the conversation rolling on neutral territory.

'Archaeology.'

There was an undercurrent of pride in the pronouncement. Barbara, an archaeologist? There were clear investigative parallels with the business she'd given up. 'So did you take up a career in archaeology?'

'Well, I raised a family.' The inference that the two were more or less the same robbed Annie of an easy reply and allowed Barbara space to turn the conversation with a tetchy look at her watch. 'I told her five o'clock on the dot.'

Twenty minutes later the sisters bickered their way out of the flat. Annie felt herself relax as sounds of them faded. The tensions must have been impossible when they worked together.

The agency and its hidden agendas were in her mind when her phone rang a little later.

'Jed's Private Investigations.'

'I should like to speak to a person called Annie Raymond,' said a high-pitched voice. 'It is so a matter of urgency and great importance.'

Annie felt her mouth curve into a grim smile. Laura Tunbridge. She resisted an urge to give the girl an immediate dressing down.

'This is Annie Raymond. How can I help you?'

'Oh Annie!' The precise tone shattered into a storm of tears. Words forced their way out between hysterical intakes of breath and huge sobs. 'Help us! You've so got to help us!'

'Laura...? What is it? Calm down. Come on. Deep breaths. Tell me what it is.'

Laura's hysterics escalated. Annie could make no sense other than 'Help us!' and strained to gather clues from the background sounds as she tried to keep up a commentary of soothing noises. Laura seemed to be out in a storm, her voice hard to hear. Annie's gaze was drawn to the big window overlooking the estuary. Nothing but the tide rippled the water's surface as the heat of the day eased itself towards evening. The sounds from the phone didn't match the calm she could see.

'Laura ... Listen to me. You must calm down.'

... *Laura's got a signal* ... A faint voice in the background.

'Who's with you Laura? Is it Kay? Mally?'

'Yes. Yes. Please help.'

Then, out of the background mayhem and the hysterical sobs, Annie picked the words, 'So awful … The smell …'

CHAPTER 8

Annie was out of the door, down the stairs and unlocking the car before she heard any break in Laura's hysteria. And then it was barely more than a pause for breath before the shrieks started up again.

'Annie … Annie … You must …'

Every nerve strained towards one goal. Keep Laura talking. Keep her on the phone. She fought back the images, the shadowy cellar for real, the rotting corpse now a mass of writhing maggots; a gang of twelve year olds walking in on it.

And what in hell had she heard behind Laura's hysterical outpouring? Muted now, the cacophony could have been a riotous party but without living participants. The images danced; decaying bodies leaping around Laura in a macabre ballet as she screamed in Annie's ear. Terry's film showed a single body, but what about the rest of the room? How many more might there be?

She must get a grip. Laura's hysteria threatened to engulf her.

'It's OK, Laura. I'm coming to get you. Try to calm down …'

A storm. Laura had been out in a storm. It was the rush of wind she'd heard, the lash of rain cascading in sheets. But where? The evening sun warmed her face, the road surface wore a haze of dust. The sky stretched out with only the slimmest brushstrokes of dusk streaking the horizon.

Instinctively, she turned east on to the main carriageway, phone clamped to her ear, struggling one-handed to attach the hands-free kit. The road was busy, too busy to drive like this. As soon as she could finish the call – which was as soon as Laura told her where she was – she could be on to the emergency services. No, not even that. She'd call Jennifer and cut the need for a whole swathe of explanation. Let Jennifer mobilize official help.

'I'm coming Laura. I'm on my way. Where are you? I'll be as quick as I can.'

'*Don't tell. Don't tell.*' A voice in the background.

'Are you in Milesthorpe?' They must be on Terry Martin's territory.

She heard Laura repeat the question. Whispers out of range. The background noises changed, became calmer and yet stronger as though the signal strengthened. The girls weren't standing still. They'd put distance between themselves and their gruesome find. Thank heavens for that, but where were they?

'Laura, where are you?'

After a pause, a different voice answered her, more in control. 'We haven't sussed out if we want to tell you. You don't know what we've found yet.'

Oh, but I do.

'I won't tell,' Annie lied. 'When I get there, we'll talk. We'll decide between us what to do. But where are you?'

'We'll meet her in Milesthorpe.'

Annie heard the whisper. The background noise had quietened. She must remember everything in case the girls clammed up. When Laura first rang, she'd been out in a storm.

'We'll meet you at Mr Balham's.' Laura's voice again, breathless but without hysteria now.

Thank heavens for the time spent scrutinizing the map, committing the major landmarks in the case to memory. Balham's farm lay just beyond the village boundary to the east. From here she must cut off the Withernsea road and head north. Milesthorpe couldn't be far. She mapped a route in her mind. 'I'll be there in five minutes.'

'So will we.' Laura's words now came out between gasps. Laura ran as she spoke. They'd been running all the time she'd driven out from Hull. How far could three twelve year olds run in quarter of an hour? Had they turned back to meet her at the scene of the crime?

'You so mustn't put the phone down!' Laura's voice screeched in her ear.

'No, no of course I won't.' Annie gritted her teeth. She didn't trust Laura's hysteria as quite so genuine as at the start of the call. It held a threat of the girls running off, going to ground, denying everything. She'd wanted to end the call and get on to Jennifer, but daren't, so kept talking until she drove down the hill towards Milesthorpe and saw three figures astride the ramshackle gate that must be the entrance to the farm.

'I can see you, Laura. Look. Up the hill.' She flashed her lights and the girls scrambled to the ground and waved back, clearly not the panicked mess they'd wanted her to believe.

Annie cut the call without advance warning. She tucked the microphone wire into her hair and jabbed the buttons to get Jennifer's number.

You have reached the voicemail of …

Shit! Either Jennifer's phone was off or she was on another call. Annie had no time to retry. She waited for the beep and spoke rapidly, tucking her head down, making a meal of backing the car on to the verge so the girls wouldn't see.

She gabbled out as concise an account as she could. 'I'm with them now at the entrance to Balham's farm,' she finished. 'But I've no idea how close we are to where they found it. Ring me back as soon as you get this.'

As she opened the car door, Annie deliberately slowed her breathing before she looked up into the faces of the three girls who crowded round.

'You've so got to help us. It was so awful.' Sweat plastered Laura's straggly hair to her scalp.

Annie recognized the other two from the church. Kay and Mally. She wondered which was which. The stocky one with short brown hair stared hard at Annie as if to judge how far to trust her. The tall one looked the oldest, and stood back, long and slender, her expression interested but without the anxiety of the others. Her hair, sweat-streaked like Laura's, hung down beyond her shoulders.

'OK,' said Annie. 'First, tell me exactly where you found … uh … exactly where you were when you rang me.'

'But we haven't sussed out if we want to tell.' The stocky girl spoke, while the tall one looked from her to Annie as if not sure whose side to take.

Laura had no reservations. 'Oh Mally, we've so got to tell.'

So the stocky one whose small eyes radiated resentment was Mally, the one who'd laughed at Terry Martin's funeral.

'People pay money to know this sort of stuff.'

'I guess you're the oldest here?' Annie turned her attention to the tall girl, wanting to shift the spotlight from Mally. She had Laura on side and if she could make the older girl take some responsibility Mally would be outnumbered and stop being obstructive.

Annie's tactic backfired. 'I'm the oldest!' Mally swelled in belligerence as she answered. 'Anyway, Kay's not thirteen yet. I've been thirteen for ages.'

'I'm nearly thirteen. It's Laura who's the baby.'

'I am so not a baby!'

'Yeah anyway, Kay's right. You act like one half the time. Always getting us into trouble.'

'I so don't, do I, Kay? I so don't, Annie. It's Mally who always—'

'You do sometimes. If you'd let Mally take Boxer—'

Kay stopped abruptly. Fierce glances were exchanged. Laura muttered, 'It's so not fair. You're a blackguard, Mally!'

'And you're a liar, Laura Tunbridge. You couldn't suss your way out of a paper bag.'

Annie took a few steps away from the simmering group and leant against the rickety gate. 'Some grown-up behaviour from all of you wouldn't be a bad idea considering what you just found.'

'You haven't sussed what we found.'

'OK, surprise me.'

The three girls looked at each other and it was Kay who spoke. 'We've found the body.'

Annie heard an edge of panic in Kay's tone as the memory came back to her. How much worse must it have been in the flesh … in the rotting flesh? All three were jumpy, it was why they sniped at each other. She must take this carefully, bear in mind what was and wasn't officially in the public domain.

'What body?'

'The one the police were looking for, stupid. You must have heard about it. We had it sussed straight away.'

'No, I haven't heard anything about a body. Tell me.'

With the big secret spilt, all three clamoured to be the one to pass on what they knew. Annie listened, sifting the core information from three simultaneous accounts. Pat had guessed it practically to the letter except that the detectives in charge hadn't been as ham-fisted as she'd implied. The leak about their interest in cellars wasn't a result of heavy-handed enquiries.

'The police got all the plans of Milesthorpe to find out who's got a cellar.'

'Where did they get the plans?'

'From the council. And Kay's sister's friend works for them at—'

Annie pretended not to notice the back-heel from Mally that shut Laura up with a gasp. Before things could dissolve into another fight, she said, 'How did you know which cellar to look in?'

'Oh, that was easy.' Mally said. 'The police kept asking about Mr Balham and if he knew Terry, so, of course, we sussed it all out at once. And now we've sussed where Terry put his body.'

But the police had searched Balham's. And anyway, Jennifer said there was no cellar. Annie chose her words with care. 'There's a cellar at Mr Balham's, is there?'

'No, course not. Haven't you sussed it yet? It took us about one minute.'

'That's so not fair, Mally. Annie doesn't know Mr Balham. She's from London.'

Christ! This village grapevine was something else.

A replay of a comment from thirty seconds ago – *we've sussed where Terry put his body*. Hope rose in a wave. The girls had smelt the corpse, she knew, but maybe they'd been spared the sight. *His* body. Not *her* body. If they'd seen it, they would know. The clothes at least wouldn't have rotted that far yet.

'Come on. You need to tell me where.' And come on, Jennifer. Check your voicemail.

'We'll show you. You'd never suss it on your own. Take us in your car. It'll take about twenty minutes.'

'How can it take twenty minutes? You got here on foot in less.'

'We're so not going back on foot. It'll be dark soon. I'm so not going anywhere near that place in the dark.'

'OK, OK.' Annie ushered them towards the car. 'I'll drive you, that's not a problem. I'm just saying that if we go the way you came, it'll be quicker than twenty minutes.'

'You can't do the cliff path in a car. We'll have to do the long way by road.'

*

Annie felt a need to move fast and hustled the girls into Pat's car. Mally sat in front with her and gave the badly timed directions of someone who'd never driven. Twice she had to stop and back the car up as Mally's 'Turn down there', came a fraction too late.

When Mally said, 'Just stay on this road now for ages. I'll tell you where to stop,' Annie put her foot down, to try to get some speed out of the car. Almost at once, her foot slammed back on the brake as the road disappeared in front of her. The car bounced alarmingly as the wheels strayed into grassy ruts. For a second she thought it would flip right over but it found the cracked tarmac surface again and righted itself.

Her heart pounded. The girls didn't seem to notice anything wrong. Mally, the non-driver, hadn't thought to mention hairpin bends. Annie forced in a deep breath. She thought of the corpse Terry Martin had filmed. Whoever the woman was, haste was no use to her now.

She concentrated to pick out the idiosyncrasies of the road ahead and modified her speed to match what she could see. The road, close to single track to start with, narrowed further, its edges ill-defined in jagged holes where heavy farm vehicles and lack of maintenance had frayed the edges of the tarmac ribbon.

After what felt like miles, Mally said, 'You need to stop along here. There's a flat bit where the gate used to be.'

Annie took a glance at the clock. Eighteen minutes. The girls' estimate hadn't been far out. It was hard to judge the twists and turns but they seemed to have driven a huge loop out of Milesthorpe and back again.

The background hiss of the sea rushing the beach far below and the crash of waves breaking, grew in volume as the four of them made their way over the uneven ground to the cliff's edge. Remnants of daylight picked out the rising moon and waves far out to sea. Annie screwed up her eyes against the rush of the wind that must blow continuously up here. She recognized the background sounds to Laura's call. Not a storm after all, just a quirk of landfall that kept a constant squall blowing. Then a form began to define itself ahead. A low black shape, angular and at odds with the landscape.

'What is it?' Annie couldn't help keeping her voice down not to disturb the ghosts she knew were nearby.

'It's the shed where Mr Balham kept his sheep when this was a real field.'

A shed? Terry Martin hadn't been inside a shed. Then she came close enough to see that the so-called shed was some kind of wartime relic. It had once been a substantial building, but it sat low, nestled into the ground. No windows. No difficulty to imagine the inside. Dark, damp ... a cellar in all but name. It stood about fifty metres from the cliff top. In the war it must have been much further back. Some manner of command post maybe.

Annie stopped. The girls were behind her. They hung back now. This was as close as they wanted to be.

All doubts gone, Annie couldn't stop the question, 'Did you go inside?'

'It's locked. Mr Balham always keeps it locked. We had that sussed years ago.'

'And anyway, Maz— Ow!'

'*Shut up*!'

Annie looked sharply across as she glimpsed Mally's foot shoot out to deal Laura a swift kick on the ankle. Mally glared. Laura's lip trembled.

'But we didn't need to go in,' Kay cut across the byplay. 'It's awful. You know as soon as you get inside the first bit.'

'I'm so not going back in.'

'I didn't say you had to. But *she* can if she wants.' Mally pointed at Annie. 'If she doesn't believe us.'

'I believe you.'

Visions leapt in front of Annie before she could fight them back. The blackened tongue … the remains of an eye … the glimpse of a ligature bitten tight … She stared towards the low building watching it shimmer and fade into the dusk. What would they say when Balham turned up in the village? And what when he was arrested? Would the woman who lay inside turn out to be someone else they knew?

She jumped at a sudden noise. It was the ring of her phone. At last! Jennifer.

The voice in her ear crackled indistinctly. Bad signal or low charge. It didn't matter. She was able to give Jennifer a concise account, and felt the weight of responsibility lift as she spoke. The girls stopped talking to listen. Laura's mouth hung open, but relief lit her eyes. Mally glowered, clearly resentful that Annie had outflanked her.

Nothing to do now but wait for the cavalry to arrive.

The scene flipped from sinister calm with only the wind and the sea as spectators to cars and shouting, high-viz jackets and powerful beams of light. Annie stood at the periphery and barely felt a part of it. Where she'd been the star player, she'd become invisible. From out of the fast-approaching night grown-ups had swooped to cluster round the three girls. Annie felt a pang of sadness that there was no one to comfort her. She recognized the police constable who'd been in the car with Scott Kerridge at the Martins. Jennifer appeared too, her movements purposeful. Everyone seemed to have a role. They all knew what to do.

'You OK?'

A light touch on her arm. Annie looked up into the face of Scott Kerridge, his expression concerned, kind. 'Yes … thanks.' She felt gratitude that he'd thought to ask.

'Get that light fixed!' someone shouted.

Her eye was drawn to the vehicles that flashed alternately bright-mute creating a pulsing blue circle centred on the narrow road. When she looked back, Scott was gone.

'Uh … Miss Raymond?'

Annie turned again and looked into the precise and rather long face of the man whose resemblance to Laura made introductions unnecessary.

'We're taking Laura home now. We were going to drop Melissa off too, but she says you've promised her a lift back to her grandfather's.'

'Yes, I can do that,' she said, taken aback.

Laura's father shook his head. 'She hadn't asked you, had she? But if you don't mind taking her, we'd be grateful. She's a bit of a wild young thing and her mother's away at the moment. I'm afraid she's been over-indulged since her parents divorced. She's Colonel Ludgrove's granddaughter. Do you know his house?'

'Yes … yes, I know where he lives.' Ludgrove, of course, was one of the names on her mental map of Milesthorpe, the friend Tremlow contacted when he found Terry Martin's body.

'I'm going to ring him and tell him that you're bringing her home. I'll explain who you are. I'm afraid he puts too much trust in young Melissa's word about where she's going or who she's with.'

He spoke into his phone as they picked their way across the grass to join the others.

Annie saw anger flare in Mally's eyes as Laura's father told her what he'd done. Clearly Mally had intended to give them all the slip and go off by herself. But where? Surely she wouldn't want to make her own way back to the village after all this, even if there were a quick route along the cliff path. It was almost completely dark now.

Annie waited until they were alone in Pat's car and had set off back towards the village. 'So how would you have got home if I hadn't given you a lift?'

'Gone with Kay,' Mally snapped.

Annie noted the reference to Kay and not Laura, the latter being out of favour probably for having pushy parents.

'Yeah, but you told Laura's Dad you were coming back with me.'

'I am, aren't I?'

Annie glanced across. Any doubts she'd had about Mally knowing the joy-riders dissolved as she looked at the girl. Mally never intended to make her way back alone from the cliff top. She had a phone and a juicy story to tempt her unruly mates with their fast cars out from Hull. That was the plan Annie and Laura's father thwarted between them. They completed the journey in silence until Annie slowed to turn into the road where Ludgrove lived.

'You can drop me here,' Mally said. 'It's just up the road.'

Annie drove to the gate. 'I'll walk with you to the door.'

'I'm not a fucking kid, you know! I can suss my way up a fucking drive!'

Annie ignored the profanities put on for her benefit and saw that even if Mally had planned a last-minute getaway, she'd have been stopped. An elderly man leaning heavily on a stick hobbled down the driveway to meet them.

'Thought I saw a car,' he greeted them.

'Can I use the net, Grandad? I want to e-mail Kay.' Mally's voice was full of bounce, no trace of the strop she'd been in a moment ago. She didn't wait for an answer but skipped past her grandfather and into the house.

'So you're the private detective they're all talking about?' The old man leant awkwardly on his stick so he could free a hand to offer Annie. 'Do come in.' He turned with difficulty and made heavy work of the climb up the three steps to the front door.

Reluctantly, Annie followed. She'd be pushing it to get back to Orchard Park and didn't want to delay any longer. She listened to Mally's grandfather's laboured breathing. E-mail to Kay? Annie didn't think so. Mally would be on to her joy-riding mates to embroider the story of the body. Would they race out here with their tatty car and blaring music to make trouble? Part of her felt she shouldn't leave this vulnerable old man at Mally's mercy. Another part felt a reluctance to cross this threshold because it led to a side of Terry Martin's story she didn't want to know. But she could spare a few minutes. Long enough to make arrangements to come back in daylight and talk to Colonel Ludgrove about the night Terry Martin died.

'Do you get much trouble with joy-riders out here?' she asked, as they entered the house.

The journey back to Hull became paradoxically brighter as the night grew darker. Country lanes, no more than narrow strips of tarmac through jungles of thick vegetation, wound their way into broader highways with road markings and streetlights. The direct route from Milesthorpe to the city led her back an unfamiliar way where neon signs and all-night garages created pools of activity in an otherwise sleeping town.

So much for the leisurely and measured introduction to the village that she'd planned, the careful cruising round the streets to locate and imprint on her mind all the addresses she'd memorized. Her mental map of the place had been flat, dotted with the square boxes that were the homes of the people she'd identified. Now she'd seen one of them, Colonel Ludgrove's; been inside even. It was a real house with a driveway and gardens, not so much square as rambling. On her way out of the village she'd passed a couple of large, old-fashioned houses tucked away across the fields, their lights showing big doors and fancy stonework. And the village itself spread far further than she'd imagined and partly sat up on the crest of a gentle hill. East Yorkshire wasn't a flat expanse. Its horizons were a long way off but the land undulated in a way that hid whole communities, and heaven knew what else. For at least a couple of weeks it had hidden the remains of a murdered woman.

Annie felt sick at the thought of it. A woman who'd met her end in a broken down building at the cliff's edge now had white-suited scenes of crime officers and the medical men who dealt in death poring over her rotting remains.

It was too late to go back to Pat's and swap the car for a taxi, but not too late for a drive round to Mrs Earle's to see what went on outside the flats in the small hours. As she headed for Orchard Park she reflected that her destination was probably the home territory of the joy-riders Mally knew.

'Joy-riders!' Colonel Ludgrove had thundered in response to her question giving a glimpse of the military authority he'd once held. 'Vandals! Hooligans! Don't give them fancy names. Call a spade a spade.'

Yes, he told her, the village had been plagued for some time with gangs from Hull racing their cars through the streets, drawing in the local youth.

'It must be a worry with your granddaughter to look after?'

'Oh, I've no worries on that score. She's a good girl, young Mel. Credit to the family name. Knows how to look after herself. Chip off the old block.'

'Will her mother be away for long?'

'No, no. Back any day now.'

Annie felt desperately sorry for him. Once a leader of men whose word was law, now helpless in the face of his own granddaughter. She imagined them together, he trying to instil in Mally all his old values; her listening with a false smile to curry favour and for as long as her boredom threshold held.

The approach to Mrs Earle's block might be the other side of the world for the contrast it offered to the lanes of Milesthorpe. No lush vegetation, just wide areas of dusty stunted grass subservient to the concrete roads and dwellings. She eased the car over the speed bumps resisting the urge to copy the joy-riders and snake round them.

She pulled into the car-park of the tower block away from the direct beam of a streetlight and settled down to wait. The clock showed five minutes to two.

For a long time there was nothing to see. Sirens whined in the distance, some came close enough that she expected blue flashing lights within sight, but none appeared. A couple strolled up to one of the maisonettes opposite and made play of letting themselves in quietly. She watched the house after the door closed, saw lights go on and off, a silhouette as someone drew the curtains together at an upstairs window. A couple returning late, keeping the noise down. Nothing surreptitious, just good-neighbourliness; at odds with her image of the neighbourhood.

Her phone rang. Annie glanced at the screen and paused. The last time she'd answered an unfamiliar number it had been Laura Tunbridge hysterical at the top of the cliff.

'Jed's Private Investigations. Annie Raymond speaking.'

'Hi, Annie. This is Scott Kerridge. I hope I haven't got you out of bed.'

Scott? She made herself hide her surprise. He must have got her number from Jennifer. 'No, I'm still working. This isn't a nine to five number, you know.'

He laughed. 'Look, I won't keep you if you're working, but I wanted to say thank you for tonight. You did a brilliant job with those kids. It was all too busy for anyone to have a proper word.'

'Oh, well … thanks for the thought. I suppose it was the right place? I mean it wasn't just a dead sheep or something?'

'It was the place he filmed all right.'

'And was it…? Was there just one body in there?'

'Just the one. Just like on the film.'

'Do you know who she is … was?'

'Too early to say for sure. We're trying to play it down if we can until we get a positive ID.'

'OK. I won't say anything.'

There was a pause. 'Um … are you doing anything tomorrow night? I just wondered … thought at least you deserved a drink after tonight. Or we could go for a meal if you like.'

Annie glanced at her watch. It was already tomorrow by almost two and a half hours. 'Yeah, thanks, that would be good. I can't be too late though. I have to be on Orchard Park in the early hours.'

'You know how to live.' It wasn't hard to envisage his face creasing into a smile. She'd imagined it enough.

For a few minutes after the call Annie sat oblivious to her surroundings. Good relations with the police were a must for an effective PI. She'd been right to accept the offer, but … but … a raft of potential complications loomed.

The slam of a car door jolted her back to the present. She sat up and stared. The white van was back. It had slipped into the car-park under the general noise of the city. She watched as the doors opened. Three of them tonight. Yesterday's two plus a big man; solid; well-dressed. There was something familiar about his appearance, but Annie was sure she didn't know him. As she watched, he stretched his shoulders, working his arms back and forth, and tossed comments across to the other two.

She lowered the window. Their voices carried easily on the night air. The big man patted his pockets. Annie caught the words, 'Do us a skin', and saw a cigarette paper exchange hands. No packages to unload tonight. When the van was locked and cigarettes lit, they all headed for the entrance.

The surrounding streets were quiet. She slid out of the car, locked it and shot across the concrete to the flats. Mrs Earle's spare key gave her access. She held back until she heard the whine of the lift and then went inside. The indicator over the blank lift doors rose steadily. No pause on six. No pause anywhere. It went all the way to the top.

With Pat's car outside, she could neither follow them up nor wait to see if they stopped off anywhere on the way back down. That was for another night. As she stepped back into the cool air she paused a moment and tipped her head right back to see to the top of the block. There must be one hell of a view from up there.

CHAPTER 9

ANNIE WOKE THE next morning to a blaze of light through the window. She rolled away from the glare of the sun and shaded her eyes as she turned her head to check the time. Ten o'clock. A late start but she hadn't been back until after three. She yawned as she got up and went through to the bathroom.

Pat had been in bed when she arrived back so there was a whole swathe of detail her boss was behind on. It was hard to schedule things like keeping Pat up to date. If asked before she arrived, she'd have said the more autonomy she was given the better job she'd do, but the reality came with an unsuspected insecurity and failed to fit the preconceptions that had put her in a busy office with people she could share worries and ideas with. What she had was a boss self-absorbed with a badly broken leg who spent half the day in bed.

She needed to know if any business had been transacted last night outside Mrs Earle's door. If not, it suggested the van was a nightly visitor and the guys did business on other floors on other nights. Later on, she'd ring Mrs Earle and find out what state the landing was in.

The voice of the guy in Birmingham murmured in her ear. *Always double-check. Don't take your clients' words for stuff; they have their own agendas.*

OK, maybe she'd call round, but she had a full schedule for Milesthorpe today and must be back before Scott showed up so she could change out of her working gear. Dowdy but practical was the only image he'd seen of her so far. Her mind skittered briefly over options. Graphite-check three-quarter trousers and white polo top had a classy touch. She had to forewarn Pat, too, and cringed inwardly at the thought of the heavy-handed comments her boss was likely to make.

As she pulled on her old jeans, she turned her mind to Milesthorpe. Now the body was found, she could go out there. She had one interview lined up already. Colonel Ludgrove, who'd turned out to be Mally Fletcher's grandfather, surprised her by not insisting on a set time. His military bearing suggested a rigid diary, but maybe Mally's arrival in his life had wrecked all that.

'Call in anytime. I'll be here. Don't get out much. Parish meeting first Tuesday of the month, nothing much else.'

He'd be no trouble. He was a lonely old man grateful for company, and that military mind would be good on detail. Three of them to deal with, Jennifer had said, and all with a different story. Ludgrove, Tremlow and Kitson, the trio who'd found the body. Annie's gut feeling was that Ludgrove was the one with the clear head. She'd take special notice of his version.

And then there was Mrs Becke, the woman who shrieked at Terry Martin on the film. Mrs Becke was her prime target.

Interviewing your witnesses in the right order could save a lot of time. She remembered the case studies they'd been shown, how the wrong order could lead to repeat visits or the wrong direction altogether.

'But how do you know in advance?' she'd asked.

'You don't necessarily,' had been the reply. 'But keep it in mind. What can one witness tell you that you might want to quiz another one about?'

Mrs Becke, a woman with something to hide who'd hated Terry Martin, had a handle on his real reasons for being in Milesthorpe, but how would she react to Annie's approach? Had Terry's death neatly concealed indiscretions that she wouldn't want raked up?

It was an accident, Annie told herself. He fell. She glanced at the closed door through which loud snores rasped and considered waiting for Pat to emerge, but Pat had a hospital appointment later today. She'd be distracted over that and if Annie were to wait until she was up and about, she wouldn't get to Milesthorpe until well into the afternoon, whereas if she got herself on the road now, she'd be back in good time to be ready for six o'clock when Scott was due to call. Not, of course, that she had any intention of planning her day around him.

The journey out to Milesthorpe was a repeat of last night's but without the tension. On impulse she turned off before reaching the village and headed for the cliff road to see what signs were left of last night's activity.

She twisted the car round the narrow lanes, their verges high with grasses. Feathery flowers shimmered in a haze that hadn't obscured oncoming headlights in the dark but that now lined the bends in the road like an impenetrable wall. Progress was slow, the journey to reach the cliff top longer than before.

It all seemed deserted. She pulled the car off the road and got out. At once the sea breeze hit and made her huddle into her thin jacket. Was this the right place? The rough grassland looked the same, the swish of waves a backdrop to the rush of the wind. But no building. She picked her way across the uneven ground until the square shape eased its way into view. She'd thought it a quirk of the darkness that it couldn't be seen from the road, but it genuinely nestled into the ground invisible from prying eyes.

She was alone. The tapes she'd seen flapping last night were gone. So they'd done all they needed to do already. Annie picked her way over the uneven tussocks of grass until she could see the walled enclosure that must once have housed Balham's sheep and before that maybe military vehicles. She imagined khaki-clad soldiers on old-fashioned motor bikes skidding on muddy ground as they delivered sealed packages to rotund men with handlebar moustaches, men like Colonel Ludgrove in his youth.

A single door led from the enclosure into the building. She slid down the grassy slope and tiptoed across the yard, although there was no one to hear her footsteps even if they'd been audible over the breeze and the crash of the waves. Annie approached the door and pulled it wide to allow in some daylight.

Terry Martin's film had made this seem a walled corridor, but it wasn't. Raised animal stalls with a few broken timbers lined either side. The concrete was cracked and broken. Green fingers of lichen and moss stretched slimy tendrils down the walls. Even after such a hot dry summer the constant spray from the sea kept the building damp. At the far end another door faced her; the blank wood seemed to watch as the daylight crept in, daring her to approach.

She had no business to be here; no need to be here, but a compulsion drew her inside and along the narrow path between the concrete stalls. This would be where Terry Martin had put the camera down, and there where he'd bent over the door struggling with the key in the lock. Where had he got that key? Why had he come here? What had he expected to find? Not a rotting body, that was for sure. Annie looked at the solid panel in front of her; far stouter wood than the outer door, less exposed to the elements. Praying it wouldn't open, she turned the handle and pushed. It held firm. She breathed a sigh of relief and turned to leave.

She'd seen the place in the film as far as she was able. It snipped off a stray end. Closure of some sort, though it had never been part of her case. This was where the line lay. This was Jennifer and Scott's territory.

Hurrying back out, she found herself looking round to be sure she wasn't watched, then she climbed the grassy slope up from the walled yard, retraced her steps to the car and headed for Milesthorpe.

The Beckes' house looked both familiar and strange. She recognized it from Terry Martin's film, but the few seconds' footage hadn't shown that this was one house in a terraced row. In the sunlight, it looked ordinary; had lost the sinister gloss the memory of the film had given it in Annie's mind.

A careful glance as she cruised past showed two figures in a downstairs room, one a bulky, broad-shouldered man, the other a slimmer female outline. She pulled up beyond the house to wait and see if one of them left. Her rear-view mirror framed the Beckes' front door. The scene in front showed her the south end of Milesthorpe. She studied the view down the hill.

Two large houses stood back from the road. She struggled to orientate them in her mind, to fit them with the view from the other side of the village. Milesthorpe was where she must work to follow in Terry Martin's footsteps. In her mind for these few weeks she had to know it as well as though she'd lived here for years. Had she seen these two houses from another angle or not? Yes, she decided, but they'd looked far grander with imposing front doors and fancy stonework. From here they were a motley collection of add-ons and out-buildings. They stood with their backs to her, yet this was the main road. Why would anyone build a house with its back to the road?

Her gaze moved further down the hill to a patchwork of fields where horses, made small by distance, shuffled about with heads down cropping the grass. Odd silvery lines crossed the big fields. Some peculiarity of the light maybe. Concrete buildings like prison blocks edged the north end of the paddocks. A figure emerged leading two more horses that were decanted into the fields and immediately put their heads down to graze.

All very Pony Club … the kids' network drives everything. Jennifer's words.

That would be the hub of it down there. That would be the place to find out more about Terry Martin's activities at Milesthorpe Show if she needed to. She reached to the glove compartment for a pair of binoculars to train on the wooden board at the head of the driveway.

Milesthorpe Riding School and Livery Yard. Prop: Ms Christina Hain.

Curious to know what she'd seen criss-crossing the grassy stretches, she swept the binoculars across the paddocks, but still couldn't tell. The glistening lines twinkled and swayed and looked even more like Christmas tinsel through the magnification of the lenses. The sharp flashes of reflected sunlight from the silvery surfaces stung her eyes.

A movement from the mirror caught Annie's attention and she looked back at the Beckes' house. A large man strode down the path and headed for a car parked further up the street. Its lights winked at him as he unlocked its doors. Annie watched closely and was as sure as she could be that this was the man Terry had filmed with Mrs Becke at Milesthorpe Show. There was nothing surreptitious about his exit. He surely was Mr Becke and not the secret lover.

As the car disappeared round the bend at the top of the road, Annie climbed out and made her way back to the house. She hadn't decided on her opening gambit, wanting to see the woman's face, to judge her expression as she set eyes on Annie for the first time. She might try the straightforward, *Hi, Mrs Becke. I'm a private detective working for …* or the less formal, *Hi, my name's Annie. I understand you knew Terry Martin….*

The door stood open. As Annie came close enough to see in, she made out Mrs Becke moving around a large kitchen table pulling plates and cups together as she swished a cloth that streaked the table top inadequately. Mrs Becke was thin, early thirties maybe, with lifeless dark hair.

Annie sensed hostility but no surprise as the woman looked up and saw her in the doorway. As she opened her mouth to introduce herself she saw a hard shell form around her intended interviewee; a shell she would never breach if she didn't make an immediate dent. She threw away the words that were on her tongue and said, 'Christ, I'd forgotten the village grapevine. You're expecting me, aren't you, Mrs Becke? I guess I should apologize for being late.'

The woman fought against a smile, but couldn't quite suppress it. 'Look, who are you? Why are you prying about that Martin prat?'

'I'm working for his parents. They don't think so badly of him, though they're probably the only ones.'

A glimmer of surprise. Mrs Becke's eyes narrowed as she tried to weigh up her visitor.

'They need more than the official enquiry gave them,' Annie went on. 'A bit of background about why he was in Milesthorpe that night. I know pretty much what sort of guy he was but I'm not out to paint the colour into every gory detail that'll make things worse for them. I just want the bare facts. Where was he those last two days? He left home on Sunday afternoon and the next they heard was a call on Tuesday evening to say he'd died.'

Mrs Becke still hovered on the brink of hostility but she seemed to relax a little. 'Just those last two days?' she murmured, as she carried a cafetière to the sink.

Whatever Terry Martin had unearthed, Annie read, it hadn't happened in those last two days. But if she wanted to get anything useful from this woman, she needed her relaxed and ready to talk, not tight and hostile. She took the chance of pushing things one way or the other. 'I don't suppose the village grapevine's good enough to tell you how I like my coffee, is it, Mrs Becke?'

The woman turned on her with a look of incredulity. For a second Annie thought she'd blown it, then Mrs Becke laughed. 'You're a cheeky cow, aren't you? Oh well, I could do with another cup myself. And for Chris'sakes call me Heather. You make me feel ancient with Mrs Becke. You're Annie, aren't you? And you're wasting your time with me. I barely saw anything of him the week before he died.'

As Heather Becke brought two cups of coffee to the table and sat down, Annie said, 'You know Terry Martin did reports for the local press?'

'He told me he could get me in the nationals. Stupid little prat. I told him I'd had all the publicity I needed. And he was six months too late anyway.'

'Publicity about what?'

Heather Becke pushed herself up from the table and went to rummage in a cupboard. 'There.' She threw a creased news-cutting on the table.

Annie opened it out. Heather and the man she'd seen leaving the house stared out at her, awkwardly posed, each with a hand pointing back indicating something about the muddy patch they stood on. It was a double-spread ... *planning dispute ... prosperous village of Milesthorpe ...* Annie glanced at the by-line. Not Terry Martin.

Heather sat back with her coffee, no sign of tension now. Whatever Terry Martin had unearthed about her, it had nothing to do with this story. 'It's all sorted now,' she said. 'I couldn't get shot of my ex until we'd cleared it all and sorted the money on the house.'

If Terry Martin's theories had any substance this new marriage wasn't very stable. Annie turned back to the page in front of her and skim read enough to get at the nub of the dispute. It hung on whether a narrow watercourse at the bottom of the Beckes' garden was manmade or natural.

'Beckes split over brook,' she murmured. Quite a snappy headline it turned out. The newspaper on the table majored on Mrs Becke as hapless victim, kept tied to her ex by a heartless local council, desperate to be properly free to live happily ever after with 'the true love of her life'. Annie wondered if the secret lover pre or post-dated the story.

'Split over brook? Yeah, he said something stupid like that.'

In her mind, Annie painted the detail of Terry Martin's motivation. He'd come across the story of the Beckes late in the day and he'd been furious. Here was a story that had had a double-page spread in one of the Sundays and he'd missed it. Here on his own doorstep. He'd done his best to revive it, trying to interest Heather in a follow-up but by then she'd got what she wanted.

'What did he say when you said you weren't interested in a follow-up?'

'He pestered for a while, then he went away. Then of course I found the little toerag had been following—'

Heather stopped abruptly. Annie was sure the picture of Heather on Terry Martin's film of Milesthorpe Show was of her with her husband and Heather hadn't appeared anywhere else on the film other than when she caught him snooping outside her house. She chose her words to be deliberately ambiguous. 'Yeah, I know. I saw some of the pictures he took. Like I say, I'm not bothered about that side of things. I've got to try and paint him like he wasn't a devious little sap for his mother's sake. All I've got so far is he couldn't keep his nose out of anyone else's business.'

'I'll say. Uh ... what sort of pictures did you see? There was nothing to make anything of in the ones he showed me.'

'No, nothing much. Nothing to make anything of, like you say. You and a guy standing talking, that's all.'

'There was nothing in it.' Heather spoke defensively. 'He was one of the guys I worked with that's all. I gave him a lift home sometimes, and a couple of times we dropped off here for something. I ... uh ... lent him a book one time. And Terry made a big thing about us being in the house for hours. We were just having coffee that's all. Anyway, it took me a while to find the book. But he found out that Jason was away and he tried to threaten me, said he'd tell him.'

Too much explanation, thought Annie, but it was nothing to her if Heather chose to have a fling with a guy she worked with while *the true love of her life* was away.

'You won't have been sorry to hear about his accident.'

'Too right. I was glad to be shot of him. He was a real hassle. He tried asking for money at one bit.'

'He was trying to blackmail you?'

'Oh yeah. See, Jason's a real hot-head and Terry had this so-called log of all the times he'd seen Mario coming into the house when Jason was away. Of course ... uh ... it was made up, but Jason would have seen red. It'd have caused no end of trouble. But you never know with Jason. He might have gone up in the air with Terry and given him a good pasting. Terry saw that and gave up on it.'

This was more than Annie had bargained for. Terry Martin had died in the midst of a blackmail campaign against Heather Becke and a guy called Mario.

'Did you see him at all after mid July?'

'Yeah, a couple of times. He was there on ... let's see, when would it be? The day after Milesthorpe Show. I remember thinking, "Oh hell," when I saw him waiting but then he went off, changed his mind I suppose.'

'You didn't see him at the show? He shot a few pictures.'

'Of me?'

'No, there was just one brief bit of you with your husband towards the end of the day. He concentrated on the horsy stuff. The kids jumping the fences.'

'Oh, he did, did he?'

Heather's tone made Annie look up sharply. Her skin tingled with the prickle of retreating blood. She hadn't expected anyone to make anything of Terry being at Milesthorpe Show.

'You want to tell Tina about that,' Heather said. 'She'll go spare. She barred him from setting a foot on her land.'

Milesthorpe Riding School and Livery Yard. Prop: Ms Christina Hain.

'How could she bar him from Milesthorpe Green?'

'Not the Green. They don't do the ponies and horses on the Green.' The tone made clear that Annie had said something stupid. 'Imagine what a state it'd be in. No, you said he filmed the jumping, the Showcross. They do that on her land.'

'Why would she bar him?'

'God knows. I don't know why she bothered with him in the first place. Little squirt.'

'You say you saw him the day after the show, the Monday. Did you see him after that?'

'Not really. I think he kept out of my way once he realized he might be in for a leathering from Jason.'

'Not really?' Annie pushed.

'Look, I bumped into him the next weekend. The Sunday it must have been. But it was nothing. He was coming out of Ted Balham's. We didn't speak.'

Coming out of Balham's that Sunday? Again Annie felt the prickle of retreating blood. In the gap between the Sunday and the Tuesday, Balham disappeared and Terry died. Accidental death? Every angle she came at it, something reared up to mock that official verdict.

'Was Mr Balham at Milesthorpe Show?' she asked.

'Ted?' Heather screwed up her eyes in thought. 'Yeah, I think so. Yes, I'm sure so. I remember seeing him.'

'Have you seen him since?'

Heather shook her head. 'He's gone walkabout, hasn't he? No, I don't remember seeing him after the show, but then why would I? The kids found a dead sheep or something up on the cliff. They were going round saying Terry had done Ted in.' Heather laughed. 'That'd be a bit of drama for Milesthorpe. He'd have loved to have had that to write up.' Suddenly serious, she looked Annie in the eye. 'It was a dead sheep, wasn't it? Everyone's saying it was a body, but there'd have been something on the news, wouldn't there?'

Yes, thought Annie, I assumed that too. She shrugged a don't-know as her mind turned to the woman, still unidentified, who had lain up by the cliff top, and thought how shocked everyone would be when the truth came out. 'Did Terry know Mr Balham well?'

'Not that I know. He was asking questions at one bit, though.'

'What sort of questions?'

'He'd asked me once how long Ted had been a church warden.'

'Why would he ask that?'

'No idea. I told him I hadn't a clue. Told him to go to Doris for that sort of stuff.'

'Doris?'

'Doris Kitson.'

Annie paused to let things sink in. She'd write it all up later, but for now she had a satisfying feel of spreading the net, grasping at the substance that had brought Terry to Milesthorpe. 'The Sunday before he died, can you remember what time you saw him?'

'Mid-afternoon. Threeish.'

The glow of satisfaction deepened. She'd started to nibble into those missing hours. Martha had seen him off just after two. 'And after that? Did you see him again?'

'Nope, not a whisper. That was the last I ever saw of him.'

After she left Heather Becke, Annie drove round the corner out of sight of the house then reached for her phone to call Mrs Earle on Orchard Park.

A befuddled voice answered and Annie had a feeling midday was too early for Mrs Earle. She asked if there'd been any disturbance the previous night.

'No!' The tone became tetchy. 'I told you that already. I told you when it is. Tuesday and Friday.'

'Are you sure? What was the landing like this morning? Any sign anyone had been there?'

'No. How many times, for God's sake! I told you. They only do Tuesdays and Fridays.'

'Have you been out of the flat yet today?'

'What would I have been out for?'

'Will you go and check the landing?'

'Oh bloody hell. What a frigging palaver.'

Annie listened to doors slam, and the sound of a television rise then fade away.

There was an echo to Mrs Earle's voice when it came again. 'There's fuck all. It's like it always is except after Tuesday and Friday. Satisfied?'

One more piece in the Earle jigsaw. Annie clicked off her phone and headed back through Milesthorpe to the house she'd visited the night before.

At Colonel Ludgrove's, it was Mally who answered her knock. 'Oh, it's you.' Mally looked her up and down then turned to shout back into the gloom of the hallway. 'Grandad, it's her.'

Annie followed Mally's retreating form into the house.

Colonel Ludgrove sat in an armchair in a dowdy living room. Annie smiled and sat on a settee opposite. She was disconcerted to see Mally plump herself down in another chair and look expectantly from one to the other of them.

'Not going out with your friends today, Mel?' her grandfather asked.

'Nah, they're grounded. Laura's dad's been telling tales again. He's a stuck-up old fart, always interfering.'

'Now, Mel,' her grandfather admonished, but his mouth curved to a smile of amusement.

'Yes, but Grandad, he is. I don't care about him always grounding Laura but he keeps sneaking on Kay, too, so I've no one to go out with. It isn't fair.'

'He rang me, too, last night. Thought you should be kept in for a day or two in case you're traumatized.'

'Huh! I'm not a wet like Laura.'

The old man chuckled and threw Annie a glance that said he was proud of a granddaughter who stood up to all-comers.

Annie was reluctant to talk in front of Mally but the girl seemed set for the day so she explained again about her job for the Martins and asked about the night Terry died.

Mally yawned. 'God, it's so boring. Dead bodies everywhere.'

'If you haven't friends coming round, why not go and get a film from the shop to watch this evening?' He turned to Annie and pointed at an untidy heap of DVDs by the television. 'Not that we don't have plenty already, but she claims she's seen the lot.'

'Well, I have. I don't mind some of them again though.'

'But wouldn't you prefer a new one for this evening?'

'Oh all right. I haven't got any money though.'

With an effort the old man pushed himself up out of his chair to reach into a back pocket and pull out a note.

'Five? Can't I have ten then I can get some crisps and stuff to have while I watch it.'

'Now Mel, there's plenty of that sort of stuff in the pantry and your mother said—'

'Oh go on, Grandad, just this once.'

With a resigned shake of his head, he swapped the five for a ten and handed it over.

'Thanks, Grandad.' Without a backward glance, Mally was gone.

He settled himself back in his chair. 'Yes, well, Mr Martin, the first of the bodies. Do you know who they found up there on the cliff, by the way? Young Mel told me it was Ted Balham. I do hope not. He was an odd cove but good company for an evening now and then.'

Unlike Heather, Colonel Ludgrove hadn't discounted the rumour. There was little point pretending.

'Sorry,' she said. 'I've no idea who it was. I don't think any identification's been made yet, but …' Annie paused, not sure how far she could go without breaching the agreement to keep things under wraps. The old man looked shrunken and forlorn. She could at least give him a crumb of comfort. 'Look, I probably shouldn't say anything so please don't quote me, but I know it wasn't Mr Balham.'

'That's good. I've few enough friends left in the village. I wouldn't want to lose one like that.'

'Did you know Terry Martin before he died?'

The old man shook his head. 'Had a call from the woman at the livery yard a few weeks ago. Said she was worried he'd been bothering young Mel. Young Mel can look after herself, but I had a word with the lad, set him straight.'

'When did you speak to him?'

'Oh, it'll be three weeks ago now, maybe more. Told the woman who runs the yard, a Miss Hain … told her to send him up to me next time he showed up. He came, too. To be frank with you, I didn't expect him. Thought his sort would just do a bunk. Put him straight. He pestered my granddaughter at his peril.'

'That did the trick, did it?'

'Oh yes. Though he didn't seem to be that bad a cove. He wrote for the newspapers. Told me he was following the village rivalries. Pony shows, you know. The big Showcross was coming up. Of course, young Mel would have been right in the running if her mother hadn't had to sell the pony. I expect she's told you all about it. I've told her not to dwell, not to bore all and sundry with family troubles, but she was very upset. They don't understand at that age. She won it the year before, you see. Broke her heart to see the beast go, but she stood up straight and took it on the chin. She spent hours out there helping her two friends.' He indicated vaguely to the window. Annie's gaze followed and saw churned and muddy ground where there must once have been an imposing sweep of lawn. At one edge was a construction of concrete blocks and poles, a clone of the obstacles she'd seen on Terry Martin's film of the ponies at Milesthorpe Show, 'She's a generous-hearted girl. They took the cup, you know, after she'd coached them. Couldn't have it herself but made sure it didn't leave the village.'

'And Terry Martin?' Annie tried to coax him away from the altar of adoration of Mally.

'Never saw him again alive. Not been home long the Tuesday when Tremlow phoned in a complete funk. Intruder in his garden. Of course it was him.'

'So you didn't see him at all in the week after Milesthorpe Show? Or the following weekend?'

'No. Don't even know if he went to the show. Said he was going to write it up, but I can't say I saw anything in the local rag.'

A sulky voice broke in from the doorway. 'Well he *was* at the show.'

Annie wondered how long Mally had been in the shadows listening, and what had happened to the putative trip to the shop. How much of her anger was at her mother for going away and leaving her behind?

'No sulks, young lady. We take what life throws.' It was the nearest to a sharp tone that Annie had heard him use.

Mally perked up at once and smiled. 'And we throw it right back.' She laughed. 'But he was at the show and he promised to write it up about us being best and he never did; the liar.'

'Did you see him at all after the show, Mally?' Annie put the question on impulse and watched Mally's gaze slide away.

'Yeah … coupla times. Grandad, can I watch a film now? When *she's* gone anyway.'

Annie tried to hide her irritation at Mally's rudeness. She needed her on side if she wanted off-the-record information on Terry Martin.

The colonel said mildly, 'Why not watch upstairs in your room? I'll be having a nap down here.'

'Oh Grandad, go on. It's a better telly down here.'

'I thought you were going to the shop to get a new film for the evening. It's such a nice day. You should be out getting some fresh air. Why not go down to the stables—?'

He caught himself not quite in time. Annie saw Mally's expression darken. The pony she'd had to sell. Nothing to go to the stables for. Was that the source of the coiled spring of rage inside her? But surprisingly no eruption came. Mally's glare lightened. 'Yeah, I will. Laura's grounded. I'll tell Tina she said I could take Boxer out. Good idea, Grandad.' She turned to Annie. 'I saw him the next weekend. He was OK. He wasn't always a creep.'

'Don't let Miss Hain catch you out in a lie, Mel.'

'Don't worry, Grandad. I'll ring Laura first.'

'Can you remember exactly when you saw him the following weekend, Mally?'

'Dunno. Sunday afternoon. I was going to meet Kay. He was just walking along.'

'Did you speak to him?'

'Mr and Mrs Tunbridge won't allow her to say yes, Mel.'

'Don't fuss, Grandad. I'll tell her not to tell them.'

'Did you speak to Terry, Mally?'

'Nah, not really.'

'What time did you see him?'

''Bout three o'clock. I told you, I was on my way to Kay's.'

'Be back in time for tea. Mrs Kitson's coming round to cook for us.'

Mally made a face. 'I hate her cooking. I'll get Tina to do me something. See you later.'

'Mel, what about your…? Oh dear, youngsters of today.' He gave Annie a resigned shake of his head as Mally disappeared in the middle of his speech. 'Maybe I'd better ring Doris. Wouldn't want her cooking for nothing. On the other hand, if I know young Mel she'll likely be back ravenous before six.'

Annie saw the lines of worry deepen across his forehead. He should never have been left in sole charge of a young adolescent, let alone one as headstrong as Mally. She felt she should leave him to have some peace while he could, but she'd barely touched on her real reason for being here.

'Could you tell me about the night Terry Martin died? I'd like to know as much about it as I can.'

'For the parents, you mean? Yes, I can understand that. I'll tell you what. You have a vehicle, don't you? We'll call round to Charles Tremlow's. You'll want to talk to him as well. Never saw action in his youth, you see. Couldn't take it. Hard to think of a man making his three score years and ten and never seen a dead body, but there it is. A bit of company'll do him a power of good.'

Annie was taken aback. Of course, she wanted to interview Tremlow, but to her own timetable, not someone else's. 'Yes, I do want to talk to him, but I wouldn't want to make things worse by dropping in unannounced. He might not be ready to talk about it.'

The colonel gave her a gentle laugh. 'I see you're old-fashioned like me, Miss Raymond, but that's not the modern way. The modern way is to talk about it, bring it all out into the open. The police offered counselling, you know. Can you believe it? Streets overrun with thieves and layabouts and they offer counselling. But no, I'll take advantage of your transport if I may, and do an old friend a favour. He needs the company. He hasn't been himself since it happened.'

As Annie watched him heave himself from the chair, she ran Mally's words through her head. Both Heather Becke and Mally had seen Terry Martin the Sunday before he died. By the looks of it, he'd come from lunch with his parents straight to Milesthorpe. He'd called on Balham. Had Balham already gone walkabout, or did he and Terry talk that afternoon?

CHAPTER 10

ANNIE KNEW FROM the map that Charles Tremlow's house lay close to Colonel Ludgrove's but he directed her round yet another loop to the bridge over the stream that bisected Milesthorpe. It was hard not to become disorientated and also absurd to think the colonel had made this journey under his own steam late at night.

'I thought it was nearer than this, Colonel.'

'No distance at all as the crow flies. Have to go right round by road, of course.'

Annie thought of the protracted journey out to the cliff the night before. 'Whoever designed Milesthorpe's roads wasn't someone in a hurry,' she commented.

'Milesthorpe was two villages years ago. No direct routes at all from one side to the other, not until they bridged the stream. Look at the older houses, you'll see they face the wrong way. Built to face the village main street, of course, but once they bridged the river, the main street became the back lane. Better in the old days. Smaller village. Good families.'

'How did you get to Mr Tremlow's that night?'

'Track from the bottom of the garden and across the field.'

'That can't have been easy in the dark.'

'Wouldn't normally go that way, of course, but the chap was clearly desperate. One does what one must in times of crisis.'

'And you'd both been out?'

'Yes, parish meeting. First Tuesday of the month. Ted Balham never turned up, but that wasn't unusual. I wasn't in the house five minutes before the telephone went. Tremlow in a blue funk. Told him to ring the emergency services; said I was on my way.'

Tremlow's house stood at the bottom of a crescent of similar houses, bathed in hot sunlight, the shadows short, reflective surfaces glinting as though a giant hand had sprinkled glitter round the street. The gardens were neat for the most part with a couple of makeshift wooden fences spoiling the overall effect. Tremlow's wore an air of genteel neglect, faded paintwork and dingy net curtains. Annie walked slowly up the path matching her pace to the colonel's. He ignored the front door and headed round the side of the house. Annie looked out down the back garden to see if the track across the fields were visible, but the vegetation was too thick and high.

At the sound of locks being drawn back she turned to the house to see a door swing open. Tremlow looked smaller than she remembered from Terry Martin's funeral, slightly bent, dark hair thinning unevenly. The skin round his face and neck hung loosely in folds, his expression haggard. Annie saw sleep deficit in eyes that looked as black as though he'd been punched.

With a fussy and nervy manner he invited them in to sit at a small Formica kitchen table.

'Charles, this is Miss Raymond. She's a private detective, looking into the death of that reporter chappie.'

'Oh dear.' Tremlow pulled at his earlobe. 'Do they think it's murder then?'

'No, no. Pull yourself together, old chap. Miss Raymond wants to know how it happened that's all. I thought we'd go through it together for her.'

'But we've done all that for the police. Why do we have to keep going over it?'

'I'll tell you what, Charles. You've not had a proper cup of tea, have you? Shall we let Miss Raymond make us a fresh pot?'

Annie looked round to locate kettle and cups. She'd had office placements where she'd made fewer hot drinks for people, but if it would get the information she needed she was happy to chuck a few tea bags about.

Tremlow glanced at her sideways. 'It's all in a bit of a state. The woman who does for me is away.'

'Miss Raymond isn't interested in domestic details, Charles.'

Yes, thought Annie, as she retrieved three cups from the heap of dirty dishes in the sink and rinsed them under the tap, she'd rather have interrogated Tremlow on her own. The colonel was used to the direct approach.

You wanted something, you barked out the order and expected to get it. But Tremlow was the sort to whom you gave free rein; let him talk about what he wanted, steer gently but don't badger for detail as the colonel did now.

'The night of the last parish meeting, Charles. You remember? You talked to me on the telephone.'

'Of course I remember. I'll never forget.'

'Tell Miss Raymond about hearing a noise outside.'

Annie lined up the cups as she listened. Tremlow had his back to her. At least he would talk in front of his old buddy. On her own, she might not have made it over the threshold. She picked up a metal tin labelled 'Tea'.

'People have been on at me for a long time about securing the kitchen door, but it's never been like that round here. What if something happened in the night? How would anyone get to me? I don't like to lock myself in.'

Annie thought back to the sounds of bolts sliding as he'd undone the door for them. She prised the lid off the tin and pulled a face. Loose tea, not bags. What on earth did you do with loose tea? She had a vague idea it needed a teapot and a complicated filter.

'I put my hearing aid in to see if I could tell where the noise had come from and there was this dreadful clatter. I said to Frank, you've got to come round, Frank. I've an intruder.'

'Did you see Terry Martin before he fell?' Annie eased the question in as she lifted a rotund china teapot from the side of the sink.

'No.'

The bald negative nonplussed her. Inside the pot lay the cold but fierce remains of the last brew. She tipped them down the sink and watched the patterns. She couldn't see the future in them but at least they told her the leaves went directly in the pot.

Tremlow's account went in loops like the roads round the village. He backtracked, changed his mind about what had happened when, and over everything he sprinkled comments about the woman who did for him.

'If she hadn't been away ... can't manage on my own ... what'll happen if she won't come back...?'

The colonel badgered Tremlow to keep him on the right track and Annie didn't know how to stop him.

'Never mind about that, Charles. Stick to the facts of the evening ... You're overwrought, that's all ... perfectly able to look after yourself ...'

'Where did it happen?' Annie asked.

'I'll show you.' Tremlow surprised them both by getting suddenly to his feet. 'Come on.'

'Now, Charles, is this necessary?'

The colonel put out a hand to stop his friend but Tremlow shook him off and marched to the door. 'D'you want to see or not?' He shot the question at Annie.

'Yes, thank you.'

Tremlow led them to the fence that separated his garden from his neighbour. 'There, look.' He pointed up at the next-door house where a metal skeleton of scaffolding clung up one corner. 'On that platform there. That's where he was standing. I saw him plain as day.'

Annie shot Tremlow a quick glance but said nothing.

'The scoundrel must have been trying to make his way round the edge to get in through the bedroom window,' the colonel said. 'That's what the policeman thought.'

'And that's where he died.' Tremlow shuddered.

Annie's gaze followed his pointing finger. A trench had been dug at the base of whatever was being done to the house. Jagged shards of concrete lay about. It was quite a distance to fall.

'Is it an extension they're having done?' she asked.

'That's right,' the colonel said, then turned to Tremlow. 'Charles, you need a nip of good malt and a few hours' sleep.'

'No, it's repairs. That house is in a terrible state.'

'Come on, Charles. I'll not take no.'

Tremlow sagged as he succumbed to the pressure of his friend's hand under his arm, and turned to the house. Annie glanced back at the scaffolding tower. 'Were they in that night, the people who live there?'

'No,' Tremlow snapped. 'I told you, she's away.'

'Don't over-excite yourself, Charles.'

'I don't believe in drink, but if it's medicinal … I haven't had a wink of sleep since that night.'

'And they're still away?' Annie's gaze ran over the scene of Terry Martin's death.

'Holiday. No one can contact them.' The colonel answered her. 'Come *on*, Charles. Don't over-excite yourself.'

Annie left the colonel fussing over his friend. He waved her off with the assurance he could call out a neighbour to give him a lift back. 'Don't you worry. Think I'd better stay on here a while.'

Annie felt troubled as she drove away. Tremlow was obviously traumatized by what he'd seen but even so his account was all over the place. He must have been a nightmare as a witness. She'd drop it into conversation with Scott tonight. Confusion she could understand, but that bald 'No' sat uneasily with the statement 'I saw him plain as day'.

Annie drove back to the centre of Milesthorpe, parked the car beside the Green and strolled through the heart of the village towards the post office and general store.

The shop window was busy with handwritten notices. Some had been there long enough that the sun had leached the words away and left only yellowing card. She paused to skim them. Items for sale from cars to puppies; services on offer … gardening … guttering … no job too small. She imagined a new notice in the middle with a photograph of Terry Martin: *Did you see this man in the week after Milesthorpe Show?*

It was no surprise to be greeted by name when she went inside. She chose a steak pasty and an apple and asked that the former be heated. While it revolved in the microwave behind the counter she chatted about Terry Martin. Of the half dozen people in the shop, they hadn't all met him, but were all eager to add their morsel to her store of knowledge.

When she asked if anyone had seen him in the week following Milesthorpe Show, several voices piped up. Annie probed for detail – where and when? What was he doing? Who was he with? Disappointingly, no one could better the 'threeish on Sunday' she'd had from Heather Becke and Mally Fletcher. From then until Tuesday evening remained a void.

Mentally she filed the information as she strolled back towards the Green.

At some stage, she must approach Doris Kitson, the third of the trio, but what could the woman tell her that she hadn't already had, however confused, from Colonel Ludgrove and Charles Tremlow? The order was important and at the moment her gut told her that Doris Kitson would be more useful in confirming the tales she heard from others, than as a source of fresh leads. Already, she'd unearthed a new angle on Terry Martin. It sat uncomfortably close to his dealings with the three girls but she didn't have to use everything she found.

She drove down the hill to the livery yard where fields and stable blocks spread out in front of her. In contrast to her reception elsewhere in the village, Annie's arrival generated no interest. She climbed out of the car into a dusty yard filled with vehicles, diesel fumes and the clatter of hoofs. She crossed to the edge of the field to investigate a strand of glitter that twinkled at her just the other side of the fence. This close she could see it was exactly what it looked like, a long strand of gold and silver Christmas decoration. Thick, heavy-duty stuff that might have been designed to dress a town centre. She reached forward to touch it, but just in time spotted the thin line of wire that tracked its path. Electric fencing disguised behind tinsel. Nothing was quite what it seemed around here.

She walked back towards the stable blocks, assuming they'd be the hub of activity, but found no real focus, just clusters of people all busy with ponies or the weird-shaped leather-bound accoutrements of the horsy world.

'Hi, Annie!'

Annie spun round at the familiar voice. Mally sat astride a small brown pony. 'Hi, Mally. Is that ... uh ... Boxer?'

'Yup. Rubbish, isn't he? But he's all right just to ride out now and then. I won't bother with him when I get my new horse. Grandad's going to suss me out a proper horse. Better than Steele even.'

Annie smiled her acknowledgement of Mally's good fortune in the new horse.

'That was Steele's.' Mally pointed to one of the stables 'He had to have the end one when he was down here 'cos he was highly strung.'

Annie, who had understood 'better than steel' to mean hard as nails realized Mally spoke of the pony that had had to be sold. If money were as tight as it seemed, she didn't fancy Mally's chances of a fine new horse. She doubted even her doting grandfather could deliver.

Before Annie could respond, a voice bellowed, 'Mally, didn't I tell you…?'

'Yes, Tina,' Mally shouted, as she spun the pony through 180 degrees and clattered off round the side of the building.

Annie looked to identify the owner of the megaphone voice and found herself facing a small, slim woman with short-cropped hair, skin-tight black jodhpurs and a T-shirt several sizes too large.

In answer to Annie's query, she said, 'Yup, glad to tell you what I can. But give me five minutes. I need to finish up.'

While she waited, Annie fell into desultory conversation with a few of the other hangers-on, mostly parents with no useful role to play as their offspring tidied away their equine charges. The people she spoke to were aware of 'an accident on a building site in the village' but none had known Terry Martin. She learnt that the field's deadly decorations were part of the ethos of the yard. Any pony stabled here must learn to be as fearful of tinsel as of lions.

'She hides the wire behind the stuff and trains them with the electric fence at full so they get a hell of a jolt.'

'Can't they just learn not to touch the wire?' Annie wondered.

'That's what they do in most yards, but Tina Hain's a bit … well … odd. She says she's not having the expense and hassle of batteries and wires in the outlying fields. She has a point, but it can cause havoc in the fancy dress if some outsider turns up dressed as a Christmas tree.'

Annie laughed as the woman moved off to collect her child.

By the time she followed Tina into the bungalow that nestled behind the stable blocks, Annie knew this would be her last interview in Milesthorpe for the day. Had she known what five minutes meant in Tina Hain's vocabulary she could have nipped back to the village for a chat with Doris Kitson. Too late for that now. She must be back in time to update Pat on all that had happened, and to explain Scott's presence before he turned up.

'Terry Martin,' Tina said, as they sat down. 'Odd little guy. I used to like him, but he got a bit creepy those last few weeks.'

'Had you known him long?'

'Oh yes. Terry did the shows for years. Did some good photos. He used to take videos and get stills off them.'

'Mally's grandfather said you'd had a word with him about Terry.'

'He remembers, does he? It was like talking to a wall. He has a real blind spot where that child's concerned. "Mally can look after herself … Mally can do no wrong." He's right of course, she's a tough nut, but Terry was what ... nearly forty? Mally's a kid. I didn't like the way he was hanging about her like he was pestering her for something.'

'Anything specific?'

'Uh ... Not that Mally would come clean about it and, of course, Terry denied it. He spun the old man a line about doing a big feature on Mally. He always could talk a big story.'

'Mally seems very angry. More so than the average girl her age. Is it to do with losing her pony? I gather it had to be sold.'

'It was the divorce settlement. It was all pretty rocky. Her mother barely managed to hold on to the house. Mally's father went to Withernsea with his new piece. Not that Mally'll hear a word against him. She was always a daddy's girl.'

'And a grandaddy's girl.'

Tina laughed. 'Yeah, too right. She has him round her little finger. Mind you, it's no wonder she's grown up like she has. It's been daggers drawn in that family for years. The old man never got on with Mally's father, always sided with his own daughter against her husband. The marriage never stood a chance. It's a wonder they lasted as long as they did.'

'I spoke to Heather Becke earlier. She told me you'd barred Terry from your land.'

Tina nodded. 'It was that business with Mally. Probably there was nothing in it. I don't know. But when I found out—'

'Found out what?'

'Look, like I said, maybe there was nothing in it, but they wouldn't say what it was about. Terry had been giving her money.'

'Mally?'

'Possibly Kay and Laura, too. I didn't like it. And when they wouldn't come clean, that was it. I wasn't risking the reputation of the stables with any funny business.'

Annie decided to end this line of questioning. Whatever was or wasn't going on Tina didn't know for sure and Annie didn't want to hear any theories. She switched to another track. 'Heather Becke was amazed when I told her Terry had filmed the horse show.'

'You mean the Showcross? He certainly didn't. You've got that wrong.'

Annie rummaged through her bag and flicked through the edited DVDs. She pulled out the one labelled *Milesthorpe Show (ponies)* and threw a glance at the TV in the corner. 'I'm afraid he did. Do you want to see?'

Tina looked taken aback, but reached for the disk and slotted it into the player. The film started abruptly into the crowds and noise of Milesthorpe Green, then cut to a young girl propping a number against a low fence.

Tina's expression darkened. 'Yes, that's the Showcross course. He's come in through the bottom gate. Look, you can see he isn't concentrating. The camera's all over the place.'

They watched the disjointed shots unfold until they reached the sequence that had amused Annie first time round, before she knew what a punch the film's finale held. Two ponies thundered towards a small obstacle and suddenly swerved out. The camera lurched as Terry Martin backed away hurriedly. Flying hoofs … mud … and then Terry tripped. Annie hadn't noticed until she'd made the edited version, but he'd backed into someone. The shot gave the briefest glimpse of a pair of legs half-tangled in his before it cut.

The film stopped.

Annie looked up in surprise. She watched Tina click a button and take the film through a jerky backward sequence. Click. Again the two ponies thundered at the obstacle. Again Terry Martin leapt back out of their way. Again he tripped. Click. Stop. Rewind.

This time through, a familiarity about the faces all but hidden under helmets and straps caught Annie's attention. She knew those riders. Kay rode the pony nearest Terry Martin, and it was Laura on the other small brown one – surely Boxer – who swerved out pushing Kay into the camera.

Tina stopped the film. Annie looked at her; read her expression. She remembered the subsequent sequence of winners and amongst them Laura Tunbridge on her small brown pony accepting a red rosette and a cup. She watched Tina closely as she asked, 'That was Mally Fletcher he tripped over, wasn't it?'

Tina nodded. 'The conniving little bastards!'

Annie let out a sigh. She'd have to bone up on the ins and outs of the rules of Showcross to know exactly what had happened but, as realization dawned, she felt a weight lift. A different reason for Terry Martin's odd hold over the three girls came on to her radar.

They'd cheated to win that cup, and he had them on film.

CHAPTER 11

'CONNIVING LITTLE BEGGARS.' Scott used similar words to Tina Hain but his tone was amused.

They sat facing each other at a wooden table outside a pub on the waterfront. The evening air was warm and still, barely a breeze from the river, just the gentle slosh of the water on to the dock wall down below. The pub nestled in a backstreet, unsuspected behind an approach of bland warehouses leading to a small irregular parade of cobbled streets, walls and railings overlooking the tamed areas of the estuary.

Scott looked different out of uniform; more solid and slightly incongruous, as though the T-shirt and jeans hadn't had an outing in years.

Conversation proved difficult, the journey into town a series of awkward remarks interspersed by long silences. Annie found his smile every bit as engaging as she'd expected and was embarrassed to meet his eye in case the flutter it produced inside her should show. They both fell back on work as an easy way to keep the words flowing.

'Tina Hain said that,' she told him. 'But it doesn't help me. I'm sorry I raked it up really. I can't say I've warmed to the three girls, especially not Mally, but they're only kids. Now I suppose they'll be in all sorts of trouble.'

'What exactly did they do? Do you know?'

'Oh yes.' Annie smiled. Tina Hain, boiling with indignation, had given her more detail than she wanted or needed. She explained to Scott about the local rivalry that demanded members of this trio were honour-bound to lift the coveted Pairs Trophy at Milesthorpe Show. 'Mally and Kay won it last year, but Mally doesn't have a pony now.' Annie explained how Boxer, Laura's pony, always refused to jump the obstacle down in the dip where Terry Martin had been filming. 'So Mally volunteered to be the person to sit down by that fence and mark the contestants as they went by. She won brownie points for that because it's not a popular job, sitting down in the dip away from the rest of the action.'

Scott shook his head. 'These things can be massively important when you're only thirteen.'

'I knew I'd uncovered something, but it says nothing about Terry's missing two days. I hoped I might get something useful from Charles Tremlow. Some idea why Terry went to the house next door maybe, but he's impossible. You must have found him a nightmare as a witness.'

Scott nodded. 'The poor old beggar was in shock, probably still is. They won't accept help, that sort.'

'So did you get a straight story of what happened that night?'

'Yes, between the three of them.'

'So, do you know why he went round there?' It was a key question in her search for Terry's lost hours, but Scott shook his head.

'No idea. Chances are he knew the house would be empty, so I doubt he went there for any legitimate reason.'

'So what happened exactly?'

'Tremlow heard him, probably the sound of him climbing the scaffolding and he called Ludgrove. Ludgrove told him to call us and he made his way round there. From what Tremlow said, Terry Martin must have fallen just before Ludgrove arrived and they both went and found him in the hole.'

'So no one saw him fall. Did Tremlow see him up on the scaffolding?'

When Scott said he hadn't, Annie told him what Tremlow had said; the bald 'no' to the direct question, then 'I saw him plain as day', as he'd pointed up at the wooden platform.

'By the time we arrived, they'd talked about it, figured out what had happened. The poor old sod's probably seen Terry Martin in his dreams every day since. But he didn't venture out until Ludgrove arrived. He locked himself in his house.'

'And Doris Kitson? When did she get there?'

'After they'd found the body. She was a bit of a godsend with the tea and sympathy bit. If it's detail you're after, she's your woman.' He laughed. 'If Martin was in Milesthorpe on the Monday, she'll know all about it.'

'What did she go to Tremlow's for?'

'Parish Council business. She'll give you chapter and verse on that too if you give her half a chance. She's the one to iron out your anomalies for you. She probably knows far more than Ludgrove about what his granddaughter gets up to.'

She'd told him about the joy-riders at the funeral; about her theories on Mally. He agreed that the rich, cosseted youth of Milesthorpe would love the spark of danger embodied in clandestine relations with joy-riders from Hull.

'One of them dropped a name that night they found the body: Maz. Could that be the guy in the car?'

Scott shrugged. 'It doesn't ring any bells. Let me know if you get anything more.'

Annie's thoughts returned to the colonel's house. 'Mally Fletcher's an ill-mannered little cow, but she's not all bad. Apparently she spent hours coaching her two friends to win the cup she'd earmarked for herself before she lost her pony.'

'Who says she was coaching them?'

'Oh, she did. I saw the mess they'd made of Colonel Ludgrove's lawn.' Annie called to mind the churned stretch of grass, the concrete blocks and wooden poles. How had the colonel felt to see his garden torn apart by Mally and her friends?

'They've a paddock at the back. Why didn't they use that?'

Annie shrugged. 'Colonel Ludgrove should never have been left in charge of her anyway. Hasn't anyone been in touch with her mother?'

'She's gone away for a couple of weeks. No one knows where. No contact number. Didn't even take a mobile with her.'

Dumped on her grandfather by her mother. Deserted by her father. It was no wonder the well of rage within Mally was so deep. Then a new meaning to Scott's words hit her. Her insides did a back flip. 'Scott, don't tell me it was Mally's mother in that building.'

'No, no.' He shook his head vigorously. 'It isn't her. Look Annie, I can't say anything until we have a positive ID, but we're pretty sure we know who it is, and it isn't her.'

Annie chastised herself for jumping to conclusions. It was the height of the holiday season. The woman who looked after Tremlow was away too. Maybe it had been her remains in that shed.

'Did you get anything off Terry Martin's other films?' she asked, suddenly curious.

'Not a bean. Nor the notebooks. An amateurish commentary on his boring life. Pretty sad really.'

'Nothing in the torn page then?'

'They all had torn pages. Most of them had been ripped to shreds.'

Annie opened her mouth on, *but not torn in half like that last one*, then shut it again, in case it sounded like manufactured drama.

Scott stared into his glass where the dregs of his beer sparkled in the evening sun, then glanced at Annie's, already empty. 'D'you fancy a walk along the waterfront? There's a pub down there where we can get something to eat.'

They strolled together, listening to squabbling seagulls shriek and swoop at the oily water. High buildings laid strips of deep shadow in their path. The heat of the day waned and the air felt cold out of the direct line of the sun. Bands of silver and gold flashed from the gently rippling surface of the water creating momentary blindness so that when Scott took her hand and Annie looked up into his face she couldn't read his expression. Real human contact felt good. She let herself enjoy the warmth of it. No point speculating on future complications when she was only here for six weeks. As they meandered through the streets, he asked about her life in London, and how she'd landed in Hull.

'I'd been looking for ages for a proper job, one that'd give me real fieldwork. It's a shame it's only a six-week placement.'

'D'you think you'll stay on longer?'

'I don't know if they'll want me. Once Pat's up and about, I doubt there'll be the work.'

'There are other employers.'

Out of nowhere a memory popped up. The three girls at Balham's gate. Kay snapping at Laura, 'If you'd let Mally take Boxer—' ... *we could have won without cheating*. Was that where the sentence headed?

'Uh-huh.' Scott gave an indeterminate grunt when she told him. Maybe he was as irritated as she'd been with Colonel Ludgrove when every conversational avenue led to Mally.

When Scott paused to look at her, one hand on the door of the pub, she expected a comment on the type of food served inside, but, after a moment, he said, 'Of course, none of it explains why *he* paid money to *them*.'

Annie braced herself for Pat's reaction as she entered the flat soon after ten. It didn't fail her.

'You're early. Not brought lover boy back? How was the hot date?'

She wouldn't rise to the bait and just called 'Coffee?' over her shoulder as she headed for the kitchen.

The first thing she saw as she brought in the cups was her Terry Martin folder on the settee beside Pat, its contents spilt on to the cushions. The TV was off. Pat sat upright, alert, even her bulk seemed smaller. Annie remembered the hospital appointment and now she'd set her mind to notice, saw that the plaster cast was different – cleaner, new. She felt a sudden compunction that much of Pat's grumpiness had been down to pain.

'How did it go at the hospital?'

'Yeah, fine. Good.' Pat was briefly surprised then turned the subject. 'Have you got enough here?' She tapped the Martin folder with her finger.

'No, not yet. I've barely chipped into those missing couple of days, but I know he went to Milesthorpe on the Sunday afternoon. I'm going to see Doris Kitson tomorrow. I meant to get to her today, but it didn't pan out.'

'Don't forget, this is an exercise in doing the best for the person we're working for. It's not an investigation into his death. It's about closure for the Martins. That means finding out where he was those last two days and putting the best gloss we can on it. Did the police find anything?'

Annie shook her head. It was clear from what Scott told her that they hadn't tried too hard. 'He vanished for two days and then he died. Because it was an accident, that's it really unless Health and Safety go after the builder.'

'You might find something in here. I got the post-mortem report.' Pat indicated a sheaf of fax paper at her side. 'He'd been drinking heavily. Way over the limit when he died. Now when you go out there tomorrow to do the Kitson woman, I want you to go back to the one you saw today.'

'Colonel Ludgrove?'

'No, the nervy one. Tremlow. See him on your own. He knows more than he's saying.'

Annie remembered Tremlow's jumpy and inconsistent account. Pat was right. Of course Tremlow knew more than he'd let on to her and the colonel. Could she get it out of him on her own? She recalled the gossip in the village shop. 'The locals are still talking about "the murder of that reporter".'

'Who do they think did it? Tremlow?'

'Hell, no. He could barely climb off his own back step, let alone up a scaffolding tower.'

Scaffolding tower? The words shot her gaze up and she read from the look in Pat's eyes that the same thought had struck them both. Pat looked down again at the papers in her hand. Annie thought of the high platform … of Tremlow's words. *I saw him plain as day.*

The flimsy paper rustled as Pat held it out towards her. Her eye skimmed the words and figures. It was Pat who put words to what was in both their minds. 'It's one hell of a climb for someone that drunk.'

CHAPTER 12

ALL THE WORRIES she'd accumulated rushed to the forefront of Annie's mind. Terry Martin had been a blackmailer. Heather Becke didn't deny being pleased he'd died. What was Terry's agenda with those three young girls? What happened during his visit to Balham's farm the afternoon he disappeared?

Before she could voice her unease, the doorbell shrilled, making them both jump.

'Oh hell, that's my taxi.' Annie leapt to her feet and looked round for her things. She'd forgotten the time.

'Keep your wits about you on Orchard Park at this time of night.' Pat paused, then added, 'And be more careful out in Milesthorpe from now on.'

Half an hour later, Annie stood in the bedroom on the sixth floor of the tower block trying to shut her mind to her disquiet on the Martin case. She looked out over the estate as it slept uneasily, its rest punctuated by occasional booms of loud music from passing cars and the background drone of sirens. She pressed herself to the glass of the window as much to avoid the smell of neglect in the room as to see out. A commentary ran on behind her.

'It's only bloody Thursday ... They're only here Friday and Tuesday ... How many bloody times...? Christ! I wish I'd never started this. You planning on being there all bloody night?'

Mrs Earle lay back on the bed, her face pallid, eyes puffy as though she'd cried, or been drinking solidly since Annie was last there. The air was warm, the room draped in a sheet of stale dilapidation. Sickly sweet perfumes fought for the upper hand with the odour of unwashed clothes.

Annie glanced across at her. The woman was a wreck. No best outcome whatever Annie delivered. She might clean the place out and get rid of the dealers, but would that deliver the precious niece and nephew or just leave a set of parents looking for a new excuse to keep their children away from their helpless lush of an aunt? She looked curiously at the woman on the bed.

'Why did you let it get this far? You could have called the police right at the start of it.'

'What, and have everyone on at me? No one wants the law sniffing round.'

'So what made you come to us?'

'It was her I wanted, not you. That Pat Thompson. When I saw her advert I thought she'd be able to do something if anyone can. And you said you could.'

'And I will.' Annie injected reassurance into her tone as she heard belligerence rise in Mrs Earle's.

'Huh! Yeah ... well ...'

There was some sense behind the woman's words. What she implied fitted with what Pat had told Annie. A link between the dealers and someone at the agency, so when Mrs Earle saw Pat apparently working as a freelance she'd had hopes Pat would have the contacts to get the guys stopped.

The grumbles behind her subsided to the back of Annie's consciousness as her attention focused on the world outside. Half past two in the morning. Her mouth curved to a smile as the familiar shape of the white van appeared and headed for the car-park.

She strained to see from the awkward angle as the van stopped and the doors opened. The shapes of the two regulars had become familiar to her. Another form climbed out too. So they'd brought number three with them, the guy from last night whose face she thought she knew. Did they come here every night? If so, could she surmise from what she'd seen that on Tuesdays and Fridays the two of them came alone? It was an interesting theory, especially if number three didn't know of the dealing.

She couldn't hide away forever trying to outguess them. It was time to get close.

The back doors of the van had been flung wide. One of them leant right in while the others stood and watched. For all their precision timing, they weren't in a hurry. If she sprinted, she might get down to the lobby before they came in. The only cover would be to crouch near the bottom of the staircase. Too far from any bolthole if they were to spot her, but why would they look? A rush of apprehension skittered across her skin making the hairs stand on end. Before she could change her mind, she skipped off out of the bedroom ignoring a muttered comment from the woman on the bed.

Beyond the security of the flat's locked door, broken lighting created dark caverns in the corners of the landing but Annie had no sense of anyone waiting there tonight. She ran down the stairs, taking them two and three at a time, swinging herself round the corners. Her insides scrunched in disgust as her hand slid through something sticky. Final flight and she slowed. No sound from below. She'd expected to hear voices, but it looked as though she hadn't been quick enough.

She went down to where she could see the lifts. One waited at ground floor level, the other rose from three to four as she watched. Missed them.

The lobby was deserted right now, but the building never really slept. It wouldn't be unusual for someone else to be here at this time, to get into the lift with the three men. Had they really gone to the top floor the other night? She moved forward towards the empty security booth and outer door. If they were still outside rummaging about in the van, she would withdraw to the stairs and—

She froze. The door clicked. Voices came at her. Cheerful, laughing banter. Too late to reach the safety of the concrete stairs. No dark corners in reach. Nowhere to hide.

She spun on her heel and leapt back towards the blank lift doors. As she did so, her hands went to her head to scrub her fingers through her hair to mess it up, to pull it forward so it straggled in her face. The backs of her hands rubbed hard at her eyes. A sour reek reminded her she'd put her hand in something on the stair rail and it was now tangled in her hair. She balked at the stench as she hung her head forward and leant against the wall.

The chatter stopped abruptly. They'd seen her. Annie concentrated on keeping an even rhythm to her breathing and gave no sign she'd registered their presence. Thank heavens for battered trainers and shabby T-shirt and jeans. With luck, her work clothes, straggly hair and unfocused red eyes marked her out as human jetsam from the sixth floor.

She saw a fat, well-manicured finger stab out at the lift call button.

A moment of silence before the machinery wheezed into life. She imagined the three men looking her up and down. Then one of them spoke, a random comment clearly continuing the exchange they'd broken off as they'd seen her, but the tone was not so free as before. She remained immobile and uninterested.

The lift door clanked open.

Fear prickled the surface of her skin. The pause was subtle, but she was clearly first in the queue. They waited for her to step inside. Head down, she shambled into the metal compartment. Any other course would focus their attention on her all the more; make them question what she'd been doing there.

She turned, head down, to reach for the control panel, but a forest of legs blocked her way. Through the prison bars of well-tailored cloth that flapped around feet clad in blindingly polished leather she saw the doors slide to. She felt her heart thud hard in her chest. The cloying aroma of aftershave blended with stale cigarette smoke and wrapped itself around her. Trapped in here she was close enough to feel the heat from their bodies.

'What floor do you want, love?' The voice that fired the question wasn't unfriendly, but had nothing of the light banter she'd heard before.

'Uh …' Annie flinched. Mustn't pick six or any other floor they didn't want her to go to. Couldn't get her head round what to say. Their suspicion rolled at her like a wave. On impulse she lurched forward and jabbed at the panel.

Her tangled hair with its vile payload pushed briefly between them. She was aware of the recoil, faces turned away. She felt relief.

As she slumped back into the corner, the relaxed chatter resumed. She tried to concentrate on it but there was nothing to bite on – a dissection of a recent rugby match and a mild debate over Big Brother. Annie raised her head a little and watched through half-closed eyes. She flicked her gaze towards the third man, the one with the bafflingly familiar air. Who did he remind her of? As her gaze focused, she felt her eyes open wide in surprise. It wasn't the same man at all. This wasn't the number three she'd seen last night. It was someone else altogether. Last night's had been a big man. This one was smaller and much older. But it wasn't that he was a stranger that shot astonishment through her. Like the man she'd seen last night, he, too, looked familiar.

She'd seen them both before, but where? She hadn't been in Hull long enough for stray faces to implant themselves on her subconscious. Could they have been in the crowd she'd pushed through that first visit? She felt she knew their faces better than from a passing glimpse in a crowd.

A lighter flicked. A moment later smoke spiralled in silver curves and she breathed in the sharpness of tobacco mixed with the sweet tang of cannabis.

When the lift lurched to a halt and the doors slid apart she couldn't be sure what floor they'd reached, but a voice said, 'There you go, love.' Hands steadied her from the back of the compartment and eased her out through the doors.

The surge of relief that coursed through her became triumph at the squeal of the doors sliding together behind her. She'd fooled them and she must only be one or two floors below the top. Straining to keep the whine of the lift mechanism at the edge of her hearing she leapt for the staircase.

The soft chatter of voices didn't register until too late. She swung round the corner and cannoned into something semi-solid, semi-soft. At once she was engulfed in a blaze of colour and overpowered by a cloud of talcum powder.

'Ow! What on earth...!'

A mountainous woman staggered back from her, eyes wide with shock. A man leapt forward. Annie raised her hands instinctively to ward off attack and saw fear light in his face. She'd run into a couple just leaving their flat. The woman was dressed in acres of voluminous flowered cotton that had grabbed Annie shroud-like and knocked her out of balance.

'I'm sorry. My fault ... wasn't looking ...' She gabbled out the words, waved her hand in a gesture of apology. The lift? Was that the sound of it stopping or was it just slowing?

'Do you realize ...' The man puffed himself out maybe to cover the fear he'd shown and set himself in front of Annie to harangue her.

It didn't matter. None of it mattered. 'I'm sorry,' she said again as she dodged round him and took the stairs in twos.

Comments followed her up the stairwell. 'Disgusting ... Leave her be ... might have a knife ...'

The lift? In an agony of suspense she fought to catch the sound of it. Had it stopped? Was she too late?

No! Another surge of triumph fought with the fire in her lungs as she leapt up the concrete stairs. It was just slowing now. She'd beaten them.

Above her was the top landing. She eased herself to the point where the glass wall from the staircase would show her the outline of their legs as they emerged. She would see which direction they took and then creep up and follow. The glass panes in their metal frames were a patchwork of old and new, yellowed and graffiti-sprayed. Perfect cover if she didn't move.

A sudden tapping startled her into absolute stillness. Someone stood waiting for the lift to arrive. The steel toecaps of his boots beat an impatient tattoo on the concrete floor. Was he waiting for three men to arrive, or was he an innocent bystander off on some late errand? Annie kept her stare fixed on the impatiently tapping foot, watched it stop as the lift clanked to a halt, saw it anticipate the opening door with a forward step.

She waited for the feet to step back again to let the lift's passengers out but they didn't. They went on in.

No one got out.

The doors began to close.

What? Annie started up as an irrational anger grasped her. They'd stayed in the lift. It was all a front. They travelled to the top floor and then down again to their real destination to fool anyone who stood at the bottom and watched the dial.

They wouldn't get away from her. Not when she was this close. She leapt up and round the corner and sprang at the closing lift doors. Too late. They slid shut.

Her chest heaved with the exertion. She looked at the blank metal wall and gasped in a deep breath, appalled at her own stupidity. The adrenalin rush of being so close and then losing them had almost cannoned her back into their midst. That would have blown her cover good and proper.

A sudden clunk. Before she could react, the doors in front of her slid apart again.

She stood face to face with a grizzle-haired man whose girth strained a battered blue boiler suit from under which a pair of steel-toecapped boots emerged. He was the lift's only occupant.

'There you go, love. Just spotted you. Hop aboard.'

Annie stammered out her thanks and stepped inside, staring into the corners as though she could possibly have failed to notice three large men had they been in there. Had they followed her out of the lift lower down? No. Impossible. And it hadn't stopped again until now. They had to be here, there was nowhere else they could be. It had to be the wrong lift. The contretemps with the couple on the lower landing had disorientated her. She should stay up here on the top floor. She should get out of the lift before it obeyed the man's command to take them right to the bottom of the tower.

But she didn't get out because she knew it wasn't the wrong lift. The sickliness of the men's aftershave held in the air. And all the way down Annie was conscious of the sweet tang of the joint they'd smoked on their way up.

CHAPTER 13

EARLY THE NEXT morning, Annie blinked her eyes open and lay motionless bathed in a clean white light. It seemed all but impossible to sleep beyond the early morning no matter how late she went to bed. Maybe it was the way the curtainless window, undersized and high on the wall, let in the dawn that flowed up the Humber with the morning tide.

Pat had been in bed when Annie returned in the small hours. She'd stood and listened to the snores from the master bedroom and considered waking her boss to tell her what happened.

They vanished into thin air … I was that close …

Drama queen….

Pat wouldn't say that. Pat would say … When she thought about it, Annie had known just what Pat would say.

You got in the lift with them! After all I've said to you. After what happened to me!

Her desperate need for sleep was overridden only by a greater need to wash the filth out of her hair, and she'd decided that whatever had happened would keep till morning. Of course they hadn't vanished. There was a perfectly logical explanation. There had to be.

And now she found her few hours' sleep had chased away last night's demons. She'd woken with a perfectly respectable theory about those three men and their so-called disappearance. Her subconscious could chew it over for a few more hours and then she'd test it out before she tried it on Pat later in the day.

Her early start had the low sun blazing bright in her face as she drove into Milesthorpe heading for the crescent where she parked outside Tremlow's house. Annie intended to get to him while yesterday's visit was fresh in his mind.

She pulled his garden gate shut behind her and walked down the path round to the back of the house where she paused to look at the tiny square of lawn fraying at the edges and the borders of weed-dappled soil. It was easy to picture Tremlow out here in his fussy way keeping order in his small plot, though he'd clearly let things slide over the last week or so. The lower half of the garden rambled wild, a path of sorts forced down one side. A footpath edged the bottom of these gardens so there would be access from down there, a shortcut from somewhere; it was the way the colonel had arrived that night.

She looked in through the kitchen window as she raised her hand to knock at the door. The sun's glare created a sharp dark-light divide in the small room. Tremlow sat at the table, hands cradling a mug, face immobile. He must have seen her but gave no sign, so she rapped her knuckles on the wood of the door.

No answer.

Gingerly she eased the door open and took a step inside. 'Mr Tremlow, may I come in?'

'I suppose you will, whatever I say.' He didn't look at her; his tone was surly.

'I'm sorry to disturb you again, Mr Tremlow, but I need a bit more information.'

'What? What do you want?'

'I'd like you to take me through the events of that evening just so I can get things straight in my head. There are a few details I'm not clear on.'

'Why should I? What right have you to ask me?'

Annie kept her voice even. 'Did you know Terry Martin, Mr Tremlow?'

'Know him? I'd seen him about. We'd all seen him hanging about asking questions.'

'What sort of questions did he ask you, Mr Tremlow?'

Tremlow swung round to throw her a furious expression. 'That's none of your business. You've no right asking me any questions. You're not the police.'

'No, but Terry Martin's mother is very upset. I just want to help her.'

'What's that to do with me?'

'I'm trying to find out what happened. She needs to know.'

'You know what happened. Everyone knows what happened. Why is everyone going over it all?'

Annie played a card she wasn't sure she held. 'Did Terry try to blackmail you?'

The reaction from Tremlow was the last thing she expected. He crumpled. Annie looked on aghast as he laid his head on his hands and sobbed. She felt terrible, as though she'd violated him, forced her way into his private space. It wasn't where she wanted to be. Through the sobs he gasped out something. She had to lean close to hear the words.

'It's all true,' he moaned. 'All of it. I didn't know what an evil man he was, but it's all true. Evil. He took money.'

Her hand reached out as though to touch him, to offer some morsel of comfort, but she felt any contact she made would be a red hot spear through him. The only thing she could comfort him with was her absence and she wouldn't go yet. She leant closer.

'What happened the night he died?'

'Who?' he sobbed. 'Who are you talking about?'

'Terry Martin. What was he doing here?'

'How should I know?'

'But why would he have come round? Had he come to see you?'

'No, no! He was next door. He wasn't in my house.'

'But why would he go next door?'

'Trying to break in, the police said.' He paused then looked up at her, his face gaunt and tortured but radiating a sly triumph as though he'd got one over on her. 'He was on that platform, you know. Just where I said.'

Annie knew she stood at the verge of Tremlow's secret but couldn't draw meaning from his words. His tear-streaked face was the mask on a wrecked man. His eyes lost focus as though his thoughts drifted off elsewhere.

'You saw Terry on the platform,' she prompted. 'And then…?'

He screeched at her, pushing his face close to hers so she felt a spray of spittle, smelt his fusty sour breath 'I didn't see him! You can tell his mother I didn't see him, all right? Satisfied? Are you satisfied? Now get out! Get out of my house!'

Annie recoiled disgusted as he collapsed again across the table, face hidden in his arms. She hadn't meant to push him to the edge like this. Yet he still hadn't told her anything that made any sense. Hating herself for it, she knew she could use the state he was in. If he would just calm down a little she'd attack again and he'd give her everything; what really happened that night; what he did and didn't see; what it was he'd hidden since that night.

There was only one way to calm him back to coherence. 'I'm leaving now, Mr Tremlow.'

She felt his relief as his trembling stilled. How long to leave him? Long enough for him to regain equilibrium. She'd return like a blackmailer who'd sworn to have taken the last ever payment. Then she'd sit down with him and demand to know exactly what it was he was hiding.

As she stepped backwards towards the door, she couldn't break her gaze from his immobile form. Would he be OK? Should she stay in the garden, try to keep an eye on him? No, the bolts would go on and she'd be lucky if he didn't call the police. But she couldn't leave him alone in this state. What if he did something stupid?

She returned to the car and pulled out her phone. What Tremlow needed was to hear the solidly rational tones of his old friend.

A clipped and reassuringly sane voice answered her call. 'Ludgrove here.'

'Colonel Ludgrove, it's Annie Raymond. I'm a bit worried about Mr Tremlow. I wondered if you could give him a call.' She told him about Tremlow's collapse, implying without speaking the lie, that she'd met Tremlow by chance and taken him home.

'Don't you worry,' said the colonel. 'The chap's highly strung, but a good sort on the whole. I'll call him on the telephone.'

Calm him, she wanted to say, just enough to be vulnerable to my questions.

As she ended the call, Annie checked the time. Tremlow could have ten minutes on the phone with his old mate, then she'd give him half an hour to settle down. That would allow her time to touch base with Doris Kitson. Today, she would use every second of her time in Milesthorpe and not allow herself to be sidetracked into delays and unfruitful dead ends like yesterday.

Doris Kitson's house offered a complete contrast to Tremlow's from the moment Annie saw it. In the middle of a small terrace, its front garden was a nightmare of ordered clutter, rockeries and mounds. Every inch of metal railing and wooden frame sported bright fresh paint in blues and greens. If the colour scheme were an attempt to blend in with the greenery and big skies, it was a comprehensive failure. Scrubbed paving gleamed between narrow borders where the geometric lines of the flower displays made Annie think of a municipal park in miniature.

As she climbed out of the car her gaze was caught by the jacket that lay on the passenger seat, an invitation to someone to smash a window to grab it. She tossed it into the boot before locking the car and making her way into Doris Kitson's front garden.

The door swung open as Annie picked her way up the narrow path. A big woman with an iron-hard grey perm stood framed in the doorway, gave a roguish smile and raised her hand to stop the speech that Annie hadn't begun to make.

'No need. No need. I know who you are. Annie Raymond, the detective. And I'm Doris Kitson of course. I've the kettle on. Now is it Ann or Annette or is it just Annie? ... Just Annie? How unusual. Do come in.'

'Thank you, Mrs Kitson, I—'

'Doris. Call me Doris. I expected you yesterday. Plain or milk?'

'Milk, thank you.' Annie sniffed appreciatively at the smell of baking that greeted her as she stepped across the threshold into the big kitchen. It looked from the cooling racks of plain and milk chocolate biscuits as if Doris expected a school trip. At one end of the wooden table, ordered ranks of uncoated biscuits waited in line to be dipped. At the other end they sat chocolate-coated and inviting.

Doris steered her to a seat and pushed across a plate of deliciously crumbly wheat rounds half obscured in not-quite-set chocolate. The kitchen mirrored the garden. Not a spare centimetre of space but everything neat and shining, a kitchen where anyone could safely eat their dinner off the floor. Germs, Annie was sure, were trained to line themselves up for execution with the battery of mops and cloths that stood ready for action in the recess under the stairs.

Doris busied herself near the sink. She poured boiling water into a teapot and placed two cups and saucers on to a tray which she carried to the table.

'Help yourself.' She waved a hand at the plate in front of Annie as she poured tea. 'Don't take sugar, do you? No, that's good. Pure poison, you know. I only ever use it in baking. These are for the carnival. You'll want to know all about young Terry I expect.'

'Uh … yes, if you don't mind. These are delicious. I talked to Mr Tremlow but he seemed very confused over what happened.'

'Yes, Charles was always highly strung. His mother sent him away to school, you know. I always think that's a mistake, don't you? And then when his wife went off like she did … I know it's nothing to people of your age, look at Frank's daughter. Mind you, that man she married … Have you come here from Charles's house just now?'

'Uh … yes.'

'And did you see a car pass you?'

'Well …' Annie thought back. The road had been quite busy. 'Yes, several.'

'A small blue saloon?'

'No, not that I remember.'

Doris tutted and shook her head. 'You should learn to observe everything around you, you know, if you want to pass muster as a detective. You've met young Mally I know, and now you've missed the chance to have a good look at her father. Now I know he doesn't live round here anymore but—'

'Um … I understand you were round at Mr Tremlow's house the night he found Terry's body?' Annie tried to haul the conversation back on track.

'Oh yes. I wanted to speak to them both. I saw Charles's car go by so I knew they were back and I wanted to know what was happening about the church gates. You'll have seen the state of them. Hanging by a thread. No? They're the ones you pass when you head for the Green if you come down from the top road by—'

'I know where you mean now,' Annie lied, as waves of detail threatened to overwhelm the rest of the morning. She would have to work hard to get what she wanted but at least there was no problem with getting Doris to talk. 'So you went round to Mr Tremlow's?'

'Well, I wanted to know. These church gates have been hanging on for long enough …'

Annie wanted to say, I thought they were hanging off. The thought made her smile.

'I'd been down to the cemetery. Just to tidy up for Elizabeth. Elizabeth Atkins, you know. She has no one, you see, and you wouldn't expect men to know what's what. I'm surprised you people weren't here then. I went to the police at the time, you know. I told them, she was right as rain only a day ago. And found dead, just like that. Her heart they said. Well, I know she had a heart condition, but that doesn't mean to say it was natural she just dropped down dead like that.'

Annie's head spun. She was torn between dragging Doris back to the night Terry Martin died and finding out more about this previously unsuspected death. Terry Martin, the woman on the cliff top and now someone called Elizabeth Atkins. She remembered Mally's comment about dead bodies everywhere. She stemmed the flow with a raised hand. 'Sorry, could you just clarify who Elizabeth Atkins is ... uh ... was?'

It's all good practice, she told herself, squeezing data out of difficult witnesses.

Annie allowed Doris to go uninterrupted through her last meeting with the mystery Elizabeth Atkins. A misgiving underlay everything that Doris said, her whole tale coloured by an unspoken suspicion of foul play. Was there anything to it? Annie might have discounted it as the imaginings of an old gossip entirely irrelevant to the case at hand, except that Terry Martin's name crept in. She'd heard no hint of anything like this before.

'Did you say that Terry Martin had been asking questions?'

'Oh yes, he asked me straight out if I was on the Parish Council—'

'I meant about Elizabeth Atkins.'

'Yes, of course, that's what I meant. Well, I mean he didn't ask outright. He couldn't, could he? He never knew Elizabeth.'

'But he wanted to know how she died?'

Doris looked puzzled. 'Not that I know of. Why would he?'

Annie paused to take a sip of her tea. Reliable as a witness, Scott had said of Doris Kitson, if you could fight through the smokescreen.

'Can I just get this straight? How long ago did Elizabeth Atkins die?'

'Just over three years. It'll be almost—'

'And cause of death was...?'

'Heart failure they said. Found dead in her bed. I didn't like it. I told the policeman at the time—'

'And she was a friend of yours?'

'More a friend of my mother's, but of course—'

'Your mother's? Uh ... how old was she when she died?'

'Let me see. She'd had her ninety-seventh birthday in the April. And she had a lovely cake. It was ...'

Annie struggled not to raise her eyes to heaven. Suspicious death from heart failure at ninety-seven. It'd make a good story for Scott, but time was getting on. She mustn't leave Tremlow too long.

She sat up straight and cleared her throat. 'About the night Terry Martin died, the night you went to Mr Tremlow's....'

'Oh yes, that's what I was telling you. You'll never believe who's just gone down there.'

'What?' Annie felt the stirrings of defeat as even this direct question led on another detour. Was she sentenced to listen to this woman ramble on forever? 'Who's gone down where?'

'Down there!' Doris spoke impatiently. 'Just before you called in. I was on the telephone ... about the church. His car must have passed you but you said you didn't see it. Young Mally's father, the colonel's ex-son-in-law. And her away. What's he doing going down there with her away, that's what I want to know.'

A connection sparked at the back of Annie's mind. 'Do you mean the house next door to Mr Tremlow's? Someone's gone down there?'

'Yes. Him. The husband. Drove down there bold as brass and her away. Frank'll have something to say if he catches him.'

The pieces clicked together. Away camping. 'Is it Colonel Ludgrove's daughter who lives next door to Mr Tremlow, who does his cleaning and things?' Had she missed something the colonel had said, or hadn't be been clear?

'And that was a come-down for her, but she hadn't a brass farthing to rub together after the divorce case.'

Annie felt as though she were hauling a heavy weight up a slope, but she'd uncovered one point of interest: the woman who 'did' for Tremlow and the colonel's daughter were one and the same. That meant Tremlow hadn't been deserted and it was someone else in the building on the cliff top.

'The night Terry Martin died?' Annie tried again with a glance at the clock. If she could prise out Doris Kitson's side, she might hone a sharper point to some of her questions to Tremlow.

'I was on my way round when it happened. I can see from the front here. The houses stand up at the back and it was close on a full moon that night. He was up on that construction the builders left. I don't think it's safe. I said to her only the week before she went away, I said I wouldn't leave a house with builders.'

'Terry Martin was up on the scaffolding?'

'That's where he fell from. And up to no good obviously. I was on the footpath at the back, almost at Charles's gate when I heard the crash.'

Needing only small prompts now to keep the story on a straight path, Doris told Annie how she'd arrived just after the colonel who was trying to get the story out of Tremlow.

'White as a sheet he was. Kept saying, "Frank, it's terrible", over and over, and "Why won't they come?" Frank had got him to call the emergency services you see, so he expected them arriving. Of course they took an age. Do you know where they have to come from now to get to Milesthorpe, it's a scandal. They have to come from—'

'Mr Tremlow must have been very upset.'

'He was in shock, of course. Frank and I went out on our own. We saw young Terry at the bottom of the hole. I said to Frank, it doesn't look good, Frank, and he checked. He said to me, I'm afraid he's had it, Doris, and I said we'd better get Charles to ring 999 again.'

It fitted with what Scott had told her. Tremlow had rung the emergency services twice.

'Do you know how he fell? Did he stumble? Did he step off the edge without realizing?'

'The metal bar gave way. We saw it up there hanging off. Shoddy workmanship, of course. Now when my neighbour had the builders in to do her roof she had a firm from town … and I'm sure she told her insurers it was the storm that took the tiles off but I know for a fact that—'

'So he was probably drunk. Terry Martin, I mean. That'll be why he fell. But why do you think he went up there in the first place?'

'Oh no, he wouldn't have been drunk. I know his parents. They're strictly teetotal.'

'Do you know them well?' Annie asked, surprised.

'Oh no, dear. Only through the church. I don't think we've ever met. You can't count the funeral.'

It didn't mean anything. Teetotal parents didn't mean their son didn't drink. He was nearly forty and he'd certainly been drinking that night. Annie told herself not to read anything into it as she pushed Doris for the detail of the rest of that evening. It matched what she'd learnt from the colonel without any significant additions.

Doris came out with Annie and walked with her to the car. 'I've somewhere to go,' she said.

Annie looked across the street in the direction of the crescent where Tremlow lived. Houses obscured her view.

'Up here.' Doris grabbed her arm and steered her up the road. After twenty metres she stopped. 'There. Look.'

Through a gap in the houses, Annie could make out the rear elevations of the buildings at the base of the crescent. She saw both Tremlow and the colonel's daughter's houses as she squinted against the glare of the sun.

They walked back together to the car where Doris said a quick goodbye and sped off. Annie sat and watched her march down the road. Off to spread the tale of her visit maybe.

In a small change of plan, she pulled out her phone and punched in Tremlow's number. A phone call might be more effective than a visit if it contained a veiled threat that she would call round if he didn't come across with the information she wanted. And it would avoid the chance of physical contact. There was something about Tremlow that repulsed her.

She listened to the ringing tone and imagined Tremlow, his hooded eyes swivelling at the sound, giving the phone a spiteful glare for disturbing him. He'd pull himself to his feet and make his way across the floor. He wouldn't hurry.

On the ninth ring it was answered.

'Yes,' said a clipped voice that Annie took a moment to recognize.

'Ah … Colonel Ludgrove. It's Annie Raymond.' Damn. The colonel said he'd phone. Maybe Tremlow had begged his old friend to come round again, instinct telling him Annie's attack wasn't finished. 'I … uh … I was worried about Mr Tremlow. How is he?'

'Afraid I can't tell you that. He isn't here.'

'Not there? But where is he?'

'Popped out to the shop maybe.' The colonel sounded uncertain. 'I had no reply when I telephoned so I came over.'

'But will he be all right?'

The colonel barked out a laugh. 'Of course he'll be all right. The chap has a temper on him. From what you told me you've riled him and he's gone to walk it off I shouldn't wonder.'

Annie remembered the upset, how she'd sensed Tremlow's humiliation at breaking down in front of her. There'd been the makings of an angry outburst in the middle of it, but … 'But he seems such a mild man.'

'And they can be the worst when they blow. You'll learn that as you grow up.' The colonel laughed again. 'Don't you worry. Tremlow's tougher than he looks. You've not done him any damage.'

'OK, thanks.' Annie ended the call and allowed herself a grunt of frustration. She could hardly tell the colonel she'd counted on having another go at his friend to find out what he had hidden about the night Terry Martin died.

A sharp rap at the window made her start up in alarm. It was Doris Kitson back again, her eyes narrowed, her mouth set in a conspiratorial smile.

'That was a short visit,' she said without preamble, as Annie slid the window down. She leant in closer so Annie could smell the chocolate on her breath. 'By the time I was round he'd already gone off again. No sign of the car. What do you make of that?'

Annie pushed back an urge to say, 'That you're an old busybody'. Doris Kitson had hurried round to see what Mally's father was up to at the ex-marital home and to gather in any gossip ready for picking. She'd now be off to spread the tale of the lightning visit leaving Annie with precious little of use in her search for Terry Martin's lost hours.

'Did you see Mr Tremlow?'

'No, no. I didn't go right down when I saw the car had gone.'

Tremlow couldn't have gone far. Annie started up the engine and decided she would scour the lanes of Milesthorpe for him.

A fruitless search ended at the village shop where she found herself greeted like an old friend. She ordered a sandwich and asked, 'Has Mr Tremlow been in? I went to call on him but he was out.'

'No, we haven't seen him this morning.'

When she left the shop, she drove once more round the village and then parked the car and set off on foot. At the bottom of the crescent she hesitated at Tremlow's gate and then went round to the back garden. Feeling like an intruder, she tried the door. Locked. She peered through the kitchen window. The room lay empty. She walked down the side of the small lawn and pushed her way through the tangle of vegetation until she reached the boundary wall. From here, there was nothing visible of either Tremlow's house or any other. The tangled bushes grew too high. At the other side of the wall ran a footpath bordered by a field high with crops.

She jumped down and looked back. From this angle, a quirk in the twisted branches of the high vegetation opened a window on the scaffolding tower. Her mind pictured Terry Martin up there.

After a moment, she turned and made off down the path, feeling hemmed in by the tall stalks to her left and the garden walls to her right. The colonel's house would be that way across the field where a rough path by a ditch led off at right-angles. She looked back. He wouldn't have been able to see anything from here, but Doris Kitson who'd come the other way had the advantage of the hill and would have had a grandstand view as she hurried round.

Annie didn't head for the colonel's, but followed the course of the ditch the other way and was surprised to find herself behind the row of houses where the Beckes lived. This, then, was the brook of Terry Martin's clever headline.

She made her way up to the road near the Beckes'. Further along was the entrance to Balham's farm, and if she were to turn up the hill and take one of the lanes that led from there, she'd be in the really prosperous end of Milesthorpe where she'd find the Tunbridges' house. She felt a mild curiosity, but had no excuse to call round, and the time she'd allotted to Milesthorpe for today was now up.

With rising frustration she tried to push aside the feeling she'd spent a whole day out here and moved no further forward. What was it she'd told Pat yesterday? Terry Martin vanished for two days and then he died. That was all she knew then and it was all she knew now.

CHAPTER 14

ANNIE HOPED THE Earle case might prove more productive. How much did she tell Pat about what had happened last night? And what exactly had happened? She had a theory on the latter and before she went back to the apartment, would test it out.

Back in Hull, Annie headed away from the river and towards Orchard Park. She drove to the tower block, left the car and headed for the lobby. Once inside, she joined two people waiting in the lift bay. When the lift doors opened and they stepped inside, she half followed, keeping her foot in the door to hold it open, and peered at the panel, swiftly counting up the buttons and looking for the discreet holes that allowed special access to key holders. She stepped back out again and allowed the doors to close. She'd seen all she needed.

Outside again, she returned to the car and cruised round the area looking for a vantage point. A traffic island in the middle of a busy junction looked about right so she pulled the car off the road on to waste ground and climbed out.

It was several minutes before a gap in the traffic allowed her to cross to the middle of the junction. Once there, she pushed her way over lumpy and uneven ground through a tangle of grass and brambles that snaked through a clump of low bushes. The fight to find a way through reminded her of Doris Kitson. Had she learnt anything from all the chatter, all the meandering diversions? More to the point, had she missed anything?

She stood in knee-high grass with the roar of traffic in her ears and the sickly tang of exhaust fumes in her nostrils. Prickles of sweat stippled her skin. A haze of pollution shimmered in the air. The heat was oppressive in town in a way it wasn't out in Milesthorpe. The temperature gauge in the car had climbed to twenty-six.

Her hands held the binoculars she'd used to watch the livery yard at the bottom of the hill in Milesthorpe. She lifted them to her eyes and focused on the distant roof of the tower block. Doris Kitson was mistaken: there was nothing wrong with her powers of observation; she hadn't registered Mally's father's small blue car because she had no reason to and had other things on her mind.

The shapes on the high roof made no immediate sense. She'd never been on the roof of a tall building to know what was normal. There could be a miniature estate hidden away, a self-contained village. She liked the idea of trees and green spaces unseen by the city below, but all she saw was a concrete landscape with a couple of small brick built huts in amongst a forest of wires and aerials.

It would be the lift machinery, things to do with the heating systems, the means to keep these blocks of hundreds of homes operating.

And that was where those men had gone. She hadn't seen them press any of the buttons, not that she'd been looking, but her memory should have shown her two sparks of light on that panel. It didn't. It showed her only one. She didn't know when they'd used the access key. Didn't care. As she'd tangled with the woman in the flowered print dress, she'd heard the lift stopping and thought she was mistaken. It had stopped on the hidden upper floor; they'd gone up to the roof.

There was an inexplicable familiarity in the high landscape. Her view was obscured by the shimmer of a heat-haze, but the angular shapes of the miniature buildings and the curves of wires that glistened like giant spider-silk threads held her attention just like the baffling familiarity of the men the dealers brought with them. She stared perplexed. Two men she'd never set eyes on before still pestered her subconscious telling her she knew them. And now this. Alien shapes far above the ground tugging at a memory that couldn't exist.

She became aware of a more constant scrutiny than the casual perusal from a stream of motorists. Dropping the binoculars from her eyes, she spun round and found herself returning the intense stare of an adolescent boy who stood on the far verge. A rush of cars separated them, but the intensity of his gaze held Annie. There was no hostility in his stare and it took a moment for her to realize who he was.

The joy-rider who might be called Maz. The one who'd disrupted Terry Martin's funeral; the one who'd shouted at her outside the tower block the first time she'd visited Mrs Earle. He looked different, younger, more vulnerable without his cloak of arrogance. What did he want?

As she watched, he held his right hand up beside his head, thumb and little finger stretched back to indicate a phone.

The message was clear. *Phone me.*

She shrugged. *How?*

He stared for a moment longer then dropped his gaze from hers and walked away. Annie turned back towards her car, dodged the traffic to get off the island and bumped the vehicle back down on to the road and into the stream of traffic. He'd gone from the verge as she drove past. The roundabout receded in her rear-view mirror and she wondered who he was, why he would think she could call him. Maybe he expected her to ask Mally for the number. But his agenda wasn't important; hers was. She needed access to the roof of Mrs Earle's tower to find out what went on up there at night.

Annie gave Pat a carefully abridged version of events at Mrs Earle's that glossed over her ill-advised ride in the lift. 'Somehow I need to find out what they do up there. Could that be where they keep the gear stashed?'

Pat remained quiet for several moments as though turning something over in her mind. She answered absently. 'No, I doubt it. Unlikely.'

Pat had muted the sound on the big television. Annie found herself watching the figures who paraded silently across the screen as though they held the secrets of the night visitors to Mrs Earle's block.

'You say they went to the top floor the night before?' Pat asked.

'That's what I assumed at first, but no, I think they went up to the roof.'

Pat shook her head. 'I should think they have a base in one of the flats.'

Annie frowned. What had made Pat say that?

'There's a fair chance,' Pat went on, 'that those two little toerags are peddling dope and whatnot without anyone else knowing. We need to find out for sure.'

Annie bent her head over the folder and flicked through the papers so she could speak without looking at Pat. 'Why don't I go up in the lift with them one night, see for sure where they go? They don't know who I am. They can't possibly know everyone who lives there or visits. I could be anyone.'

'No way!' Pat's tone was sharp enough to snap Annie's gaze up to meet hers. 'I mean it, Annie. You're not to try any silly tricks.'

But I already have … She hovered on the brink of confessing to Pat what she'd done, but, as she hesitated, Pat pulled the file open again and flipped through the papers. The moment passed. Annie ran her tongue over lips that had suddenly dried. 'What should I do then?'

'Watch the top-floor lift bay. No heroics. Just watch. I'd like to know for sure which flat they use. I can make enquiries from here if you find me that.'

'OK. I'll see what I can do tonight.'

Pat was wrong, she was sure of it. Nonetheless, she would do as she was told, wait discreetly on the staircase and watch through the patchwork of reinforced glass. She wouldn't see the lift doors open or hear anything other than the whine of the lift going on up to the roof.

Pat flipped the file closed and pushed it aside. 'How's it going with the Martins? Did you get anything out of Tremlow?'

Annie gave Pat a shamefaced smile. 'No, I really messed up there.' She told Pat of Tremlow's collapse, of her plan to give him space to compose himself before she went back. 'I completely misread him. He did a runner.'

Pat shrugged. 'It happens. Don't beat yourself up. You can catch up with him again. What else did you get?'

She told Pat about her time in Doris Kitson's kitchen, about Doris rushing off to try to catch Mally's father at the ex-marital home, then her fruitless search for Tremlow and finally her walk round the lanes and tracks seeing for herself the routes taken by Colonel Ludgrove and Doris Kitson the night Terry Martin died.

'Tell me again,' Pat said. 'Who exactly saw Terry Martin on that scaffolding and who didn't?'

'Ludgrove didn't. He came at Tremlow's house from the back and from across the field. You can't see a thing because of the bushes. Doris Kitson did. She came from the other direction, from down the hill. You can see the back of the crescent quite clearly.'

'And Tremlow himself?'

'No. According to Scott, Tremlow locked himself in his house until the colonel arrived.'

'But he told you he did see him?'

'Well, yes. That is, he said both. He was all over the place. Scott thinks he probably sees Terry in his nightmares.'

'There's no doubt that Terry was up there though, is there?'

'No; Doris Kitson saw him and anyway, there's nowhere else he could have fallen from … Oh shit!' Her line of reasoning skidded to a sudden halt.

'What is it?' Pat prompted.

'Doris Kitson's pretty old. I mean, she's full of energy and all that, but she's getting on a bit. And it was dark.'

'What are you saying? Could she have seen Terry Martin on that scaffolding or not?'

'Oh yes, she could have seen that there was someone on that platform, and once she got there and found Terry in the hole, she'd have assumed it was him, but ...'

Pat looked troubled. Annie saw her flick the Martins' file open and finger the distinctive paper that held the post-mortem report; the report that implied Terry was too drunk to climb. Someone had been on that platform. Terry had died in the hole beneath.

'Pat, what if it wasn't Terry that Doris saw? What if there was someone else there that night?'

CHAPTER 15

Annie felt suddenly breathless, both excited and uneasy. 'Pat, if I'm right about this, he might have been pushed.'

Pat puffed out her cheeks as she hauled herself upright on the settee. 'Christ, I hope not. We don't want that sort of complication.'

'What should we do? I'm seeing Scott tomorrow. Should I—?'

'Hell no. At least not yet. Let me think.'

Pat tossed the TV remote from hand to hand and eventually said, 'No one wants a murder case. You'll make yourself very unpopular if you spring it on them and they take it up.'

'Yes, but if ...'

Pat raised a hand. 'Think it through. They've one murder on their hands already. You sew enough doubt that they take it up then they're into all manner of hassle, more cancelled leave, trying to dredge up resources, all that stuff. And if they go through all that and you're wrong you end up without any credibility. You become the hysterical tart who cries wolf.'

Drama queen!

'I know you're only here a few weeks but you've built up a good relationship with a couple of the local plods one way or another. You don't want to wreck that. It could be useful.'

Only here a few weeks. The words burnt painfully into the tension of Annie's theories about Terry Martin. She'd put everything into these two cases and begun to feel she belonged here, but of course she didn't.

'Saying that,' Pat went on, 'you'd better watch it with the guy. I don't want any pillow talk; anything leaking out about the agency.'

Indignation wrenched Annie's mind away from thoughts of her future career. 'What d'you mean, pillow talk? I've only known him five minutes. And anyway,' she snapped, with an added layer of umbrage at the way

Vince had brought her here as a skivvy, 'I don't know anything about the agency.'

'I'm just saying be careful. Now let's get back to Terry Martin. Go through the timings for me again.'

Annie went over everything she'd squeezed from Heather Becke, Tremlow, Doris Kitson and the colonel and tossed in the shreds of gossip she'd picked up around the village.

'OK,' Pat said. 'You need to go back and walk the key routes. Be precise, follow exactly in their footsteps, figure out just how much they could have seen. Do that first and see where we get.'

'And I can have another go at Tremlow, too. It's obvious what's happened isn't it? He saw someone all right, but he's not saying who.'

'Hold your hosses. Don't run away with this. If we get a shred of evidence to say things weren't as straightforward as the official report, it isn't our case any more. But let's test the theory first.'

'But if he is protecting someone, why would he be doing it?'

'It's someone he cares about, or it's someone he's frightened of.'

'Terry Martin was trying to blackmail him.'

'Terry Martin's the one person he isn't trying to protect. Terry Martin's dead.'

'But ... well, it means Tremlow's blackmail-able.'

'True. And that's something your mates in blue can dig out if and when we break it to them their holidays are under threat.'

'I'll nip out tomorrow morning and check those routes.'

Pat laughed. 'You're allowed weekends off, you know, and if you're staying in this business you want to learn to take them when you can. Some cases don't give you much time out. And when you go, you should go at the same time of night so you get the conditions they had. You won't get the right light if you go in the morning.'

Pat was right, but Annie was reluctant to change her plans for Saturday. Scott was coming round about three o'clock to show her more of the area. He'd said with a laugh, showing the smile she couldn't resist, that she hadn't seen the best of it with Orchard Park and Milesthorpe. They were to make an evening of it.

'It'll keep till next week,' Pat said. 'Terry Martin'll be no less dead for being pushed. You've worked some long hours this last week. You've done well. Have a couple of days off.'

Annie returned Pat's smile pleased at this praise. At the same time she itched to get back out to Milesthorpe to test her theories. What use did she have for time off at the moment? Today ... tomorrow ... next week ... it was all the same to Terry Martin. But she decided to slip out tomorrow morning anyway. She'd be back before Pat woke.

*

Her theories about Terry Martin burnt bright enough to cover the chill of the night air as she made her way out to the taxi later. They were on their way and too late to turn back when she remembered that her jacket lay in the boot of Pat's car outside the flat.

'You take care up there at this hour. I wouldn't let my daughter come here at this time of night, you know.'

Annie smiled. The driver, sixtyish, large head partly bald, had countered his stereotype the first couple of trips she'd made with him and been monosyllabic. These last two nights though he'd opened up and told her something about his family.

'I'll be OK. We have training for this sort of thing.' She knew the words stretched the reality of her few days in Birmingham; but she spoke with a well of pride in her profession and he nodded, taking it all in.

He dropped her at the entranceway. It was too early for the white van, but she knew there'd be customers already huddled in the shadows of the sixth-floor landing. She stepped into the lift and hit the button for floor seven.

When it stopped and the doors slid apart, she stepped out and peered down the stairwell to the inky blackness of the floor below. A rustle of soft words in the darkness played like the whisper of a breeze through undergrowth. They didn't matter tonight. Her target was higher.

She climbed the stairs, alert for trouble and trying to get a feel for the building and all its tiny communities. Not a single landing had escaped modifications to its toughened glass panels. In some, it was a single mismatched square. In others, the patchwork glass was studded with wooden panes and graffiti. The light swayed between standard brightness from ordinary bulbs through dim fitful beams that escaped paint-sprayed covers to pools of blackness where fittings were smashed.

Concrete stair followed concrete stair. A burst of shrieks and giggling halted her as a gaggle of young girls burst out of a flat and jostled down past her, their scant clothing like daubs of paint across their skinny bodies. It was the early hours of the morning, but in this concrete cocoon she could be anywhere … anywhen. She paused to rest when the blood in her legs ran like lead. It took longer to reach the top than she'd estimated and, when she arrived, a glance at her watch showed her the white van might be drawing into the car-park right now.

Five minutes later, the mechanical whine told her the lift was climbing beyond the upper floors. This was it. She watched through cracked glass, knowing there'd be nothing to see, knowing they'd go up beyond her reach. It slowed, clanked to a halt. Shock rushed the blood from her skin. The metal doors slid apart.

Two pairs of legs emerged. She knew the shoes well after the long minutes she'd spent staring down at them in the lift. They stepped out on to the landing and headed left. Hardly daring to pull in a breath, she crept up the stairs and peered after them. She heard laughter as the two men headed for the far end of the corridor.

She caught half a remark, '… said to that Peter Levy on the TV …' another laugh, before the rattle of a key in a lock drowned out what they said. The overheard name stopped her for a moment. Did it sound familiar? Then the sounds she heard banged on to her consciousness. A key in a lock. Another key in a lock. And then another. And another. How many damned locks did this door have – and why?

After they disappeared inside she crept closer. There was a spy hole that she put her eye to but was met only with darkness. She tried an ear to the door but could hear nothing. Temptation rose to knock and see what happened, trust to the lucky star that had protected her this far. But no, Pat would kill her if she tried anything so foolish. She took note of the number and retreated.

Inside the lift, the cloying scent of after-shave fought with remnants of chemical cleaner and the hot machinery smell. She watched the light track her path down the building and tensed as floor six approached. The clients waiting there would expect the lift to stop, but the downward movement carried her smoothly past. She punched the taxi driver's number into her mobile.

The car-park was empty of people but had acquired the smouldering remains of a small saloon car while she'd been inside the building. The acrid smoke drifted across; the sharp tang cut into her nostrils making her screw up her face. She prowled the concrete surface keeping a wary eye on the surrounding streets. So Pat was right. They had a flat up there on the top floor, a well-secured flat, but she wouldn't abandon her theory. They'd been on the roof last night.

She craned her head back and looked up at the outline of the building against the pale moonlight. That first night she'd been up there watching down on them. Tonight, she was at ground level looking up. Memory showed men with packages whose weird shapes fought back as they manhandled them towards the building; then spider-thread wires high above the city glinting through the lenses of the binoculars.

The distant sound of a siren cut into her thoughts. A car approached. Her taxi.

As she stepped forward to intercept its path, the memory popped up like the replay of a single frame of a film. Sharp as flint for a second, then gone in a burst of light. At once, she spun round and looked up again, straining to see anything beyond the bare outline of the roof's edge. Her mind's eye superimposed the view from the traffic island where she'd squinted up through sunlight to the high roof. Cut to a sordid flat, photographs culled from a difficult angle.

The toot of a horn sounded the driver's impatience. She turned to climb into the taxi and, like seeing an odd-shaped piece of jigsaw in amongst a heap of similar pieces, her mind made the match.

She still had no idea what she'd been looking at, but the shapes were the same. Whatever the two men had taken up in those packages the first time she watched them was now on the roof of the tower block and visible to anyone who took the trouble to look.

Back at the flat Annie waved a companionable goodbye to the driver and jogged across to Pat's car to retrieve the jacket she'd left in the boot. The Orchard Park puzzle must be close to solved. She didn't understand much of what she'd found, but felt she held almost all the pieces. The flat on the top floor; the trips to the roof; the dealing when the two men were on their own. Between them she and Pat would slot everything into place.

She opened the boot, stared nonplussed at its emptiness then spotted her jacket in a tight ball in the corner. She'd shaken it out and slipped it on before recalling the careless gesture with which she'd tossed it in there outside Doris Kitson's. No way had it rolled itself up like that. It hung awkwardly at one side. She reached into the pocket and pulled out a torn cigarette packet ripped and refolded into a cube. Unfolding it gingerly because she knew she hadn't put it there and inside Pat's car boot it sure as hell hadn't got there accidentally, she felt anger rise. A mobile phone number was etched into the card with a largely ink-free pen.

The boy at the traffic island. *Phone me.* His presence in Withernsea hadn't been coincidence. He'd known Terry Martin. She needed to speak to him and now she had the means. The little bastard had not only left her his number, he'd cocked a snook by showing he could break into her car.

CHAPTER 16

ANNIE MARCHED THROUGH to the kitchen the next morning as light streamed in giving everything a fresh new sparkle helped by a scouring from Barbara the day before. There was no sign of movement in the street outside, but the distant rumble of traffic accompanied the rattle of the kettle as it came to the boil.

The little git with his phone number cast a small shadow. She was curious but not convinced he'd have anything of use. For some reason, he needed her. For now, he could wait. The barb of apprehension was having to confess to Pat how he'd passed on his number.

The deep aroma of coffee wrapped itself round her. She wanted to get out to Milesthorpe and test her theories. No way could she have left it till Monday.

A voice boomed into her ear from close behind. 'Make that two cups.'

Annie leapt with the shock. Pat stood in the doorway, her bulk all but blocking the light from the other room.

'I'm coming with you.'

'What? But…?'

'You *are* going to Milesthorpe, aren't you?'

Annie could only nod as she felt for a second cup. She wanted to say, you can't come with me, but, of course, Pat could go where she pleased.

By the time they were on the road, Annie's astonishment had dissolved. It felt good to have someone to share her thoughts and theories. They talked about Tremlow. The winding lanes on the approach to the village were easier to navigate because the roadside undergrowth had been cut and lay in yellowing heaps. They passed a small tractor that dragged a giant egg whisk behind it fluffing up the grasses as it went by and filling the car with the smell of fresh hay.

Pat sneezed.

Annie took advantage of one of Milesthorpe's many loops and came at Doris Kitson's road from the top so as not to pass her house and have their presence broadcast. She eased the car to a standstill and pointed between the houses.

'That's the crescent where Tremlow lives. There, can you see the scaffolding?'

Pat nodded.

They sat in silence. Annie kept her stare on the backs of the far houses. She could make out both Tremlow and his neighbour's, but if there were anyone up on that scaffolding now, could she identify him?

Sunlight hit the buildings with the white intensity that presaged a baking hot day. Milesthorpe's few trees waggled their leaf-ends acknowledging the closeness of the sea and the constant breeze.

'Well you'd certainly see someone from here,' was Pat's verdict.

'But could you see who it was?'

'Maybe. If it was someone I knew.'

'In moonlight, not daylight?' Annie tried to imagine the scene against a night sky. 'Doris Kitson's sharp as a knife, but she's getting on. She wears glasses. He'd have been against the house wall and that would have been in darkness. I don't think she had a cat in hell's chance of seeing who it was.'

'Security lights?'

'I don't know.' Annie felt foolish because she should have checked.

'Let's go and see.'

'And if there aren't?'

'You want to have another go at Tremlow, don't you?'

'Yes. The sooner the better. I'm sure I can get him to talk.'

*

As she pulled up the car at Tremlow's gate, Annie cast a doubtful look at the uneven path round the side of the house.

'He seems to live in his kitchen round the back. Let me go and rouse him and I'll let you in through the front door.'

Annie left Pat struggling out of the car and made her way down the side path. The bushes that grew in the shadow of the house brushed their glistening leaves wetly against her. She took a few steps down the garden and turned back to the house which she raked with an intense stare. No sign even of a conventional outside bulb, let alone security lights that might have lit the next-door elevation. The colonel's daughter's house under the same inspection produced the same result. Annie felt a surge of triumph.

Gotcha, Mr Charles Tremlow. You saw someone that night, someone you knew well enough to recognize in the dark. And it wasn't Terry Martin. Now let's find out who you're covering for.

She peered through the kitchen window. The room was empty, so she knocked a brisk tattoo on the door and waited. Had he seen her and decided to lie low? She wasn't having that. He would come out and face her if she had to drag him.

The door yielded to her and she stepped inside. The kitchen felt as empty as it looked. No trace of recent activity. No background smell of tea brewing or toast crisping.

'Mr Tremlow,' she called, surprising herself at a nervy edge to her voice. No answer.

Triumph faded into apprehension as Annie crept through to the front of the house. Empty rooms greeted her. She looked for cups, used ashtrays, recent indentations in the cushions. Nothing. What was she to make of the unlocked door? He'd claimed he didn't like to lock up, yet the day she'd visited with the colonel he'd been behind more bolts than a high security prison. She looked at the staircase, listened for any sound from above, and felt reluctance to ascend. Instead, she turned to the front door and pulled back the bolt. Pat stood at the gate and made her way down the small path as she saw Annie.

'He's not here. Not a sign. But I haven't looked upstairs yet.'

They made fleeting eye contact. 'Go on up,' Pat said. 'I'll wait here.'

Annie climbed the stairs, all her senses alert and straining upwards. She listened for breathing or snores. Was there a trace of anything in the air? What was that stale smell? Would it burgeon into something more sinister? Would she find him up here huddled in a corner hiding from her ... or something worse?

The stairs led to a tiny landing and three closed doors. The first was a small bathroom that smelt sour and decayed. The next was a box room. A bed-frame and bare mattress sat beneath a pile of miscellaneous junk. No sign anything had been disturbed recently. The third room was bigger, clearly the master bedroom. An old-fashioned double bed fought for domination of the room with a dark wood wardrobe. A matching dressing-table stood across the window, its mirror blocking the sun, making the room oppressive and gloomy where it could have been airy and light.

The bed was unmade, the sheets might once have been white. A constriction in her throat made Annie gulp to swallow as she stepped inside the room and pulled the wardrobe door open. Nothing more sinister than the smell of age greeted her.

She felt certain now she was alone in the house and let out a breath she didn't know she'd been holding. Out on the landing, she gave the ceiling a glance. A small square loft access hung above her, but she could see it hadn't been used in months.

Pat was in the open doorway as she came down.

'No sign upstairs.'

'I've just had a look in the garage. It's empty. Does he have a car?'

'Yes, I think so. I'm sure so. Doris Kitson mentioned it.'

'He's gone out. Leave everything as you found it. I daresay one of the neighbours'll report us when he gets back. Put a card in the kitchen on your way out. Let's see if he calls back. There's no point pretending we weren't here. No chance of hiding anything in Milesthorpe.'

Unless, thought Annie, you're Terry Martin and about to die. Then you can hide yourself for two whole days and a bit.

'We could drop in on the colonel. He might know something.'

'OK, go on your own. Casual visit. Just passing. That sort of thing. Take me to the other end of the footpath that runs along the back of the houses. I'll see what I can find.'

Annie didn't like the idea of Pat stumbling about on an unmade path on her own. It was a long way from here to the nearest Accident & Emergency department. But she couldn't voice her fears without sounding like a fussy elder sister so drove back to Doris Kitson's road and searched for the access point. It came as a pleasant surprise, neatly marked with a metal bollard and tall sign that pointed down a long narrow stretch of tarmac.

'Thought so,' said Pat. 'It's the old railway. I won't go far. Don't be longer than ten minutes. I'm not supposed to stand on this thing too long.'

There was no answer from the colonel's house so Annie returned to the footpath a few minutes later and looked along to see where Pat had got to. The sun made a shiny ribbon of the smooth surface. A group of cyclists melted into the far distance as the path curved round out of sight. Walkers dotted the length of the track. Pat's lopsided gait wasn't hard to distinguish. She'd travelled a fair way, but was now heading back towards the car. Between her and Annie were two girls on ponies, their backs to Annie, heading towards Pat who hobbled awkwardly, head down.

Annie was filled with a sudden certainty that they would knock their ponies into Pat as they passed her. She took in a breath to shout a greeting to Pat, to signal to the girls they were watched, but before she could make a sound, the two riders turned their ponies off the tarmac strip and made them pick their way in single file along the lumpy gravel that edged the path. It was Laura and Kay. Annie thought she recognized Boxer too. Kay's mount, a fat orangey version of Laura's was probably the one in the film who'd knocked Terry Martin down. Now she knew who they were it seemed natural they should have given Pat right of way. If Mally had been with them maybe it would have been different.

Unfinished business there. What had they done for Terry Martin? He'd had the film for blackmail and money for bribes.

As Pat reached her, Annie said, 'The colonel wasn't in. Did you notice two girls on ponies go past you just now. They're the ones who cheated on Terry Martin's film.'

Pat glanced back, then, with laboured breathing and grunts of effort, tottered the last few steps and hoisted herself into the car where she slumped into the seat with an enormous sigh. 'Christ! That was hard going. So your other old man wasn't home either. I doubt I made it far enough down that track. You'll need to have a look later.'

Annie wasn't sure it mattered anymore. Doris's eyes couldn't be good enough to make out Terry Martin at night against that wall: Tremlow was the key.

'Walk it through sometime.' Pat lay back, eyes closed, clearly exhausted. 'Details matter. Never forget that. But next week's soon enough. Let's get home.'

As Annie reached for the key her phone rang. She looked at the screen and turned to Pat in surprise. 'It's Colonel Ludgrove.'

'Awfully sorry I missed you. Saw you walk away and couldn't get to the door in time. Can't think how I missed your knock, but the ears are not as sharp as they were. Do pop back. I'm not too late, am I? Took me a while to find that card you left. Young Mel's been looking for something on the telephone table and you can imagine the chaos.' He gave a laugh under which Annie heard a note of defeat.

'Well, actually I was just on my way back to town. It wasn't anything important. I was just passing.'

'No, please. I'll feel I've offended you. Ignoring a visitor. Can't think how it happened.'

Annie turned a helpless look to Pat who signalled an OK gesture.

'Fine, I'll be a couple of minutes. But I really can't stay long.'

Annie pulled up the car out of sight of the colonel's house. 'I'll park here,' she said. 'So he doesn't see the car and hassle for us both to come in.'

Pat nodded. 'Suits me. I've had my exercise for the day.'

'I'll be as quick as I can.'

'Don't cut it short on my account. See if you can get anything out of him about Tremlow.'

When Annie saw the colonel she had no difficulty understanding why he'd missed her the first time although he carried on apologizing all the way to the living room as he waved her to a chair. His face was drawn, his hair tousled. The crisp military neatness she remembered was replaced with crumpled clothes and an air of neglect. He almost looked as though he'd just finished some vigorous exercise, but had clearly been asleep and didn't want to admit to it. It didn't seem fair to start straight in on an interrogation about Tremlow so she asked at random, 'Have you managed to contact your daughter yet?'

He shook his head. 'I'll be frank with you. It's becoming a bit of a strain. I'm not saying a word against young Mel. She's a good girl, but she's a youngster and I'm not as young as I was. It's a job keeping up with her at times. Now you've time for a quick cuppa before you rush off?'

'Well, really I shouldn't …'

'I won't take no. Don't worry, it's already in the pot brewing.' As he spoke, the colonel turned and headed for the door. Annie listened to his footsteps recede down the lino of the hallway. He called out something, the words disjointed as they floated back to her. '… little nip … keep the cold out …'

She sprang to her feet and followed him to a big kitchen. He stood in front of two steaming cups and twisted the top off a brandy bottle.

'No, Colonel, I can't. I'm driving.'

'Just a small one to keep the cold out?' There was a pleading tone in his voice. She felt desperately sorry for him. Mally must be giving him hell.

'No, really, I mustn't. My boss is waiting in the car outside.' It was a risk that she'd now have to fight against Pat being dragged inside, but she couldn't abide the taste of brandy and the thought of it in tea made her feel ill.

'Ah, I see.' The colonel gave her a conspiratorial look. 'Don't want him smelling it on your breath. Quite understand. Ah, well. Tea'll be welcome anyway.'

'Don't let me stop you,' Annie said, as he put the bottle aside unopened.

He laughed. 'Drink on my own during the day? Good heavens no. That's the slippery path.'

Annie smiled and pretended to believe him. No mystery now why he'd slept so soundly. She wondered if he'd been much of a drinker before he'd had to cope with Mally.

'I called in really to know if you'd seen Mr Tremlow. He wasn't in.'

'Not sure where he'll be. I think Doris said she'd seen him driving out of the village.'

Annie made a move to carry the two cups through, but he waved her aside and took them himself. 'Was there anything special you wanted him for?'

'Yes, there was. Did you know that Terry Martin had been blackmailing him?'

'Good Lord! I'd no idea. Why didn't he tell me? I'd have sorted the blighter out. What was it about?'

'I was hoping you'd tell me.'

'Oh, I see.' He paused in thought. 'It must have been the business with his wife. Bad business. She ran off with a travelling salesman.'

'I thought that was years ago.'

'It was. Hasn't lessened the shame for poor Charles, I'm afraid. He hates the idea of people knowing. I expect the young chap threatened to put something in the newspapers. Not that people these days care a fig for that sort of thing. Been through it myself with the daughter. Not pleasant, but you take it on the chin.'

Annie hoped she wasn't about to make a big mistake. 'There's something else, Colonel. I'm afraid it looks as though Mr Tremlow lied about the night Terry Martin died.'

'Good Lord! Charles lied? What do you mean?'

She outlined her theory that Tremlow had seen someone else up on the scaffolding. 'Mrs Kitson saw someone up there, but she couldn't have seen who it was. We've just been to check. And Terry Martin was drunk, really drunk. I'm not sure he was up there at all.'

'No no, you're wrong about that.' The colonel looked puzzled. 'Well, I see what you mean. Yes, Charles was a bit cagey but …' He picked up his tea, stared into the depths of the cup with a wistful look that Annie read as regret for the lack of brandy, and put it down untouched. Then he sat upright and nodded decisively. 'Yes, I can see it now. You're absolutely right. Of course he didn't see anyone up there. He's vain. It's his downfall. He heard Doris's account and adopted it for his own. Blind as a bat at night. He wouldn't have stopped to get his spectacles. He was in a panic. When he was out there he wouldn't have seen a thing.'

'The police told me he locked himself in his house.'

'I believe he did after he'd rung me, but he told me he'd been out there. You see, he thought it was a neighbour's dog come to dig up his border. Bane of his life those dogs.'

'So it could have been someone else that Mrs Kitson saw up there?'

'No no. It was the Martin chap all right. I saw him myself from the bottom of the path. Land drops away. Look up from there and that whole contraption they've set up stands out against the sky.'

Annie felt deflated. He was right. From the top of the path where Doris had seen him, he'd have been in darkness, but from nearby, not only was the angle steeper, the colonel would have been close enough to see exactly who was up there. She remembered how the branches parted to allow a small but clear view of the scaffolding tower.

'And there was no one else up there?'

'No. He was on his own.'

'You didn't see him fall?'

'Well, no. That would have happened when I was at the back coming up towards the garden. You can't see from there because of the bushes.'

Annie knew just where he meant. 'Did you hear anything? Doris Kitson said she heard the crash.'

The colonel looked embarrassed. 'Afraid I can't say for certain. Some of that undergrowth is very tangled and the hearing isn't what it was.'

That was that. Annie mentally berated herself for a stab of disappointment. Far better that it had been a simple fall. Her gaze strayed to the window that looked over the churned grass, the concrete blocks and wooden poles where Mally had coached Laura and Kay on their ponies. 'They've made a real mess of your lawn,' she observed, thinking of Terry Martin and forgetting about Mally's cheating. She could have bitten through her tongue the moment the words were out, but the colonel smiled.

'She's a little scamp at times. But she had those two girls up and down by that hedge; over that contraption I don't know how many times. The poor beasts must have been jumping it in their sleep by the time she'd finished. Did the trick though, didn't it?'

Annie let out the breath she'd been holding. She didn't know what action Tina might take over the cheating but thankfully nothing had reached the colonel yet. No way would she be the one to break it to him.

He still hadn't touched his tea. She suspected the brandy bottle would be out again the moment she left. In fact, she sensed he wanted her gone now. Probably he wanted some rest before Mally turned up. Time to go and tell Pat that the Terry Martin theory was in tatters. She downed the last of her tea and stood up. The colonel made no move to stop her.

CHAPTER 17

SCOTT DROVE HER west then north showing her parts of the city she hadn't seen before. Evidence of a seafaring past was mostly marked as symbols integral to new buildings. Circular windows in modern façades flashed the sun's light back at the city. A modern pub in a housing estate lay on the site of the real Timber Dock where, years ago, he told her, huge logs floated submerged until seasoned and ready for use.

'You don't remember it, surely?'

He didn't, but his grandmother had told him all about Hull in the early years of the last century. Queen's Gardens, now in the heart of the city, had once been a natural harbour. 'People were very iffy about the idea of filling it in and building on it. Even now they have a terrible time building into the clay. There's nothing underneath, nothing to pin anything to. Most of the buildings are on huge concrete rafts.'

She smiled because the city's past seemed to mean a lot to him, but his words resonated with more recent events. Nothing underneath, nothing to pin anything to. She'd grasped for substance in the Terry Martin case and found only a false foundation. Would Orchard Park, so close to resolution, crumble in the same way? The cityscape had talked to her from the start. She'd woken on her first morning to the view across a calm surface on a treacherous shipping lane. Her journeys out of Hull took her past security gates at an ordinary roundabout and led to villages where houses stood with their backs to the road as though holding on to secrets that casual observers mustn't share. Nothing much to see, but so much hidden.

'What's that?' She pointed to the giant sculpture of a ship slipping beneath the waves that she'd spotted on her first evening in the city.

'The Deep. It's an aquarium thing. Sharks and all that.'

The drive through areas of the town she hadn't seen or suspected caught her interest. Sweeping tree-lined roads gave glimpses of imposing dwellings behind high walls and mature densely planted gardens. She felt the contrast with the areas she'd come to know. Orchard Park with its cracked jigsaw of concrete streets simmered against the shaded velvety tarmac of these more prosperous areas. She saw patterns she recognized from the hopscotch of moves she'd made when a student. Familiar areas in a city she'd never explored. Like the men on Orchard Park. Familiar faces on people she'd never met.

'What's up?'

'I was just thinking; it's like London really. In miniature.'

And just imagine if she'd rushed to him with her theory about the mystery man on the scaffolding. *Drama queen*! She'd been as bad as Terry Martin chasing his big stories.

'Do you miss London?'

'No, not at all.' The readiness of her answer surprised her. It was true. London seemed an age away.

'So, will you stay when the six weeks is up?'

'It's not that simple. I can't stay without a job.'

'You don't have to work for Sleeman. There are other firms ... other jobs. How come you know him anyway?'

Something in his tone alerted her to history between him and Vince. It startled her. Something else she hadn't suspected. She stole a sideways glance. He stared ahead, eyes narrowed.

'I answered a job advert. Why?'

'Just wondered. You don't know him well?'

She blew out a sigh and thought of the wing and prayer that had carried her here. 'Hardly at all. I've only met him a couple of times.'

'But you work at the agency in town? While you're not out and about, that is?'

This had morphed into an interrogation. Silently she closed down the shutters. In theory they trod the same professional line of the law, but she knew all about the suspicion between parallel professions. 'Just routine stuff,' she murmured, then continued on before he could speak again, 'How about you? D'you think you'll stay in the force? What made you join up? You never look enthusiastic when I see you in uniform.'

He shrugged and she waited for him to explain how he'd fallen into it for want of anything better to do, but he surprised her. 'My grandmother bought me a policeman's helmet when I was two. It's my earliest memory. I've never seriously considered anything else.'

Annie turned to him with a spontaneous smile. It echoed her own aspirations so perfectly. Never seriously considered anything else. He'd had the courage of his certainty where she'd failed in hers. She'd kept her ambitions a secret because they were tied up in confused early memories and meant talking about her family. People invariably jumped to the wrong conclusions.

Her upbringing hadn't been textbook, but whose was? She and her father had been strangers for years. He hadn't been able to cope with her mother's death, not that she'd known it at the time, being too young to understand adult despair. She felt no resentment that he'd palmed off his small daughter on to his sister-in-law, too old even then to raise a child. There were no psychoses or stress disorders battling within her, but people wouldn't believe it.

'We didn't starve,' she used to say in the days when she talked about it at all. 'I wasn't born into a famine-stricken war zone. I was looked after.'

So she'd nursed her passion for the world of private investigation like a shameful secret. She'd let her elders and supposedly betters discuss her future career. She'd even joined in. If she'd only been upfront in the days when there were people around able and willing to help, maybe she'd have all the right bits of paper now and be setting up her own business. She remembered the excitement of landing her first temporary post in a PI's office. It was a big city firm; she no more than coffee-maker and gopher, but the excitement still glowed as a physical memory though the job had been gone in a fortnight. It remained as a line on her CV, a talisman more than a position of substance. Two weeks in a *real job* at last.

She'd told her aunt; remembered the buzz, the elation. 'It's a big firm.' The exhilaration shone out of the simple statement.

'Never mind, dear. It's all experience. You'll soon get a proper job.'

Crushed.

'What are you thinking about?' Scott's words cut into her musing.

'Nothing.'

'Come on. You were laughing at me when I told you about the helmet my grandmother bought me. Then you looked really down. It was like a cloud going over the sun.'

She had to explain because she couldn't leave him thinking she'd laughed at his memories. 'It made me smile because it sounded so much like it was for me. I don't remember a time I didn't want to be a private investigator.'

'What was it for you, a toy spy-glass and funny hat?'

She laughed and murmured, 'Don't be daft.'

'There must have been something. PIs don't usually hit the radar till you get older.'

He didn't sound as though he was about to analyse her, or to mock. He just sounded interested. In a move that felt like unclipping a safety rope, she told him that her mother had died and she'd been sent to live with her aunt. 'When I look back on it, my need to be an investigator feels like the only thing I took with me to my aunt's house.'

'Did your father hire a PI to look into your mother's death?'

He said it so simply, as though it were the easiest thing in the world to talk about.

'I've always assumed so.'

'And how ... uh ... how did your mother die?' She sensed his sideways glance.

'I don't know. No one talked about it. I've never tried to find out.'

She tensed ready to field the usual outburst, that people must have talked to her about it, why hadn't she asked questions ... but he just nodded as though he understood.

'Were you living with your aunt before you came to Hull?'

'Christ, no. I got out years ago.' She laughed at her own words. 'That makes it sound awful. It wasn't. She was fine. I was happy there.'

It was true, she had been as happy as any of her peers when just a child, but despite material comfort, the sedate atmosphere of her elderly aunt's world stultified the teenager in her. She'd scrabbled through college prospectuses looking not to kick-start her career but for any course that would take her far away and into a bustling metropolis.

'Do you see much of her nowadays?' Scott asked.

'No, not really. I was on a tight budget when I left to go to college so I knew I wouldn't be able to visit regularly.' She remembered the buzz of standing alone on a station platform in London, aged seventeen, her case at her feet. 'And now it's even harder. Soon after I left, she moved to a residential home so there isn't really anywhere for me to stay.'

She thought back to the shock that had coursed through her when her aunt told her the news. *It's time I had a real retirement, dear. Someone to look after me for a change. But I wanted to see you safely off my hands first.* Shock had turned into the realization that she'd valued a place to call home, even if she hadn't wanted to be there much.

'It must have come as a bit of a shock,' Scott said, his tone matter-of-fact.

'It was a bit. She was at sea with all the technicalities of college and me going away. She knew I'd taken a room in hall, but she didn't realize that meant I'd counted on the option of going home in the long holiday if I couldn't afford to stay. But it was OK. I'd got my own life and I soon found myself a place.'

She remembered the awful spell of sordid bedsits, of feeling rootless and cut adrift, but she'd picked herself up, found better places to stay.

'So what did you do at college?'

Wasted my time, Annie thought, whilst silently thanking Scott for his change of topic. 'Computing. It was supposed to make me marketable.'

'Did it?'

'It helped get me temporary posts, but it meant they shoved me into IT, so I stopped mentioning it on my CV, which didn't help at all because it made it look as though I hadn't any qualifications to speak of.' She laughed, thinking back to the frustration of first realizing this. 'Hey, maybe I should sign up with your lot if I can't get fixed up with anything else.'

'Not round here you won't.'

'Why not? It could be fun trying out the other side of the coin. Being a PI should be a good grounding for a police officer.'

'People usually do the reverse career move. Just don't join up round here. Go back to London.'

'Why? Do you find it that bad?'

'It's all right for me, I'm a man.'

She felt her jaw drop as she stared across at him. Had she moved 200 miles north or 200 years back in time? The conversation skirted a side of Scott she might not want to see. She'd accepted his invitation mainly because she thought she liked him, but also because she wanted his take on Terry Martin. If he turned into someone she didn't like after all, questioning him would become deceitful.

The car climbed a hill past a barrack-like hospital. Annie glanced at the Portakabins scattered in the grounds of imposing old buildings. Functional side by side with imposing … tattered hardboard … polished stone. Was it the converted remains of a stately home, or had it once been an asylum, and did tortured ghosts shriek in the fabric of the carved stonework? So much hidden …

Scott said nothing as he slowed at the top of the hill to manoeuvre the car out on to a roundabout that took them to a wide river of tarmac sweeping its way up between fields and trees. Abruptly, they'd left the city behind.

'It was my dream,' he said. 'Always. I can't remember not wanting to wear the uniform. I thought about it all the time, but in some ways I never thought about it at all. I mean that it wasn't until the reality hit me that I knew what the dream was all about. Like my whole life hung on making it in, then I had to face the truth of it. Like going hell for leather down a wide road and suddenly you can't see what's ahead. It all looked like plain sailing and then you don't know where the hell you are. Courtland Road was where reality hit for me.'

'Courtland Road?'

'It's where you go for local training.' A thought cut into sombre reflections and he flashed her a smile. 'It's on Orchard Park.'

She smiled back recognition of a shared experience.

'You do two-week stints in between all the other stuff. Physicals, law study, out on the beat, all that.' He paused as the traffic congealed round a tractor and trailer. 'There was only one woman in the group I was with out of a couple of dozen. We were a good way into it. Six months at least.' The tractor pulled over and they streamed past with the rest of the cars. 'One of the cases she'd been on had blown up and she was called out.'

'Called out?'

'Called out of the room. You all sit round in this big room. A couple of the guys made some stupid comments. 1970s stuff about the way she looked. All she was doing was walking out of the room, for God's sake, but they made it into a big deal. You could see it got to her. I thought they'd get a real slap down from the guy in charge, but he joined in. It kind of hit me in a way … I don't know, hard to describe. Almost like they'd punched the guts out of my childhood dream. I know it was silly, but it was the first time I'd really stood back and thought, hang about, is this really what I want to do? What if I've spent my whole life blinkered on this one thing and it isn't what I wanted it to be.' He gave a hollow laugh. 'I got over it, but it bugged me. It still bugs me.'

'And it's worse here than other places?'

He shrugged. 'I'm pretty sure there's better forces. We had to liaise with West Mids not so long ago. They were a joke at one time, but they've cleaned up their act. At least that's how it seemed. She left, the woman who was at Courtland Road with me.'

'Jennifer Flanagan seems fine with it all.'

'Yeah, if you're a woman like Jen you can hack it. She doesn't let anyone get to her.'

This conversational detour had run its course, Annie decided, as a chalk-board sign outside a pub – *Happy Hour* – focused her thoughts. 'Scott, you know the guy who fell off the house, Terry Martin? How did he climb up there? His blood alcohol was through the roof.'

'How do you know that?'

'Why shouldn't I know it? Is it classified?'

A look of annoyance briefly clouded his features and he shrugged. 'If you'd seen the drink-drive cases I've seen, you wouldn't bother to ask. People do incredible things, then they just flop down unconscious. Or dead in his case.'

'But as drunk as that? Didn't anyone think it was odd?'

'It explained why he was clumsy enough to fall.'

Annie opened her mouth to respond, but was cut short by a muffled ring from her bag.

'Sorry,' she murmured, pulling out the phone and glancing at a number she didn't recognize. 'Annie Raymond.'

A gruff voice spoke from the phone. 'You're supposed to call me.'

The boy. She felt irritation tense her lips. 'Yeah and I might when I'm ready.'

'Yeah, but I need you to do something.'

'You don't lack nerve, I'll give you that. What is it?'

'You've gotta meet me. An' I'll show you.'

Annie toyed with calling him Maz. That would shock him. 'Actually, I haven't *got to* do anything. Tell me what you want and I'll decide.'

'Nah, listen. You gotta come and meet me.'

Annie glanced at Scott. 'I might call you back, but I'm not talking to you now. I'm with someone.'

'Who?' Wary now.

'The police.'

'Uh … See you then.' Annie laughed at the alacrity with which he ended the call.

By reminding her of Orchard Park, she found the boy had crystallized something in her mind. Pat had said, you're allowed weekends, but she would go back to Orchard Park tonight. Not by taxi. Just quietly in Pat's car and wait to see who turned up on Saturday nights. The alternative of a few extra hours' sleep was attractive, but she wanted the full picture. Details mattered.

Scott pulled off the road and into the car-park of a small pub. 'We can get something to eat here. I wanted to take you further out really but …' He glanced at his watch. 'I can't be late back tonight. This bloody job. It is what I want to do but it plays havoc with any sort of social life.'

Annie smiled and put her hand on his arm. 'That's fine, don't worry. I have to go out on a case later, too.'

She was glad he wasn't too pushy. She didn't want to be rushed. There was a frisson to being in his presence and she found herself looking forward to seeing him, but underneath that there was unease because she still wasn't sure whether she liked him.

Annie woke the next morning far too early. It had been late when she came in after sitting yawning outside Mrs Earle's block until the white van appeared, a minute or two late, and disgorged three men. Her theory strengthened with every visit. Two men on dealing nights, three every other. But not the same third man. Who were they? Why did she think she'd seen them before? The man last night had been in shadow from van to entranceway. She hadn't had a good look. If she had, maybe she'd have found him a complete stranger.

She'd planned a lie-in but once she'd woken, she knew sleep wouldn't return. The boy had demanded a call. Odds on, he'd be dead to the world somewhere, but she said she'd call him and it would serve him right to be roused at this hour.

The phone rang for a long time before a croaky and befuddled voice said, 'Yeah?'

Annie smiled. 'Hi,' she said brightly. 'I said I'd ring back. So what's it all about?'

She expected curses, but after a moment's mumbling, he got his act together. 'You're that Annie from the investigation place, right?'

'Yes, and you're Maz, aren't you? What do you want?'

A small gasp of surprise confirmed her guess. Then his words came quickly, his tone anxious. 'It's about that guy, Terry. That Terry Martin. You'll meet me, won't you? Look, they can't stick him for it now, can they?'

'Can't stick him for what?'

'They can't stick him for doing in that Balham guy.'

It interested her that rumour stayed with the original theory that Terry Martin had murdered Edward Balham despite lack of official word about the body. She'd thought the silence might have got the grapevine working overtime with new theories. It hadn't even leaked that it had been a woman's body.

'It weren't nowt to do with me,' Maz went on. Then, as a begrudged concession, 'And it weren't nowt to do with them either.'

'Who's them?'

'Mally and them. I mean they're not going to pin it on them, are they? Posh kids like that. But it weren't nowt to do with them anyway.'

'And what was it to do with you?'

'Nowt. That's what I'm telling you. But they can't stick it on Terry no more, can they? And you've to stop them stitching me up.'

'If Terry Martin's guilty, there's no reason at all they shouldn't … uh … stick it on him.'

'Yeah, but they like to get someone in what they can knock about a bit. You can't have no fun with a dead guy. She were right mad at you for taking her back to her grandad's but she said you listened. The others said you listened too. I need someone what'll listen.'

Annie considered this. Maz was worried probably for some spurious reason, but the three girls had vouched for her as someone to trust, so he wanted her to have his side of whatever it was. It all sounded like nebulous fears, but there was one aspect that interested her. What did Maz know about Terry Martin?

'So will you meet me?' he asked.

Instinct told Annie she needed to grill him face to face, but she wanted it to be on her terms not his. When she hesitated, he went on, 'I can easy get a car and come to you. You don't have to go to no trouble.'

She didn't doubt that. 'Well, just hold on a bit. We'll talk about that in a minute. What is it you need to show me?'

'I can't say. But I'll show you. See, I know I done wrong when I got it for them, but I didn't do no murder and I'm not having them stick it on me.'

Maz was at the edge of agreeing to admit to a lesser crime because he'd been scared witless to find himself close to a murder. It was so clearly against his nature – and probably nurture – to admit to anything that Annie found herself with a sliver of something close to respect for him for doing it. Then she remembered Bill Martin outside the church in Withernsea and she pulled herself up. OK, she thought, let's hear you show you're a better person than the crass git who disrupted a funeral.

'Tell me about Terry Martin.'

Maz told her he and Terry Martin had been 'mates'. Terry had 'done stuff' for him. He'd been to the Martins' house in Withernsea. It became clear Terry had used Maz the same way he'd tried to use the girls in Milesthorpe. Maz, far more streetwise, probably managed to squeeze regular money out of Terry with a steady supply of borderline useful information.

He hadn't taken Mally to the funeral. 'She went with someone's grandad. I weren't going to go in. I don't go with all that churchy stuff – load of cobblers. Mind, Terry'd started hanging about the church in Milesthorpe. I dunno what that were about. I played some of his music, special. That's why I went.'

Annie found her preconceptions in a heap on the floor. Was this for real? Was it some clever double-bluff to get her on side? He sounded sincere. Had Bill Martin been right, the sudden disruption had been a mark of respect to his son? She could see Maz in a completely different light if he'd gone to Terry Martin's funeral specially to play some of Terry's favourite music. Hardly a tactful tribute the way he'd done it, but it showed him from a different angle.

When he went on to tell her about hearing from Martha Martin that she wanted her son's death investigated, he had a bigger surprise for her.

'It were me what give her Pat Thompson's advert. I knew she'd come a cropper when Sleeman's mate legged her down the stairs, so I thought she wouldn't do no damage. I didn't know what had happened to Terry. And I weren't planning on taking no blame for it. Didn't know she'd send you. Listen, I've told you everything … nearly. Will you meet up? I'm not taking the rap for this.'

Annie didn't intend giving him notice so he had time to plan an ambush. 'Well, I'll have to think about it—'

She stopped. The far door had opened and Pat hobbled in. Annie snatched the phone from her ear and pressed it into her shoulder, irrationally sure for a second that Pat had overheard what Maz said about Vince.

Pat's look held the annoyance of someone pulled from sleep too early. She held her own phone between thumb and forefinger. 'It's your faithful plod,' she said. 'He tried your phone, says it's engaged. He insists it won't wait.'

What on earth? Annie reached for the handset Pat held towards her. 'Scott?'

'Annie? Listen, I didn't want you to hear this from anyone else. Charles Tremlow's dead. He's topped himself.'

CHAPTER 18

ANNIE GASPED IN a breath, confusion overwhelming her. A picture slammed on to her consciousness. Tremlow broken, slumped on his kitchen table. Tremlow dead?

Had he done it because of her?

'Why, Scott? How? Tell me what happened.'

'I can't, Annie. I don't know what happened. No one knows yet. I shouldn't be ringing you, but I didn't want you hearing it from anyone else. I don't know what time I'll get away. There's a stack of loose ends here.'

'Are you at his house?'

'No.' She felt the extra layer of worry in his tone. 'Annie, you mustn't come out here. I shouldn't be telling you this.'

'I won't. I won't. I just need to know. Oh my God!'

'Listen, Jen should be off duty in an hour. They've no reason to keep her on. Give her a ring. She'll have got to hear about it by then; she'll know whatever there is to know. I have to go.'

Annie didn't think to say thank you until his voice had gone. She stared at the silent handset, watched as Pat reached out to take it back. A hollow carved itself out inside her. She felt stunned. A faint chirrup from the phone still pressed to her shoulder roused her. She remembered Maz.

'Uh huh?'

She heard his desperation in a detached way, heard him promise her information, frantic to hold her. She heard herself say yes to a meeting, but knew it was only to get him off the line. He knew it too. She clicked the phone off to the sounds of him trying to pin her down to a time.

A jolt ran up her spine as she sat down hard on the settee. She heard clumping footsteps and the clink of china on the tiled surface of the low table. The tang of coffee snaked around her.

'Here.' Pat's voice was curt. 'Drink that. Tell me about it later.'

Before Annie could stammer out a word of thanks Pat had hobbled back to the bedroom.

Why had he done it? She, Annie, had killed him. She knew it. He couldn't stand the humiliation of her having broken him. Yet she still didn't understand.

His story had been confused but hadn't had that much of a lie in it. She couldn't begin to get inside his mind. She thought of the others – Heather Becke, Doris Kitson, the colonel, Tina Hain, the three girls. Reading them was a piece of cake; emotion lay naked on their faces. But Tremlow might as well have been an alien.

One hour. Jennifer wouldn't be off duty for another hour. She cupped both hands round the hot drink warming herself against a sudden chill.

Her phone lay on the table top. Must remember to charge it later. Would she really go to meet Maz? Thoughts paraded automatically as she grabbed at anything to keep Scott's call out of the forefront of her mind. Why hadn't Maz called straight back? Was he wise enough on some level to know it would do no good? It gave her a glimmer again of something below the brittle arrogant surface. Did he have anything for her? Was it a trap where she'd find herself surrounded by grinning faces crowing over her stupidity? What was the worst he could do? He was no killer, just an amateur car thief, a boy who wanted to impress and who'd found the perfect foils in Mally, Laura and Kay.

The next sixty minutes crawled by until time slowed to a stop. Annie closed her eyes and counted off the final 300 seconds because they wouldn't leak away by themselves.

Jennifer answered on the third ring. 'Oh, Annie … Hello?'

Annie felt her heart thud dully at the sound of Jennifer's voice. The surprised tone told her Scott hadn't been in touch and she wasn't expecting a call. It seemed presumptuous to expect Jennifer to meet her, to talk police business, without Scott having paved the way.

'I wondered if you'd like to come out for a coffee. It's not often we're both off-duty at the same time.' She tried to keep her tone bright, as though the suggestion were the most normal thing in the world.

'That's a kind thought, Annie, uh … Actually, I'd planned on … Still, I suppose … Yes, why not? Thanks.'

Well might Jennifer sound surprised. The request was without precedent. And she mustn't make Jennifer feel ambushed once they were together, so she added, 'Sad about poor Charles Tremlow, isn't it?'

'The guy from Milesthorpe? Why, what's happened?'

Annie's heart dropped like a heavy rock in still water. Not only had Scott not been in touch, Jennifer didn't even know about it. Their meeting became an unnecessary waste of time. She cast about for a way to rescind the invitation Jennifer hadn't wanted to accept. There wasn't one.

Annie sat in Starbucks near the station hugging a cup of coffee not half so fierce as Pat's brew. Jennifer arrived ten minutes later. It was the first time since Terry Martin's funeral Annie had seen her in civvies. Jennifer wore her hair loose. It straggled over the shoulders of a flowery blouse. The untidiness and fussy material sat awkwardly with Jennifer's stately form; the ill-matched skirt at just the length to suggest dowdiness rather than make the most of her long legs. But for all her awkward manner Annie could see Jennifer was comfortable in her own skin. Maybe that was the clue to Scott's comment about 'women like Jen'.

Jennifer's demeanour was more animated than Annie expected after the phone call. As she approached the table, she looked round to make sure they weren't overheard, and said, 'I made enquiries about Charles Tremlow after what you said. Yes, isn't it awful? Have you any idea why he did it?'

I know why he did it. 'Uh ... no. Let me get you a drink. Coffee?'

When she sat down again, Annie asked, 'Where did they find him?'

'In his car on the cliff road outside Milesthorpe. I wonder what drove him to that?'

Annie swallowed hard. *It was me. I did it.* 'Is it definite that it's suicide?'

'Oh yes, I think so. Why?'

'I just wondered. You hear of these things. Odd sorts of deaths that turn out to be accidents.' Annie felt compelled to press the point, to find a way out of the guilt.

Jennifer gave her a hard look. 'Not in this case. Hosepipe from the exhaust. There'll have to be a post-mortem and everything. Why are you so keen it shouldn't be suicide?'

Because if it is, I did it. 'I just hate to think of anyone in that much despair, and he didn't seem like someone who'd do that.'

'What do people who do that seem like? You never know with people. There's so much hidden beneath the surface.'

So much hidden ... The phrase sent a chill down Annie's spine. 'But could he have been killed by whoever killed the woman in the building on the cliff?'

That hard look again. 'No. No, definitely not.'

'How can you be so certain?'

'I can't say much but we know what happened there ... We know who did it. We need to confirm it, that's all.'

'But there's been no fuss. There's a killer loose.'

'No, there isn't,' said Jennifer. 'The person responsible is dead. Look, you mustn't say anything, not yet. It's just that there's been a problem getting a definite ID. Trying to trace family, all that ...'

Jennifer's voice tailed off. Trying to trace family. The words stopped Annie for a moment. It seemed a long time since she'd given the dead woman any thought in terms of her being a person with family. There might be parents, children, a husband. What did you say to people? Your daughter ... your wife ... her body lay hidden for weeks ... when we found her she was half rotted.

She sat up suddenly. What did Jennifer mean, the killer was already dead? 'But Jennifer, you can't mean Terry Martin did it? He couldn't have. He—'

'I can't tell you anything else, Annie!' Jennifer's words cut through with enough authority to silence her.

There was an awkward pause, then a phone rang. They both reached for their bags, but it was Jennifer's handset that flashed an incoming call.

Annie chewed on what Jennifer had let slip. Terry Martin? No, it couldn't have been. Terry Martin chased shadows. He didn't strangle women. The answer was in her head. She needed time to calm down and think it through rationally. She and Pat would suss it out between them when she got back.

Annie became aware that Jennifer's gaze was on her as she finished her call. She looked up into a steady stare that stood the hairs on her arms to attention.

'One of my colleagues said he'd keep me posted on any news.'

'And?'

'They've found a note. Charles Tremlow left a note.'

Emotion flooded Annie like fallout from an explosion. Unstoppable. Culpability, like shrapnel, flew out from the words Tremlow left behind. 'What did he say?' It was a whisper.

'Said he couldn't live with it.'

What was Jennifer saying? Why was her voice so flat and calm? Why didn't she come right out and accuse Annie of pushing an old man over the edge.

'It's Terry Martin,' Jennifer said. 'Tremlow's confessed to killing Terry Martin.'

CHAPTER 19

ANNIE WATCHED HERSELF twist the key in the lock of the apartment, click down the handle and push open the door. Stunned disbelief fought guilty relief for dominance. If it were true that Tremlow had killed Terry Martin then his suicide wasn't her fault.

Pat, in the middle of an enormous yawn, looked up as she entered and further distorted her face by way of greeting. She let the full extravagance of the yawn take its course then said, 'OK, let's have it. What did lover boy want? Storm in a teacup or something important?' Before Annie could answer, Pat shot her a piercing look and added, 'It doesn't look like quite the calamity it was this morning.'

'Well, I suppose …' Pat was right, the guilt had lifted. It didn't feel half so bad. 'In one way, it's worse.'

Annie gave Pat a brief summary of events, ending with the call Jennifer received while they were together. 'He killed Terry Martin,' she finished. 'He confessed to it in his suicide note.'

Pat's eyebrows rose in surprise. 'Christ, there's a turn up. What did the note say exactly?'

'I don't know. Jennifer didn't say.'

'So there was something in your theory, after all.'

Not much, thought Annie. She hadn't come close to guessing Tremlow's secret. The killer he'd protected was himself. She'd majored on mystery men on the scaffolding tower, the drama queen leaning towards the unnecessarily dramatic as usual.

'I mean it, Annie,' Pat said. 'Something got at you; told you it wasn't as straightforward as it looked. You've got the right instinct. Don't discount it.'

Annie looked up through the window out across the estuary, a panorama on a world that bustled on unmoved by Tremlow's death; unaware he'd ever lived.

'The Martins'll have to be told,' she said.

Pat nodded.

'But told what exactly, and when and who by? Should I go out there now before the police get there?'

'You could, but I'd advise you to wait, see if you can find out more. They'll want to know how it happened, what the note said. If the police get there first, it won't do any harm.'

Pat hadn't told her what to do, she'd advised her. This was her case now; her decisions to make. She thought she'd already had that authority and now recognized she hadn't been ready for it. The weight sat heavy on her shoulders, but didn't crush her. 'They'll have to reopen the enquiry into Terry's death, won't they?'

'Yeah, might disrupt your social life a bit, but it shouldn't be too resource-hungry with the killer off the books.'

Annie acknowledged the comment with a small curl of her lip. 'It was my fault Tremlow died, you know. If I hadn't pushed him the way I did, he wouldn't have done it.'

'Don't get hung up on if-onlys, Annie. They never brought anyone back to life. What was that about the first murder, about that killer being dead too? They can't have meant Terry Martin did it, can they?'

'That was my first thought, but it wasn't him. I know exactly who it was. Terry knew too. It was Edward Balham, the missing farmer. I don't know how they know it's him, or how they know he's dead, but I'm sure that's who Jennifer meant.'

'Yes, I think you're right. That copper saw something on the film the first time we ran it for him. Maybe Balham's been on their books for a while. And who knows what they found when they searched the site. Balham probably topped himself too.'

'Why the secrecy?'

'I suppose they want to identify the poor cow they found up there. And Balham could have thrown himself off the cliff. It can take time for a body to wash ashore.'

'That's why there was no big murder enquiry then. They knew right from the start the killer was dead.' She wished Scott would trust her with this sort of stuff. After all, she hadn't broken any of his confidences.

'Poor buggers. They've not only got Tremlow on their hands, they've an unidentified murder victim, a family to trace and another missing body. And not one of them young or glamorous enough to attract extra resources. It always makes me glad to be this side of the line when things like this happen.'

Me too, thought Annie. Not that beggars could be choosers in her own position, but at least she had the perception of choice. Scott and Jennifer had to do anything and everything they were ordered to do.

Memory walked her back along the paths and pastures of Milesthorpe, from the track behind the houses where the remnants of a sea breeze reached a couple of miles inland, to the fierce gale at the top of the crumbling clay cliff. Tremlow had chosen to die up there just a spit from the first murder scene. Did Tremlow know what Balham had done? Had Terry Martin gone round there to confront him? It was all conjecture.

'Before I go out to see the Martins,' she said. 'I'd like to see if I can get a look at Tremlow's suicide note.'

'You're going to try sweet-talking the faithful plod?'

'Well …' Annie bridled at the way Pat voiced what was in her mind. 'I know he was involved when Tremlow was found, and unless anything else has happened, he should be off duty this afternoon.'

'You want me out of the way, do you?'

'No, no. We'll go out.' Annie held up her hand. She hadn't meant that at all. She'd thought vaguely in terms of another walk by the river.

Pat looked up to a corner of the room, gaze unfocused, then said, 'I need to have a word with Babs about Orchard Park; that flat number you gave me. I'll give her a ring. She can take me round to her place. He's more likely to come up with the goods if you're on your own.' She paused and then ended on a speculative note, 'You might have seen the last of the Earle case when Babs and I have done. Now get on the phone and get lover boy round.'

Annie wanted to say, don't solve it without me. I want to be in on the end of it, but closed her mouth, the words unsaid. It was Pat's call. She could only hope to get the full story later. She turned to her phone and clicked out a text to Scott.

Can u come 2 flat when u finish? Q to ask u.

While she interrogated Scott about Tremlow, Pat would get together with Barbara over that address at the top of the block. She remembered Maz's words. *… when Sleeman's mate legged her down the stairs …* and how Vince had brought news about the job being cancelled. Between them she and Pat had reignited it behind his back. Annie had a feeling it was coming full circle and about to join up with Vince again.

*

By the afternoon, the apartment was warm, comfortable and empty. Annie tried to quieten a flutter in her stomach. She told herself it wasn't the thought of seeing Scott, of spending time with him here with the place to themselves that unsettled her. It was the idea of trying to trick him into giving her what she wanted about Tremlow's suicide note if he wouldn't discuss it with her. She wasn't sure she could do it.

When the door buzzer sounded, she took in several deep, measured breaths and didn't hurry on her way to let him in.

'Hi, thanks for coming. Sit down. What d'you want to drink? Tea? Coffee?'

He settled for a soft drink. 'It's been a hot day. It's not pleasant dealing with a body in this heat.' He sat back in the chair and looked around the room. 'Nice place this. I didn't really notice before.'

'It wasn't the sort of visit where you take note of the fittings.'

'What was it you wanted to ask me?'

'It's about Charles Tremlow. I'm going to have to talk to Terry Martin's parents. I want to be a position to answer their questions if I can, so really I just wanted to know what he'd said.'

'In the note, you mean?' Scott shrugged. 'He didn't give us much really.'

Annie caught him in a brief glance towards his jacket where it lay over the back of the settee. Her mind raced over possible scenarios that could have brought him here with the note still in his possession. Maybe his partner dropped him off but left him with the evidence to deliver later. He'd taken time out to pick up his own car on the way but not stopped for long enough to change out of anything but the more overt elements of his uniform. At any rate she hoped those were uniform trousers. She didn't want him to have quite such bad taste in clothes. She waited for him to elaborate, but he just said, 'Did you get in touch with Jen?'

'Yes, we had coffee, but she didn't know about it till I told her. So how did it happen? Did Terry confront Tremlow about the body on the cliff?'

Terry Martin head to head with Charles Tremlow? It was hard to see Tremlow coming out best in a fight against anyone, although Terry had been very drunk. Annie saw Scott shrug as he weighed up what he should and shouldn't say. It annoyed her. Hadn't she been open with him about the things she'd found?

'We only have the note. It was short. It wasn't an essay.'

'What did it say exactly?'

'I can't tell you.'

Annie fought to hold on to a relaxed smile. Couldn't tell her! This was too much. She wouldn't let it show. She intended getting her hands on it and knew just how. She led the conversation away from the note.

'So it was the car exhaust thing, was it? Why did he go up on to the cliff?'

'Less chance of anyone finding him in time, I suppose. Poor old sod. He was a bit of a prat but harmless.'

Annie laughed her disbelief. 'Harmless? I thought he'd confessed to a pretty gruesome murder.'

'He did, but the way he told it, it could have been an accident. He just hit out. Didn't realize what he'd done.'

So the note had given some detail. She wondered if she could spin the conversation out enough to tease the morsels from him bit by bit. She tried to picture what he described. 'I can't imagine a punch from Tremlow laying out a rabbit, let alone a full grown person.'

'No, he hit out with a stick. He said where he'd hidden it and it looks like it's for real. There's congealed blood on it. It's in the lab now.'

'Where had he stashed it?'

He was silent for a moment. Weighing up whether or not he's *allowed* to tell me, Annie thought angrily, but held on to her smile. Maybe the smile did the trick. Maybe the information came under the doesn't-matter-who-knows category.

'In his loft,' he told her.

'But—' Annie stopped. She'd been about to blurt out that it couldn't have been. She'd stood beneath that loft access. 'Uh … When did he put it there?'

'Who knows? Same night I suppose.'

She remembered the trapdoor. It hadn't been touched in months. The image was clear in her mind. 'I don't think he could have done.' She gave him a summary of how they'd called round; how she'd searched the house. 'Not exactly searched,' she amended. 'I was just checking he was OK. The loft access caught my eye. I remember noticing it hadn't been opened in ages.'

'I don't know that we've a reported sighting after that. You might have been the last person to see him.'

'But we didn't see him.'

Scott's face relaxed into a smile. 'We've really not looked into it yet beyond a brief chat with a couple of neighbours.'

Annie smiled back. She didn't suppose resources would stretch too far for Tremlow, not with an unidentified murder victim and Balham still not found, dead or alive.

'The loft thing's useful,' he went on. 'He didn't say when he'd stashed it.'

He'd relaxed so much, she felt emboldened to say, 'But you can't show me the note?'

'Sorry, no.'

Bastard.

She smiled extra sweetly and glanced at her watch. 'Not to worry. Listen, I'm expecting Pat back any minute with that sister of hers.' Her words brought a certain immobility to his expression. The two sisters were a double act that didn't make for relaxing company. 'They won't stay long.

Let's go through to my room. We can keep out of their way. D'you fancy a beer?'

Annie had known from first setting foot in it that her room was tiny, but it wasn't until she led Scott in and closed the door, she realized just how small it was. There was no chair, no room for one, to invite him to sit on. They both had to sit on the bed.

This was appalling, their sudden proximity, what he must make of it? She'd meant him to make assumptions about this invitation into her room, but the way the walls pressed in made the enticement all too blatant.

She'd intended to settle him comfortably with his beer, then slip out of the room briefly on some excuse. I'll just nip and get my bag … She only needed seconds. She could work through his pockets quickly, grab a look at the note. One rapid skim read would lodge it in her head. But they weren't settled comfortably. He hadn't taken the ring pull from his beer. The tension was palpable. She scrabbled desperately for something to say, something that would get a conversation going, allow the stress to ease.

'So it's definitely suicide?' She wasn't in any doubt about the answer, but the question was there in her head. It was the one she'd asked Jennifer.

'I can't see the coroner coming up with anything else. Annie…?'

His answer was hurried, distracted. She felt the change of direction as he spoke her name.

'Jennifer told me it couldn't have been anything to do with the woman in the building,' she gabbled out, speaking across him. 'But could it? How sure can you be?'

'Very sure.' He spoke calmly, damn him, and with an undercurrent of amusement.

She busied herself with the ring-pull in her beer can, hoped he'd follow her lead and open his. Her mind blanked. There had to be more to say about the case. She concentrated on making space on the tiny bedside cupboard. 'The killer was Edward Balham, wasn't it?' She shot the question almost at random, her nervousness showing in more hostile tones than she'd intended. 'Um … I mean the woman on the cliff.'

'Annie …'

'OK, OK, you don't have to say anything. I know it's under wraps till you get a positive ID.'

This would be so much easier if she didn't fancy him; if she hadn't fancied him from the first time she'd looked at the grim expression on his face and known how a smile would light him up. Motives sat uneasily together. The flimsy excuse of being out of Pat's way; the obvious intention of inviting him into her bed; and the real reason of separating him from his jacket and Tremlow's note.

'D'you think Tremlow knew what Balham had done?' She sought to stay in the safer refuge of messy deaths. 'I mean, could that have been what Terry confronted him about that night?'

'Not that I know of. He wrote a suicide note, not a life story.'

'I wonder how he nerved himself up to it. He seemed so fearful.'

'No mystery there. He was drunk. If he'd survived, he'd be facing a drink-drive charge. He must have been almost as drunk as Terry Martin.'

Annie remembered the comment – *I don't believe in drink* – with which Tremlow had accepted the colonel's offer of a nip of whisky. *Oh no, he wouldn't have been drunk* – Doris Kitson about Terry Martin.

Aware that Scott had bent towards the floor to put his beer down, Annie glanced across wanting to read his expression while he wasn't watching her. But as though he'd guessed what she'd do, she found his face turned towards her, a smile meeting her gaze. No mistaking the look he gave her. She looked down, feigned interest in a non-existent stain on her jeans, as she felt her heart pound. This wasn't the way she'd planned things.

'Uh … drunk, was he? I didn't get the impression he was much of a drinker usually, so—'

'Annie?'

He'd moved closer to her. She couldn't look up. 'Uh huh?'

'This is a pretty small room, isn't it?'

'Yes, but …'

'How about we leave the population of Milesthorpe outside just for now?'

He reached across her and lifted her beer can out of her grasp. She watched his hand, fingers long and slender, as it placed the can into the space she'd so painstakingly cleared on the bedside table.

The move brought his body close to hers. She gulped and felt a shiver run down her insides. Her psyche played traitor, told her it didn't matter about finding out whether she liked him or not. She wanted him more than the note now. When his hand touched her face to move it round to his, she didn't resist, let him take control. He held still for a moment, their faces almost touching, so close his features blurred. He kissed her softly until she began to kiss him back and then he pulled her close as her hands went to his head to drag him into her, to devour him as avidly as he devoured her.

Annie surfaced from a deep sleep. A feeling of wellbeing enveloped her. Her face formed itself into a smile as she turned her head. Scott lay beside her, his head resting back into the pillow, his mouth slightly open as he snored gently. He must have been tired enough before she'd enticed him through here. He lay on his back, out for the count, and looked as though he'd sleep for hours yet. She flexed her fingers wanting to reach over and run the back of her hand gently down the side of his face as he slept. But she mustn't risk waking him. This was her opportunity to find out what Tremlow had said about Terry Martin.

Getting out of bed without waking him wasn't a problem. He'd taken up the centre of the mattress and left her barely clinging to the edge. One outflung arm was across her. She eased herself sideways from under it and slid to the floor where she gathered up her clothes and crept out.

With her hand on the door to the living room she was met with a sudden vision of Pat and Barbara walking in to find her naked rifling through the pockets of someone else's coat. Scott slipped into the image, appearing half-dressed and yawning. Pat would laugh, but the thought of Barbara's face made Annie stop to pull on her clothes and straighten them down.

She'd slept deeply but not for long, and was confident Scott wouldn't wake for ages. His jacket lay over the back of the settee. Her hands ran themselves quickly through the outer pockets and found nothing of significance. She reached inside and felt her eyebrows rise at the number of inner pockets that met her touch. How many pockets did a person need for heaven's sake! Zips, Velcro, buttons.

It was the rip of the Velcro that melded into the click of a door.

Annie's head shot up expecting to see Barbara, but the door to the hallway remained shut. Oh no! She felt the flush of guilt rush up her neck and face as she turned.

Scott stood behind her, his expression hard. Not half-dressed as in her mental image, she noted inconsequentially, but fully dressed. He even had his shoes on. She knew he'd come through that door with a smile on his face, but the sight of her with his jacket had obliterated it and left only amazement and anger.

'What the fuck are you doing?'

Even if she could have controlled her expression, she couldn't pretend she'd been doing anything other than going through his pockets.

'Well, I have to go and face the Martins with all this. I need to know what happened.' She tried attack as a belated form of defence.

His expression didn't soften. It grew an air of incredulity and worse, a measure of distaste as he stared at her. 'What are you talking about?'

'Why couldn't you have just shown me the note? He said something about those two missing days, didn't he? I need to know. His mother needs to know.'

'The note?' He looked blank for a moment. 'You mean the old guy's suicide note? I don't have it.'

'You don't...? But when I asked about it you looked at your jacket.'

'Oh, I looked at my jacket, did I?' She saw cold anger suffuse him as his voice rose. 'A single look and the great detective surmises that I'm with-holding evidence from her. Bloody drama queen! And what did you surmise from the way I looked at *you*? No need to answer that one, is there? Is that how you get all your evidence?'

'No, it wasn't like that ...' She stopped, because he was right. It had been like that, but not the way he implied.

He marched across towards her and, with a scything sweep of his arm, snatched the jacket from her hands as he headed for the outer door.

As she opened her mouth to try to speak, he cut across her. 'I heard the note read out, OK? I never even got to hold it.'

'You didn't...?'

In the open doorway to the hall, he turned and looked her up and down. His words came in measured tones. 'There was nothing about Martin's missing two days. He heard him out there, heard him come down from the scaffolding platform. Sounds like he didn't fall, he jumped, or something fell from the platform. Tremlow grabbed the stick and went out in a panic. Hit out and found he'd killed the guy. And before you ask, it's not clear whether he pushed the body into the hole or if it just fell. Whatever he hit his head on down there disguised the blow from the stick. If he'd burnt it, no one would ever have known.'

Stunned at his open contempt, she felt his words carve out a void inside her. He stared at her hard as though waiting for her to speak. No words would come.

'That's what you wanted, isn't it? Will it do?'

'Will it...?'

'Well, I've no cash on me.' He spun on his heel and strode out.

It took Annie a second to understand, then she hurled herself after him into the hallway and shrieked. 'Fuck off!' at the door as it slammed behind him.

Tears of anger and humiliation stung the backs of her eyes. The bastard! She'd show him. Should have stuck with her instinct. So much for not being sure if she liked him or not. She was sure now. And the bastard had called her a drama queen! She didn't care what he thought of her. She really didn't. The only emotion he spawned within her now was fury.

Tremlow's note. She had what she needed. Nothing else mattered.

She pictured Scott's smile, the way he looked at her when he relaxed. Deep inside there was a nub of hurt that wouldn't harden into anger.

CHAPTER 20

AFTER THE ECHO of the door slamming and the stomping footsteps receded, Annie was left in a silent bubble that was the empty apartment. She turned slowly, let her gaze move from the still of the room to the expanse of water outside.

Pat and Barbara would be home soon. She tried to rehearse the conversation. Pat was bound to ask, did you get lover boy to cough up the goods, or something like that.

Her shoulders straightened. She had the information and would meet Pat's eye unflinchingly. 'Oh yes, I know what was in the note ...' Well, perhaps she wouldn't meet her eye; maybe she would busy herself in the file, pretend to be distracted as she answered. 'Uh ... what's that? Oh, Tremlow's note? Yeah, sure, I've got what I need on that ...' She tried to talk herself through a scenario where she answered Pat without embarrassment flooding her until she glowed like a beacon; where there was even a slim likelihood of Pat failing to notice something was wrong. No chance. Not now, not so soon after Scott had walked out like that, the bastard!

She had to get out, to get something else in between now and the inevitable discussion with Pat to blunt the edge of what had happened with Scott.

So much for her useful contacts. Scott wouldn't speak to her again and nor would Jennifer once she'd heard Scott's side. One week she'd been here: she told herself the next five couldn't pass quickly enough.

It was with a moment's misgiving that she grabbed her phone. She ought to leave it on charge. A glance at the screen decided her it would last out. Pat might want to ring her and she wouldn't mind having the initial conversation about Tremlow's note by phone rather than face to face.

She ran down the stairs to the car, not able to relax until she was out on Hedon Road and beyond the risk of running into Pat and Barbara returning. As she drove along the dual-carriageway that swept her east out of Hull, her hands tapped impatiently on the wheel. This had become a familiar route, but today its 40 m.p.h. limit irritated her. She wanted to put her foot down, to increase the distance between her and that awful moment when Scott had walked in on her going through his pockets.

Small factories and business units hid the huge estuary behind a bleak industrial landscape. So much hidden ...

Salt End roundabout, with its forbidden exit road to the chemical works, slipped by. The limit dropped to 30 m.p.h., then rose again to 40. Stupid bloody road, twisting and turning through an endless parade of settlements. Thorngumbald melted into Camerton without a break. Trees, a vein that snaked through the built-up area, thinned to nothing. On and on. Keyingham, Ottringham. Anger rose, even against Tremlow. If he hadn't done this, she wouldn't have invited Scott round. Why had Tremlow done it? How dare Scott call her a drama queen! Where had Terry Martin disappeared for two and a bit days?

Signs she'd passed every time she came this way now jarred on her consciousness. *Sunk Island ... Fort Paull ...* Who had ever needed a fort out here? What use an island that had sunk? Even the landscape mocked her.

At last, a familiar white oblong sign appeared propped in the hedge. Its peremptory order, *Visit the Lighthouse*, signalled the Withernsea boundary and the end of her journey.

She should have waited for Pat to come home to tell her about Tremlow's note. It was too soon to come to the Martins with her fragments of information. As she pulled up outside the house, she wondered about setting off again and heading back to the city, but she saw a shadow move behind the heavy curtains. Martha had spotted her.

Both Bill and Martha met her in the hallway.

'There's been a development,' Annie said. 'I don't have all the details but I thought I'd let you know.'

'Come through and sit down, love.' Bill waved her towards the small sitting room.

She took her seat in Terry's chair and told them about Tremlow; how his body had been discovered that morning and how he'd left a note in which he'd confessed to killing Terry.

'But he's a church warden,' Bill said, bewildered.

Annie looked to where Martha sat at the end of the small settee, her face as still as though someone had pressed a pause button. It took only a second to realize why she couldn't read anything of Martha's feelings; Martha herself didn't know what she felt. It was one blow too many. In the turmoil of the day's events Annie had forgotten that Tremlow might not be a stranger to the Martins. The church was a tight network across the area.

'Did you know him well?' she asked.

Bill shook his head. 'I don't think we ever met him, did we, Martha?'

'And the other two who were there that night, Colonel Ludgrove and Doris Kitson, did you know them?'

'No, love. We never met any of them. We know of them, of course, through the church.'

Annie breathed an inner sigh of relief. She didn't analyse why it would be worse to have handed over this news if they knew their son's killer, but it would have been. She waited for the flood of questions. Why? How?

Bill grasped the arms of his chair and pulled himself to his feet. 'Tea'll be brewed by now.' He looked neither at Annie nor his wife as he spoke then clumped out of the room.

Annie saw that he wasn't going to ask anything she didn't volunteer. The structure of his life to date didn't allow it. Until this awful calamity, he'd swum with the tide, done as he was told and bowed to authority in whatever guise it came. Out of his depth now, he could only flounder along and accept whatever the tides washed over him.

Annie watched him leave the room. She wanted Martha to follow. They needed each other and they needed their own space without her sitting in the middle of it. She began to rise. 'I'll go now, but if you want—'

'Wait.' Martha's upraised hand stopped her. 'Did he … the man who did it … did he say where our Terry was on the Monday?'

'No,' said Annie. 'Just what happened on the Tuesday evening.'

'You say he left a letter?'

'A suicide note, yes.'

'Have you read what he wrote?'

'No, but I spoke to one of the policemen who was involved. I made sure I got everything from him.'

'Will we be able to see it?'

'I don't know. I expect the police will come here to tell you about it.' She saw Martha's lips purse. They'd had enough of officialdom on their doorstep. 'You should ask them. I might be able to get hold of it later. It depends who they release it to. I'll try.' As she spoke, Annie wondered who Tremlow had addressed his note to. Had he any family? She didn't think so. Maybe it wasn't addressed to anyone.

'What do you think?' Martha stared at her hard. 'Did he really kill our Terry?'

'Well, he said so ... it seems consistent with ... The police think ...' Annie floundered as Martha's words painted a picture in her mind of Tremlow hitting out in blind terror. She tried to imagine how it might have happened but a viable scenario wouldn't gel. And she still hated the feel of those two blank days.

'It's only just come to light,' she told Martha. 'I'll make more enquiries. I'll find out more about Mr Tremlow.'

Martha looked up at her, the expression in her eyes overshadowed by the heavy weight of defeat that the loss of her son had etched there, but something else too. Just for a second, the light of battle sparked. 'I want to know,' she said. 'I want to know where he was those two days.'

She feels it, too, thought Annie. Not an investigator's muscle in her body, but a mother's instinct has faced her the same way I'm looking. There's something wrong about all this. Very wrong.

She thought back to the last time she'd seen Tremlow and scoured her mind for a report from anyone of a positive sighting between then and his being found this morning. Someone must have seen him. Of course they must, she just didn't know about it.

Drunk like Terry and neither of them drinkers. Missing like Terry for just over two days. It was a good thing it was unequivocally suicide, because there was a limit to how high the coincidences could stack up before they began to fall down.

As Annie left the Martins', the breeze that stroked her face held the first chill of early evening. The street lay empty, but within a stone's throw the sea-front would still be packed. On impulse, she drove the short distance to the sea and parked by the high sea-wall.

She leant on to the wall, elbows on the rough stone surface, chin cupped in her hands. The North Sea spread in front of her, the sun glinting off incoming waves as they rushed the shore in small explosions of white frothy foam. Children raced about, their laughter and shrieks overlying the rhythmic swish and rush of the waves' ebb and flow.

Even here at the edge of the sea and with the first chill of evening in the air the day lay heavy as though the atmosphere was over-laden with the sun's heat. Annie looked up and saw clouds a long way off in a sky that had begun to boil. There'd be a storm in the next twenty-four hours.

The sea and sky with their direct link to the beginning of time put perspective on to her immediate worries. She might have stood there a long time soaking up the ambience of a summer's day winding down, but the familiar chirp of her phone cut in. She stood up straight and stretched her arms before pulling the mobile from her pocket and glancing at the screen. It was Pat, but that was fine. She was ready to talk now.

'Where are you?'

'Just outside the Martins' in Withernsea.' It was true to within a few hundred yards.

'Oh right, you've decided to go and see them. OK. You're coming back here though, aren't you, before you go on anywhere else?'

'That's what I had in mind. Why?'

'I just need a word, that's all. What time will you be back?'

Annie bit back a question, suddenly realizing what it was Pat wanted to tell her and knowing she didn't want to hear it. She glanced at the time, crossed her fingers and said, 'Not sure. I could be with the Martins for a couple of hours.'

Pat had been to see Barbara. They were to discuss Orchard Park. Pat had told her she might have seen the last of the Earle case. Annie knew she shouldn't do it, but she wanted one more trip to that tower block. She didn't want the case pulled from under her like this. And as long as Pat hadn't explicitly told her not to go there, what harm could it do to have one more look?

If Pat found out, Annie would say, I thought you meant me to come back when I'd finished work for the evening – you know, the Martins, Mrs Earle ...

The bumpy concrete of the tower-block's car-park bounced the car as Annie pulled in. It was packed. For the first time ever, she had to manoeuvre the vehicle to get into a space. She'd never seen it so full. Pat had drummed into her that she mustn't leave the car unattended here at night, but it was barely evening and there would be safety in the number of vehicles here just now. Her watch showed just after seven o'clock and she'd won herself two extra hours when Pat thought she was in Withernsea, but she wondered if there was anything useful she could do with them. What she needed was to swap her early evening hours for later ones, but could think of no means to make the trade.

A sudden rapping on the window inches from her face made her start up in alarm. Scott!

The face staring back into hers flinched at the hard glare she gave it. Of course it wasn't Scott. What had made her think it? It was more obvious than that. The joy-rider, Maz. He'd been frantic to talk to her when she'd cut him off. In all that had happened since, she'd forgotten him, but he hadn't forgotten her. Desperation had brought him within arm's length. She lowered the side window a short way.

'They won't be 'ere tonight,' he said. 'It's Sunday. They don't do Sundays.'

She held her expression steady – neither friendly, nor threatening. How did he know who she came here to watch? How come he knew so much about her? Some of it could have come from the girls in Milesthorpe but not all.

Maybe this wouldn't be a wasted journey after all. She'd hear him out but anything she gave him would come at a high price and he'd pay her in advance.

As she climbed out of the car, he took a step back, on guard for attack. She stood with one hand on the top of the open door and looked towards the tower block, first the entrance then right up to the high roof that stood out against the veins of dusk across the sky. She sensed his hesitation. The direction of her stare wasn't lost on him.

'You want something from me,' she said, not looking at him. 'Then you'd better have something good to offer in return.'

'There's summat I need you to keep safe.'

'What is it? And what do I get for it?'

'Say you'll keep it and not say owt, and then I'll tell you.'

'What's in it for me?'

He hesitated. 'I'll show you the setup. Up there. I've got keys. No one comes on Sunday. Is that why you're here?'

This was beyond what she'd expected. Could he be on the level? An offer to see the top flat while it was empty. It wasn't a chance she could pass up. Did he know that? Was she snapping at hooked bait...? The car...? She shot him a look, then stared again at the high building.

'I'll see no one touches the motor,' he said, anticipating her.

He turned away, put finger and thumb to his lips and emitted a low piercing whistle. A pool of shadow by the edge of the concrete broke up and became two small figures. Children aged about ten, Annie judged, sex indeterminate. They approached warily, eyes on the boy who seemed to swell in height and breadth as he assumed authority over them.

'You know whose motor that is?' he barked out in a low voice.

The two small figures tipped their heads towards Annie in unison.

'Nah,' said Maz, crooking a finger and beckoning them closer. 'I'll tell yer whose it is.'

He leant to whisper in their ears and Annie saw their eyes widen. Their stares rested on her again but this time with unmistakable respect. Whatever name he'd given them, Annie suspected it wasn't Pat Thompson.

'OK. It's safe now.' The boy turned back to Annie with a throwaway comment over his shoulder. 'Anyone comes near, make sure they know.'

He set off towards the building. Annie took a couple of seconds to weigh up the risks, then slammed the car door, clicked the key fob to lock it and followed him.

The entrance lobby pulsed with activity and laughing crowds. They jostled through the throng, people all dressed-up, eyes blurred with the slight haze of an afternoon of drip-fed alcohol. The pristine crispness and flamboyant style of the clothes they pushed past marked this the aftermath of a wedding. The lift was packed, too, but the crowds melted away at floor nine, chatter and laughter replaced by the hum of machinery; when they arrived on the top landing they were alone.

Annie walked with Maz, heard the jingle of keys as he delved in his pocket. She watched in detail the pantomime she'd listened to in the early hours of Saturday morning. A key in a lock. Another key in a lock. And then another. How many damned locks did this door have and why?

Now she knew how many and would soon know why.

'Why all the locks?'

'Need time to get out if there's a raid, don't they? There's like as not guys in what won't want hauling into the nick, be all over the telly an' all that. Reinforced steel.' He banged his fist on to the door panel. 'You'll not ram yer way through that.'

OK, that wasn't perfect sense, but she'd let it do for now. She stepped inside and looked round. It was a smaller apartment than Mrs Earle's and, beyond the entrance lobby, fitted out so it bore little relation to conventional living space with none of the usual boundaries to show where living room became bedroom. The air was cool, the atmosphere antiseptic. The mismatched furniture was sparse. Three functional armchairs and two hard-back chairs in amongst tables topped with electronic equipment. Wires looped across the open spaces. Headphones dangled untidily from chair arms. Some semblance of normality remained in what was left of the kitchen. A bin overflowing with pizza boxes, a stack of stained mugs, a jar of Kenco Rappor on its side, contents heaped out on the draining board.

She saw Maz hunch his shoulders as he saw the mess, felt surprise that he noticed, then as he made a stack of the dirty boxes and carried them through to the main area she realized that his role in the setup included mucking out the place. It made sense that he was just a gopher.

'So what the hell is it?'

He stared at her. Amazement and doubt crossed his features. He thought she already had the answers. She read in his expression that if he'd known how little she knew, he wouldn't have brought her here. Too late now.

'Radio, innit?' His voice was sulky.

She understood and swung round again to take in all the setup. Pirate radio. She'd known a couple at college who'd done a bit of broadcasting out of their rooms at hall. That had been amateur stuff, nothing like this. She had no idea that pirate radio could be this sophisticated. Whoever ran this little lot had plans ... big plans. No way they intended to sit out their lives at the top of this block.

Tuesdays and Fridays – that was, early hours Wednesdays and Saturdays – two guys operated this setup on their own. And that's when they put a few spare minutes into their little sideline, their little drugs' store on the sixth floor. She stared again at all the equipment. It had cost serious money both to set up and to run.

She would get the details from Maz and listen in, later tonight. With the setup they had here and ... She stalled her own train of thought to slot another piece into the puzzle. Those odd-shaped packages. Suddenly, the shapes made sense. She knew just what she'd watched the two guys bring to the tower that first night. Aerials. Yes, with the size of the aerials they now had on the roof she'd pick them up from the other side of the city no problem.

Was it drugs money that financed them? Yet their sixth-floor activities were sordid small-time stuff. High-risk too, to use a regular venue like that landing. And right on the doorstep of the operation they took such trouble to protect. She looked again at the door. All those locks. And now she looked from this side, all those steel bolts.

'How scared are they of being bust?' she asked.

He pulled himself up basking in the reflected glory. 'Yeah, real scared. They've some mint gear stashed. 's a real finite setup. Big names an' all.'

Big names? Mentally she struck her forehead as she remembered the times she'd felt frustration at Pat for always having the TV playing. How many times had she had those faces almost in her grasp and felt the blare of the television wipe them from her mind. It hadn't been that at all. That's where she'd seen them, those bafflingly familiar third parties who arrived with the white van on non-drug nights. Celebrity faces. Not big mega-celebs but big enough and just off mainstream. She'd clocked their pictures in the music press; on local TV. These were names big enough to have red-carpet treatment when they came to the area, and this setup was big enough to tempt them in to do guest spots. Big enough and secure enough.

The jigsaw grew, piece by piece. Not quite a complete picture yet but surely close, very close. All the time, this kid had been a goldmine, and there might be more to get out of him so she'd keep him on side.

'Oh yeah,' he told her, his sulks left behind in the face of her close-to-speechless astonishment and taking advantage of a fresh audience to boast to. 'Yeah. It's for real. Look at this lot. They gotta shift it quick, it's real mint stuff. Don't want to lose it. An' whoever's here, they need time, see? Door like that'll give 'em long enough.'

'But where would they go?' The reinforced door, after all, was the flat's only exit.

'Oh, they've a kick-through to the next flat, and a way down from there. An' they could always go up and get the lift off the roof.'

'Up? How?'

His face now wore the self-satisfied look of one about to impress his public. 'Come and see this.'

She followed him to a space behind the kitchen and through a door to the veranda. She recognized the layout from Mrs Earle's. The small tarmacked rectangle was empty but for a metal contraption lying on the swept floor. As she stepped out, the air changed, the whistle of the wind zipped round the apex of the building. At this height it became a different world.

The balconies didn't protrude far from the face of the building so when she stepped to the railing and looked down it was on to a sheer drop to a world in miniature that made her gasp and step back.

Maz smiled a superior smile and made a flashy approach to the edge which he peered over with swaggering indifference. Annie ignored this, annoyed with herself for showing weakness in front of him, but then couldn't hold back a gasp as he lifted the metal contraption and hoisted himself up so he straddled the inadequate balcony rail.

His turn to ignore her as he lifted the thing over his head pushing it up beyond the top of the gap. Annie clapped her hand to her mouth, couldn't stop herself. He stood up now, balancing on the rail, one arm against the ceiling as though that would save him if a sudden gust whipped stability from under him. Impulsively, she leapt forward and grasped a handful of material near his waist ready to haul him in if he lost balance.

He threw her a casual, 'Cheers.'

But it wasn't his safety in her mind at all. She'd grabbed hold to save herself the horror of his falling in front of her, plummeting down to splat on the concrete below. This close to an unguarded edge it was too easy to imagine herself slipping over. How would it feel at the instant of realization, the point of toppling too far to get back again? She shuddered and shifted her weight further back from the direction of the drop.

'There. That's it, see?' He twitched suddenly loosening her grasp and she saw his feet fly free of the rail out into midair.

Her instinct was to leap back. Then she was ashamed as she saw him peer down at her from where he hung apparently secure from some handhold out of her sight. She stepped forward again and peered upwards. The metal contraption was now a robust-looking ladder that hooked on to something up above. It took his swinging weight without trouble though she saw a look of alarm cross his features as a gust of wind buffeted him. His feet scrabbled for purchase on the rail as he lowered himself down. She grabbed a handful of denim at his thigh and pulled him in.

'Ta.' He tried for nonchalance but couldn't disguise his breathlessness. 'It's a piece of piss getting up, but it's a bit tricky getting back in.'

She could believe it. 'And they've actually used that as a route out?'

'Nah, but they could. They did that ladder thing to get up to do the aerials first off when they didn't have a key to the lift.'

'What's holding it?'

'It fits on the maint'nance rail.'

'Maintenance rail?'

'Fer repairs and that. Holds the cradle.'

They were dedicated for sure. It would have to be life and death to get her outside on to that makeshift ladder. No way would she risk her neck at this height for an aerial.

The boy cleared his throat and glanced back. 'I'll get that back in a bit.' To get the ladder back, he'd have to straddle the railing again. Not so reckless and devil-may-care as he'd have her believe.

Fine. His problem. 'The guys who do the radio, the gophers I mean, not the names. They deal drugs twice a week.'

He looked vaguely surprised. 'Is that why you been watching?'

She nodded. 'Why do they do it? It's high-risk. They'll be caught.'

A look of contempt crossed his features. 'They're pissheads.'

It was roughly the conclusion she'd found herself heading towards. She looked at Maz. She wanted more from him but it was time to let something flow the other way. Keep him on side. 'OK. What is it you want from me? Quid pro quo.'

The quid pro quo clearly puzzled him, but he caught the sense and asked, 'You'll do it then?'

'I don't know what it is yet.'

'Yeah, but I've showed you the setup, haven't I?'

'OK, if I can, I'll do it. What is it?'

He went for an inner jacket pocket and pulled out two envelopes. He looked at one of them as if he'd never seen it before but then gave an irritated huff of recognition and put it on one side. The other he cradled in his hands.

'We never used it. Never once.' His tone was earnest, almost pleading. 'Listen, you can do forensics an' all that, that'll prove it. We never used it. But like as not if the cops get hold of it they'll fit us up. Fit me up. They'll not touch the posh kids. And I'm not taking the rap for that out there. I 'ad nowt to do with any of it.'

Annie fought bafflement as she looked at the odd-shaped metal rod he passed to her. Her gaze rested for a moment on the other envelope he'd set aside. The words 'Annie Raymond' were printed on it in neat script.

'That's nowt,' he said impatiently. 'That's just some crap letter she wrote you. It's that you've to deal with.' As he spoke, he picked up the other envelope and held it out to her. She would quiz him on it in a moment. For now, she put it into her pocket and looked again at the object he wanted her to take away.

It looked like half a key. A large oddly shaped one. She turned it over in her hand then gave up. 'What is it?'

He spoke with a hint of exasperation. 'It's a key to that place. I only did it cos they wanted me to. No one's used it. I told you. By the time I'd got it done, they got all screechy and said they didn't want it. I was going to chuck it in the drain but what if they found out I'd had it done? If you have those forensics done on it you can prove I never used it. But if the cops get hold, they'll fit me up. They said you was OK over that stuff with the body.'

Annie pieced it together. The three girls considered her a safe pair of hands because she'd gone to meet them without telling anyone the night they'd found the body in Balham's shed. It hadn't occurred to them it was only because she couldn't find anyone to tell. And they'd got Maz to do something … what? Oh hell! Of course. 'That's a key to the building on the cliff, isn't it? How did you get it? Why did they want it?'

'They used to follow him, see. But he always kept it locked. So I said it'd be a piece of piss to get in and we give it a go. Tried to open it up but it's a better lock than you'd think. He's had it done special. So I says I'd get a key made up and I followed him. This right big fancy key it was, then I just nipped into the house later on when he was down the yard doing stuff and I got the shape of it.'

'Like an impression in a bar of soap?' Annie was amazed.

'Soap's no good. You can get this stuff like Blu-Tack and you oil it so it don't stick. Got some off me uncle and he made the key up for me.'

'Didn't he ask what it was for?'

'I told him it were a lock-up. He thought it were just for ornery robbing.'

Ordinary robbing? That was OK, was it? She took another incredulous look at the device then put it into her pocket with the envelope.

'You never used it?'

'Never. On me mam's life. I only got it done 'cos o' them. They …' She didn't doubt his sincerity and she could probably put words to the motives that now baffled him. He'd have had those girls hanging on his words in horrified admiration at the thought he could steal an impression of a key and get a copy made. But what should she do with it? Keep it like he asked? Hand it over to the police? He had a point, they wouldn't give him an easy time if they knew its provenance.

'Oh shit!' He was on his feet, the colour gone from his face.

'What? What is it?'

'Someone's coming. You gotta hide. You gotta get out.'

She heard it, too, now. Footsteps from outside. He hadn't secured the reinforced door. There was no time to be bought that way. Clearly he knew who it was. The wave of fear that radiated from him had her on her feet. She dived for the kitchen area where she eased herself out on to the small veranda and held the door open a crack to listen through.

'What the fuck are you doing here?'

Her heart plummeted to her feet. She knew that voice.

'I just come to clean up, Mr Sleeman. I didn't get it all done last night.' She heard him rattling the pizza boxes.

'The fucking door was open, you cretin. What are you playing at?'

'I only jus' got here, Mr Sleeman. I were just gonna shut it.'

'You lying little git. I saw the light from down below. You've been here a good while. And not done much cleaning to show for it. What have you been doing? Robbing stuff, I suppose. Empty your pockets!'

'Nah, I 'aven't, Mr Sleeman. Honest. There's nowt in me pockets. I were just 'aving a sit down. I were tired is all.'

'I told you to empty your pockets. And when I've done with you I'm going to check this place over so you may as well help yourself out and come clean.'

Annie froze from the inside out as she listened to Maz's whiny voice plead with Vince. There was nothing in his pockets. Anything he wanted to be rid of he'd already passed on to her. He was stalling Vince deliberately to give her time to get away.

She gulped. Time to get away ...

Where was this kick-through to the adjacent flat? Was it anywhere she could reach? Of course not. And the very term, kick-through, implied noise not a clandestine escape.

Anyway, so what if Vince found her here? Wasn't she on a job for his agency? She fought to win the argument with herself. A job for his agency. A job he'd had cancelled. Pat and that giant plaster cast.

When Sleeman's mate legged her down the stairs ...

If Annie were pushed right now, she didn't have the safety net of a concrete staircase. She had a sheer drop to assured death. But he wouldn't push her. Why should he? Why was he here? What was his role in it all? Another piece in a jigsaw she suddenly had no interest in completing.

Maz's voice whined on. He wouldn't divert Vince for ever. She had to do it. Now. Don't think. Just do it. She'd seen him swinging there quite secure.

She tried to swallow, but her mouth had dried.

Clinging to the rail, she eased one leg up on to it, then the other. Felt the awful instability of clinging to too thin a handhold. She had to get her hands off the rail, up above her head, on to the ladder. She couldn't do it.

She moved nearer the side wall. Maybe with that to balance her ... Holding her breath, looking anywhere but down, she managed to stand up on the rail, one hand now pushed up on the ceiling of the small veranda. Weight leaning inwards. Daren't look out, not even upwards, but she must if she were to grab the lower rung of the ladder.

Quick glance up, smothering the gasp of a snatched breath. She inched along, hand pressed to the rough surface of the ceiling.

About there now, just the right point to reach out into the air ...

She crawled one of her hands along the stippled concrete ... felt at the changing texture as it neared the outer edge. Her jaw began to shake, the chattering of her teeth was involuntary. Either she got down now and faced Vince, or she must make one bold grab for that rung.

She tried to tell herself that whatever Vince chose to do, it had to be less risky than hanging over a sheer drop at this height. But this intimacy with her own mortality didn't allow her to kid herself. No way could she trust Vince to save her from an 'accidental' fall. Here she was at the heart of something he'd worked to keep hidden. Tiny memories flashed by ... his cold eyes ... his lack of interest in her as a person. Scott and the way he'd said, 'You don't have to work for Sleeman.' The only witness was Maz and Vince would have no worries about keeping him quiet.

Her chest constricted, the deep breaths she tried to take stalled themselves. She counted anyway. One ... two ... three ... Praying it wasn't her last moment on earth, Annie loosed her hand from the security of the concrete surface, reached up and round the corner, above where she could see. Her weight had to move with it, to tip towards the emptiness.

Her fingers felt cold metal, closed on it, grasped it tight. Without stopping to think out the next move, knowing that she could use the momentum, she let her other hand follow. Her hands gripped tight. Her feet barely danced on the rail. She was outside the shelter of the building, buffeted by the wind, helpless. No way back.

Maz with his longer legs could have used the rail to boost himself up. She had nothing, just the strength in her arms to rely on. She hauled up, felt the sting of blood in her mouth as she clenched her teeth too hard. Another gasping breath, a quick look up to locate her target and she let go with one hand and grabbed for the next rung up.

Got it. A bit of leeway now to rest on one elbow and let the pounding in her chest slow. But she mustn't let herself stop. Other hand up to the next rung ... and the next ... and at last her feet found purchase on the bottom of the ladder and she could breathe freely into the buffeting wind.

Now she'd stopped to catch her breath she could see exactly where she was. On the short makeshift ladder that was hooked ... barely ... over the steel rail at the roof's edge. A horrible vision came to her that one more move and it would slip free and send her plummeting down.

She must get right up on to the roof as quickly as possible. Up there it was safe.

After one more attempt at a deep breath, a flexing of muscles, she turned her head sideways and glanced down.

The whole world swam around her. There was nothing ... nothing between her and the tiny patchwork estate far below. Tiny figures scurried about their business, never looking up. She fought back an urge to scream, but the breath had rushed out of her body. Clutching at the ladder, eyes squeezed tight shut, she couldn't suppress a whimper as a gust hit her and the metal swayed.

For a moment she curled in on the certainty that she couldn't move ... that she must stay still and cling to this flimsy support. If Vince saw her ... A vision flooded her mind. Vince appearing above her, reaching out to loosen the ladder ...

There was one way to go. She didn't stop even to try for the deep breath that should signal decisive action. She moved one hand up to the top rung. One foot up. Other hand. A heart-stopping pause at the edge of the roof, at the perimeter of safety. In this pummelling wind, how to make the critical move needed to get from the side of the building to the top. No handholds. She must let go and throw her body weight forwards and over, but what if a circling eddy of wind chose that moment to tip her back again, out beyond the reach of the thin metal frame?

She knew if she didn't get over the edge immediately, she'd freeze and never move again. The tightness in her chest rose to her throat. She pushed up with her feet and hurled herself forwards and over with a force that sent her headfirst into something hard and unyielding. Instinctively she flattened herself to the surface and lay still as the sharp pain in her head subsided.

After a moment when the surface beneath her remained solid, slowly and very cautiously, she sat up and looked round.

It was flat. The top of a box. She'd expected a wall round the edge, but there was just the maintenance rail the boy had told her about, a steel girder round the edge to hold the cables for maintenance cradles. She'd imagined a forest of tiny buildings holding the machinery that kept the whole tower alive, but there was just one unevenly shaped protuberance to house the tops of the two lifts and whatever else the building needed up here. Body firmly pressed to the surface of the roof, she eased herself round. And there right in front of her was the aerial she'd seen them bring that first night.

One thing she could be certain of; she would stay up here and starve before even considering going back down the way she'd come up.

CHAPTER 21

ANNIE CLOSED HER eyes and let her head fall forward until her face rested against the rough surface. What had she done? A tremor took hold of her that had nothing to do with the chill of the breeze. Scott's words burnt across her mind. *A single look and the great detective surmises* ... What had the great detective surmised this time? A single snarl in Vince's tone and she'd assumed what – that he'd kill her? She tried to recreate her sudden fear. Unexpectedly, a sliver of it remained.

She lifted her head. The promise of a storm that she'd seen out over the sea in Withernsea swirled high in the sky. It gave her a sudden boost of energy.

Within a hair's breadth of death, but she was alive.

Would Vince really have pushed her from the high balcony? She'd hidden from him and she'd found what he'd wanted hidden from her. She'd crossed a line, shown what she could do when she had to. She'd never forget how it felt to hang over that drop. Every detail would stay with her, every nuance. It might be the start of a nightmare or a source of inspiration. She was too hyped up to tell.

Now she'd got over the need to crouch down into the tarry surface, she stood up straight, let the wind try to drag the hair from her head as it lashed round the strange world up here. The city lay spread out below her. It couldn't see her but she could see it.

Tell me your secrets, she urged.

She laughed. As the gusts grabbed the laughter from her throat and whipped it away, she laughed louder, shouted out to the world that she was alive.

The need to be practical pulled her up and she reached into her inside pocket for her phone.

'Pat, it's Annie.' The strange high from where she'd shouted out over the city dropped her without warning. Her voice wobbled.

'Annie? What's up? What's happened? Where are you?'

Facts. Stick to the facts. 'I'm on the roof of Mrs Earle's tower block.' Why didn't the howling of the wind grab the catch in her voice and dissolve it into the sky before it reached across the airwaves to Pat?

'On the...? Sounds like you're in a railway tunnel. What the fuck are you doing up there!'

How could she begin to answer that? 'Look, can I tell you later? The thing is ... can you get me down?'

'What d'you want me to do? Come round with a rope and crampons? How did you get up there? Can't you go back the same way?'

Flashback to a spinning landscape. Sharp intake of breath. 'No. I need someone to bring the lift. Someone with an access key.'

'Does it need a key from the top?'

Brilliant! Whoosh! Right back on that high. Was it the bullying air currents that affected her mood so unpredictably? And why hadn't she thought of checking the lift first? She spun round, gaze speeding over the roofscape as she spoke. 'I don't know. I'll check.' She ran towards the nearest of the two structures.

As she approached, the door in the side wall swung inwards. Annie skidded to a halt and flattened herself round the back of it. The high still held her. No fear, just grim satisfaction that if it were Vince, she'd outflank him before he'd taken in a breath. Despite almost wishing to see the man who – if her earlier fears were founded – could only have come up here to finish the job, she let out a sigh when the slight figure emerged. It was Maz. Vince must have gone and he'd come to look for her. She stepped into view and saw relief spread across his face as he beckoned.

'It's OK,' she told Pat. 'I can get at the lift. I'm on my way. We'll talk when I get back.'

As she clicked the phone off, she caught the words, 'Count on it.'

'Quick, quick,' Maz hissed at her with frantic hand signals. 'You've gotta get out before he knows.'

He dashed across the roof surface towards the ladder. So that's what had brought him up here; he wasn't on a rescue mission. Vince was still around but diverted for long enough for Maz to retrieve the ladder.

As the lift door opened on the top floor, he jabbed at the ground floor button in a show of gallantry and told her to, 'Gerrout quick. He don't know you been here. Watch out in the car-park. He's gone to get summat.'

Annie smiled and let him dash off, but as the doors began to slide shut, she stepped out between them and stood once again on the top landing. She moved back from the lift, away from the entrance to the flat. She waited.

It was a while before the lift returned. She was ready for it, calm now. She watched Vince step out, heard angry mutterings below his breath, saw him march towards the flat.

She let him disappear inside, then walked towards the reinforced door confident that he wouldn't invite her in. The spy hole faced her as she knocked. She made sure she was visible to anyone looking through it.

Bolts slid back, locks clinked. The reinforced panel opened a crack and Vince's face appeared, glaring into hers.

'What the hell are you doing here?' His gaze raked her up and down and she realized that she'd brought a lot of the roof with her. She'd just have to hope the garbage she wore wasn't identifiable as roof debris.

'I followed you.'

He looked shocked and then amazed. Before he could speak, she went on, 'I want to talk. Shall I come in, or shall we go back down?'

Breath held now because there was no way she'd cross the threshold of this flat ever again. But he must believe she didn't know what was in there. And this time it wasn't him catching her out, she'd caught him. For all he knew, she had backup. Surely, he wouldn't risk anything silly.

'I'll come down,' he snarled.

At once, Annie said, 'I'll see you in the car-park,' and rushed off so as to get the lift before he'd got his act together. She didn't want to have to stand in that small box with him on the journey down the building.

Less than five minutes after she'd made her way back to Pat's car, Vince appeared in the entranceway. His tall, solid form sauntered across the concrete expanse. In front of the car he paused to give her a hard stare then he walked round to the passenger side and climbed in.

'Well?'

She told him about the drug dealing, about Tuesday and Friday nights.

He didn't try to contradict her and only interrupted to ask questions about the timing, the amounts, who bought the stuff. She didn't have answers to most of it. He sat looking out through the windscreen. It was impossible from his face to get any sense of how he felt, how much was news, how much he already knew. Somewhere inside her Annie had the impression she'd shocked him.

The seesaw of emotion held Annie in its grip as she drove back across the city. By the time she pulled up outside the apartment block, she felt nervy and on edge; wished she'd never made the call to Pat. She needed the security of the nearest place she had to home, but wanted to be alone, not to have to explain. Not yet.

Half a hope that Pat would be engrossed in a film died as she clicked the door open. Pat's greeting was bawled at full volume. 'I told you to come straight back after you'd seen the Martins.'

Annie thought about the excuse she'd rehearsed as she'd sat in the car in Withernsea. It no longer had any substance, but she used it anyway. 'I thought you meant …'

'No, you bloody well didn't!'

'How should I know what you mean?' Annie yelled back. 'You never tell me anything!'

'You're employed to do as you're bloody well told!'

The argument raged back and forth until Pat suddenly sat up and stared hard into her face. 'Have you taken something? You're all over the place.'

'No, of course I haven't. What do you take me for?'

'Then what's the matter with you?'

'It's being on that roof. Have you any idea how bloody high it is?'

'Did you go and look over the edge? You did, didn't you? Idiot. What did you do that for?'

'No I didn't. I mean not like that.'

Flashback … the ladder … the awful stretch to reach it.

'You've gone white as a sheet,' Pat said. 'You didn't say how you got up there. I assumed the lift. Was it the lift?'

She shook her head.

'Then how?'

'Off the veranda of their flat.'

'Jesus! You idiot! What the fuck possessed you? You could have been killed!'

'You think I don't know that?' Annie screeched out the words and slammed out of the room. In the bedroom she paused. What was the matter with her? She looked down at her hands. They shook and felt cold as though she'd crawled through snow. She'd never felt like this before … never done anything like this before. A wonderful rush of triumph took the shivers right up through her body. She must get off this rollercoaster. She'd pushed beyond some sort of limit, shown just what she could do. But forget it … it would never happen again. Never. Where was the route to equilibrium? In normality. Getting out of these mucky clothes covered in streaks of oil and tar from the rooftop would be a good start.

Ten minutes later she re-entered the living room. 'Sorry about that. I ...'

'OK, no sweat. Tell me what you found. What is it they've got up there?'

Annie breathed out a sigh. Somehow she and Pat were on the same wavelength when it came to what really mattered and what could just be left.

She told Pat what she'd found, how she'd identified the familiarity of the faces she'd seen.

'Pirate radio?' Pat said. 'I see.'

Annie looked up sharply. Pat's tone seemed to find logic in what she heard, but when she didn't elaborate, Annie went on, 'Then Vince turned up.'

'Shit! Did he see you?'

'See me!' Annie felt the emotion rise once again. 'Hell, he tried to push me off the roof.'

'What! Vince tried to push you off the roof?' Pat looked horror-struck.

'Well no, but ... but he would have if he'd found me. I'm certain he would.'

'But he knows you were there?'

'No, he didn't see me in the flat. He doesn't know I've been in there.'

'Thank God for that. Vince might have been mad at you, Annie, but he isn't an animal. He wouldn't have pushed you off a roof. You leap to some dramatic conclusions.'

'But where does Vince fit in?'

It seemed a long time before Pat replied. 'There was some paperwork Vince sent me a while ago. I don't want to go into the detail. Suffice to say things had been a bit fraught between us all. It looks like the agency owns that flat. By the look of it, Vince has set up his nephew there.'

Annie struggled to piece together what Pat was saying. Was this about misuse of company funds or something more? She tried to guess where it led. 'You told me someone from the agency tipped off whoever ambushed you. Are you saying it was Vince?'

'Oh no. That was just by the way. I doubt if Vince has a clue about the drug dealing.'

Annie opened her mouth, then shut it again. Pat didn't know she'd talked to Vince after her adventure on the roof. She hadn't meant not to tell her, but with all the turmoil in her mind, it had happened that way.

'One of the others is involved,' Pat went on. 'And probably knows about the dealing too. He's likely the supplier. Vince'd kill him if he found out.'

'So should we tell Vince?' Annie eased the question in wanting to confess to the car-park discussion on the back of a 'yes' from Pat.

'Hell, no. Let's keep this under wraps. Pirate radio? I wonder.'

So much for that. 'What do you mean? It *is* a pirate radio. I saw the setup. And those guys they take up there, one of them's been on the local TV, and

I think I know the other from the music press. Whatever their sins, they've made a name for themselves. You don't get names like that on air without a good audience.'

Pat shrugged agreement as though Annie had missed the point. 'I don't want to go into it any further, Annie. Whatever Vince is up to I don't want to know. I'd lay odds he doesn't know that the little twats are dealing drugs though, putting his setup at risk.'

'It is a pirate radio,' Annie persisted. 'Even if it's something else too.'

'Oh yeah, I'm not saying it isn't. One of the guys you clocked, the ones doing the dealing, I can't swear to it but I'm pretty sure it's Vince's nephew, favourite nephew, I should add. Vince took him under his wing when his brother died. It all adds up. The lad always had ambitions in the music business. It's the sort of thing Vince would do for him, but there'll be a payoff for Vince in it, and like I say, I don't want to know what that is.'

'But what if the agency's involved?'

A troubled look crossed Pat's features. 'Not your problem,' she murmured.

'I'll help if I can.'

'Yes, I know.' Pat made an effort to shake off a cloud of gloom, and smiled across at Annie. 'You're a good kid. Vince hadn't a clue what he'd got when he hired you.'

Annie thought back to the way Vince had ordered Maz about in that flat, the way he'd waltzed in as though he owned the place, the way Maz had recognized him. A classy pirate radio setup for the son of his dead brother? It half added up and half didn't. Vince's cold eyes. All that equipment. Pat was right. At this early stage in her career, she didn't want to tangle with a pro like Vince. This was a boundary she didn't need to cross.

'We need to back off the Earle case, don't we?'

'It's a shame really given how far you got. We won't be able to bill her now. She'll be pleased about that at any rate.'

'I'll drop her keys back in sometime and let her know.'

It was an unsatisfactory end to her very first case, but she'd try and see it as a useful lesson in how things panned out. Expect the unexpected, someone had told her, probably the guy in Birmingham. He was right.

Late that night, she and Pat slumped in front of a film. Annie had no interest in the drama that unfolded on the screen, but was glad of the distraction that meant she could sit in silence with her own thoughts. She lay back in the chair, closing her eyes then opening them again, practising for sleep although it felt foolish and irrational. The dizzying swirl of a miniature landscape far below lay in wait for her at the edge of slumber. Conscious, she could push it away, but as she floated into sleep would she spin back into the nausea of hanging over that drop?

Get up ... walk across the room ... get undressed ... go to bed ... sleep.

The longer she sat, the more tiredness seeped into her and the more enticing the prospect of a night in the chair became.

A click from somewhere behind jerked her to full awareness. A key turning in a lock. Footsteps in the lobby. A heavy tread she'd recognize anywhere. Vince!

She shot to her feet, gabbled out to Pat, 'I'm off to bed. Good night,' and bolted for the sanctuary of her room.

Once safe in the tiny room, she sat on the bed, door ajar so as to hear what went on. Muffled voices ... the film playing out behind them. Vince's growl ... Pat's snappish responses.

The events of the day raced up from behind and swept over her. Leaden tiredness laid itself across every fibre of her being. But no, she couldn't think about sleep. Any minute, one of them would shout her name, call her back through. When they did, she'd obey, because the alternative was having Vince come to get her. She lay back on the pillows. Not to sleep, just to rest her body. She was determined to stay alert for the summons.

CHAPTER 22

AS ANNIE WOKE, relief filled her. The bright morning sunlight streaming through her window had driven the demon of Vince away. There was relief too that she felt refreshed. After yesterday, she hadn't expected to sleep at all.

She thought about Orchard Park, about two young guys hiding behind the indulgent uncle of one of them; about a pirate radio hiding behind the façade of an ordinary flat; and about those huge aerials masquerading as necessary accoutrements to illegal music broadcasts. So much hidden ...

Case closed.

This was the opportunity to put all her efforts into finding where Terry Martin had been. He had to have left his footprints somewhere in those two days. Tremlow, too. Where had he been since Friday?

If she followed Tremlow's footsteps, she felt she'd have a handle on Terry's missing hours. Tremlow was surely a creature of habit and the person to know his habits was his old friend, Colonel Ludgrove. As soon as morning reached a reasonable hour, she picked up her phone to make the colonel a concerned call to express her condolences about his friend.

The voice that said hello wasn't the one she expected, or wanted.

'Oh ... Hi, Mally. It's Annie. Can I speak to your grandad?'

'Grandad isn't well. I'm not to disturb him. Can you ring later?'

No surprise there. The old man was worn out with caring for his grand-daughter in amongst all the chaos of first Terry Martin and now Tremlow's death.

'That's OK. It wasn't important.' It was on the tip of her tongue to quiz Mally on Terry Martin and the money that had changed hands, but she held back. If she were to question them, it must be casually, informally and appear to be unplanned, because they were minors and could get her into real trouble.

She knew just the place to find them. Not even the fallout from the cheating would keep them out of the saddle. She knew that because she and Pat had seen Laura and Kay out riding on Saturday. All she needed was a reason to talk to Tina Hain again. The stables were an ideal place to hang about unchallenged. She clicked out Tina's number.

'I wondered if I could pop out and run through things with you again. All that business at Milesthorpe Show.'

'Those blasted girls. Yes, no problem. I've the three of them in for a lesson this afternoon, but I'm free afterwards.'

'Laura, Kay and Mally?' Annie felt her fist clench in triumph. She'd have some answers by this evening.

When Pat clumped through from her bedroom later, Annie was ready with the coffee pot. She stood back and watched from a distance until she judged Pat's caffeine level high enough, and then told her about her plan to go to Milesthorpe, to quiz the three girls.

'Be very careful. Have you got a legitimate excuse to talk to the Hain woman?'

'Yes, I'll ask her about the cheating. Not that there's anything more I need to know, but it's part of what Terry Martin was doing.'

'OK, but remember. Delicate handling. These things can backfire.'

'I'll call and give Mrs Earle her keys back on the way.'

Pat sighed. 'Vince had a point. There was never a cat in hell's chance of getting anything out of her. Jobs like those should be invoiced up front.'

Annie didn't like the note of defeat in Pat's voice. It was all tied up with Vince and family feuds.

'So then I'll just have the Martins' case,' she said eventually. 'Unless anything else has come in?'

'No, sorry. I've had enough of going out on a limb. No more adverts. I know what you're thinking. This suicide thing: it wraps up the Martin case, too. But don't worry. Vince said he wanted you for six weeks and I'll hold him to it. There's an outside chance—'

'What? Chance of what?'

'Look, I don't want to get your hopes up. Vince dropped in last night after you'd gone to bed. He half hinted he might find you something. But I probably shouldn't even mention it. He won't do anything about it, but he wouldn't have said it if you hadn't impressed him. I assumed he thought you were sitting round here playing general factotum, but he must have been keeping a closer eye on you than I realized.'

This must have sprung from their friction-laden conversation in the car on Orchard Park. Vince had told Pat he was impressed with her? It was the last thing she expected. 'What did he say?'

'He said he'd like to have seen you in action a bit more. That if he'd seen you through three meaty cases with a good result on each, then he'd have offered you a job with the agency.'

'Why three?'

'Because he knows there's no chance of you doing it, so he'll never have to deliver.'

'I suppose we could advertise again. See if we can bring anything in.'

Pat laughed and Annie knew she hadn't taken the suggestion seriously.

'Before I go, I need to show you this key.'

Annie told Pat how Maz had had the key made. 'The Milesthorpe girls, thank heavens, got cold feet about taking it off him.'

Pat took it from her and turned it in her hand letting the light glint from its different faces. 'It's a nice job,' she said.

'Should it go to the police?'

'Yeah, I think so, but keep it with you for when you have a go at those kids. Spring that on them and they might blurt out all sorts. Ah, was that the door?'

Annie turned to see the door open and Barbara's bulk fill the gap. 'Hi.' She gave Barbara a smile and raised a hand in acknowledgement.

In return, she received a glare and a grunt.

'You're early,' was Pat's greeting.

'I have to be early to get you out of your pit, or we'd never get anywhere. We've things to talk about.'

'I'm ready. I've been waiting for you.'

'You were complaining I was early a minute ago.'

'Well, that's no ...'

Annie eased herself out of the room and slipped into her bedroom to get Mrs Earle's keys. She had no illusions that she'd get anything approaching gratitude for her efforts, but handing over the keys would be a kind of closure to what had, after all, been her first proper case.

She tossed Maz's key in her hand. There would be a betrayal of trust in giving it to the police, but what other option was open? She'd have liked to hand it to someone she could talk to informally. Twenty-four hours ago that would have been Scott. Now, she didn't even know if Jennifer trusted her.

While she waited in her room, half aware of the sisters arguing their way out of the flat, Annie pulled together the clothes she'd ruined in her foray on to the roof. She wondered if the tarry substance would come out. She pulled off the loose bits and checked through the pockets. Screwed-up paper tissues and an envelope.

An envelope? Of course, Maz had handed it over just before they'd talked about the key. Then Vince arrived and events snowballed on under their own momentum. What had Maz said? *Some crap letter she wrote you.* One of the girls, obviously, but which one?

She slit it open and stared at it, puzzled. A torn page … except it was whole. The paper was flimsy. It was old-fashioned fax paper. One of them had fed a torn and partly scorched page through an old fax machine and sent her the result. The only non-fax-copy elements were the words 'see e-mail' written in a round childish hand in the top corner.

A few part-words remained undamaged either by fire or the rip in the copied sheet. They were hard to decipher. Annie squinted at them as she walked through to Pat's room where she switched on the PC.

Mally. She would put her money on the letter being from Mally. But there was no e-mail from Mally, or from any of them.

She turned the machine off and looked again at the murky fax. Pat's reading glasses lay on the desk. Annie used them as a magnifying glass. The page had been torn through the middle of a line but some of the half-letters became decipherable as the lens enlarged them. She made out z-a-b. Then a smudge and t-h. Then the word 'at'.

Zabath at? Zabeth at? At where? There was something earlier that might be an E.

A shiver ran across her skin as she realized what she was looking at.

E—zabeth At. Before the page had been torn and then burnt, it had said Elizabeth Atkins. The woman Doris Kitson told her about; the woman Terry Martin had asked about although he hadn't known her.

What one of the girls had fed through the fax machine was the missing half page from Terry Martin's last notebook.

CHAPTER 23

ANNIE STARED AT the page. Here was her handle on Terry's missing days. Elizabeth Atkins. Who had ripped the page out and tried to burn it? When? How and where had the girls found it?

She itched to get on the road at once, but knew her meeting with Mally, Laura and Kay must seem accidental. This afternoon at the stables she'd have a captive audience. It was all tied in with the church connection she kept hearing about. Doris had mentioned it. Maz, too.

If she had to spend all night at those stables interrogating the three girls, she'd do it. She wouldn't end the day without answers.

As she drove to Orchard Park, theories spun in her head, but nothing added up. It wasn't until she stepped out of the car and saw the bulk of the tower in front of her that she was caught by a sudden constriction in her throat as though the structure itself watched her, ready to draw her in and force her back up to its highest point. She looked up and up until she faced out the height of the building ... waited for the flashback of panic, but the memory was a panoramic view out over a city that couldn't see her. Unexpectedly, the feeling inside was power, not fear.

She walked into the lobby and jabbed the lift call button. It was automatic to pull in a breath as the lift jolted to a halt on the sixth floor, to give herself a lungful of air to avoid breathing in the stench of the landing.

Noise banged into her as she stepped out, expelling the held breath as she skipped to avoid an open paint pot. Instinctively her hands rose to meet a threat, then she realized there was no menace here just the overpowering thump of music and nostril-stinging tang of fresh paint. People everywhere. A thin youth in baggy overalls swung a wide paintbrush at the wall from the top of a stepladder; another balanced on a contraption that gave him access to the patchwork of glass and hardboard that separated the landing from the stairwell. Repairs and refurbishment. Was this a special refit for the sixth floor, or part of some maintenance juggernaut that rolled up and down the building across the seasons?

None of the half-dozen gangly figures in overalls took any notice so she picked her way round their ladders and knocked at the door of Mrs Earle's flat. The key was in her hand but she was reluctant to use it knowing Mrs Earle would be comatose on a bed inside. Letting herself in to spy on the men in the van was different. She knocked again louder.

The door opened a crack. It wasn't Mrs Earle who peered out, but her brother. His expression was surly, his face unshaven. He looked her up and down and said, 'She ain't here,' just the way he'd greeted her the first time she'd called.

She made her decision on the spot. She'd come to see the woman, to try to explain things face to face. She'd tried. That was enough.

'I've come to return her keys,' she told the man, thrusting them at him.

He took them from her with a grunt and shut the door. She stood there for a moment. It was a disappointing way to end the case, but she shrugged and turned away.

Mrs Earle had gone from her thoughts before she was back in the car. Her mind teemed with the implications of the page one of the girls had sent her via Maz. She was early for her appointment with Tina, but no one would notice in the busy stable yard. She pulled the car in between a gleaming Shogun and a battered Trooper and stepped out into a patch of mud. The storm that had threatened since yesterday evening, hadn't broken yet. Someone had been busy with a hosepipe. The ground at her feet sparkled with scraps of tinsel. The air was heavy with the smell of horses and cut grass.

A fat pony plodded its way towards her the other side of the fence, but as she watched, its head shot up, its eyes opened wide and it bounded away. Annie felt a jolt of alarm. What had panicked it? A woman marched past with a bundle of heavy-duty tinsel glittering in her arms, Tina's eccentric method for subduing her charges with festive spirit.

She walked down the track towards the stable blocks, her gaze raking every corner, looking for the girls. Tina emerged from a door in a wall and raised a hand in greeting.

'My last appointment didn't turn up,' said Annie, 'so I'm a bit early.' She spoke the lie to Tina's back and saw the woman was too busy shouting orders across the yard to take in what she said. Early had no meaning round here, but Annie guessed that late was a cardinal crime.

'Come and talk while I plait up, if you like,' Tina threw over her shoulder.

Annie followed to one of the big stables and watched as an enormous beast, four times Boxer's size submitted to some complicated work on its mane.

'What have you decided to do about the three girls?' she asked. 'I was talking to Colonel Ludgrove and it was clear he knew nothing about the cheating. I don't want to put my foot in it.'

'Officially I'm doing nothing. I don't want any talk outside the stables.' Tina gave a vicious tug at the horse's mane. Annie watched the animal brace its neck. 'The Tunbridge brat is trying to pull a fast one, but she'll get a rude awakening when I get my hands on her this afternoon. I've the reputation of the stables to keep up. It's a knife-edge business these days, running a place like this. There are people who'd take advantage.'

'So they get away with it?' Not that Annie cared, she just wanted Tina to keep talking.

'No way. I've threatened all three of them to within an inch of their lives. I suppose Laura'll spill the beans to Ma and Pa at some stage, but they won't want it broadcast. And I've barred them all from riding out for a fortnight. They're to have a lesson with me in the school once a week. First one today. That'll quieten them down. They'll have to shell out extra, too.'

'But Laura and Kay were out on their ponies on Saturday. We saw them.'

'Yes, I know.' Tina spoke with barely suppressed anger and another tug at a handful of coarse hair. The horse gave Annie a reproachful look. 'I hadn't had the chance to speak to them and they slipped out. Laura didn't bring Boxer back, the little minx. She had it figured I'd ground her.'

Annie felt frustrated disappointment at Tina's words. 'She'll not turn up this afternoon then, will she? None of them will.'

'Oh, they will. She acts without thinking, that child. If she wants to keep her footing in the area, she'll not cross me. I could have her out of the Pony

Club. I haven't gone running after her. She'll have to come down this after-noon and eat humble pie.'

'What will she have done with Boxer?'

'They all have stables at home. She probably took him to Colonel Ludgrove's to start with, but she might have taken him to her place. Her parents are away. I'd put money on Mally being in on it. Mally can get away with murder while she's with her grandfather.'

'Won't Kay be in on it, too?'

'She wasn't at the time, no. Kay came back. She told me Laura had nipped round to Mally's and she'd be back later. Kay's no actress. I'd have seen it if she'd been trying to pull the wool.' She glanced at her watch and then out over Annie's shoulder to the yard beyond. 'They're late. Probably huddled round the corner talking tactics.'

By the time Tina had finished with the big horse and come back out of the stable, her expression was hard. 'I don't know what they think they're playing at, but they're not getting away with it. D'you have a phone on you? I'll get on to the Dearloves, Kay's people.'

Annie handed her phone across and followed Tina as she raced across to shout more orders at more people and horses, whilst speaking into Annie's phone.

'Yes … yes. OK, thanks.'

She clicked it off and handed it back. 'Kay's in bed ill. That explains why she isn't here.'

'Isn't Laura staying with her?'

'No, she's gone to Mally's while her parents are away.'

'I thought her parents disapproved of Mally?'

'Yes, especially with her mother away. They know Colonel Ludgrove's too old to cope. But the girls will have done as they pleased once Laura's parents had gone.'

'I had the impression Laura was better friends with Kay than Mally.'

'You never know who's best friends in that trio. Mally can be a bit wild, but she's not bad for Laura. Laura gets wrapped in cotton wool. If she were a bit bolder they might not have needed to cheat. I blame Mally's father. He promised to take her part of the time, but then gave her some cock and bull story about a business trip. Then again, Ludgrove can't abide him so he'd keep hold of Mally just to prove a point.'

A point that might be the death of him in the end, thought Annie, remem-bering the drawn features.

Tina led Annie to the house and picked up her own phone. 'I'll try Ludgrove, but it looks as though they aren't going to show.'

Annie struggled to hide her frustration. She had to find a way to talk to those girls.

'No reply.' Tina put the phone down. 'But still, it'll mean you haven't had a wasted journey. I've time to tell you whatever it is you want to know.'

Annie smiled and cast about for a question with a credible link to Terry Martin that would get Tina on to the technicalities of her horses. Then she could let Tina rabbit on for long enough to make her visit seem legit.

'I don't understand why they cheated or how it worked,' she lied, knowing that Tina's anger had burnt so bright when she'd discovered it, she wouldn't remember what she had and hadn't already told Annie.

Tina explained again that Boxer was near-phobic about the concrete blocks that made up that particular obstacle. 'Mally tried to coach Laura to get him to jump them in line with Kay. I think they got him going in the colonel's garden, but he wasn't going to touch them in the dip in the field. That's why she had her little insurance policy of stewarding that fence so she could mark them clear and trust to luck no one noticed.'

'Why didn't it work in the field if it worked at Colonel Ludgrove's?'

'It looks different, smells different. He's an odd little tyke. He'll trust a rider with most things, but not those blocks. He jumps blind with Laura, no problem.'

'Blind?' Annie imagined the small pony with a flapping cloth blindfold.

'When they can't see what's at the other side, where the land falls away, or it's just too big to see over. A pony that trusts its rider'll jump anyway.'

'Why in that bit of the garden? Why couldn't they have used the proper paddock round the back?' Annie, who just wanted Tina to keep talking and who'd never had a garden in her life, felt a measure of indignation on the colonel's behalf at the wreckage they'd left of his lawn.

Tina laughed. 'Have you tried shifting one of those blocks? That's why we always have that jump down in the dip.'

'Where do they come from?' Annie asked, suddenly curious. Now she thought about it, memories popped up everywhere. Those elaborate painted structures in Doris Kitson's garden were based on the same shape. 'They're all over Milesthorpe.'

'There are loads of them up on the cliff where the camp was. Military thing. It was abandoned some years ago. Most of it's fallen over now. Heaven knows what they used them for but once Milesthorpe cottoned on, there were car suspensions groaning with the things. I don't know how many people put their backs out. You can still see them all along the cliffs, right up to where poor old Charles Tremlow popped his clogs.'

It jarred to hear Tina speak about him so casually. 'That'll be a blow to Mally's grandad, won't it?'

'Oh yes. It's like the end of an era to see that trio gone. We called them Last of the Summer Wine. Charles Tremlow was the timid one. And Balham was the scruff. I don't know what the colonel'll do for company. He won't even have the church to fall back on now Tremlow's gone. Doris'll grab his place as church warden. She's been after it for years.'

That church connection again. Annie took a surreptitious look at her watch. She'd done enough now for the visit to appear genuine.

From Tina's, she headed to Colonel Ludgrove's. She couldn't target Kay, who was ill, and didn't know what she'd say to the colonel, but she had to try and find at least one of the girls.

Annie knocked at the colonel's door and listened to the sound echo through the house. After a moment, she heard Mally's voice, 'It's all right, it isn't Tina. It's Annie,' and understood why Tina's call hadn't been answered.

The door opened and Annie followed Mally through to the living room.

'No, no. Don't get up,' she said to Colonel Ludgrove, who huddled in a chair by the unlit fire. 'I heard you weren't well. Are you feeling better now?'

'Oh, not so bad. Old bones, you know. Not as young as I was. Just got up as a matter of fact.'

Mally slumped ostentatiously into a chair, lower lip protruding.

'I've just been down to the stables,' Annie said. She ignored the poisonous glance Mally shot her and smiled at the girl. 'Tina expected you this afternoon.'

'Huh! Go on my own and have old Hain in my face? No thank you. I'll wait till Kay and Laura can go, too.'

'Isn't Laura here?'

'Nah, she was going to stay, but that old fart Tunbridge got all sniffy just 'cos we're poor now and made her stay with Kay.'

'Mel!' The colonel's tone snapped Mally upright in the chair. 'There's no need for that talk.'

'Sorry, grandad.'

Annie found herself unsure whether it was the insult to Mr Tunbridge or Mally claiming to be poor that had earned the rebuke.

Mally looked subdued for a couple of seconds, then began, 'Dad says ...' only to be interrupted by her grandfather.

'Your father's a renegade, a wastrel.'

Annie shifted in her chair, uncomfortable that the family feud should be played out in her presence and that Mally's father should be denigrated in front of his daughter.

'He's not, grandad. He had to go on a business trip. He couldn't help it.'

The colonel gave a contemptuous sniff. 'He didn't look very businesslike when I saw him the other day.'

Mally pounced on this bait. 'When did you see him? Where?'

'A day or two ago, talking to young Laura.'

'Why didn't he come to see me? That's not fair.'

For the first time, Annie found her sympathies veering the other way. Mally was only thirteen; it wasn't fair to goad her about her father like this. She decided to drop a small bombshell into the exchange.

'I'm glad you're feeling better, Colonel. I wonder if I could ask you about this?'

She pulled the key from her pocket and held it out for them to see, watching closely to see how Mally reacted. Nothing. They both stared blankly. It matched Maz's assertion that the girls had never seen it.

'What is it?' Mally asked.

Annie gave an abridged account of Maz handing it over to her. Mally shrank in her chair. The colonel looked aghast.

'I need to know the truth,' she ended, 'before I decide what to do next.'

Mally leapt to her feet. 'I think you're stupid and you should just mind your own business.' She flounced to the door.

'Back here, Mel, and face the music,' the colonel said.

To Annie's surprise, Mally obeyed. There was some code between them that Annie had yet to crack.

'Here, young lady.' The colonel spoke without anger but with a firmness that Mally complied with. The girl stood on the hearth rug in front of him, her gaze down at her feet. 'An explanation.'

'It's Mr Balham. People said they didn't know where he went walkabout. Well, we knew 'cos we saw him up there. We tried to get in but it was real well locked.'

'And where did this scoundrel from Hull come into the picture? I've warned you about people like him.'

'I ... uh ... we ... One of us ... it was probably Laura ... told Maz about it and so we showed him. It looks old but Maz said Mr Balham had new locks on and all that. We just wanted to see in. You can't see through the gap at the back. Then we showed Maz where Mr Balham lived. Maz told us to, and Maz saw the key and he said he could get us a copy made.'

'And did this young vagabond break into Mr Balham's house?'

'We didn't tell him to; we didn't go in the house.' For all Mally's discomfort, she couldn't disguise her admiration for Maz's bravado. 'He said he'd got the key but we said we didn't want it.'

The colonel looked thunderous and Mally for once remained subdued. Annie couldn't second guess what sat worst with the colonel, the stalking of his friend Edward Balham or Mally's association with Maz.

'I'm obliged to you for bringing this to my attention, Miss Raymond. So's young Mel. She could have taken the whole business to the police, Mel, and then where would you be? Say thank you.'

Mally's sullen gaze met Annie's. 'Thank you,' she muttered.

Annie itched to ask about the faxed page, but knew she was on thin ice with this interview already, and didn't know which of the three had sent it with Maz. She'd go back to him and get the facts straight.

She tried a more oblique angle, and asked, 'What was Terry Martin to do with it?'

The colonel stared at her. 'What did that scallywag have to do with any of this?'

'I thought Mally said something about him,' Annie lied, watching the girl closely.

Mally looked blank and then indignant. 'Nothing. He had nothing to do with any of it. We didn't know anything about him killing Mr Balham in that shed.'

Annie saw a look of pain cross the colonel's features at this mention of his friend. Annie was glad she'd told him it wasn't Edward Balham in the building on the cliff, but of course he knew his old friend was missing. Maybe he'd already connected him to the murder.

She murmured conventional condolences about Tremlow and they had a stilted exchange. The colonel struggled to hide how uncomfortable he was at a close friend taking a coward's way out.

As Annie rose to go, the colonel looked up at her. 'May I keep the key?' he said. 'I'll see it gets back to Ted Balham.'

The key would never get back to Ted Balham because he was dead. Annie wouldn't be the one to tell the colonel. But it wasn't a bad compromise. She hoped Pat would agree as she handed it over.

CHAPTER 24

THE PLAN FOR clandestine interrogation of the three girls hadn't worked out, but Annie knew just where to go for information on Elizabeth Atkins.

'Annie, I wasn't expecting you today,' said Doris Kitson. 'Is it about poor Charles?'

'There was something else I wanted to ask you, but yes, it's tragic about Mr Tremlow. I wonder what made him do it.'

'He was always highly strung. You'll sit down for a cup of tea, won't you? His mother sent him away to school, you know.'

'Yes, you told me that before.'

'It's always a mistake. Now promise me you won't send any of your children away to school. Well, you won't, will you? Not with the example of poor Charles in front of you. And then his wife, too. A travelling salesman.'

'It was all such a long time ago, though,' Annie pointed out, as Doris waved her to a seat at the scrubbed wooden table.

'Ah yes, time. A great healer but a great deceiver too. Of course, I shall step into the breach. It'll be hard but I'll manage. I'll have to delegate. What's that new word they all use now? Subsidiarity. That's what we need round here if the Christmas Fayre isn't to suffer.'

Annie said nothing. Had Doris completely lost her marbles or was she, Annie, not as fluent in Milesthorpe-speak as she'd thought. Christmas

Fayre? It was barely August. She cleared her throat. 'Doris, last time I was here, you told me something about a friend of yours. Elizabeth Atkins.'

Doris placed a tray with teapot, cups, saucers and milk jug on the table. 'Elizabeth died years ago, dear. You wouldn't be interested in her.'

'You told me you weren't satisfied her death was from natural causes.'

'Well, maybe I was hasty. She was quite an age. It's all been very upsetting, what with Charles and everything. And now people are saying Ted's died. Is it true? Did they really find him in that building on the cliff? Do you know about it?' Doris spoke fretfully.

So word had begun to leak out, but Annie wouldn't pour fuel on the rumour fire. 'As far as I know he hasn't been seen for about three weeks, but that's all I know. What have you heard?'

'Oh, just people gossiping. You know how they do. Three weeks though. It's a long time. He hasn't been off for this long before.'

Just like the colonel, Doris was distracted and not the robust person Annie had first met. 'About Elizabeth Atkins,' she prompted.

'Yes, dear. Elizabeth died a rich woman and she left a considerable sum of money to Milesthorpe Church.'

The church again. Annie tried to think herself into Terry Martin's head. Had he known Elizabeth Atkins before she died?

No, Doris was clear on that, but she might have talked to Terry Martin about Elizabeth. 'He was interested in the church wardens.'

'What have the church wardens to do with it?'

'She left her money in trust and they have it to administer.' Doris shook her head. 'If only she'd left it to someone more practical … Those gates …'

Annie took it that by someone more practical Doris meant herself, and thought back to the paperwork she'd seen in some of the offices where she'd worked.

'In my experience …' It felt odd to talk about previous experience. She didn't think she had any. Maybe those bits of jobs had taught her something after all. '… money left in trust can take years to untangle.'

Doris sniffed, clearly of the view that it wouldn't have taken her two minutes.

When Annie arrived back into Hull, and let herself into the apartment, she heard Barbara's voice from the living room. 'He's been at it since Dad first got ill.'

'Come off it. I'd have seen it. You can't mean …'

A rustle of paper. 'Look at that.'

'Where did you get that?'

'I was in the agency offices this morning. Six a.m. Long before any of those shysters were up and about.'

'Christ! I can't believe he's doing this. He promised Dad he'd look after the business for me … for us.'

'Junk the sentimentality, Patsy. He has. Hell, he'd junked it while Dad was still alive. All he's looking after is number one.'

'The bastard! I'll kill him!'

'You damned well won't. Not if you don't want to lose the whole lot. Do you realize how dicey our position is?'

Annie found herself stalled in the hallway. She hadn't meant to overhear all this and couldn't just walk in on it. Her priority was the Martins' case, and she had to speak to Pat about it no matter what family crises were ongoing. She crept back to the outside door, eased it open and slammed it shut. At once the voices stopped. Good. She'd walk in as though she didn't know Barbara was here.

'Hi.' She entered with a smile.

Pat glanced up. Barbara narrowed her eyes.

'Pat, one of the girls from Milesthorpe got her hands on the missing page from Terry Martin's notebook.'

'Oh yeah?' Pat struggled visibly to pull her mind back to Milesthorpe. 'Right, yeah, those three girls. Did you get the goods from them?'

'I only saw one of them.' Annie explained the circumstances; the letter Maz had passed on, but could see that Pat was distracted. 'Look, I didn't get a chance to ask about the fax thing. D'you mind if I check my e-mail? It might have come through by now.'

'Sure.' Pat waved her through to the big bedroom, clearly happy to have her out of the room.

Annie sat at her boss's desk, in amongst the clutter of the room, and turned on the PC. She drummed her fingers whilst bits and bytes reached out across networks to make their connections. She logged into her e-mail and ran her gaze down the list of new messages. *Viagra... Cialis... Your loan is approved... Best prices ...* All spam. Nothing from any of the girls.

She sat up suddenly. Of course there wasn't. Where would they get her e-mail address? She'd given them her card, which was Pat's card with her number written on. Her phone number but Pat's e-mail. She bounced up from the chair.

'Pat ... Pat!' As she burst back into the living room she realized she'd interrupted again and this time less tactfully for her intrusion being unintended. She tried not to notice the blankness in the two faces that turned to her. 'I need you to check your e-mail.'

She tried to be rational and unemotional in her explanation but knew she came across as breathless and immature.

'OK.' Pat heaved herself out of the settee and balanced herself on her crutch to hobble to the bedroom.

Annie tried to hover at her shoulder but was squashed back by a look.

The wait seemed interminable, then Pat said, reading from the screen, 'From Laura Tunbridge. No subject. That sound like the one?'

'Yes, that's it. What does it say? I'll—'

'I'll redirect it, OK?' Pat's fingers pecked at the keyboard. She heaved herself to her feet again and hobbled back out of the room.

Annie hurled herself back into the chair in front of the desk and played the Alt+Tab sequence to switch back to her own e-mail.

Sender: Laura Tunbridge.

She clicked it open.

It's what we got money for.

No salutation. No formal schoolgirl style. Laura had been in a hurry.

So Terry had paid them for information on Elizabeth Atkins, but what would they have known about an elderly woman who died over three years ago? She daren't e-mail back. She mustn't leave that kind of paper trail. But she wondered about the Dearloves. Could she ring with some excuse about a message from Tina?

Tina had rung the Dearloves on her phone. She clicked through the call register until she found the number. 'Hello, I'm sorry to bother you but I understand Laura Tunbridge is staying while her parents are away.'

'No, sorry. She does sometimes but our daughter's ill so she's staying with another friend.'

'Would that be Melissa Fletcher?'

'That's right, but her parents are away too. She's staying with her grandfather.'

Annie ended the call feeling puzzled and rang through to the colonel's. Mally answered.

'Hi Mally. It's Annie. Can I speak to your grandfather?'

'He's asleep. I'm not to disturb him.'

'That's OK. Mally, is Laura staying with you while her parents are away?'

'Nah. I told you before. She was going to but she went to Kay's.'

'When did her parents go?'

'Yesterday. Anyway, I didn't want her here.'

Annie held her tone in neutral. 'And what about Boxer? Is he in the stable at your grandfather's?'

'No, he's at Tina's.'

Annie didn't press the point because Mally wasn't hiding anything. Laura had sent the e-mail on Saturday afternoon. Annie and Pat had seen them out with their ponies in the morning. She thought back to Tina and the pony Laura never brought back. She supposed Laura could have taken it to all manner of places.

She tried to recreate Laura's movements. Saturday afternoon, she sent the e-mail. Sunday, she stayed with her parents until they left. Wouldn't they have dropped her off wherever she was to stay? Kay's illness might have complicated matters. Annie worked through Mally thinking Laura was with Kay and the Dearloves thinking she was with Mally.

It didn't matter what angle she came at it, Laura had been missing all night.

CHAPTER 25

ANNIE FELT DREAD rise up inside her. This was no faulty deduction like the non-existent second man on the scaffolding; no mad panic like the one that swept her up when she heard Vince berating Maz. She hadn't misread this one. A young girl was missing.

The low voices of Pat and Barbara still murmured from the living room, but Annie held back from rushing in there. Pat was distracted. It would mean explanations, time lost.

Her hand reached for the phone, hesitated, drew back. Who could she call? Scott? What would he say? Would he take her seriously? Jennifer? What had Scott told her?

If she dialled 999 they'd want explanations she couldn't give. Are you a relative ... a friend ... a neighbour...? She clapped her hands to her face in frustration. Who?

Of course, Tina Hain. Tina would take her seriously. She'd tell Tina; let her get on to the police.

As soon as Tina picked up the phone, Annie blurted out the story. 'The Dearloves think she's at Colonel Ludgrove's,' she ended, 'and vice versa.'

A weight lifted from her as she shared the facts, but that was nothing to the relief she felt on hearing Tina's first words.

'Oh Lord! Has she pulled that stunt again? That explains Boxer.'

Tina wasn't worried. Laura was OK. 'What do you mean?'

'This is Laura all over. It's because she's in trouble.' Annie listened to Tina explain. Laura had run off before. 'She took her pony and went to an aunt who lives about twenty miles away.'

Annie felt her knotted muscles untangle themselves, but knew she must verify Laura's safety for sure before she went to bed tonight.

'The first time it happened,' Tina said, 'she gave her parents the worst fright of their lives. When she arrived with the aunt, she said her parents knew where she was and the aunt let her stay over and didn't ring because it was late. The police were called out. It was chaos.'

'She's done this more than once then?'

'Oh yes. There was a good gap after the first time, but then she did it again because she'd had a row about something. Then it was set to be her stock reaction to anything not going her way. But the last time – back in the spring – her father went on ahead to the aunt's and waited till she turned up. He tried to find her on the way, but she went cross-country. He took the box and was there to stop her the moment she appeared on the drive.

Apparently he bawled her out so loudly she nearly wet herself. He didn't let her go in the house. He loaded the pony straight in the box, Laura in the car and drove them both straight home. It's probably the first time she ever had a proper bawling out and we thought it had stopped her.'

'But of course with them being away at the moment...?'

'Yes, that's what I'm thinking. I'll bet the aunt's already been in touch. Look, I have to nip up into the village, I'll call in on Ludgrove and the Dearloves and just double check. I'll call you back.'

'Yes, please. That would be a weight off my mind.'

Annie stood up, turned off the computer and went back to the living room. She gave Pat a brief summary of what had happened. 'Tina's going to ring me back when she's made enquiries.'

'Run off and no one's noticed.' Pat laughed. 'Poor kid. It's always frustrating to have your grand gestures fall flat.'

A silence fell. It was clear that whatever business was being conducted in this room was far from over. Annie was an unwanted third party.

'I'll nip off out,' she said, and headed for the door. Relief about Laura had let Mrs Earle into her thoughts. The Neanderthal brother might not have handed over the keys. She knew it was irrational and not the way to conduct business, but Orchard Park had been her very first real case and she wanted face-to-face closure.

The refit of the sixth-floor landing was complete. Annie paused to look round at the bright walls, the fresh new paint, the polished glass panels in the partition. She felt a compulsion to savour it. What must the residents feel who were in and out every day? Was it better or worse to see how it could be when they knew what it would be like tomorrow night?

Annie knocked at the door of the flat. It swung open and Mrs Earle stood in front of her. Music and colour pulsed out. She recognized the light glaze of alcohol in Mrs Earle's eyes but nothing else was familiar. Everything shone with bright colours, including Mrs Earle who was dressed in yards of flowered material, her hair packed on her head and studded with glittery baubles. The flat was full of people, all shapes and sizes. She'd arrived in the middle of a party.

'Come in. Come in.' Mrs Earle's tone was effusive as she grabbed Annie's arm and pulled her inside.

Annie stared at the gleaming polish on the furniture, the fresh smell of the place, the way everything was ordered, making it a homely welcoming space. She found herself surrounded by grinning faces and almost knocked off balance as a gang of small children raced through the throng at knee-height on some mission of their own.

'Have a drink. Have a drink.' A giant glass of layered blue and purple liquid was thrust into her hand. Her other hand was enveloped in a huge hot palm. The meaty fingers closed around hers.

She looked up at Mrs Earle's burly brother who gave her an uneven-toothed grin as he raised her hand above her head and shouted over the din. 'This is the one what did it. Cleared 'em out. And not a scrap of muscle on her.' He pinched her upper arm and laughed. 'Friends in 'igh places, eh, love?'

Annie laughed back and surreptitiously pushed the garish glass behind a pot plant on a shelf at her side. So the refit was of lasting duration. She felt her face crease to a grin as she realized what had happened. Vince had stepped in here. Of course he had. The refit was his bribe to the sixth-floor residents to keep them quiet. He'd provided his favourite nephew with a sophisticated setup in that top flat and the guy had jeopardized it with some amateurish dealing on his own doorstep. Vince must have been livid. She had no desire to know the detail because she wouldn't like Vince's methods no matter how cheerful the outcome.

'I know you've come for your money, love.' Mrs Earle was at her elbow again. 'And you've earned it. I'll be honest, I didn't think you 'ad a cat in hell's chance of shifting them, but fair do's.' As she thrust a slim wad of notes into Annie's hand, a sly smile slid across her features. 'It's a bit short,' she said, 'but you can call round in a week or two and I'll have the rest.'

Annie returned the false smile as she pocketed the money. She wouldn't be back. She knew it and Mrs Earle knew it.

A blood-curdling shriek made her jump. Two small children battled briefly round her legs and then raced off. Mrs Earle smiled fondly after them. 'Just look at them bairns. Having the time of their little lives, bless 'em.'

As she sauntered across the sixth-floor lobby to the lift bay on her way out, Annie looked round. Someone else would move in and wreck the place she supposed, but maybe not for a long time. Whatever was in her pocket was all the cash she'd get and however much it came to was that much more than Pat expected out of the job.

She shunned the stairs and jabbed the lift call button. It was no penance to wait on this landing now. Good result.

Her phone rang as she drove across the city. She fiddled to attach the hands-free and took a quick look at the screen. Tina Hain.

'Hi Tina. Has she turned up?'

'No, she hasn't.' The tension in Tina's voice made Annie decide to pull over to take the call. 'No one knew she'd gone till I called in. Kay's mother called the aunt but she hasn't seen her. She's been away. She's only just back. Laura wouldn't have bargained on that.'

'But you've got to get the police.'

'Don't worry, that's the first thing we did.'

'What did they say? Do they know what's happened?'

'They still think she's done her usual stunt, but had to hide out somewhere with the aunt being away. They think she'll turn up there if she doesn't turn tail and come home. They're talking to anyone who talked to Laura at the weekend.'

That nearly included her and Pat. Something nagged at Annie, but she couldn't bring her thoughts into line. The awful notion dawned that Laura's e-mail might have had a role in her decision to bolt. Was she hanging about all Sunday waiting for a reply?

'Have you any idea if she planned it before her parents went, or if something happened to trigger it after they left?'

'Oh, it was planned OK. And planned to disrupt her parents' trip, too, but she overplayed her hand. I think Kay was supposed to notice she'd gone and raise the alarm before they left, but of course she was ill.'

Annie didn't follow Tina's reasoning. 'What d'you mean?'

As Tina explained, Annie tried to remember what she'd assumed and why. Someone had told her Laura's parents left on Sunday. She'd made assumptions, hadn't dug out the detail. *It matters.* Something hammered at her. She listened to Tina tell her how the Tunbridges made this trip every year. They always left early on Sunday morning. Laura was taken to whichever friend was to have her and goodbyes were said on Saturday afternoon. No one now was quite clear when the Tunbridges thought the handover had taken place, but they'd clearly got on with their packing and preparation on Saturday evening assuming Laura was tucked up in her temporary berth.

'I'm sure she expected either the Dearloves or Colonel Ludgrove to ring her parents on Saturday night to say she hadn't turned up, but however it happened, everyone thought she was somewhere else. She hasn't been seen by anyone since Kay carried on down the railway to come back here and Laura cut across the fields supposedly to go to Mally's.'

'Oh my God, but me and Pat saw her and Kay riding down the railway.'

'I suppose you should tell the police then, but there'll be no shortage of witnesses to them riding out. It's where the little minx went next that we need to know. I shouldn't be too hard on her. She'll be scared to death after being out at night in the open. She'll never do it again after this. But really, Annie, there's no need to worry too much. She's safe with Boxer. Even if she gets lost, he won't. And now we're out looking for her, she'll be found in no time.'

'OK, well, thanks for letting me know. Will you ring me the minute she's found? I don't care what time it is.'

Annie set off again for Pat's, but it took no more than a couple of minutes for the clamour that whirled in her mind to spiral down into a terrible spike of fear. She screeched the car to a halt as though Laura herself had stepped out into the road. The front wheel bumped up the kerb and rolled back. She felt the jolt, felt her jaw drop as she worked it out.

Last seen Saturday lunchtime? It was now late Monday afternoon.

Terry Martin ... Charles Tremlow ... For two days and a bit they'd vanished from sight and then they'd died.

Laura Tunbridge had been missing for two days already.

CHAPTER 26

Annie leapt up the stairs to the apartment, burst through the outer door and dived straight into the living room. She stopped, taking in the scene in front of her.

Barbara, on all fours, hung over a swathe of paperwork spread out on the floor around her. Pat balanced awkwardly over the edge of the settee to watch her sister.

Barbara shot Annie a hostile glare. 'Oh, it's you.'

'Well, don't take it out on her,' Pat snapped. 'She's the one who uncovered it.'

They both turned their attention back to the mass of documents.

'See there ... and there ...'

'Where? Move your hand. I can't see. Is that...?'

Annie's gaze ran across the complex mass of papers, tables of figures, lists, dense official-looking text. She couldn't take it in, didn't know how to cut through it with her own news.

'Uh ... Hi ... sorry ...' She spoke without direction, without expecting to be heard as she picked her way across the paper maze and headed for the sanctuary of her room.

Telling Pat wasn't the priority. It could wait. But what she'd worked out couldn't. She clicked through her phone for Jennifer's number.

You have reached the voicemail of ...

Shit! Should she leave a message? What to say? She ended the call before Jennifer's voicemail message finished. She had to call Scott. There was no alternative.

'Annie?' His voice was guarded, cold.

'Scott? It's about Laura Tunbridge. She's missing.'

'Yes, we know that.' His tone was measured. 'We're already dealing with it.'

'Yes, but it's linked.'

He didn't try to hide a heavy sigh. 'How do you mean, Annie?'

'To Terry Martin and Charles Tremlow. And maybe the woman on the cliff too, I don't know. But—'

He interrupted, his tone curt. 'Do you have information about Laura Tunbridge that we need to know?'

'Well ... I'm not sure ... I ...' She should have rehearsed this. 'I just want you to know you have to take it seriously.'

'Annie, when a twelve-year-old girl goes missing, especially for this length of time, we take it seriously. Have you any new information?'

'No, but—'

'Do you know where Laura is?'

'No, but—'

'Then keep your nose out and let us do our job. OK?'

Before she could articulate a response, he ended the call. She thumped the bed in frustration. He hadn't understood. None of them realized the urgency. Anger at Scott mixed with the fear she'd be proved right. She must go out to Milesthorpe, find someone who'd listen to her, find something that would show she was right. But she'd looked for Terry Martin's missing days in Milesthorpe and found nothing. Where to head for, where to focus? She fell back on to the bed, hands over her face trying to find a way through.

The ring of her phone shot her back upright. Jennifer!

'I've spoken to Scott, Annie. I'm sorry I missed your call. I'm supposed to keep my phone off at the moment, but listen, you mustn't worry. We'll find her.' Jennifer's tone was kinder than Scott's, but it wasn't kindness she needed.

'But Jennifer, you need to think about the others. There's a link. Laura's been gone for two days just like they were.'

'We won't leave any stone unturned. We're on the case here. Now, I don't want you to pass this on to anyone, but it might help set your mind at rest. She's done this before.'

'I know that, but it's two days, Jennifer.'

'She was out all night the first time.' Jennifer sounded annoyed at how much Annie already knew.

'Yes, but she was safe at her aunt's. This is different.'

'The only reason she hasn't been found is that no one's been looking.'

'Jennifer, listen to me. There's more to it. How could she possibly stay hidden for two whole days?'

'No Annie, you listen to me. I know you don't mean any harm, but you haven't gone into the detail of this. On previous occasions she's gone to great lengths to hide.'

'But Jennifer, two days?'

'Did you know about the time they knew she'd set off for her aunt's? They tried to catch her on the way and they couldn't. These are people who know the area and knew where she was going. She managed to avoid them. She knows the countryside round here. She's done pony treks. She's been all over the place with those other girls. It might not look a huge area but there are all the big country estates, Burton Constable, Wassand, all round the Mere, the old army ranges. Without anyone actively looking for her, she'll have found it easier to hide than she bargained on, but she's bull-headed. We've talked to a lot of people. She'll stay under cover for sheer obstinacy.'

'But two days, Jennifer. Someone should have seen her.' Annie heard the plea in her tone, knew that Jennifer's logic had won the argument. It made no odds. The certainty knotted tighter inside her.

'Chances are plenty of people have seen her,' Jennifer went on. 'But no one's given it a second thought. A girl on a pony. She's probably been seen by people who know her, but why would they bother? She hasn't officially been missing. Listen, Annie, I don't mean to be unkind, but melodramatics aren't going to help anyone, much less Laura.'

Annie admitted defeat. Jennifer said all the right things and she supposed she and her colleagues did all the things they should, but underlying it all was the conviction they had it wrong. They wouldn't find Laura.

She felt bleak as she clicked off the phone and trailed back into the living room where the scene was more chaotic than when she'd left it a few minutes ago.

'Ah yes, Annie ...' Pat looked up.

Annie took her chance while she had Pat's attention and dived into the conversation to tell her about Laura.

A troubled expression flashed across Pat's features. 'Tunbridge? Sorry, I should have said when you first came in. I was tied up in this lot. There's a message.'

A sudden rush within her had Annie gulp in a breath. 'What do you mean? Has Laura been in touch?' Apprehension churned her stomach. This could be very good or very bad.

'It's on the answer-phone.'

Annie dived for the machine.

It was Laura's father asking for Annie by name. 'We're on our way back. We want you to take on a case for us. It's urgent. We're not satisfied with the police investigation. Please ring as soon as you get this message.'

They'd sensed it too. No doubt the police had been more tactful with Laura's parents than Jennifer had been with her, but they were her parents. They knew Laura. They'd have sensed the misdirection at the core of it.

Mrs Tunbridge answered her call. Annie heard the worry in every word she spoke. The background noise of traffic came through too. She hoped they'd drive carefully.

'We're on our way back. We'll be a couple of hours at least. I don't believe she's run off this time. She wouldn't stay out this long. You must help. We don't care what it costs. I have a terrible feeling about this.'

'I'll do everything I can. Is there anything you can tell me, anything that might help? When did you last speak to her?'

'It was when she rang on Saturday afternoon to say she was at the Dearloves and they were all going out.'

At the Dearloves? But Kay had already been tucked up in bed ill on Saturday afternoon. Laura had made that up. Where had she really called from?

'We know now she wasn't there. We've been in touch with her friends, with anyone who might know where she is. That's how we got your number. Laura talked about you. She trusted you. The police said they can trace the phone records to see where she rang from on Saturday, but it's no good. She'll have used her mobile. Listen, we want you on the spot. You're to use our house as a base. We leave a key with a friend in the village, that's how the police got in, but we've rung and told her to let you have the key. She knows you. Doris Kitson. The police have been into our house and searched already, but I'd be happier to know you'd done it too.'

She wouldn't find Laura there. But a base with a landline was a good idea. She thought of the e-mail.

'Can I check her PC?'

'Of course. Hers is the bedroom on the right at the top of the stairs. The police may have taken it. You don't think she's met someone on the internet, do you? We warned her time and again about that sort of thing.'

'No, I don't think it's anything like that. But I'd like to check her e-mails.' Annie thought of the e-mail to Pat – minimal. Maybe Laura had been more verbose to a close friend.

Annie gave Pat as good an explanation as she could in the few seconds it took to grab the car keys and dive back out of the apartment. She accelerated along the now familiar route out of Hull and swung the car off the main road. The quickest route to Milesthorpe was on the back roads. Wind buffeted the car as the storm that had been threatening to break the heat-wave rumbled low overhead. The sky darkened and the air grew heavy.

She headed straight for the prosperous outskirts of the village. Doris would have planted herself at the heart of the drama and be waiting at the Tunbridges' house, Annie was sure.

There were no lights at this end of the village. She had to slow as she peered into the dark looking for the turning into their lane.

Suddenly, a figure was in the road in front of her, its arms waving.

Annie slammed her foot down on the brake. Shock coursed through her. She jerked up the handbrake and scrambled to untangle her seat belt as she leapt from the car.

'What the hell...? Mally? Mally, what are you doing? I nearly ran into you.'

Mally's face was tight with emotion. Her hair blew across it in the strengthening wind. 'You got to help me. You've got to. It's not my dad. It's nothing to do with my dad.'

'Calm down, Mally. Of course I'll help you. What is it? Come on, get in the car and we'll go to Laura's house.'

Mally knew something. She must keep her here, keep her safe, get her to the official enquiry. Jennifer … Scott …

'No.'

As Annie reached out to put a reassuring hand on the girl's arm, Mally backed off. Annie looked into her eyes as a gust of wind spiralled round them. Mally pushed the hair out of her face and shot Annie a hostile stare. 'I won't. They'll stop me. I'll go by myself if you won't come with me. It isn't my dad; they all think it's my dad.'

Annie knew what had nagged at the back of her mind when Tina had said, 'They're talking to anyone who talked to Laura.' She remembered Mally's outburst when she heard her dad had been seen talking to Laura. But wasn't he supposed to be away? The police needed to talk to Mally's father. *They all think it's my dad*. Hadn't he been involved in a surreptitious visit to the ex-marital home? Someone had told Doris he'd been seen entering the house next door to Tremlow's, but, by the time she'd hurried round, he'd gone. There was more to this.

'Mally, do you know where Laura is?' Annie found herself having to raise her voice to counter the rising whistle of the wind.

'She's all right,' Mally shouted back. 'I know she's all right.'

Scott had asked if she had anything they needed to know. She did now. Mally's father. What was his place in all this? What did Mally know? She mustn't let the girl disappear. Two and a bit days. Time was nearly up for Laura.

'Mally, where is she?' Annie took a step towards the girl but again Mally backed off.

'I didn't say I knew where she was.' Mally set her bottom lip in a stubborn pout. 'I just said she's OK. I know she is. Will you come with me and not tell anyone?'

'Yes, I will,' Annie lied. 'Get in the car. It's going to pour down soon. You can direct me.'

'No, you can't get there by car. Leave it here.'

'I can't. It's in the middle of the road.'

'OK, move it to the side then, but hurry up. I'm going to make a phone call and I don't want you listening in.'

Mally stalked to the far side of the lane and ostentatiously turned her back. Annie leapt for the car and had the earpiece in her ear before Mally thought to turn back to watch her. She wanted to ring Jennifer, but Jennifer had her phone turned off. It had to be Scott. He answered at once as she backed the car awkwardly, keeping her face turned away from Mally's line of sight.

She spoke before he could say anything. 'Scott listen, I think Melissa Fletcher's father's involved in all this. He—'

His angry tone cut across her 'We're on to it, Annie. His father-in-law's told us about him. For God's sake, leave things alone. Is he with you?'

'No. I don't know Mally's father. I wouldn't recognize him.'

'Not him. Her grandfather. He's gone out looking for his granddaughter. We told him to stay put … Christ, no one in this village will stand still for a second.'

'But Mally's with me. She—'

'Well, thank God for that at least. Are you in Hull?'

'No, we're in Milesthorpe.'

'What the hell are you doing out here? I told you … Oh, never mind. Take her to the Dearloves' house at once.'

'But, Scott, I think she's—'

He shouted across her. 'Take her to the Dearloves', Annie. Or to the Tunbridges'. Jen's round there. Whichever you're nearest to. Just do it! Now!'

'Scott, will you listen? I—'

This time she interrupted herself. Footsteps. Mally was back. Sod Scott and his heavy-handedness. She clicked the phone off. Right off. Mally knew something and it was vital Annie find it out before Laura ran out of time. As soon as she knew, she'd get Mally, or the information, or both back to the official enquiry.

Mally didn't speak, just jerked her head in a follow-me gesture and turned to jog back up the lane.

Annie matched step with her. As they reached the top and turned down the hill towards the centre of Milesthorpe, big raindrops began to splat down around them. Mally increased her pace. Annie followed. This was the hill she'd driven down when Laura had called her to say they'd found the body. Through the encroaching dusk she made out the ramshackle gate that was the entrance to Balham's farm. Instead of slowing to follow the turn in the road, Mally took a sprint at the gate and vaulted it. Annie clambered over. Another set of clothes wrecked.

It wasn't easy to keep Mally in view. Dusk pooled into dense shadow between the farm buildings. The girl ahead of her clearly knew her way through here blindfold. It rained in earnest now, only the high barn walls offered any protection and that was gone as Mally scrambled over a wall and led Annie on to a grassy track out into the open.

As they ran, the storm blew harder. She heard her own laboured breathing mirroring Mally's. 'Where are we going?' she panted.

The girl just said, 'Come on.'

A stunted tree and part of a hedge marked a junction in the track. Mally threw herself into the hedge and lay back against the spiky hawthorn. 'Hurry up. Hurry up.' She muttered the words as though to herself.

Annie ducked into the little shelter the hedge had to offer noting out of the corner of her eye a moss- and creeper-covered shape at her feet. One of those blocks again, abandoned in the bottom of the hedge as though someone had carried it this far and could go no further.

'Hurry up!' Mally growled.

'I'm here,' said Annie.

'Not you. Kay.'

'Kay's ill.' As she spoke, Annie heard footsteps patter along the grass. Someone approached from the other track. Annie recognized Kay's slender form and, as the girl drew close, took in the lank hair plastered to her face and head not only with the rain but with sweat. Kay's face flushed red from whatever illness still had her in its grip.

Oh no, she'd hijacked both of them. When Scott found out …

'I had to climb out of the window,' Kay said to Mally.

So it was Kay whom Mally had called. It would do no good to order Kay back home. The three of them stood in the rain, braced against the force of the wind. Kay looked from one to the other of them. 'What is it?'

Mally glanced at Annie, then back at Kay, but met neither of their stares as she said, 'I've found Boxer.'

Kay gave an excited jump and clapped her hands. 'That means you've found Laura. Where, Mally? Where?'

'I'm taking *her*.' Mally jerked her head towards Annie. 'You can come too if you want.'

Boxer? If Mally had really found Boxer … but the girl held something back. She had to go along with her further than this. Mally looked resolute but scared. Annie fingered the phone in her pocket. It would do no good to call anyone now. If Mally legged it, she'd be left empty-handed and no nearer Laura.

'Come on.' As Mally shouted and set off again at a run, Kay followed and Annie ran behind them.

A sudden flare of lightning lit the landscape. Annie saw they were more exposed than she'd realized. She struggled on over uneven grassy hillocks as thunder rumbled around them. Her calf muscles protested the underlying upward gradient. She half-registered the angular shapes that grew at intervals from the side of the track. Whatever military use this land had once been put to, it had needed concrete blocks to trail some long-lost boundary. They were near the sea's edge, climbing up on to the grassland above the crumbling clay cliffs. That lightning flash had shown her seething white-crested waves down below. She had time to note that the cross-country route from Milesthorpe to the sea was way shorter than going by road.

As the gradient steepened, they slowed. Then Mally slumped down in the mud breathing hard.

'Wait a bit,' she said, as first Kay and then Annie collapsed beside her. 'We'd better keep quiet.'

Another diffuse sheet of lightning swept over them bathing everything in a short burst of white light. Their stares were drawn up towards the sea, invisible now they lay on the ground, but audible as the waves crashed into the cliffs below them. Probably undermining the land beneath us, thought Annie.

The lightning picked out a silvery line that hovered just above the track in front of them. Tinsel blown all the way from Tina's and caught here in the scrub. Annie looked into Kay's face. The girl gazed towards the sounds of the sea as though not quite on the same planet as her companions. Her face glowed an unnatural blotchy red. Her stare was so intense that Annie followed the line of it and made out some kind of barrier fencing off a dangerous part of the edge. A branch wedged across more of those omnipresent concrete blocks.

Annie heard Kay's hands and knees squelch in the mud as the girl turned to crawl towards the sound of the sea. She dived forward and pulled her back. 'No, Kay. Don't go near the edge. The storm's too strong. It's dangerous.'

She knew too well the way the wind could whip away all stability at the edge of a precipice. The rain dripped down her back running a freezing track across her sweat-soaked skin. Kay shouldn't be out in this.

'We need to go down here.' Mally slithered in the mud following a downward incline away from the cliff's edge leaving the strand of tinsel glittering behind them as a shaft of moonlight escaped the storm clouds. Annie kept close to the girl. There was some relief in having the rain lash the back of her head now instead of her face, but water ran down the neck of her jacket as though from a tap. Without the glow off the sea, the landscape ahead vanished into the darkness. They almost came up against a low wall before its shape grew from the shadows. Over the rush of the waves and the roar of the wind Annie made out the unmistakable sounds of an animal snuffling about.

'There, that's Boxer,' Mally whispered.

Part of Annie wanted to stop now and get on her phone to call for help, but something in Mally's tone stopped her. She had to be sure. All ponies looked much the same, but she'd seen Boxer several times and was fairly sure she could recognize him. 'I want to see him closer up,' she whispered back.

Kay sat in the mud and stayed put. Mally and Annie crept closer. Annie half wished for a bigger moon, but at the same time wished for no moon at all so she could be sure they were invisible as they pressed themselves low in the sodden grass and slid forward towards the wall.

They heard the clack of hoofs on concrete as the pony moved, its outline crossing their line of sight. Annie saw it in silhouette, heard it chuckle in its throat as it put its head down. She hadn't a hope of distinguishing it from a beach donkey but Mally gave a sudden start.

'But it *is* Boxer,' she blurted out.

Annie felt her heart begin to pound in reaction to the wave of fear she sensed from the girl beside her. Mally knew they'd find a pony here but she'd had no idea it was Boxer. What was she playing at? Why had she led them here?

'Come on,' Annie hissed, taking charge and backing off away from the low wall towards where they'd left Kay. Mally scrambled after her.

When they'd retreated up the slope, Annie put her arms round both girls huddling them all close together. Mally's shivers were more than the lashing wind and rain warranted. The heat from Kay was abnormal but the high blush was gone from her cheeks as though the moonlight leached the blood out of her. As Annie spoke, she fought to keep her tone neutral.

'Why did you bring me here, Mally?' Suddenly she knew the question wasn't why. '*Who* told you to bring me here?'

Even in the scrappy moonlight, Annie saw the colour drain from Mally's face as she looked first down into the gloom towards where they'd seen Boxer and then back towards the cliff top. She saw Mally and Kay exchange glances. Kay's face, now wan from her illness, turned paler in the silvery light.

Whatever the two girls had worked out between them, they wouldn't share it. Annie guessed it was a dawning realization about Mally's father.

Annie thought of Jennifer, of the police search for Laura. They'd cast a wide net. Jennifer had mentioned Burton Constable and Wassand. They were way off course, far to the north of Milesthorpe when they should be east. She replayed Scott's scathing comments about the great detective and knew she'd been right all along. Right about Terry Martin. Right about Tremlow. She'd even been right about what Vince could have done to her in the heat of temper. Now she had to be right about Laura before it was too late.

Laura was here. Nearby. And Annie had been lured here, too. She couldn't blame Mally. The girl's motives had been to protect her father.

She released the two girls and pulled out her phone, tried to shield it from the driving rain so she could see the screen, and called Jennifer.

The ring tone crackled, broke up. She took the phone from her ear and pressed the buttons again.

'You'll not get much of a signal up here,' Kay said. 'We couldn't.'

We couldn't? She realized she knew exactly where they were. On the cliff side of the building where the murdered woman's body had been found. She'd never seen it from this angle. That pen where Boxer ambled about was the walled enclosure she'd crossed that day after the body was taken away.

The two girls watched her in silence.

She lifted her phone again and stared at the screen. It had to work. Terry Martin was silenced for what he knew. Tremlow too. He'd been about to tell her something and it was clearly more than that he hadn't had his glasses on that night. And Laura had found the missing page from Terry Martin's notebook. She had to ring Scott. She'd just talk over him if he tried to silence her.

It took a second to realize what she saw in front of her. Oh no ... Please, no. Battery low. She'd forgotten to charge it. It could give her no more than a few seconds. No time to waste stabbing at buttons. Return last call. She jammed it to her ear and prayed silently to whatever god grumbled its displeasure from the skies above her.

The ring tone crackled but it didn't cut out.

You have reached the voicemail of ...

Oh Jennifer! No. Where are you? 'Jennifer, you must ...' but the phone had gone dead.

She looked down the slope into the gloom. Boxer was in that enclosure at the side of the building. She remembered the dank corridor, the raised stalls to either side and the slimy green fingers of lichen and moss that reached down the walls. At the far end was a sturdy wooden door behind which a rotting body had lain.

Boxer was outside. Laura must be inside. And she'd given away the key to Colonel Ludgrove.

When she focused again on the girls it was to see Mally's rain-streaked face looking up at her, expression stunned.

She pulled them close again, heard Kay's laboured breathing, felt the fire from the girl's body. 'Tell me about the building. Everything. How can I get in? Is Boxer shut in? Where's the gate?'

'Straight down from here.' Kay pointed into the darkness, her voice slurred. 'If you go straight you'll get to the side of it. On your left'll be the yard bit where they used to put the sheep. That's where Boxer is. The first door goes off the yard bit and the locked door's inside.'

Yes, thought Annie, I know about that. 'Is there any other way in.'

'No, but there's a gap in the wall at the back.'

'How do I get to it? Can I see inside the building? Is it big enough to get in?'

'You can't see in. We think there's sacking or something covering it inside. You just feel along the back wall and you'll come to it. You'd be able to see in a bit probably if there was any light inside. We never saw anything. We never came at night.'

Annie looked again at her useless phone. Even if she could call anyone, help would come too late. Laura's two and a bit days were up. She was on borrowed time.

'You want to phone the police, don't you?' Mally's tone was sombre.

'Yes, of course. We have to. And it's what you two are going to do now while I go down there.'

'We'll come with you, Annie.'

'No, Kay, you mustn't. You must go back until Mally's phone works properly. How far did you have to go that night you called me?'

'We used Laura's phone,' said Kay. 'Mine and Mally's wouldn't work at all, would they, Mally?'

Mally shivered as she reached into her pocket. 'D'you want this?' Annie looked at the object in Mally's hand. The key Maz had given her. 'I took it out of Grandad's pocket, but Annie you mustn't tell. You won't, will you?'

'I won't.' As Annie felt the key in her hand she felt a surge of something that felt like fear but approximated optimism. She could get through that door. Get Laura free before … before whatever was going to happen was scheduled to happen. But Laura's time was up. It was already too late. There was no point in doing anything unless she moved fast.

'Please,' she begged the two girls. 'You must go back. Call the police.' As she begged, she knew they wouldn't phone and speak to an anonymous voice. They'd go all the way back to Milesthorpe before they told anyone. 'Do you remember Jennifer Flanagan? That nice policewoman. Ask to speak to her. Or a man called Scott Kerridge. He's Jennifer's friend. He'll know how to help. Now go on. Quick.'

Kay wiped her hand across her face. 'We have to go back to the edge of the cliff,' she said.

'Yes, you have to go that way.' Annie agreed, wondering what had prompted Kay to state the obvious. 'Take care. The wind's strong.'

Neither girl took any notice of her. Annie saw through the last vestiges of light that they stared hard at each other. Some byplay that she couldn't understand sizzled between them.

After a moment, Mally gulped and then spoke. 'It's not my dad.' It was a whisper.

'No, I expect it isn't,' Kay replied, in a voice that sounded as though it deliberately humoured her friend.

'It isn't!' Mally insisted.

'But we've got to clear the way,' said Kay.

Annie couldn't stay to help them and didn't have time to try to work out what they were talking about. They'd turned in the right direction. 'Phone Jennifer Flanagan, Mally,' she urged. 'And look after Kay.'

With terrible misgivings, she pushed them into starting the scramble back up to the path at the edge of the cliff, then she turned and began the muddy slither back down towards the building.

CHAPTER 27

ANNIE MADE OUT Boxer's outline as the pony shifted his weight and took a step forward. For a moment he stood bathed in a pale silver light as the moon pierced the storm clouds. In front of him was a net like those Annie had seen at Tina's, but it wasn't stuffed with fodder; it hung limply from the wall. Boxer placidly picked strands of hay from the ground. Wisps blew from his mouth and eddied around the yard. In close to the building, he had some shelter from the worst of the squall.

As the storm threw clouds across to shroud the moon and the scene darkened, Annie thought back to Tina's words. 'She's safe with Boxer. Even if she gets lost, he won't.' And there stood Laura's symbol of safety wearing a saddle and bridle as though all ready to set off with his rider. But even through the gloom and driving rain Annie could see the leather was soaked through. The stirrups swung beside the pony as he moved. How long had he stood there?

If Laura were inside and if Annie could get her out and on to her pony …

She looked at the entrance to the yard. A pole was balanced across. It would be the work of a moment to lift that clear.

The first door, the one that led to the corridor Terry Martin had crept down, was a dark outline in the far wall. A perfect trap. She remembered how it felt to sneak inside in the daylight and tried to imagine herself creeping down into the yard, slipping through that door … She couldn't.

She eased back and made her way through the wet grass towards the other end of the building feeling along the wall as she went. The wind screamed, but in the shelter of the wall, couldn't batter her as well as it wanted. The rain made up for it. A relentless barrage pounded down. Then, as her hands began to track along the cold, wet surface of the building proper, a soft moaning reached out to her over the howling of the storm. She saw a dark shadow like a gash in the wall. The gap Kay told her about. And the low keening she could hear could only be Laura.

When she reached the slit in the wall, Annie pressed her ear to the sodden surface and heard the subdued wailing. It was all that was left of long burnt-out hysterics. Low cries, barely sobs. What state was the poor child in? How long had she been in that hellhole?

The gap was no more than a fissure where the cement bed crumbled away from between two uneven slabs of concrete. Annie found she could slip a hand through but there was no chance to get inside or to get Laura out. The despairing sound seemed right beside her, but that might be the echo from the cave-like structure.

Could she risk calling out?

She pulled her hand back and pressed her face to the opening straining for any glimpse of the interior. Kay said it was covered with sacking. Annie eased herself sideways into the wall to get the longest reach, and gingerly stretched her arm through. Her hand went beyond the concrete of the wall, felt flimsy material that trailed on her skin like spiders' web and then touched cold metal, some sort of wall bracket. She walked her fingers along it. They pushed up against something warm and soft.

There was a shriek from inside as she recoiled. Oh my God! Laura!

'No, Laura. It's OK. Be quiet. It's Annie. I've come to get you out. It's OK.'

After the first petrified shriek, Laura quietened, as though too exhausted to scream. What had she been through these last two days? Annie could almost lose her fear of the dark corridor in her determination to get this child out of her prison.

She reached back in through the gap. 'Laura, it's Annie. I'm going to reach through and touch your arm. I've come to get you out. The police are on their way.' Please God.

'Annie?' Barely a whisper that Annie couldn't be sure she'd heard.

'Yes, I'm going to get you out. Just keep calm.'

'But my arm's in this thing.' As Laura spoke, her voice broke up into sobs.

'I know it is. I'll get it out. Who locked you up, Laura?'

'I don't know. I was waiting for Mally then I woke up in here. Annie, get me out. I'm frightened.'

Annie knew she had to keep the girl talking. 'Is your other hand tied?'

'It so isn't fair, Annie. I want to go home.'

'I know, Laura. I'll get you out. Please tell me, is your other hand tied? Are your legs tied?'

While she talked, Annie felt as best she could round the metal of the wall bracket.

'No,' Laura sobbed. 'It's so not fair. It hurts my arm.'

'Are you sure, Laura? This is really important. Try and tell me. Is it just one hand that's tied?'

Annie kept up the questions to distract Laura and keep her calm, but she also needed to know because the wall bracket holding Laura was old and loose. She was sure she could jiggle it out far enough for Laura to slide her hand free. And if sliding her hand free would release her properly, then Annie could creep back round and down that corridor knowing that if she could get the door open, Laura had a chance to get away. A tremor ran through her as she saw herself wrestling with the key in the lock, just as she'd seen Terry Martin do on the film, but now she pictured a figure in the darkness behind her watching, waiting for the moment to grab her and push her inside the trap with Laura. If she were prepared for it, she might be able to hold out long enough for Laura to run back down the corridor, get on to her pony's back and away. If she could only stop Laura's fear pinning her inside the dark cave.

'Laura, have you heard anyone else nearby?'

'No, Annie, not for ages.'

The killer had imprisoned Laura and left her, but he'd be back to finish the job. She had to work quickly and somehow, while she worked Laura's arm free, she must coach her to have the courage to run. Because once Laura was in the saddle no one would catch her on this terrain.

'Laura, listen carefully. I'm going to get your hand out of here and then I'm coming to unlock the door. Boxer's waiting outside.'

At once, Laura's half-sobs changed to rapid breaths that made Annie fear the girl would hyperventilate herself into a faint. 'Annie … Annie, get me out. I knew he was still out there … I knew it …'

Annie felt excitement rise inside her. The thought of her pony nearby would bolster Laura. Whoever put her in here should have freed the pony to wander off but had maybe been afraid the loose pony would alert people. Laura must have been persuaded to ride him here. That's where she'd gone after she'd left Kay on the old railway. No. No, it wasn't. It was where she'd been persuaded to go after she'd e-mailed Annie. When had she found the torn page and made a copy for Maz? She couldn't stop to work it all out now.

'It's important to keep calm, Laura. Keep calm for Boxer.' Annie gritted her teeth as she pulled at the bracket through the narrow opening. The angle was almost impossible, but she could feel it loosening. Now she must rehearse Laura in the detail of her escape, because it was possible she'd have to do it all on her own while Annie struggled to hold back a killer. Don't think about it. Focus on the girl.

'Now listen, Laura. When I unlock the door, you come out as quickly as you can and get to Boxer.'

'I'll wait for you, Annie.'

'No, no. You mustn't wait for me.'

'I'll be frightened on my own. I so won't go on my own.'

Annie knew Laura would panic if she hinted the killer might be close. She sought for inspiration as the sharp sting of the rain hit the side of her head and water poured down her face. 'You must take Boxer straight home, Laura. He's been standing out in the rain. He needs his warm dry stable. You'll take him straight home, won't you, Laura?'

'Oh yes. Yes, I will. Poor Boxer. Let me out, Annie. Quickly.'

'No, Laura, don't pull yet. Let me loosen it further. Laura, when you get outside … this is really important, Laura … when you get on Boxer you need to go out of the yard here. And then you must go along till you get to the track, then turn towards the sea and you can get to the cliff path.'

'Yes, I know Annie. I've done it loads of times.'

Annie smiled in the darkness as she redoubled her efforts with the metal bracket. Of course Laura knew. She *had* done it loads of times. 'Hold still, Laura. Nearly there.'

'I saw Terry in Mally's house with Mr Tremlow.'

'It doesn't matter now, Laura. You can tell me later.'

'It was after Mally's mum had gone away. Mr Tremlow so shouldn't have taken Terry in there. It's not his house. He shouldn't have taken him, should he, Annie?'

'No, Laura, he shouldn't.'

'I went to call for Mally. I forgot she wasn't there. And I saw them.'

'What were they doing, Laura?'

'Terry said, "It's Mrs Atkins's money isn't it?" And Mr Tremlow called him a blackguard. What's a blackguard, Annie?'

'Blackguard? I think it'll have been blaggard. It's an old-fashioned swear word.'

Laura babbled on as Annie gritted her teeth in frustration at the awkward angle, the pounding of the rain and the pain in her arm as she struggled with the ancient structure.

'I didn't tell Mally 'cos she was horrid about the Showcross. It wasn't my fault. It was clever of me to make a copy of that paper like that, wasn't it, and send it with Maz?'

'Yes, Laura, very clever.'

'It was what Terry wrote when Mally stole him the papers about the church. Then I decided to sneak it back after I'd e-mailed you so no one would know.'

So she'd been caught trying to put the torn page back. Annie wondered where. It didn't matter for now. She imagined *someone* twisting their mouth to a false smile, pretending not to notice what they'd seen; questioning Laura gently so she spilt all she knew.

She wrenched the metal bar, grunting at the effort needed to get any sort of purchase on it; wincing as the awkward position shot a shaft of fire up her arm.

'Why did you come up here with Boxer, Laura?'

'Mally said to come up here quick as I could and not let anyone know.'

'Mally told you?' Mally had lured them both? But the girl had been genuinely surprised to find Boxer.

'She left me a message, but I came as quick as I could.'

A message? Annie would lay money it was a message Mally knew nothing about.

She yanked at the bar, heard Laura's sudden intake of breath as the jarring movement jerked her arm, was aware the girl held back an instinctive cry of pain. As she kept up the pressure and felt the decades-old wall give up its hold bit by bit, Annie kept talking almost at random. Anything to distract the girl from her predicament.

'Who was here when you arrived, Laura?'

'No one.' The girl's voice sounded puzzled. 'Just a hay-net for Boxer and a drink for me. I was ever so thirsty, Annie. Then I got sleepy and I don't remember.'

Did that make it planned in advance, or just very quick thinking by someone taking advantage of circumstances and Laura's parents being away?

Annie thought of Mally leaping out in front of her car. Everyone knew everything in Milesthorpe; and by then the place was boiling with news of Laura's disappearance. Doris Kitson knew Annie was on her way to the Tunbridges'. If Doris knew, Milesthorpe knew. Who was aware that Annie had a copy of the torn page? Was that the reason Mally had been used to lure her up here? Or was it just that she homed in on the truth step by step, millimetre by millimetre, and must be stopped. It didn't matter now. None of it mattered now.

What mattered was to keep Laura talking. Once she'd freed her arm, she wanted the girl to feel her way across a pitch-black room where a rotting corpse had lain not so long ago. It would be good if Laura didn't remember that.

Laura's earlier words were an irrelevance, but they seeped into Annie's consciousness. Mally didn't live at the colonel's, of course she didn't. Her house was where she lived with her mother, next door to Tremlow. Annie had known all along but somehow hadn't adjusted her mental image. The house with all the work being done. *We're poor now …*

'Try it now, Laura. Can you get your arm out?' Annie felt Laura pull against her. For a moment she thought the bracket might hold firm but suddenly the strain slackened.

'I'm free.' It was a whisper. 'Hurry up, Annie. Hurry and unlock the door.'

'Keep calm, Laura. Boxer's waiting for you.'

Annie pulled her hand out of the gap, grazing it painfully on the rough surface of the concrete. She stumbled along the side of the building sliding in the mud, running blind now. The last of the light had been swallowed in the storm.

Boxer was no more than an outline down below her. She was aware his head shot up as she looked over at him, but then he returned to his search for stray wisps of hay. Annie slid herself over the low wall and dropped down beside him. She made for the pole blocking the entrance.

'Stay here, Boxer. Don't wander off,' she whispered, and lifted the pole away from the gap.

She crept to the outer door. It creaked as she pulled it towards her. She prayed that the gale hid the sound as she slipped through into the dark corridor. At once, the noise of the storm melted into the background behind the thick walls. The air stilled. The silence wrapped itself round her too closely, too intimately, as her footsteps traced Terry Martin's.

She took the dark stretch step by step with Terry Martin's film in her mind's eye, knowing the raised stalls lay in the blackness beside her, every shadow dense enough to hide a body. Terry Martin's killer could be close enough to reach out and touch her as she crept past.

The big door, the backdrop to the only sight she'd had of Terry Martin, loomed large ahead of her. His silhouette had bent over this door twisting a key. Now Annie reached out with an identical key to the same door and found Maz's uncle's handiwork all but swallowed by the lock. She had to bend close as she held the key with finger ends and tried to turn it. As she struggled with it she realized Maz hadn't broken into Balham's farmhouse to get a copy of the key for the girls: he already had the impression from doing the same task for Terry Martin. How much had Terry paid him for that?

The sound of the key in the lock must have filtered through the stout wooden panels.

'Hurry. Hurry.' She heard Laura's fists pound on the other side of the wood.

'Hush, Laura, please hush.' She couldn't make Laura hear without shouting louder than she dared and desperately centred her efforts on the stubby key. Once she'd pushed it home, it turned sweetly. Maz's uncle knew his craft. She pushed the big door and felt it give under the pressure.

'Quiet, Laura. You must keep quiet.' The girl was out as soon as the door was wide enough for her to squeeze through. She shot past Annie and raced towards the thin line of light from the outer door. Annie heard her stumble on the uneven ground as she hurried after her. It had been wasted worry that Laura would hang back and wait for her. The girl had forgotten her in the rush of freedom from her prison. Annie hurried after her, too aware of the clammy stones of the building closing in.

Outside, the storm had lost its intensity. The rain poured down without a hurricane to whip it to a stinging force that hit from all directions. Pale moonlight filtered through, turning the yard into a stage, the surrounding scrubland an amphitheatre where anyone might sit back and watch through the dark.

'Boxer!' Laura flew at her pony and embraced his neck.

'Get on his back, Laura. Quick. Get going.'

Laura seemed paralyzed as though shock had switched her to a different dimension. 'Oh, his saddle's all wet. He's soaked. He's ...' Laura reached into her pocket for a hanky to dab at the wet leather.

'For God's sake! Get on his back!' Annie rushed at Laura and lifted her at the pony, half throwing her on to it. 'Go on. Get going.'

Even once aboard, Laura couldn't seem to grab the urgency above the niceties of arranging herself in the saddle and untwisting the reins. Careless of the danger from hoofs or teeth, Annie grabbed a handful of leather strapping somewhere near Boxer's nose and dragged him round to face the way out of the enclosure, then she dived behind him and slapped his rump with all the energy she could muster.

Almost crying in frustration as the rain stung her face and the wind cut through to her skin, Annie hit out again and again. The pony ambled across the concrete with Laura crooning, 'Boxer. You're safe. Poor Boxer ...'

Then, through the rush and roar of the storm and the waves lashing the shore, Annie heard a tiny sound from somewhere nearby. Like the snapping of a twig in the darkness beyond the wall.

CHAPTER 28

'RUN, LAURA!'

At last, something speared panic through the unnatural calm. Boxer leapt forward. Laura screamed. In a clatter of hoofs they were gone. Annie had a momentary impression of the pony disappearing into the night then she dived for the deep shadow of the wall.

A surge of triumph took her. Now she was alone with whoever was here in the darkness, but Laura was out of the trap. Pressed into the wall, she eased herself along, desperate for the safety of open country.

Rain swept across her in waves, the wind found strength again to howl at the rush of the sea. As the moon's light was obscured, definition leached from the scene. Reflected phosphorescence from distant waves danced weird shapes in front of Annie's eyes. She fought for memory of the yard's layout as she felt her way.

Under everything she could hear the rapidly receding hoofbeats heading for the track. Make him run, Laura. Make him run.

Water and mud poured down the face of the wall. She could barely get any purchase but grabbed at the loose bricks and forced herself to climb.

Just at the top where one last effort would take her over, a hand reached out of the darkness, grasped her upper arm and heaved her up and over the wall.

Annie cried out in fright, thought her heart would burst from her chest the shock was so great. At once the hand released her and a voice hissed from the shadow, 'Keep the noise down. He's not far away. This way, Miss Raymond. Quick.'

She scrabbled to her feet, fought for breath as she squinted to see the man who'd appeared from nowhere. 'What the hell…?'

'Quick. No time. He's on his way.' The figure turned to go, his form dissolving into the dark.

Annie scrambled after him, thoughts spinning. Colonel Ludgrove. He'd come up here to find Mally. What instinct had brought him? This must be about Mally's father. And where was he?

She was aware the colonel stumbled worse than she did. This would kill him for sure. How had he known? Why couldn't she focus? What must they do?

He stopped and waited for Annie to catch up. She stood beside him, listened to his rasping intakes of breath. He stared in the direction from where all sight and sound of Laura had vanished and wheezed out, 'D'you think she'll make it?'

'Laura? Oh yes. She knows these tracks, Colonel. She'll follow the quickest way back home.'

'Hope so. Galloped off like a trouper. Don't know how she got free, but …'

'She was locked in. I had a key.'

She heard him chuckle. 'That granddaughter of mine, eh? Resourceful young lass.' The wind whipped the words away. She had to lean close to hear him. 'Young Laura, will she hold her nerve, keep the beast at a gallop?'

'Oh yes, no one'll catch her now. Come on. We need to get back to the road.'

His breathing had eased. She'd lead him back. He must have a car here.

Where were the police? Mally and Kay should have been on to Jennifer by now. Laura was safe. That was the thought to hold to. She'd be on auto-pilot for home. Down the slope from the building ... on to the side track up towards the cliff.

Full gallop up the slope and then ...

And then turn right, but his path would be barred by a silvery strand of Christmas tinsel. *Danger! Lions!* He'd been taught to be terrified. He'd leap shy of it. What would be there in front of him? Two concrete blocks with a pole wedged between them. The obstacle he'd been taught to jump in his sleep.

Annie felt her insides turn to ice; her heart begin to pound. Boxer flying up that slope.

'Oh my God!' She clenched her fists. 'Colonel, she's going into a trap. We've got to stop her.'

Annie took a step. Which way? She couldn't see in the darkness. The colonel's hand was on her arm. 'This way,' he barked.

Yes, he was right. Head for the only landmark they could see. The smudged outline of the cliff's edge where it drew a line between land and sea.

'Laura!' she screamed, careless of hidden listeners, knowing the sound wouldn't carry, knowing it was too late.

As she ran, ignoring the colonel's laboured breathing behind her, she strained to hear through the increasing rush of the waves as they neared the edge. Too late. Too late.

The colonel tried to keep up with her, his face a grimace of pain as he clutched at his chest. She couldn't help him, could only gasp out, 'Stop, Colonel. Wait there. I'll come back to you.'

Tina's words. 'Boxer'll jump blind.' Over the obstacle ... over the edge ... Laura, given to running away with her pony, would be found dead at the foot of the cliff.

She stumbled on, knowing she couldn't reach the spot before they did, knowing they must be there already.

But she'd heard no scream. Surely they'd scream when Boxer with all that training flew over that tiny obstacle and took them both to their deaths far below.

Oh, but he wouldn't. A sudden surge of hope. Concrete blocks were lions too. For all Mally's hard work he'd only ever jumped that fence in the colonel's garden.

And Mally ... Kay ... *Clearing the path*. Christ, that's what they'd meant. Kay had recognized it at once. And Mally had gone to pieces. Couldn't cope with what her father had planned.

What sort of mind planned that? As she slid and staggered over the rutted ground, Annie knew she hadn't worked it out because it could never have been the plan to frighten the pony over the edge with Laura on its back. But that was what would happen. She knew the answer was there for her to think out. It didn't matter. No time. All she could think was that she was too late.

Laura's fate lay with Mally and Kay now.

The clay grabbed her shoes and clung on, weighing her down. She cursed the rain that flew into her face, salty and stinging, obscuring everything ahead.

A sheet of lightning flashed across the sky. For a second the scene lit up like day. They were there. Further away than she'd realized. All of them. On the slope near the edge. She caught half a glimpse of a pony struggling on its side in the mud ... three small figures. Then the black of night and the pounding of the rain swallowed them, leaving the image imprinted on her mind.

'They've made it!' She turned to the colonel in triumph. 'Boxer fell in the mud. We were heading the wrong way. We have to get to them.'

'Yes,' said the colonel. Just yes.

A tiny gap opened with the relief of seeing them all alive; a gap through which another thought was able to snake in. Mally's father. It needed no thinking through; the idea arrived fully-formed in her mind.

He'd been away ... seen nothing of the Showcross ... wasn't a welcome visitor at his father-in-law's house. Why would he embezzle money to spend on his ex-wife's house after such a messy divorce? Who had sat and watched those girls with Boxer ... up and down ... up and down ... Who had control of Elizabeth Atkins's money? Terry Martin and his obsession with the church wardens ...

And how had a man in the throes of a heart attack kept pace with her?

In the fraction of a second it took for the story to slot into place in her mind, Annie tried to turn.

Strong hands gripped her arms from behind, twisted her body till her feet were almost off the floor.

She screamed out. At once the world tipped from under her and she found her face pressed into the mud. No room for any thoughts except how to breathe. He'd suffocate her here. She felt herself gag on the pooled rain-water. The pain of his weight on her back speared through her as it forced her into the ground.

At the moment of panic, as she tasted salty clay, his grip slackened, the weight was gone. She had enough leeway that instinct almost had her struggle to her feet.

No. She clung to the security of the muddy ground.

He'd fooled her long and often enough. At last – too late? – she could read him. He needed her on her feet so he could drag her the last metre to the edge. She mustn't suffocate in the mud. Modern forensics were too good to risk that. But if she were found dashed to pieces by the waves, who could say what made her fall? He was so strong. No glimmer of the frail old man she thought she'd come to know.

He'd used Mally to lure her up here, but he'd arrived too late to trap her; hadn't expected her to free Laura.

He might not be frail, but he was old. He held still. Getting his breath back. Annie clung to the security of the muddy surface alert to the hands that held her. Both hands. While both hands held her down, he couldn't hit her.

'Is that what you did to Terry Martin? Hit him first then toss him in that hole?'

She spoke into the mud with no expectation of being heard, but his voice answered her. Down here close to the ground, they'd found their own refuge from the storm.

'Good Lord, no. Leave things to chance? Hit him in the first place of course. Had to silence him. He wasn't a drinker, you see. Couldn't have got it down him easily if he'd been fully *compos mentis*.' He laughed softly. The sound sent bolts of panic through her. 'Clever forensics might have found an earlier head wound, but they wouldn't find a mismatched time of death. Died maybe ten minutes before his so-called fall.'

Poor, foolish Terry. Annie knew now why he'd gone to the colonel, even knew who had sent him. Mally, who'd seen him 'threeish' on the Sunday, had sent him to her grandfather and to his death. She remembered the fractured conversation as the colonel had prevented Mally's answers to Annie making any sense. Terry had spent his missing hours comatose in the colonel's house, or maybe his daughter's.

It was you on that scaffolding, Colonel.

Irrationally, she wanted to scream it at him. You that Doris saw up there, loosening the metal rail as a reason for Terry's fall. But Terry was already dead below.

She remembered the look in Tremlow's eye as he'd said, 'I saw him plain as day'. Glasses or no, Tremlow knew who he'd seen.

Her mind flitted from point to point across the things she now knew. Where was his weakness, what could she say to distract him, to put him off balance?

The track blocked with harmless silver glitz was a trap for Boxer, not for Laura. He intended the pony to gallop up there to leave its tracks for someone to find. If Boxer, frightened, went over the edge, all the better. If not, he would have made his way back tired and soaked. It would have taken nothing to carry Laura up to the edge and throw her over into the darkness of the storm.

She'd had a few more hours than Terry Martin and Tremlow to get the alcohol out of her system. Terry Martin and Tremlow could die drunk without undue comment: a girl like Laura couldn't.

'But, Colonel, she's just a child.' She hadn't meant to speak the words aloud; knew better than to plead with him. 'It's too late, Colonel. The police are on their way.'

His reply came somewhere close to a laugh. She'd asked Laura who had locked her up. Laura didn't know.

No one had seen him. Or rather they'd all seen him and not noticed. The finger pointed at his son-in-law. If he could rid himself of Annie he might yet make it. She felt the pressure ease again. She nerved every muscle in her body. He intended using what she'd said, pretending to relent, giving her half a chance to rise because this was deadlock and time was running out.

Oh, now the smokescreen's lifted, Colonel, I can read you so easily.

She must use this to get free. He mustn't know she'd sussed him.

'Quiet!' His weight rammed down on the back of her head, forcing her face into the mud. She struggled to breathe, strained to hear what was going on.

A voice had cut through the night, up close.

'Grandad...?'

Mally!

'It was her, Mel. You did well to get her here. And I'm afraid she's in cahoots with that scoundrel your mother married.'

'But Laura was really here, Grandad.'

'You stole the key from me, Mel.'

'I'm sorry, Grandad. I'm sorry.' Mally's voice rose in panic. Annie knew the odd relationship between them had been play-acting. What she heard now – Mally's terror of him – was real.

'Then make amends. Here, hold her down like this. I won't be long.'

In a spike of pain to her lower back that made her groan aloud, the weight shifted. It was Mally holding her now. Mally, terrified of her grandfather like she'd been all along. All that loutish behaviour in front of him had been what he wanted to paint the picture of the frail old man who could barely cope; the front he put on for the gossips of Milesthorpe and the interfering woman who asked questions about Terry Martin.

Mally's grip was strong, but not quite so strong as her grandfather's. Annie lay very still, let Mally relax just a little. When she made her move she must be sure of it.

She heard the colonel's voice barking out instructions, the sense of them carried off on the storm.

'Dad's not here ...' Mally's voice was small.

'He's here somewhere, Mel.'

Annie understood. Did Mally? Her father was on his way here, panicked by some message about his daughter. The colonel intended him to appear in time to take the blame for all this.

It couldn't work. It was too late, surely. The frail old man versus the prime suspect up here on the moor. Annie's body in the sea. Could he keep Mally quiet?

'Hold firm, Mel, but keep clear.'

More voices far off. Too far off to bother with.

Annie played comatose. A fraction of a second more ... as long as she dared ... cringing inwardly at the image of something heavy crashing towards her.

And then she twisted out of Mally's grip.

Halfway to her feet, off balance, the colonel came at her.

The rocks and crashing waves spiralled below. In one dizzying rush, she was back on top of the world, high above the city. Invincible. She read every move before he made it. He would grab her as she dived to get away from the crumbling earth at the lip of the precipice, but she didn't go that way. She leapt back into the danger zone, getting round him. The storm might try to tip her over, but it acted without malice, she knew all its moves. She knew her face smiled as their stares locked; she tasted the power. He was the one who floundered now.

She worked with the eddies of the storm, keeping low. He tried to grab out at her, paradoxically needing to drag her away from danger so he could push her over without going with her.

And even now she'd underestimated him. She'd been so sure she could snatch the fraction of a second that was all she needed, but he read her. He knew power too.

Voices from the darkness. She couldn't take an iota of attention away even to think out the need to shout to them.

But another voice rang out. 'Over here!' Mally shrieked. 'Over here!'

'Mel!' her grandfather roared.

The instant his attention slewed to his granddaughter, Annie leapt for safety. She saw him lunge out at her, felt his hand rake its way down her arm. He seemed right there with her, but she knew she was a fraction ahead.

A hair's breadth from safety she heard a gasp and was aware of one of his legs sliding out on the slick clay as he lost his footing. She threw herself back from the hand that grabbed out at her. In the moment of twisting away, their eyes met. An instant frozen in time. Realization. No way back.

She squeezed her eyes shut. Didn't want to see. In her mind she gabbled out the words, already rehearsing her script. *It happened so quickly ... dark ... it was dark ...*

An angry howl dragged the strength from her as his form disappeared, swallowed up into the night and the crashing of the waves.

All that was left was the high breathing of someone who'd sprinted beyond their capacity, someone close by.

'Annie?' Jennifer's voice had barely the strength to breathe her name.

Annie let herself sink back down into the mud. All her power to read the vagaries of the storm had vanished. She held tight to the grass beneath her and slithered backwards away from the edge. She was aware of Jennifer beside her, keeping low, moving the other way wanting to see over.

'They called you then. Thank God. I wasn't sure they would.'

'Who? No one called me. You tried to leave a message on my voicemail.

Couldn't make out what you said, but I heard the sound of the sea before you cut out. It made me think of the night we found the body up here. I guessed where you'd be.'

As Jennifer reached the edge, the winds howled their unease and a pale moon slid into view spreading a ribbon of silver across the sea. Annie imagined a momentary glistening edge to the body far below before the waves crashed in to obliterate the sight and the storm whipped a dark cloud across to shroud the scene.

She heard Jennifer's gasp of surprise. 'But it isn't him. That isn't Melissa Fletcher's father.'

'I know.' Annie lay on the mud, hands shaking as they clutched tight to tufts of grass. Without haste she let in the idea she was safe 'It's her grandfather. It's Colonel Ludgrove. I didn't realize … not till too late anyway.'

She thought she'd been so clever … built up a picture no one else had seen … but details matter. And she'd missed so much.

The sea breeze became a jagged hand scraping across her back, freezing the sweat on her skin, making her shake in earnest. She rolled over and forced herself to her feet. Her eyes told her that people raced about shouting, that vehicles bumped towards them over the rough ground, but the rush of the waves and the wind overlay everything as though no other sound would ever pierce this landscape again.

As soon as she'd wrapped herself in the security of the thought, an unearthly cry sliced through the air, cutting out the best efforts of sea and sky. Annie started up in alarm, was aware of Jennifer beside her, face ashen. She spun round to the source of the noise. Mally stood alone, pose rigid as though paralyzed in some bizarre act of pagan worship, eyes turned skywards, arms and hands raised twisted, clutching an invisible foe. The only movement was in her face that contorted as she let out scream after scream.

CHAPTER 29

ANNIE WATCHED AS people rushed towards Mally. After her first shock, she stopped and allowed her mind to remember. Everything. Details matter.

The sodden form of Kay, leading an equally sodden Boxer, plodded across her line of sight. Someone she didn't recognize strode up to take the pair in hand. Annie looked round for Laura and saw her sitting on the grass, as oblivious as Kay to the shrieks that rent the night air. She walked over to her.

'Come on, Laura. Let's get to the road and find somewhere warm.'

Laura allowed herself to be raised to her feet. Annie supported the shivering girl and led her back towards civilization.

She reflected later that it had not been by any plan on her part. It was the detail that teemed in her mind, the things she had to get straight. And because in the end these had drawn her to Laura and not to Mally, the sight that greeted the Tunbridges as they leapt from their car almost before it had skidded to a halt on the verge, was of their daughter being led out of the hellhole with Annie at her side, arms wrapped protectively around her. In the mêlée that followed, the hugs, the gasps over Laura, Annie felt her hands wrung and her shoulders squeezed as expressions of gratitude tumbled out. She knew she had her third case. Vince would be furious.

In the rush of emotion with which Laura and her parents collided, Mrs Tunbridge grabbed her daughter. 'Oh Laura ... how ... what ... where...?'

Laura gabbled out her own confused account in a torrent of words, as events teetered back towards equilibrium. Annie stayed at the periphery of the family group and listened intently.

After the day that Laura had seen Terry Martin in Mally's house with Charles Tremlow and heard their conversation, she'd taken special note of what went on there. Because she and Mally had been at loggerheads over the cheating at the Showcross, she hadn't shared what she'd overheard, but the track at the bottom of the crescent was a bridleway, a popular route for the girls on their ponies. Laura had seen smoke from the chimney of the Fletchers' house and gone round later to investigate. Back doors were rarely locked in Milesthorpe, not even the colonel's daughter's with the comatose victims inside. Laura had sneaked in unnoticed the first time and although she'd missed the horrors that lay in the garage, had recognized the scorched half page and pulled it from the grate. She'd decided to copy it through a fax machine.

If only she'd sent the original with Maz, she wouldn't have tried to return it to the grate and been caught by the colonel who, in what must have been a panicked bout of quick thinking, made up the message from Mally to get Laura up to the prison where he could first subdue and then kill her.

Annie fought to get her head round the cold calculations of the man who'd set himself up as a pillar of the community. Events had snowballed on to him. Just as he felt confident enough to use Elizabeth Atkins's money, Terry Martin came on the scene asking awkward questions, then Tremlow saw more than he should. While he dealt with him, Annie was in his face and Laura showed up with the incriminating page. If he hadn't been prepared to throw in the towel at that stage, nothing would have stopped him, and what had happened at the cliff's edge was for the best.

And now, there were things she must do.

'Could I borrow your phone?' she asked Mr Tunbridge, hoping his mobile would find a network up here by the road.

She called Pat to tell her what had happened, to let her know where she was.

The right thing for her to do now was sit tight with the Tunbridges until the confusion eased. The police would want to question her, to get all she knew. She was pretty sure they hadn't yet figured out why Colonel Ludgrove had done it, but she could tell them that. First thing though was her duty to the Martins.

It was far too late at night, but she couldn't leave it. The ring tone buzzed in her ear for a long time before Martha's voice, befuddled by sleep, said, 'Hello. Who's that? What is it?'

'It's Annie Raymond. I've news for you. Can I come round?'

A pause, then, 'We'll be waiting.'

Annie handed back the phone. 'Mr Tunbridge, could I ask you to do me another favour?'

With his help she was able to slip away unnoticed. He drove her back to where she'd parked the car in Milesthorpe. She thought back to the colonel's kitchen. Those two cups of tea. After he heard Pat was outside waiting, he'd changed his mind about the nip of brandy – was that to mask the taste of what he'd already put in it? He'd carried the cups through and hadn't touched his.

Would she have disappeared and turned up two days later dead in Pat's car with a pipe from the exhaust? Pat might have wondered, but could only have said she didn't know Annie well. Cursory enquiries would have shown her virtually penniless and homeless; the product of a fractured childhood. Yes, the colonel had lost his one chance there.

As she pulled up outside the house in Withernsea, the door opened to reveal Martha wrapped in layers of cotton nightdress and the rough sack-like material of a long bulky dressing gown. For just a fraction of a second she paused and stared hard at Annie. Then she pulled the door wide and said, 'Come through.'

Annie glimpsed her own profile in the hallstand as she stepped inside. Her hair stuck out like a spiky halo framing a face smeared with mud. No wonder Martha had had to check to be sure it was her. As she followed her to the small sitting room she became aware of the huge clods of clay that still clung to her shoes, the swathes of mud that stiffened her clothes. Dirt and grass rained down on to the carpet with every step.

She stopped. Surely Martha hadn't meant her to come in, to violate the pristine neatness of her home.

'Come and sit down, love.' Bill's voice summoned her from where he sat in his usual armchair, bundled in the same rough material as his wife and with striped pyjama trousers emerging from beneath the identical dressing gown.

She stared at them, felt the damp that seeped through to her skin, looked at the spotless moquette of the empty armchair.

'You said you had news,' Bill prompted.

They didn't care about the mud, or the state she'd leave the furniture in; all they cared about was that she had news. She stepped forward carefully trying to dislodge as little loose stuff as possible and picked up a newspaper from the table. Spread open, it was reasonable protection for the fabric of the chair. It crackled as she sat down on it.

'I don't know when it started,' she told them, 'but Terry had worked it out. He'd confronted Mr Tremlow with evidence that the work on the house next door was paid for from the money Elizabeth Atkins left to Milesthorpe Church.' Annie imagined Tremlow horrified, rushing to the colonel for reassurance that Terry had it wrong.

'Tremlow wouldn't have suspected the colonel, not at that stage. And I don't think Terry did to start with. He thought it was Edward Balham, the other church warden.' As she spoke, Annie thought of the still unidentified body in the building on the cliff. She intended having the full story now from either Scott or Jennifer. And if they wouldn't play ball then there were plenty of things she wouldn't tell them in return.

As she unravelled the tale for the Martins, Annie saw it more clearly in her own mind. Terry's obsession with the church wardens, the ones who'd been left in control of Elizabeth Atkins's legacy, made sense now.

'It was just the right focus,' she told them. 'No one else had spotted what was going on.'

'Why didn't the others know? Weren't they all in charge of that money?'

She told them about the elderly trio; Last of the Summer Wine; a bit of a joke. Balham, who was retired from everything except some nominal oversight of the farm that operated as efficiently with as without him. Whether Balham's extracurricular activities in that building by the cliff had any bearing, she didn't know. Tremlow, nervy, ineffective, happy to do as his assertive friend told him until he found himself covering for a murder. Then there was the colonel. A leader of men, whose daughter brought shame on the family and near bankruptcy with her high living and divorce settlement. Likely the colonel had killed Elizabeth Atkins once the paperwork was straight enough for him to get hold of the money. Doris was probably right. No one would ever know now.

Yes, she thought, Terry had been on the point of uncovering the fraud, until his ill-judged pursuit of Balham had derailed him.

'Terry must have had the whole story ready to roll,' she said, 'but Colonel Ludgrove caught up with him.'

'How did he kill our Terry?'

Annie's mind raced over what she now knew, sorting fact from supposition. The Martins didn't want theory, they wanted facts, so she presented it to them that way. She was pretty sure she had it right.

'Terry bumped into Melissa Fletcher that Sunday in Milesthorpe. He asked her about Edward Balham and she directed him to her grandfather.

She ran wild but she knew where her grandfather's boundaries lay. She was wary of crossing his friends and Balham was one of his friends. One of the other girls had told Terry about the building on the cliff, but Melissa had found him some paperwork on Elizabeth Atkins's legacy. She had no idea what it meant.'

'So what happened that Sunday?'

'Terry went to confront the colonel.' That was the theory that made Terry look brave and decisive. More likely he'd gone to dig for detail on Balham.

She told them how the colonel had knocked Terry out and fed him alcohol to keep him comatose as he came round, and noted a rapid nod of agreement from Bill. They knew he wasn't a drinker and this lifted the slur. She wondered what other drug the colonel had used. Something that made him keep his victims alive for two days to get it out of their system. She'd need to find out about that.

'Where was he those missing two days?'

'In the Fletchers' house. The colonel took him there unconscious from his own house.' Having felt the colonel's strength, Annie had no problem with presenting this theory as fact. Terry had probably been bundled into the boot of the car. The house next door to Tremlow's, like Tremlow's own, had an integral garage so no problem getting him in. And, of course, the colonel would be an expected visitor looking after the place while his daughter was away. Even with its ever-open doors, Milesthorpe was the sort of place where everyone had everyone else's key. The colonel had a key to Balham's, including to the shed on the cliff. It must have been a nasty moment for him when Annie produced a copy he hadn't known existed.

And it was Annie who'd signed Tremlow's death warrant when she'd rung the colonel about his friend. As she and Pat searched the house, poor Tremlow must have been next door drugged, maybe in his own car in the Fletchers' garage.

'So the man who confessed? He didn't kill our Terry?'

'No, but the colonel got him to go out in a panic with a weapon that night and hit out. He might have thought he'd done it at first. The colonel must have been there all along. That business about Tremlow ringing him up, about him struggling his way across the fields was just lies. Tremlow knew by then that Terry was right about the church legacy. The colonel tried to keep him quiet by persuading him he'd killed Terry.'

Annie wondered what the colonel had said.

We'll leave him in the hole. Pretend he fell from the scaffolding. Look, there's a loose bar up on the platform.

But Tremlow had seen the colonel up there. The shock of it all had made him a wreck.

Annie thought back to what Scott had said about Tremlow's confession. 'The way he told it, it could have been an accident. He hit out. Didn't realize what he'd done.'

Didn't realize because he hadn't done it. The colonel must have had a terrible shock when Doris Kitson turned up so suddenly and promptly. Luckily for him Tremlow was in too bad a state to unburden himself to Doris and her version backed up the colonel's story.

Annie thought she might have a final cup of tea in Doris's immaculate kitchen. She'd like to bet it was the colonel himself who told her Mally's father had been seen heading for the ex-marital home the day of Annie's first visit. Annie hadn't seen the small blue car because it had never been there to see. It was the colonel who'd upset Mally by claiming his ex son-in-law had talked to Laura. All along he'd strewn the seeds, just in case.

And it might have worked.

Yes, she'd prise some dates out of Doris. When did Mally's parents' marriage hit the rocks? When was it clear they were about to slide into the financial mire? She'd like to bet there was a correlation with Elizabeth Atkins's promised legacy. Doris had been right. Annie felt ashamed now she'd ignored her theories about a suspicious death just because the victim was in her nineties.

'The man who killed our Terry, he's dead now? He fell off the cliff?'

'Uh … yes.' Annie didn't meet Bill Martin's eye. 'Yes, he lost his footing when he tried to push me over the edge. There'll be media interest in all of it,' she went on. 'But if you want to you can refer the newspapers to me, I'll verify the facts with them.'

'How will the papers treat him now?'

Annie thought of all the things she'd uncovered about Terry Martin, about all the ways the truth might be spun. She thought about the main players. How would pensioners from the rural wasteland to the east of Hull fare against news stories from the more accessible parts of the country? Terry Martin couldn't compete for coverage in the nationals. There was too much real news about. And, as the slightly unsavoury character he'd been, the respectable local press would ignore him, but Pat had contacts. Annie felt confident she could seed a good local interest angle with them.

'As a dedicated journalist who died for his craft,' she said.

It wouldn't last. It wasn't real consolation. But Annie would remember the smile of satisfaction on Martha's face that had found some reflection in Bill's when he looked at his wife. And she knew she'd done the best it was possible to do for them.

When she arrived back at the flat in the small hours, Annie found both Pat and Barbara in the living room sitting opposite each other with a tray on the table between them. It was clearly one of Barbara's creations with a lace cloth, neatly arranged biscuits on a plate and coffee in a pot.

Barbara looked Annie up and down. 'Coffee? Or d'you want to get showered first?' Although she didn't quite smile, she managed not to look unfriendly.

'Uh … thanks. I'd love a coffee.'

'She'll clog the drains,' Barbara said to Pat, as she leant forward to the tray. 'Go on. Tell her.'

Pat sat up straight. 'Barbara and I have had … what shall we say? A frank exchange with Vince. We're parting company.'

'What's happening to the agency?' Annie surprised herself at how much she cared what became of Pat's family business.

'Unfortunately Vince gets to keep the business and the name, but we had enough of a legal stake left to screw a financial settlement out of him.'

'Another few months' leeway and we wouldn't have got that.' Barbara narrowed her eyes at Pat as she spoke, and handed Annie her coffee.

'Well, don't look at me. It was never my bag to keep an eye on that side of things. You were supposed to do that.'

'Not after I'd left. Don't be ridiculous—'

Annie interrupted. 'What are you going to do?'

'We're going to set up on our own, go for the jobs that the big boys aren't interested in. It's what Dad did in the first place. He always said there was a market to be carved out if you worked at it. Vince isn't bothered. He just wants the money to keep rolling in.'

Annie pretended not to see the glance that speared between Pat and Barbara. She thought about the roof of the tower block. With aerials that size, their transmissions could reach out to the estuary and beyond, but she'd bet if she went back to the roundabout now she'd see nothing on that roof. Vince would have shifted the whole operation. And right now she could see the sense in leaving him to it, but maybe one day the sisters would go head to head with him again. For now, it was enough that Pat had seen through him.

Pat glanced at Barbara and nodded towards Annie. Barbara cleared her throat before she spoke. 'We've no security to offer, but the money we've screwed from Vince'll keep us afloat a while. We're going to give it a go. If you want to come on board, you can, but all we're offering is hard work, crap money and no security.'

'Well …'

'Don't answer now. Have a think. Oh, and by the way, the law's after you.'

'The law…? Oh right, yes, they'll want a statement, I suppose.'

'Your faithful plod was going spare; thought you'd done something stupid.'

'Why would I do something stupid?'

'I told him he was being a prat. Anyway, I said I'd ask you to call him when you turned up.'

'Well it's far too late now. I'm knackered. I'm going to have a shower and go to bed. I'll go down tomorrow.'

*

Annie gave her statement the next morning to a police sergeant she didn't know and an unsmiling PC Greaves.

Scott turned up at the flat soon after she arrived back. She assumed he'd been waiting for her. He'd taken the trouble to change out of his uniform. Even his trousers looked normal. He sat in the chair next to Annie. Pat sat opposite them rummaging through her big bag, not looking inclined to move.

After a moment, he spoke, his tone diffident. 'Uh ... I'm sorry, Annie. I said things I shouldn't have.'

He didn't quite manage to meet her eye, but then she couldn't quite meet his as she said, 'That's OK, I expect I deserved some of it. Um ... how are those girls? Kay Dearlove wasn't well at all.'

'OK. They're all OK.'

'And what about Mally? Has anyone found her mother yet?'

'She was never lost. Her grandfather was in daily contact, so was the girl. They didn't breathe a word to her of what had happened. Melissa told us it was so her mother wasn't worried. That was the line her grandfather gave her.'

'So her mother wasn't a part of it?'

'Oh no, doesn't look like it. Ludgrove handed her the chance of a break when he decided he had to be rid of Terry Martin. Told her to go off for a fortnight with the new boyfriend. I don't think he'd acknowledged the guy before so she snatched at it. She should have been back this weekend but he told her to stay on, said that Melissa was going to spend a week with her father.'

Pat looked across at Scott. 'I wonder why he didn't send Melissa with them.'

'I doubt they'd have stayed away five minutes crammed in a mobile home together. I gather the mother's boyfriend was daggers drawn with the girl. She wouldn't acknowledge his existence. And I think her grandfather found her useful. She did as she was told. We won't dig too deeply there. She's only a kid.'

Annie digested this without comment and asked, 'Where was her father?'

'He'd been away on business.'

'Just like he said. I heard the colonel imply to Mally that he'd made that up so as not to have to take her.' And he'd seeded various sightings over the week. He'd had his fall guy prepared if anyone veered away from the idea of Terry Martin having died in a fall and Tremlow being a suicide.

'How far away is Mally's mother? Will it take her long to get back?'

'She's back already. She was on a campsite further up the coast. A bit of a dim cow, if you ask me. The daughter has more to her.'

She certainly does, thought Annie, remembering the chaotic scenes at the cliff top. Aloud she said, 'That's hardly fair, Scott. It must have been an awful shock for her. What about the ex-husband, is he on his way back?'

'He's back, too. He got some garbled message from his ex-father-in-law about his daughter being in trouble and rushed back.'

'He was supposed to be on the spot to take the rap, wasn't he?'

'I guess so.'

Annie let the sequence of events run through her mind. She wanted to move the conversation away from Mally. 'Did Colonel Ludgrove know what Balham got up to in that shed?'

Scott shook his head. 'No.'

'So Terry Martin hadn't really sussed it out, had he? He'd come close, then he'd been sidetracked by what he found up there on the cliff.'

'He'd come too close for the colonel to let him go.'

Annie felt a hollow inside her that was partly anger at the damage the colonel had wrought and partly sorrow for those to whom he'd caused the most devastation. 'Terry Martin never stuck at anything,' she said. 'If the colonel had just kept his head down, some other cause would have taken him right out of Milesthorpe.'

Pat heaved herself to her feet and fixed Scott with a stare. 'That letter the old guy Tremlow wrote, it was a confession wasn't it, not a suicide note at all?'

He nodded. 'Looks like it.'

Annie wondered if the colonel had persuaded him to write it or found he'd done it, and pounced on the opportunity. She thought of the words Tremlow had spat out. 'I didn't know what an evil man he was ... he took money.' Of course he'd meant the colonel, his trusted old friend, not Terry Martin.

Pat embarrassed Annie with a knowing wink as she stomped off to the kitchen where Barbara was busy. Their muffled guffaws and low-voiced chat created an awkward backdrop.

Scott glanced uneasily over his shoulder and kept his voice down as he said, 'When did you cotton on it was Colonel Ludgrove? Jen said you figured it before he died.'

Annie thought for a moment. Information should flow both ways. 'Will you tell me who the woman in that building was?'

'OK, but you go first.'

She looked into his eyes, decided he was on the level – he'd better be – and told him about the false trails the colonel had laid for her. 'The village grapevine had it all over Milesthorpe that I was looking into Terry Martin's death. He had me sussed from the off, but it didn't fall into place for me until I was up there with him. Another metre and I'd have been over the edge before I'd figured it.'

He reached out to grasp her hand. 'Oh Annie, I'm so relieved you're safe. I'm sorry I didn't believe you.'

She let him hold her hand while an awkward silence grew between them. He broke it by saying, 'Will you talk to Jen? She says she wants to resign.'

'Resign? Why?'

'I don't know. She won't say anything except that she doesn't know what happened up there on the cliff. She doesn't think she can stay on.'

Annie slid her hand out from Scott's grasp and sat still for a moment. When she spoke, she picked her words with care. 'Will you tell her that I know what she thinks? And tell her I don't think it happened that way. I was on the spot. I saw everything. She shouldn't resign. She's good at her job.'

He looked baffled. 'But what's it about? And can't you tell her yourself?'

'And can you also tell her that I don't want to talk about that night. Not yet. So I'd rather you took the message. And I'd rather not talk about it now.'

She saw his puzzled expression and braced herself to resist his interrogation. Then his gaze became unfocused as though he was working it out for himself. Annie held her breath. Could he piece it together? No, he could only guess.

'OK,' he said at length, and gave her a nod as though they'd sealed a bargain.

She made him repeat her message to Jennifer word for word until he had it right. Then she said, 'Now come on. You promised. The body in the shed. Who is it?'

'It's who we thought it would be all along. Balham.'

'Edward Balham?' She stared at him. 'But ... but it can't be ... It was a woman. The clothes ...'

He shook his head. 'I thought it was a man's body all along.'

'Is that what you saw on the film that first night?'

'Not first time through,' he admitted. 'I thought I saw the glimmer of a wire above the body. It hadn't been strangled. It had been hanged. Then I thought if it's a guy, wearing all that lacy stuff, then it's pretty clear what's happened. It's not the first one I've seen. It's more common than you'd think.'

'Auto-strangulation? Is that what it's called?'

'Something like that.'

It rang vague bells with Annie. Odd reports here and there. 'So that's why he went walkabout. To wear women's knickers and semi-strangle himself in a dark shed?'

'Yep. We even found the chair. A rickety old thing. The more rickety the chair, the greater the thrill. That's why so many of them end up hanging themselves. Balham's chair was textbook.'

'And people get turned on by it?'

'So they say. I don't see it myself.'

'Why the delay?'

'We've had a real hassle getting a firm ID. No family. Decomposed corpse. But we have now. It's definitely him.'

'So it was never a murder then?'

'Not even suicide. The verdict'll be accidental death.'

Annie remembered the hard look Jennifer had given her that day in the coffee bar when she'd referred to odd sorts of deaths that turn out to be accidents. Jennifer thought she was fishing about the body in the building. An idea occurred to her. 'The Milesthorpe grapevine was right all along. They always had it as Balham's body.'

'Speaking of grapevines, I heard that you persuaded Sleeman to use some muscle to clear out a drug problem in one of the blocks on Orchard Park.'

Annie owned the achievement with a nod of her head, but when he pressed for detail of who, where and when, she said. 'It's settled now. Let's just leave it at that.'

She almost congratulated him on his grapevine, but decided it was too flippant at this delicate stage.

It took her thoughts to Vince. Impulsive, dangerous ... livid at the revelation of what his nephew was mixed up in. Not that he wanted him on the straight and narrow, she was sure. It was that he didn't want him involved in something so sordid and small.

'Look, I know I said things about Sleeman,' Scott said, 'but I don't mind you working for him if that's the sort of influence you have.'

Bloody cheek, she thought. Who's he to mind or not?

Mrs Earle, the Martins, Laura Tunbridge. Her three cases. What would it be like to have a secure berth to launch her career from? She needn't get involved in the dodgy stuff or stay with Vince any longer than she need to get herself on her feet. Of course, he'd only ever made his three-cases comment to Pat. He hadn't actually offered her a job yet.

As for Scott, well, it could be worth allowing herself to accept his apology and seeing if she could educate him into the twenty-first century. He had the raw materials in him.

'I might be staying on,' she said.

At once, his face relaxed into the smile that had attracted her even before she'd seen it. 'That's good. Maybe we could ... uh ... meet up sometime?'

'Maybe.'

'If you're staying on, you'll need someone to show you round the place.' She smiled back at him. 'I suppose I will.'

After he'd gone, she reflected on what he'd said about Jennifer and how much she'd seen. It had been dark, stormy. Jennifer couldn't have been sure. Scott would say to her that Annie didn't think it happened that way and Annie was there on the spot. She saw everything.

Hopefully Jennifer would leave it at that. Annie couldn't see what might be gained from raking it all over. It had been a traumatic night for them all. For some, like Mally, it had been the culmination of several traumatic years. And what she'd said was the exact truth. She knew what Jennifer thought might have happened. And she, Annie, didn't think it happened that way. She'd seen the small foot flash into view, kick the colonel's leg from under him so he lost balance there at the top of the cliff. No, she didn't think Mally had pushed her grandfather over the cliff, she knew for sure the girl had done it.

Annie slipped through to her room to sit in peace and sort her thoughts. She lay back on the bed, only wanting to relax, and didn't realize she'd slept until an hour later when voices roused her.

Almost before she woke, she sensed the atmosphere of hostility.

Pat's voice shouted, 'And I'll have those bloody keys back.'

From the jangle of metal landing on a hard surface, it sounded as though she'd got them. Annie smoothed down her clothes to the background of Barbara's raised voice, and then Vince's.

'It's not your car, it's mine. You've got plenty out of this settlement to get your own transport.'

Annie made no attempt to keep quiet as she shut her bedroom door and approached the living room. She stepped into a silence, aware they'd all reined back at her entrance.

Pat on the settee, cradling an unopened packet of biscuits, gave her a nod of acknowledgement. Barbara tossed an all-purpose surface cleaner spray from hand to hand. Vince took in a breath and paused before turning to her as though he needed a moment to change gear.

'There you are, Annie. I've kept a distance while you've been here.' He could say that again. 'I wanted to see how you shaped up before I made any decisions. Now I've made my decision. I know you don't have all the bits of paper, but I never thought much to bits of paper. You've shown what you can do.' He paused as though expecting her to speak. When she said nothing, he went on, 'You've courage and a good instinct. It's a useful combination. You've earned yourself a place in the team. Good basic salary, good bonuses if you earn them. Have a long weekend and come down to the office middle of next week. Take the car down to London and pick up your stuff if you want. In fact, you may as well keep the car. You're going to need one anyway.'

A vision reared up in front of Annie. She thought of all the people who'd told her to grow up and look for a proper job. Not for the first time, she played out a fantasy of returning in triumph in a tailored suit and a flash car. The sleek BMW was the fantasy made real. *It's just a small agency. Good salary plus bonuses ... The car? Yes, it's mine. Goes with the job.*

She felt the smile creep across her features. Vince was still talking, saying he felt he'd come to know her ... liked her style ...

'I've learnt a lot about you,' he said.

She mustn't let him go on. 'I've learnt a lot about myself over the last week.'

Vince laughed, the first friendly laugh she'd heard from him. 'I'll bet you have. You never thought you could face down a homicidal maniac, did you?'

Annie looked up at him and thought about a seven or eight hour round trip just to lord it over past acquaintances. No way. She had a life to live. But maybe a trip to see her father would be a good way to start this new chapter and tie some loose ends from the past. It was time she found the courage to ask him how her mother died.

'No, it wasn't that,' she told Vince. 'It was other things. Personal stuff. I always knew I had it in me to meet a challenge. Now I want the chance to build on it. I want something that inspires me; that I really have to work for. But I don't want to stagnate. The bits of paper, as you call them, are a part of it. They mean digging deeper into how things work, getting to grips with the detail. Matching theory to practice. You might not care about them, but they're important to me.'

'If it's a matter of funding ...' Another first. An edge of uncertainty to his tone.

'No, it's not the money. As I'm given the choice, I want to be in on building something from the start, facing the real challenge of risking everything on it. So I appreciate the offer but I have to turn it down. And if your offer's still open, Pat ... Barbara ... I'd like to accept.'

Vince looked round at them all. Pat on the settee feeling for the tag to open her biscuits, Barbara with her spray cleaner held up like a weapon, Annie standing in front of him. There was no hostility in his expression and his voice was friendly as he said, 'You'll be out of business in six months.'

Annie walked with him to the door to see him out, a gesture that this was her territory now more than his.

'We might indeed,' she said. 'But that was just another challenge they could offer and you couldn't. No hard feelings.'

His look of complete bafflement made her laugh as she walked back to the living room to rejoin her new team.